THE WOODS OUT BACK

Spearwielder's Tale

R. A. Salvatore

OPEN ROAD
INTEGRATED MEDIA
NEW YORK

ISBN: 978-1-5040-8058-3

This edition published in 2023 by Open Road Integrated Media, Inc.
180 Maiden Lane
New York, NY 10038
www.openroadmedia.com

THE WOODS OUT BACK

PRELUDE

"You were caught fairly and within the written limits of your own rules," Kelsey said sternly. His sharp eyes, golden in hue and ever sparkling like the stars he so loved, bore into the smaller sprite, promising no compromise.

"Might that it be time for changing the rules," Mickey the leprechaun mumbled under his breath.

Kelsey's golden eyes, the same hue as his flowing hair, narrowed dangerously, his thin brows forming a "V" over his delicate but angular nose.

Mickey silently berated himself. He could get away with his constant private muttering around bumbling humans, but, he reminded himself again, one should never underestimate the sharpness of an elf's ears. The leprechaun looked around the open meadow, searching for some escape route. He knew it to be a futile exercise; he couldn't hope to outrun the elf, standing more than twice his height, and the nearest cover was fully a hundred yards away.

Not a promising proposition.

Always ready to improvise, Mickey went into his best posture for bargaining, a leprechaun's second favorite pastime (the first being the use of illusions to trick pursuing humans into smashing their faces into trees).

"Ancient, they are," the leprechaun tried to explain. "Rules o' catching made for humans and greedy folk. It was meant for being a game, ye know." Mickey kicked a curly-toed shoe against a mushroom stalk and his voice held an unmistakable edge of sarcasm as he completed the thought. "Elfs were not expected in the chase, being honorable folk and their hearts not being held by a pot o' gold. At least, that's what I been told about elfs."

"I do not desire your precious pot," Kelsey reminded him. "Only a small task."

"Not so small."

"Would you prefer that I take your gold?" Kelsey warned. "That is the usual payment for capture."

Mickey gnashed his teeth, then popped his enormous (considering his size) pipe into his mouth. He couldn't argue; Kelsey had caught him fairly. Still, Mickey had to wonder how honest the chase had been. The rules for catching a leprechaun were indeed ancient and precise, and, written by the wee folk themselves, hugely slanted in the leprechaun's favor. But a leprechaun's greatest advantage in evading humans lay in his uncanny abilities at creating illusions. Enter Kelsey the elf, and the advantage is no more. None in all the land of Faerie, not the dwarfs of Dvergamal nor even the great dragons themselves, could see through illusions, could separate reality from fabrication, as well as the elfs.

"Not so small a task, I say," Mickey iterated. "Ye're looking to fill Cedric's own shoes—none in Dilnamarra that I've seen are fitting that task! The man was a giant . . ."

Kelsey shrugged, unconcerned, his casual stance stealing Mickey's rising bluster. The human stock in Faerie had indeed diminished, and the prospects of finding a man who could fit into the ancient armor once worn by King Cedric Donigarten were not good. Of course Kelsey knew that; why else would he have taken the time to catch Mickey?

"I might have to go over," Mickey said gravely.

"You are the cleverest of your kind," Kelsey replied, and the compliment was not patronizing. "You shall find a way, I do not doubt. Have the faeries you know so well do their dance, then. Surely they owe Mickey McMickey a favor or two."

Mickey took a long draw on his pipe. The fairie dance! Kelsey actually expected him to go over, to find someone from the other side, from Real-earth.

"Me pot o' gold might be an easier barter," the leprechaun grumbled.

"Then give it to me," replied a smiling Kelsey, knowing the bluff for what it was. "And I shall use the wealth to purchase what I need from some other source."

Mickey gnashed his teeth around his pipe, wanting to put his curly boot into the smug elf's face. Kelsey had seen his bluff as easily as he had seen through Mickey's illusions on the lopsided chase. No leprechaun would willingly give up his pot of gold with no chance of stealing it back unless his very life was at stake. And for all of the inconvenience Kelsey had caused him, Mickey knew that the elf would not harm him.

"Not an easy task," the leprechaun said again.

"If the task was easy, I would have taken the trouble myself," Kelsey replied evenly, though a twitch in one of his golden eyes revealed that he was nearing the end of his patience. "I have not the time."

"Ye taked the trouble to catching me," Mickey snarled.

"Not so much trouble," Kelsey assured him.

Mickey rested back and considered a possible escape through the meadow again. Kelsey was shooting down his every leading suggestion with no room for argument, with no room for bargaining. By a leprechaun's measure, Kelsey wasn't playing fair.

"You shall accept my offer, then," Kelsey said. "Or I shall have your pot of gold here and now." He paused for a few moments to give Mickey the chance to produce the pot, which, of course, the leprechaun did not do.

"Excellent," continued the elf. "Then you know the terms of your indenture. When might I expect my human?"

Mickey kicked his curly-toed shoes again and moved to find a seat on the enormous mushroom. "Sure'n 'tis a beautiful day," he said, and he was not exaggerating in the least. The breeze was cool but not stiff, and it carried a thousand springtime scents with it, aromas of awakening flowers and new-growing grass.

"Too beautiful for talking business, I say," Mickey mentioned.

"When?" Kelsey demanded again, refusing to be sidetracked.

"All the folk o' Dilnamarra are out to frolic while we're sitting here arguing . . ."

"Mickey McMickey!" Kelsey declared. "You have been caught, captured, defeated on the chase. Of that, there can be no argument. You are thus bound to me. We are not discussing business; we are . . . I am, establishing the conditions of your freedom."

"Sure'n yer tongue's as sharp as yer ears," mumbled Mickey quietly.

Kelsey heard every word of it, of course, but this time he did not scowl. He knew by Mickey's resigned tone that the leprechaun had surrendered fully. "When?" he asked a third time.

"I cannot be sure," Mickey replied. "I'll set me friends to working on it."

Kelsey bowed low. "Then enjoy your beautiful day," he said, and he turned to leave.

For all his whining, Mickey was not so unhappy about the way things had turned out. His pride was hurt—any self-respecting leprechaun would be embarrassed over a capture—but Kelsey was an elf, after all, and that proved that the chase hadn't really been fair. Besides, Mickey still had his precious pot of gold and Kelsey's request wasn't overly difficult, leaving plenty of room for Mickey's own interpretation.

Mickey was thinking of that task now as he sat on the mushroom, his legs, crossed at the ankles, dangling freely over its side, and he was thinking that the task, like everything else in a leprechaun's life, just might turn out to be a bit of fun.

"It cannot be," the sorceress declared, pulling away from her reflecting pool and flipping her long and wavy, impossibly thick black hair back over her delicate shoulders.

"What has yous seen, my lady?" the hunched goblin rasped.

Ceridwen turned on him sharply and the goblin realized that he had not been asked to speak. He dipped into an apologetic bow, fell right to the floor, and groveled on the ground below the beautiful sorceress, whining and kissing her feet piteously.

"Get up, Geek!" she commanded, and the goblin snapped to attention. "There is trouble in the land," Ceridwen went on, true concern in her voice. "Kelsenellenelvial Gil-Ravadry has taken up his life-quest to forge the broken spear."

The goblin's face twisted in confusion.

"We do not want the people of Dilnamarra thinking of dead kings and heroes of old," Ceridwen explained. "Their thoughts must be on their own pitiful existence, on their gruel and mud-farming, on the latest disease that sweeps their land and keeps them weak.

"Weak and whimpering," Ceridwen declared, and her icy-blue eyes, so contrasting her raven-black hair, flashed like lightning. She rose up tall and terrible and Geek huddled again on the floor. But Ceridwen calmed immediately and seemed again the quiet, beautiful woman. "Like you, dear Geek," she said softly. "Weak and whimpering, and under the control of Kinnemore, my puppet King."

"Does we's killses the elf?" Geek asked hopefully. The goblin so loved killing!

"It is not so easy as that," replied Ceridwen. "I do not wish to invoke the wrath of the Tylwyth Teg." She winced at the notion. The Tylwyth Teg, the elfs of Faerie, were not to be taken lightly. But Ceridwen's concern soon dissipated, replaced by a confident smile. "But there are other ways, more subtle ways," the sorceress purred, more to herself than to her wretched goblin.

Ceridwen's smile only widened as she considered the many wicked allies she might call upon, the dark creatures of Faerie's misty nights.

ONE

THE GRIND

WHRRRR!

The noise was deafening, a twenty-horsepower motor spinning eight heavy blades. It only got louder when a chunk of scrap plastic slipped in through the creaking hopper gate and landed on that spinning blur, to be bounced and slammed and chipped apart. In mere seconds, the chunk, reduced to tiny flakes, would be spit out the grinder's bottom into a waiting barrel.

Gary Leger slipped his headphones over his ears and put on the heavy, heat-resistant gloves. With a resigned sigh, he stepped up on the stool beside the grinder and absently tipped over the next barrel, spilling the scrap pieces out before him on the metal table. He tossed one on the hopper tray and pushed it through the gate, listening carefully as the grinder blades mashed it to ensure that the plastic was not too hot to be ground. If it was, if the inside of the chunks were still soft, the grinder would soon jam, leaving Gary with a time-consuming and filthy job of tearing down and cleaning the machine.

The chunk went straight through, its flaky remains spewing into the empty barrel beneath the grinder, telling Gary that he could go at the work in earnest. He paused for a moment to consider what adventure awaited him this time, then smiled and adjusted his headphones and gloves. These items were his protection from the noise and the sharp edges of the irregular plastic chunks, but mostly they were Gary's insulation from reality itself. All the world—all the real world—became a distant place to Gary, standing on that stool beside the grinder table. Reality was gone now, no match for the excitement roused by an active imagination.

The plastic chunks became enemy soldiers—no, fighter jets, variations of a MiG-29. Perhaps a hundred of the multishaped, dark blue lumps, some as small as two inches across, others nearly a foot long, though only half that length, lay piled on the table and inside the tipped barrel.

A hundred to one, both bombers and fighters.

Overwhelming odds by any rational estimate, but not in the minds of the specially selected squadron, led by Gary, of course, sent out to challenge them.

An enemy fighter flashed along the tray and through the hopper gate.

Slam! Crash and burn.

Another one followed, then two more.

Good shooting.

Work blended with adventure, the challenge being to push the chunks in as fast as possible, to shoot down the enemy force before they could get by and inflict damage on your rear area. As fast as possible, but not so fast as to jam the grinder. To jam the grinder was to be shot down. Crash!

Game over.

Gary was getting good at this. He had half the barrel ground in just a couple of minutes and still the blade spun smoothly. Gary shifted the game, allowed for a bit of ego. Now the enemy fighters, realizing their enemy, and thus, their inevitable doom, turned tail and ran. Gary's squadron sped off in pursuit. If the enemy escaped, they would only come back another time, reinforced. Gary looked at the long line of chunk-filled barrels stretching back halfway through the large room and groaned. There were always more barrels, more enemies; the reinforcements would come, whatever he might do.

This was a war the young man felt he would never finish.

And here was a battle too real to be truly beaten by imagination, a battle against tedium, against a day where the body worked but the mind had to be shut down, or constantly diverted. It had been played out by the ants of an industrialized society for decades, men and women doing what they had to do to survive.

It all seemed so very perverted to Gary Leger. What had his father dreamed through the forty-five years of his working life? Baseball probably; his father loved the game so dearly. Gary pictured him standing before the slotted shelves in the post office, pitching letters, throwing balls and strikes. How many World Series were won in that postal room?

So very perverted.

Gary shrugged it all away and went back to his aerial battle. The pace had slowed, though the enemy still remained a threat. Another wide-winged fighter smashed through the creaking gate to its doom. Gary considered the pilot. Another man doing as he had to do?

No, that notion didn't work for Gary. Imagining a man being killed by his handiwork destroyed the fantasy and left him with a cold feeling. But that was the marvel of imagination, after all, for to Gary, these were no longer pilot-filled aircraft. They were robot drones—extraterrestrial robot drones. Or even better, they were extraterrestrial aircraft—so what if they still resembled the Russian MiGs—piloted by monster aliens, purely evil and come to conquer the world.

Crash and burn.

"Hey, stupid!"

Gary barely heard the call above the clanging din. He pulled off the head-phones and spun about, as embarrassed as a teenager caught playing an air guitar.

Leo's smirk and the direction of his gaze told Gary all that he needed to know. He bent down from the stool and looked beneath the grinder, to the overfilled catch barrel and the pile of plastic flakes on the floor.

"Coffee man's here," Leo said, and he turned away, chuckling and shaking his head.

Did Leo know the game? Gary wondered. Did Leo play? And what might his imagination conjure? Probably baseball, like Gary's father.

They didn't call it the all-American game for nothing.

Gary waited until the last banging chunks had cleared the whirring blades, then switched off the motor. The coffee man was here; the twenty-minute reprieve had begun. He looked back once to the grinder as he started away, to the piled plastic on the dirty floor. He'd have to pick that up after his break.

Victory had not been clean this day.

The conversations among the twenty or so workers gathered out by the coffee truck covered everything from politics to the upcoming softball tournament. Gary walked past the groups, hardly hearing their talk. It was too fine a spring day, he decided, to get caught up in some discussion that almost always ended on a bitter note. Still, louder calls and the more excited conclusions found their way through his indifference.

"Hey, Danny, you think two steak-and-cheese grinders are enough?" came one sarcastic shout—probably from Leo. "Lunch is almost an hour and a half away. You think that'll hold you?

". . . kick their butts," said another man, an older worker that Gary knew only as Tomo. Gary knew right away that Tomo, and his bitter group were talking about the latest war, or the next war, or the chosen minority group of the day.

Gary shook his head. "Too nice a day for wars," he muttered under his breath. He spent his buck fifty and walked back towards the shop, carrying a pint of milk and a two-pack of Ring Dings. Gary did some quick calculations. He could grind six barrels an hour. Considering his wages, this snack was worth about two barrels, two hundred enemy jets.

He had to stop eating so much.

"You playing this weekend?" Leo asked him when he got to the loading dock, which the crew used as a sun deck.

"Probably," Gary spun about, hopping up to take a seat on the edge of the deck. Before he landed, an empty milk carton hopped off the back of his head.

"What'd'ye mean, probably?" Leo demanded.

Gary picked up the carton and returned fire. Caught in a crosswind, it missed Leo, bounced off Danny's head (who was too engrossed with his food to even notice), and ricocheted into a trash bin.

The highlight of the day.

"I meant to do that," Gary insisted.

"If you can plan a throw like that, you'd better play this weekend," remarked another of the group.

"You'd better play," Leo agreed, though from him it sounded more as a warning. "If you don't, I'll have him"—he motioned to his brother, Danny—"next to me in the outfield." He launched a second carton, this one at Danny. Danny dodged as it flew past, but his movement dropped a hunk of steak to the ground. He considered the fallen food for a moment, then looked back to Leo.

"That's my food!"

Leo was laughing too hard to hear him. He headed back into the shop; Gary shook his head in amazement at Danny's unending appetite—and yet, Danny was by far the slimmest of the group—and joined Leo. Twenty minutes. The reprieve was over.

Gary's thoughts were on the tournament as he headed back towards the grinding room. He liked that Leo, and many others, wanted him to play, considering their interest a payoff for the many hours he put in at the local gym. He was big and strong, six feet tall and well over two hundred pounds, and he could hit a softball a long, long way. That didn't count for much by Gary's estimation, but it apparently did in many other people's eyes—and Gary had to admit that he enjoyed their attention, the minor celebrity status.

The new skip in his step flattened immediately when he entered the grinding room.

"Now you gonna take a work break?" snarled Tomo. Gary looked up at the clock; his group had spent a few extra minutes outside.

"And what's this?" Tomo demanded, pointing to the mess by the catch barrel. "You too stupid to know when to change the barrel?"

Gary resisted the urge to mouth a sharp retort. Tomo wasn't his boss, wasn't anybody's boss, but he really wasn't such a bad guy. And looking at his pointing hand, with three fingers sheared off at the first knuckle, Gary could understand where the old plastics professional was coming from, could understand the source of the bitterness.

"Didn't teach you any common sense in college?" Tomo muttered, wandering away. His voice was full of venom as he repeated, "College."

Tomo was a lifer, had been working in plastics factories fully twenty years before Gary was even born. The missing fingers accentuated that point; many older men in Lancashire were missing fingers, a result of the older-design molding machines. Prone to jams, these monstrosities had a pair of iron doors that snapped shut with the force (and appetite, some would say) of a shark's jaws, and fingers seemed to be their favorite meals.

A profound sadness came over Gary as he watched the old man depart, limping slightly, leaning to one side, and with his two-fingered hand hanging freely by his side. It wasn't condescension aimed at Tomo—Gary wasn't feeling particularly superior to anyone at that moment—it was just a sadness about the human condition in general.

As if sensing Gary's lingering stare, Tomo spun back on him suddenly. "You'll be here all your life, you know!" the old man growled. "You'll work in the dirt and then you'll retire and then you'll die!"

Tomo turned and was gone, but his words hovered in the air around Gary like a black-winged curse.

"No, I won't," Gary insisted quietly, if somewhat lamely. At that point in his life, Gary had little ammunition to argue back against Tomo's cynicism. Gary had done everything right, everything according to the rules as they had been explained to him. Top of his class in college, double major, summa cum laude. And he had purposely concentrated in a field that promised lucrative employment, not the liberal arts concentration that he would have preferred. Even the general electives, courses most of his college colleagues breezed through without a care, Gary went after with a vengeance. If a 4.0 was there to be earned, Gary would settle for nothing less.

Everything according to the rules, everything done right. He had graduated nearly a year before, expecting to go out and set the world on fire.

It hadn't worked out quite as he had expected. They called it recession. Too pretty a word, by Gary Leger's estimation. He was beginning to think of it as reality.

And so here he was, back at the shop he had worked at part-time to help pay for his education. Grinding plastic chunks, shooting down enemy aircraft.

And dying.

He knew that, conceded that at least that part of Tomo's curse seemed accurate enough. Every day he worked here, passing time, was a day further away from the job and the life he desired, and a day closer to his death.

It was not a pleasant thought for a twenty-two-year-old. Gary moved back to the grinder, too consumed by a sense of mortality and self-pity for any thoughts of imaginary battles or World Series caliber curve balls.

Was he looking into a prophetic mirror when he gazed upon bitter Tomo? Would he become that seven-fingered old man, crooked and angry, fearing death and hating life?

There had to be more to it all, more reason for continuing his existence. Gary had seen dozens of shows interviewing people who had come close to death. All of them said how much more they valued their lives now, how their zest for living had increased dramatically and each new day had become a challenge and a joy. Sweeping up the plastic by the catch barrel with that beautiful spring day just inches away, beyond an open window, Gary almost hoped for a near-death experience, for something to shake him up, or at least to shake up this petty existence he had landed himself into. Was the value of his life to be tied up in memories of softball, or of that one moment on the loading dock when he had unintentionally bounced a milk carton off of Danny's head and landed it perfectly into the trash bin?

Tomo came back through the grinding room then, laughing and joking with another worker. His laughter mocked Gary's self-pity and made him feel ashamed of his dark thoughts. This was an honest job, after all, and a paying job, and for all his grumbling, Gary had to finally admit to himself that his life was his own to accept or to change.

Still, he seemed a pitiful sight indeed that night walking home—he always walked, not wanting to get the plastic colors on the seats of his new Jeep. His clothes were filthy, his hands were filthy (and bleeding in a few places), and his eyes stung from the dark blue powder, a grotesque parody of makeup, that had accumulated in and around them.

He kept off the main road for the two-block walk to his parents' house; he didn't really want to be seen.

TWO

THE CEMETERY, THE JEEP, AND THE HOBBIT

A cemetery covered most of the distance between the shop and home. This was not a morbid place to Gary. Far from it; he and his friends had spent endless hours in the cemetery, playing Fox and Hounds or Capture the Flag, using the large empty field (the water table was too high for graves) in the back corner for baseball games and football games. The importance of the place had not diminished as the group grew older. This was where you brought your girlfriend, hoping, praying, to uncover some of those "mysteries" in a Bob Seger song. This was where you sneaked the *Playboy* magazines a friend had lifted from his father's drawer, or the six-pack someone's over-twenty-one brother had bought (for a 100 percent delivery charge!). A thousand memories were tied up in this place, memories of a vital time of youth, and of learning about life.

In a cemetery.

The irony of that thought never failed to touch Gary as he walked through here each morning and night, to and from the grind of the grinder. He could see his parents' house from the cemetery, a two-story garrison up on the hill beyond the graveyard's chain-link fence. Hell, he could see all of his life from here, the games, the first love, limitations and boundless dreams. And now, a bit older, Gary could see, too, his own inevitable fate, could grasp the importance of those rows of headstones and understand that the people buried here had once had hopes and dreams just like his own, once wondered about the meaning and the worth of their lives.

Still, it remained not a morbid place, but heavy with nostalgia, a place of long ago and far away, and edged in the sadness of realized mortality. And as each day, each precious day, passed him by, Gary stood on a stool beside a metal table, loading chunks of scrap plastic into a whirring grinder.

Somehow, somewhere, there had to be more.

The stones and the sadness were left behind as soon as Gary hopped the six-foot fence across from his home. His tan Wrangler sat in front of the hedgerow, quiet and still as usual. Gary laughed to himself, at himself, every time he passed his four-wheel-drive toy. He had bought it for the promise of adventure, so he told others—and told himself at those times he was feeling gullible. There weren't a lot of trails in Lancashire; in the six months Gary had

owned the Jeep, he had taken it off-road exactly twice. Six months and only three thousand miles clocked on the odometer—hardly worth the payments.

But those payments were the real reason Gary had bought the Jeep, and in his heart he knew it. Gary had realized that he needed a reason to go stand on that stool and get filthy every day, a reason to answer the beckon of the rising sun. When he had bought the Jeep, he had played the all-American game, the sacrifice of precious time for things that someone else, some make-believe model in a make-believe world, told him he really wanted to have. Like everything else, it seemed, this Jeep was the end result of just one more of those rules that Gary had played by all his life.

"Ah, the road to adventure," Gary muttered, tapping the front fender as he passed. The previous night's rain had left brown spots all over the Jeep, but Gary didn't care. His filthy fingers left a blue streak of plastics' coloring above the headlight, but he didn't even notice.

He heard the words before his mother even spoke them.

"Oh my God," she groaned when he walked in the door. "Look at you."

"I am the ghost of Christmas past!" Gary moaned, holding his arms stiffly in front of him, opening his blue-painted eyes wide, and advancing a step towards her, reaching for her with grimy fingers.

"Get away!" she cried. "And get those filthy clothes in the laundry chute."

"Seventeen words," Gary whispered to his father as he passed him by on his way to the stairs. It was their inside joke. Every single day his mother said those same seventeen words. There was something comfortable in that uncanny predictability, something eternal and immortal.

Gary's step lightened considerably as he bounded up the carpeted stairs to the bathroom. This was home; this in his life, at least, was real, was the way it was supposed to be. His mother whined and complained at him constantly about his job, but he knew that was only because she truly cared, because she wanted better for her youngest child. She couldn't imagine her baby losing fingers to some hungry molding machine, or covering himself and filling up his lungs with a blue powder that was probably a carcinogen, or a something-ogen. (Wasn't everything?) This was Mom's support, given the only way Mom knew how to give it, and it did not fall on deaf ears where Gary Leger was concerned.

His father, too, was sympathetic and supportive. The elder Leger male understood Gary's realities better than his mom, Gary knew. Dad had been there, after all, pitching World Series into the letter sorters. "It will get better," he often promised Gary, and if Dad said it was so, then to Gary, it was so.

Period.

Gary spent a long time in front of the mirror, using cold cream in an attempt to get the blue powder away from the edges of his green eyes. He wondered if it would be there forever, vocational makeup. It amazed him how a job could

change his appearance. No longer did his hair seem to hold its previous luster, as though its shiny blackness was being dulled as surely as Gary's hopes and dreams.

Much more than blue plastic washed down the shower drain. Responsibility, tedium, and Tomo all went with the filthy powder. Even thoughts of mortality and wasted time. Now the day belonged to Gary, just to Gary. Not to rules and whirring grinders and cynical old men seeking company in their helpless misery.

The shower marked the transition.

"Dave called," his father yelled from the bottom of the stairs when he exited the bathroom. "He wants you to play for him this weekend."

Gary shrugged—big surprise—and moved to his room. He came back out in just a minute, wearing a tank top, shorts, and sneakers, free of his steel-toed work boots, jeans thick with grime, and heavy gloves. He got to the stairs, then snapped his fingers and spun about, returning to his room to scoop up his worn copy of J.R.R. Tolkien's *The Hobbit*. Yes, the rest of the day belonged to Gary, and he had plans.

"You gonna call him?" his father asked when he skipped through the kitchen. Gary stopped suddenly, caught off guard by the urgency in his father's tone.

As soon as he looked at his dad, the image of himself in forty years, Gary remembered the importance of the tournament. He hadn't really known his father as a young man. Gary was the youngest of seven and his dad was closer to fifty than forty when he was born. But Gary had heard the stories; he knew that Dad had been one heck of a ball player. "Could've gone pro, your father," the old cronies in the neighborhood bars asserted. "But there wasn't no money in the game back then and he had a family."

Ouch.

Play by the rules; pitch your World Series in the post office's slotted wall.

"He's not home now," Gary lied. "I'll get him tonight."

"Are you gonna play for him?"

Gary shrugged. "The shop's putting a team in. Leo wants me in left-center."

That satisfied Dad, and Gary, full of nothing but respect and admiration for his father, would have settled for nothing less. Still, thoughts of softball left him as soon as he stepped outside the house, the same way thoughts of work had washed away down the shower drain. The day was indeed beautiful—Gary could see that clearly now, with the blue powder no longer tinting his vision—and he had his favorite book under his arm.

He headed off down the dead-end road, the cemetery fence on his right and neighbors he had known all his life on his left. The road ended just a few houses down, spilling into a small wood, another of those special growing-up places.

The forest seemed lighter and smaller to Gary than he remembered it from the faraway days. Part of it, of course, was simply that he was a grown man, physically larger now. And the other part, truly, was that the forest was lighter, and smaller than it had been in Gary's younger days. Three new houses cut into this end of the wood, the western side; the eastern end had been chopped to make way for a state swimming pool and a new school; the northern edge had been cleared for a new playground; even the cemetery had played a role, spilling over into the southern end. Gary's forest was under assault from every side. Often he wondered what he might find if he moved away and came back twenty years from now. Would this wood, his wood, be no more than a handful of trees surrounded by asphalt and cement?

That thought disturbed Gary as profoundly as the notion of losing fingers to a hungry molding machine.

There was still some serenity and privacy to be found in the small wood, though. Gary moved in a few dozen yards, then turned north on a fire road, purposely keeping his eyes on the trees as he passed the new houses, the new trespassers. He came up to one ridge, cleared except for the remains of a few burned-out trees and a number of waist-high blueberry bushes. He kept far from the ridge's lip, not because of any dangerous drop—there were no dangerous drops in this wood—but because to look over the edge was to look down upon the new school, nestled in what had once been Gary's favorite valley.

The fire road, becoming no more than a foot-wide trail among the blueberries, dipped steeply into a darker region, a hillside engulfed by thick oaks and elms. This was the center of the wood, too far from any of the encircling roads to hear the unending traffic and packed with enough trees and bushes to block out the unwelcome sights of progress. No sunlight came in here at this time of the afternoon except for one spot on a west-facing, mossy banking.

Privacy and serenity.

Gary plopped down on the thick moss and took out his book. The bookmark showed him to be on one of the later chapters, but he opened the book near the front, as he always did, to consider the introduction, written by some man that Gary did not know named Peter S. Beagle. It was dated July 14, 1973, and filled with thoughts surely based in the "radical" sixties. How relevant those ideas of "progress" and "escape" seemed to Gary, sitting in his dwindling wood more than fifteen years later.

The last line, "Let us at last praise the colonizers of dreams," held particular interest for Gary, a justification of imagination and of his own escapism. When Gary read this introduction and that last line, he did not feel so silly about standing by the grinder shooting down alien aircraft.

His sigh was one of thanks to the late Mr. Tolkien, and he reverently opened the book to the marked page and plowed ahead on the great adventure of one hobbit, Mr. Bilbo Baggins.

Time held no meaning to Gary as he read. Only if he looked back to see how many pages he had flipped could he guess whether minutes or hours had passed. At this time of the year, the mossy banking would catch enough sun to read by for two or three hours before twilight, he knew, so when his light ran out it would be time for supper. That was all the clock Gary Leger needed or wanted.

He read two chapters, then took a good stretch and a good yawn, cupped his hands behind his head, and lay back on the natural carpet. He could see pieces of the blue sky through the thick leaves, one white cloud lazily meandering west to east, to Boston and the Atlantic Ocean fifty miles away.

"Fifty miles?" Gary asked aloud, chuckling and stretching again. Here with his book, it might as well have been five thousand miles. But this moment of freedom was fleeting, he knew. The light was already fading; he figured he might have time for one more chapter. He forced himself back up to a sitting posture—he was getting too comfortable—and took up his book.

Then he heard a small rustle to the side. He was up in an instant, quietly, crouching low and looking all about. It could have been a field mouse or, more likely, a chipmunk. Or maybe a snake; Gary hoped it wasn't a snake. He had never been fond of the slithery things, though the only ones around here were garters, without fangs or poison, and most of them too small to give even a half-assed bite, certainly not as nasty a nip as a mouse or chipmunk could deliver. Still, Gary hoped it wasn't a snake. If he found a snake here, he'd probably never be able to lie down comfortably on the mossy banking again.

His careful scan showed him something quite unexpected. "A doll?" he mouthed, staring at the tiny figure. He wondered how he could possibly have missed that before, or who might have put it here, in this place he thought reserved for his exclusive use. He crouched lower and moved a step closer, meaning to pick the thing up. He had never seen one like it before. "Robin Hood?" he whispered, though it seemed more of an elf-like figure, sharp-featured (incredibly detailed!), dressed in woodland greens and browns, and wearing a longbow (a very short longbow, of course) over one shoulder and a pointed cap on its head.

Gary reached for it but recoiled quickly in amazement.

The thing had taken the bow off its shoulder! Gary thought he must have imagined it, but even as he tried to convince himself of his foolishness, he continued to watch the living doll. It showed no fear of Gary at all, just calmly pulled an arrow from its quiver and drew back on the bowstring.

Oh my God! Gary's face crinkled in confusion; he looked back to his book accusingly, as though it had something to do with all of this.

"Where the heck did you come from?" Gary stuttered. Oh my God! He glanced all around, searched the trees and the bushes for something, someone with a projector. Oh my God!

It seemed like the trick of a high-tech movie: "Help me, Obi-Wan Kenobi, you're my only hope."

Oh my God!

The doll, the elf, whatever it was, seemed to pay his movements little heed. It took aim at Gary and fired.

"Hey!" Gary cried, throwing a hand out to block the projectile. His reality sense told him it was just another trick, another image from the unseen projector. But he felt a sting in his palm, as real as one a bee might give, then looked down incredulously to see a tiny dart sticking out of it.

Oh my God!

"Why'd you do that?" Gary protested. He looked back to the tiny figure, more curious than angry. It leaned casually on its bow, looking about and whistling in a tiny, mousey voice. How calm it seemed, considering that Gary could lift one foot and crush it out like a discarded cigarette.

"Why'd . . ." Gary started to ask again, but he stopped and tried hard to hold himself steady as a wave of dizziness swept over him.

Had the sun already set?

A gray fog engulfed the woods—or was the fog in his eyes? He still heard the squeaky whistling, more clearly now, but all the rest of the world seemed to be getting farther away.

Had the sun already set?

Instinctively Gary headed towards home, back up the dirt road. The . . . the thing—oh my God, what the hell was it?—had shot him! Had fricken shot him!

The thing, what the hell was it?

The smell of blueberries filled Gary's nose as he came up over the embankment. He tried to stay on the path but wandered often into the tangling bushes.

The sudden rush of air was the only indication Gary had that he was falling. A soft grassy patch padded his landing, but Gary, deep in the slumbers of pixie poison, wouldn't have noticed anyway, even if he had clunked down on a sheet of cement.

It was night—how had he missed the sunset?

Gary forced himself to his feet and tried to get his bearings. The aroma of blueberries reminded him where he was, and he knew how to get home. But it was night, and he had probably missed supper—try explaining that to his fretful mother!

His limbs still weary, he struggled to rise.

And then he froze in startlement and wonderment. He remembered the pixie archer, for the sprite was suddenly there again, right before him, this time joined by scores of its little friends. They danced and twirled around the grassy patch, wrapping Gary in a shimmering cocoon of tiny song and sparkling light.

Oh my God!

Sparkling. The light blurred together into a single curtain, exuded calmness. The fairie song came to his ears, compelling him to lie back down.

Lie back down and sleep.

THREE

SYLVAN FOREST

It was day—what the heck was going on?

Gary felt the grass under his cheek. At first, he thought he had simply fallen asleep, and he was drowsy still, lying there so very comfortably. Then Gary remembered again the sprite archer and the dance of the fairies, and his eyes popped open wide. It took considerable effort to lift his head and prop himself up on his elbows; the poison, or whatever it was, weighed heavily in his limbs. But he managed it, and he looked around, and then he became even more confused.

He was still in the blueberry patch; all the trees and bushes and paths were in the places he remembered them. They were somehow not the same, though—Gary knew that instinctively. It took him a moment to figure out exactly what was different, but once he recognized it clearly, there could be no doubt.

The colors were different.

The trees were brown and green, the grass and moss were green, and the dirt trail a grayish brown, but they were not the browns, greens, and grays of Gary's world. There was a luster to the colors, an inner vibrancy and richness beyond anything Gary had seen. He couldn't even begin to explain it to himself, the view was too vivid to be real, like some forest rendition by a surrealistic painter, a primordial viewpoint of a world undulled by reality and human pollution.

Another shock greeted Gary when he turned his attention away from his immediate surroundings and looked out over the ridge, at the landscape beyond the school that had stolen his favorite valley. He saw no houses—he was sure that he had seen houses from this point before—but only distant, towering mountains.

"Where did those come from?" Gary asked under his breath. He was still a bit disoriented, he decided, and he told himself that he had never really looked out over that ridge before, never allowed himself to register the magnificent sight. Of course the mountains had always been there, Gary had just never noticed how large and truly spectacular they were.

At the snap of a twig, Gary turned to look over his shoulder. There stood the sprite, half a foot tall, paying him little heed and leaning casually on its longbow. "What are you?" Gary asked, too confused to question his sanity.

The diminutive creature made no move to respond; gave no indication that it had heard the question at all.

"What . . ." Gary started to ask again, but he changed his mind. What indeed was this creature, and this dream? For it had to be a dream, Gary rationally told himself, as any respectable, intelligent person awaiting the dawn of the twenty-first century would tell himself.

It didn't feel like one, though. There were too many real sounds and colors, no single-purposed visions common to nightmares. Gary was cognizant of his surroundings, could turn in any direction and see the forest clearly. And he had never experienced a dream, or even heard of anyone else experiencing a dream, where he consciously knew that he was dreaming.

"Time to find out," he muttered under his breath. He had always thought himself pretty quick-handed, had even done some boxing in high school. His lunge at the sprite was pitifully slow, though; the creature was gone before he ever got near the spot. He followed the rustle stubbornly, pouncing on any noise, sweeping areas of dead leaves and low berry bushes with his arms.

"Ow!" he cried, feeling a pinprick in his backside. He spun about. The sprite was a few feet behind him—he had no idea how the stupid thing got there—holding its bow and actually laughing at him!

Gary turned slowly, never letting the creature out of his glowering stare. He leaned forward, his muscles tensed for a spring that would put him beyond the creature, cut off its expected escape route.

Then Gary fell back on his elbows, eyes wide in heightened disbelief, as a second creature joined the first, this one taller, at least two feet from toes to top, and this one, Gary recognized.

Gary was not of Irish descent, but that hardly mattered. He had seen this creature pictured a thousand times, and he marveled now at the accuracy of those images. The creature wore a beard, light brown, like its curly hair. Its overcoat was gray, like its sparkling, mischievous eyes, and its breeches green, with shiny black, curly-toed shoes. If the long-stemmed pipe in its mouth wasn't a dead giveaway, the tam-o'-shanter on its head certainly was.

"So call it a dream, then," the creature said to him "and be satisfied with that. It do not matter." Gary watched, stunned, as this newest sprite, this leprechaun—this fricken *leprechaun!*—walked over to the archer.

"He's a big one," the leprechaun said. "I say, will he fit?"

The archer chirped out something too squeaky for Gary to understand, but the leprechaun seemed appeased.

"For yer troubles, then," the leprechaun said, and he handed over a four-leaf clover, the apparent payment for delivering Gary.

The pixie archer bowed low in appreciation, cast a derisive chuckle Gary's way, and then was gone, disappearing into the underbrush too quickly and completely for Gary to even visually follow its movements.

"Mickey McMickey at yer service," the leprechaun said politely, dipping into a low bow and tipping his tam-o'-shanter.

Oh my God.

The leprechaun, having completed its greeting, waited patiently.

"If you're really at my service," Gary stuttered, startled even by the sound of his own voice, "then you'll answer a few questions. Like, what the hell is going on?"

"Don't ye ask," Mickey advised. "Ye'd not be satisfied in hearing me answers. Not yet. But in time ye'll come to understand it all. Know now that ye're here for a service, and when ye're done with it, ye can return to yer own place."

"So I'm at your service," Gary reasoned. "And not the other way around."

Mickey scratched at his finely trimmed beard. "Not in service for me," he answered after some thought. "Though yer being here does do me a service, if ye follow me thinking. Ye're in service to an elf."

"The little guy?" Gary asked, pointing to the brush where the sprite had disappeared.

"Not a pixie," Mickey replied. "An elf. Tylwyth Teg." He paused, as if those strange words should mean something to Gary. With no response beyond a confused stare forthcoming, Mickey went on, somewhat exasperated.

"Tylwyth Teg," he said again. "The Fair Family. Ye've not heard o' them?"

Gary shook his head, his mouth hanging open.

"Sad times ye're living in, ye poor lad," Mickey mumbled. He shrugged helplessly, a twittering, jerky movement for a creature as small as he, and finished his explanation. "These elfs are named the Tylwyth Teg, the Fair Family. To be sure, they're the noblest race of the faerie folk, though a bit unbending to the ways of others. A great elf, too, this one ye'll soon be meeting, and one not for taking lightly. 'Twas him that catched me, ye see, and made me catch yerself."

"Why me?" Gary wondered why he'd asked that, why he was talking to this . . . whatever it was . . . at all. Would Alan Funt soon leap out at him, laughing and pointing to that elusive camera?

"Because ye'll fit the armor," Mickey said as though the whole thing should make perfect sense. "The pixies took yer measures and say ye'll fit. As good yerself as another, that being the only requirement." Mickey paused a moment, staring reflectively into Gary's eyes.

"Green eyes?" the leprechaun remarked. "Ah, so were Cedric's. A good sign!"

Gary's nod showed that he accepted, but certainly did not understand, what Mickey was saying. It really wasn't a big problem for Gary at that moment, though, for all that he could do was go along with these thoroughly unbelievable events and thoroughly unbelievable creatures. If he was dreaming, then fine; it might be enjoyable. And if not . . . well, Gary decided not to think about that possibility just then.

What Gary did think about was his knowledge of leprechauns and the legends surrounding them. He knew the reward for catching a leprechaun and, dream or not, it sounded like a fun course to take. He reached a hand up behind his head, feigning an itch, then dove headlong at Mickey and came up clutching the little guy.

"There," Gary declared triumphantly. "I've caught you and you have to lead me to your pot of gold! I know the rules, Mr. Mickey McMickey."

"Tsk, tsk, tsk," he heard from the side. He turned to see Mickey leaning casually against a tree stump, holding Gary's book, *The Hobbit*, open before him. Gary turned slowly back to his catch and saw that he held Mickey in his own two hands. "Sonofabitch," Gary mumbled under his breath, for this was a bit too confusing.

"If ye know the rules, ye should know the game," Mickey—the Mickey leaning against the tree—said in response to Gary's blank stare.

"How?" Gary stuttered.

"Look closer, lad," Mickey said to him. "Then let go of the mushroom before ye get yer hands all dirty."

Gary studied his catch carefully. It remained a leprechaun as far as he could tell, though it didn't seem to be moving very much—not at all, actually. He looked back to the leaning leprechaun and shrugged.

"Closer," Mickey implored.

Gary eyed the figure a moment longer. Gradually the image transformed and he realized that he was indeed holding a large and dirty mushroom. He shook his head in disbelief and dropped it to the ground, then noticed *The Hobbit* lying at his feet, right where he had left it. He looked back to Mickey by the tree trunk, now a mushroom again, and then back to the dropped mushroom, now a leprechaun brushing himself off.

"Ye think it to be an easy thing, catching a leprechaun?" Mickey asked him sourly. "Well, if it was, do ye think any of us'd have any gold left to give out?" He walked right next to Gary to scoop up the strange book. Gary had a thought about grabbing him again, this time to hold on, but the leprechaun acted first.

"Don't ye be reaching yer hands at me," Mickey ordered.

"'Twas me that catched yerself, remember? And besides, grabbing at the likes o' Mickey McMickey, ye just don't know what ye might put them hands in! Been fooling stupid big folk longer than ye've been alive, I tell ye! I telled ye once . . . what did ye say yer name was? . . . don't ye make me tell ye again!"

"Gary," Gary answered, straightening up and taking a prudent step away from the unpredictable sprite. "Gary Leger."

"Well met, then, Gary Leger," Mickey said absently. His thoughts now seemed to be fully on the book's cover, "Bilbo comes to the huts of the raft elfs," an original painting by Tolkien himself. Mickey nodded his approval, then opened the work. His face crinkled immediately and he mumbled a few words under his breath and waved a hand across the open page.

"Much the better," he said.

"What are you doing to my book?" Gary protested, leaning down to take it back. Just before he reached it, though, he realized that he was putting his hand into the fanged maw of some horrid, demonic thing, and he recoiled immediately, nearly falling over backwards.

"Never know what ye might put yer hands into," Mickey said again absently, not bothering to look up at the startled man. "And really, Gary Leger, ye must learn to see more the clearly if we mean to finish this quest. Ye can't go playing with dragons if ye can't look through a simple illusion. Come along, then." And Mickey started off, reading as he walked.

"Dragons?" Gary muttered at the leprechaun's back, drawing no response. "Dragons?" Gary asked again, this time to himself. Really, he told himself, he shouldn't be so surprised.

The fire road, too, was as Gary remembered it, except, of course, for the colors, which continued with their surrealistic vibrancy. As they moved along the path towards the main road, though, Gary thought that the woods seemed denser. On the way in, he had seen houses from this point, the new constructions he always tried not to notice. Now he wanted to see them, wanted to find some sense of normalcy in this crazy situation, but try as he may, his gaze could not penetrate the tangle of leaves and branches.

When they came to the end of the fire road, Gary realized beyond doubt that more had changed about the world around him than unnoticed mountains and dense trees and strange colors. This time there could be no mistake of perception.

Back in Lancashire, the fire road ended at the dirt continuation of the main road, the road that ran past his parents' house. Across from the juncture sat the chain-link cemetery fence.

But there was no fence here, just more trees, endless trees.

Mickey paused to wait for Gary, who stood staring, open-mouthed. "Well, are ye coming, then?" the leprechaun demanded after a long uneventful moment.

"Where's the fence?" Gary asked, hardly able to find his breath.

"Fence?" Mickey echoed. "What're ye talking about, lad?"

"The cemetery fence," Gary tried to explain.

"Who'd be putting a graveyard in the middle of the forest?" Mickey replied with a laugh. The leprechaun stopped short, seeing that Gary did not share in the joke, and then Mickey nodded his understanding.

"Hear me, lad," the leprechaun began sympathetically. "Ye're not in yer own place—I told ye that already. Ye're in me place now, in County Dilnamarra in the wood called Tir na n'Og."

"But I remember the blueberry patch," Gary protested, thinking he had caught the leprechaun in a logic trap. Surprisingly Mickey seemed almost saddened by Gary's words.

"That ye do," the leprechaun began. "Ye remember the blueberries from yer own place, Real-earth, in a patch much like the one I found ye in."

"They were the same," Gary said stubbornly.

"No, lad," Mickey replied. "There be bridges still between yer own world and this world, places alike yer blueberry patch that seem as the same in both the lands."

"This world?"

"Sure that ye've heard of it," Mickey replied. "The world of the Faerie."

Gary crinkled his brow with incredulity, then tried to humor the leprechaun and hide his smile.

"In such places," Mickey continued, not noticing Gary's obvious doubt, "some folk, the pixies mostly, can cross over, and within their dancing circle, they can bring a one such as yerself back. But alas, fewer the bridges get by the day—I fear that yer world'll soon lose its way to Faerie altogether."

"This has been done before?" Gary asked. "I mean, people from my world have crossed . . ."

"Aren't ye listening? And have ye not heard the tales?" Mickey asked. He grabbed his pipe in one hand, plopped his hands on his hips, and gave a disgusted shake of his head.

"I've heard of leprechauns," Gary offered hopefully.

"Well, where are ye thinking the stories came from?" Mickey replied. "All the tales of wee folk and dancing elfs, and dragons in lairs full o' gold? Did ye not believe them, lad? Did ye think them stories for the children by a winter's fire?"

"It's not that I don't want to believe them," Gary tried to explain.

"Don't?" Mickey echoed. "Sure'n ye mean to say 'didn't.' Ye've no choice but to believe the faerie tales now, seeing as ye've landed in one of them!"

Gary only smiled noncommittally, though in fact he was truly enjoying this experience—whatever it might be. He shook his head at the thought. Whatever it might be? Oh my God!

He asked no more questions as they made their way along footpaths through the marvelous colors and aromas of the sylvan forest. He did stop once to more closely regard the leprechaun, shuffling up ahead of him. Mickey crossed over a patch of dry brown leaves, but made not a whisper of a sound. Gary moved up behind as carefully as he could, noting his own crunching and crackling footsteps and feeling altogether clumsy and out of place next to the nimble Mickey.

But if Gary was indeed an intruder here, the forest did not make him feel so. Birds and squirrels, a raccoon and a young deer, skipped by on their business not too far from him, paying no attention to him beyond a quick and curious glance. Gary could not help but feel at home here; the place was warm and dreamy, full of life and full of ease. And to Gary, it was still entirely in his mind, a fantasy, a dream, and perfectly safe.

They arrived many minutes later at a small clearing centered by a huge and ancient oak tree—Gary figured it to be located on the spot normally occupied by downtown Lancashire's Dunkin' Donuts. Apparently the leprechaun had set out with this destination in mind, for Mickey moved right up to the tree and plopped down on a mossy patch, pulling out a packet of weed for his pipe.

"A rest?" Gary asked.

"Here's the place," Mickey replied. "Kelsey's to meet us here, and then ye're on with him. I'll take me leave."

"You're not coming with us?"

Mickey laughed, nearly choking as he simultaneously tried to light his pipe. "Yerself and Kelsey," he explained. "'Tis his quest and not me own. Rest and don't ye be testing. I'll give ye some tips for handling that one." He paused to finish lighting the pipe, and if he went on after that, Gary did not hear him.

A song drifted down from the boughs of the great oak, high-pitched and charmingly sweet. It flittered on the very edges of Gary's hearing, teasing . . . teasing.

Gary's gaze wandered up the massive oak, seeking the source.

Teasing . . . teasing.

And then he saw her, peeking around a thick lower branch. She was a tiny thing by human measures, five feet tall perhaps and never close to a hundred pounds, with a pixieish face and eyes too clear and hair too golden.

And a voice too sweet.

It took Gary a moment to even realize that she was naked—no, not naked, but wearing the sheerest veil of gossamer that barely blurred her form. Again, that edge-of-perception tease.

"What are ye about?" Gary heard Mickey say from some distant place.

The melody was more than a simple song, it was a call to Gary. "Come up to me," the notes implored him.

He didn't have to be asked twice.

"Oh, cobblestones," moaned Mickey, realizing then the source of Gary's distraction. The leprechaun pulled off his tam-o'-shanter and slapped it across his knee, angry at himself. He should have known better than to take so vulnerable a young human near the haunting grounds of Leshiye, the wood nymph.

"Get yerself down, lad," he called to Gary. "There's not a thing up there ye're wanting."

Gary didn't bother to reply; it was obvious that he didn't agree. He swung a leg over the lowest branch and pulled himself up. The nymph was close now, smelling sweet, singing sweet, and so alluring in her translucent gown. And her song was so inviting, promising, teasing in ways that Gary could not resist.

"Get yerself gone, Leshiye!" Mickey yelled from below, knowing that any further appeals he might make to Gary would fall on deaf ears. "We've business more important than yer hunting. Kelsey'll be here soon and he won't be pleased with ye. Not a bit!"

The nymph's song went on undisturbed. Gary tried several routes through the branch tangle, then finally found one that would lead him to his goal.

A huge snake appeared on the branch before him, coiled and hissing, with fangs all too prominent. Gary stopped short and tried to backtrack, eyes wide, and so frantic that he nearly toppled from the branch.

Still, Leshiye sang, even heightened the sweetness of her song with laughter. She waved her hand and the snake was gone, and as far as the entranced Gary was concerned, the serpent had never appeared. He started up the tree again immediately, but now the branches began to dance under him, waving and seeming to multiply.

Gary looked down at Mickey, guessing both the serpent and now this to be more of the leprechaun's illusionary tricks.

"What are you doing?" he called down angrily. "Are you trying to make me fall?"

"Leave her be, lad," Mickey replied. "Ye're not for mixing with one of her type."

Gary looked back at the nymph for a long, lingering while, then turned back sharply on Mickey. "Are you nuts?"

Mickey's cherubic face twisted in confusion over the strange phrase for just a moment, but then he seemed to recognize the general meaning of the words. "And block yer ears, lad," Mickey went on stubbornly. "Don't ye let her charms fall over ye. Ye must be strong; in this tree, her home, I've no magics to outdo her illusions."

The leprechaun's warnings began to make some sense to Gary—until he looked back at the nymph, now reclining languidly on one stretching branch. Gary looked all about helplessly, trying to sort some safe way to get through to her.

Leshiye laughed again—within the melodic boundaries of her continuing song. She drew her powers from the tree—this was her home base—and she easily defeated Mickey's illusionary maze, leaving the correct path open and obvious before Gary's eager eyes.

Mickey slapped his tam-o'-shanter against his knee again and fell down to the moss, defeated. He could not win the attention of a young human male against the likes of a wood nymph. "Kelsey's not to be liking this," he muttered quietly and soberly, not thrilled at facing the stern and impatient elf with still more bad news.

Leshiye had taken Gary's hand by then, and she led him higher into the tree, just over the second split in the thick trunk area to a small leafy hollow.

"Oh, well," Mickey shrugged as they disappeared from sight. "I'll just have to go out and find another one fitting the armor." He tapped his pipe against the tree and popped it into his mouth, then took out Gary's book and sat down for a good read.

FOUR

THE ELF

The elf's expression soured as he neared the small field surrounding the giant oak tree. Mickey was there, as arranged, sitting against the tree, intently reading a book. But Mickey was alone, and that was not according to the plan.

"Just like a bunch o' dwarfs to go off chasing some long-lost treasure," the elf, with his sharp ears, heard Mickey mutter lightheartedly. "Never could resist a gem or bit o' gold and always claiming that it was their own from the start!"

Mickey looked up then, sensing the elf's approach. "And a good day to ye, Kelsey!" he declared, not bothering to rise.

"Where is he?" Kelsey demanded. "I have gone to great trouble to make all the arrangements in time and Baron Pwyll is not a patient man. You agreed to have him here today."

"And so I did," Mickey replied.

There came a high-pitched giggle from above. Kelsey knew the forest at least as well as Mickey, and seeing the leprechaun holding the strange book and hearing the call from above, he looked up at the towering oak and quickly figured out the riddle.

"Leshiye," Kelsey grumbled.

He turned back to Mickey, still absorbed by the book. "How long has he been up there?"

Mickey put a hand over his eyes to regard the position of the sun. "Two hours, by now," he said. "He's a scrapper, this one!"

Kelsey didn't appreciate Mickey's lightheartedness; not where his life-quest was concerned. "Why did you not stop him?" the elf demanded, his golden eyes flashing with anger.

"Think what ye're asking," Mickey shot back. "Stop a healthy young man from getting at a nymph's offered charms? I'd as soon try to catch a dragon in me hat"—he pulled off his tam-o'-shanter and held it out upside down in front of him—"and make the beast warm up me dinner stew."

Kelsey couldn't argue against the leprechaun's claims of helplessness. Nymphs were a powerful foe where young men were concerned, and this one, Leshiye, was as skillful at her seductive arts as any in all Tir na n'Og. "Is he the proper size to wear the armor?" Kelsey asked, obviously disgusted.

On Mickey's nod, the elf dropped the longbow off his shoulder and began scrambling up the tree. Mickey just went on reading. If Kelsey could handle it, then fine, that would mean less work for the leprechaun. And if not, if Gary was too far gone to be rescued, then Kelsey certainly couldn't blame Mickey for the failure, and Mickey would at least be able to get the elf to give him more time in his hunt for another suitable man. Either way, it didn't bother the leprechaun—very little ever truly bothered any leprechaun. It was a sunny warm day, with good smells, good sights, and good reading. What else could a leprechaun ask for?

He settled back against the tree and found his spot on the page, but before he could begin reading again, a sneaker plopped down upon his head and bounced to the ground next to him.

"Hey!" he cried, looking up. "What are ye about, then?" A second sneaker came bouncing down, straight at Mickey, but he quickly pointed a finger and uttered a single word and the shoe stopped in midair a foot above his head, and hung there motionless.

There came the sound of scuffling up above, a complaint, which Mickey recognized as Gary's voice—the scrapper was still alive, at least—and suddenly Leshiye's singing sounded not so happy. Nymphs held little power over the Tylwyth Teg, the leprechaun knew, for the elven folk were not taken by enchantments and illusions as easily as were humans. Mickey nodded and shook his head helplessly, in sympathy with the nymph—it was that same resistance that had allowed Kelsey to catch Mickey and start this whole adventure in the first place.

A moment later, Gary came over the lip of the leafy hollow, followed closely by Kelsey. Gary cast a mournful look at what he was leaving behind, but the pointy sword tip at his back overruled Leshiye's pull on him. He moved slowly, picking his way down the tree, and kept looking back over his shoulder. Kelsey, obviously agitated and knowing that he had to get Gary as far away from the nymph as quickly as possible, prodded him along none too gently each time.

Leshiye came out behind them then, singing still.

"Get back in your den!" Kelsey yelled at her. He spun about, his gleaming sword up high and ready.

Leshiye, naked and vulnerable, stubbornly held her ground.

"Don't hit her!" Gary snapped at Kelsey. "Don't you dare!"

Kelsey turned and calmly slipped his foot across Gary's. A subtle twist sent Gary tumbling from the branch, the last ten feet to the ground. Without giving the human another thought, the elf spun back on Leshiye and warned again, "Get back in your den!"

Leshiye laughed at him. She knew, and Kelsey knew, that the elf's threat was a hollow one. No member of Tylwyth Teg would ever strike down a creature of Tir na n'Og, and Leshiye the wood nymph was as much a part of the forest as any tree or any animal.

Kelsey slipped his sword back in its gem-studded scabbard, scowled once more at the nymph, just for good measure, then skipped down the tree so lightly and easily that Gary, recovering down below, blinked in amazement.

Almost immediately, Leshiye's singing started up again.

"Be quiet!" Kelsey yelled up at her. "And you," he growled at Gary, "straighten your clothes and come along!"

Gary looked at Mickey, who nodded that he should obey. He picked up one shoe, then bumped his head on the other, noticing it for the first time. It remained hanging in the air where Mickey had magically held it. Gary expected to find some invisible wire supporting it, but it came freely into his hand when he tentatively grasped it.

"How?" Gary started to ask, but he took Mickey's sly wink as the only explanation he would ever get.

"Hurry along!" Kelsey demanded.

"Who the hell is he?" Gary asked Mickey. Kelsey swung about immediately and stormed over, his clear eyes shining fiercely, and his shoulder-length hair, more golden than the eyes even, glistening brightly in the sunlight Kelsey was fully a foot shorter than Gary, and a hundred pounds lighter, but he seemed to tower over the young man now, enlarged by confidence and open anger.

"There I go again," Mickey said, slapping himself off the side of the head. "Forgetting me manners. Gary, lad, meet Kelsey . . ."

Kelsey showed Mickey a look that bordered on violence.

"Kelsenellenelvial Gil-Ravadry," Mickey quickly corrected. "An elf-lord of the Tylwyth Teg."

"Kelsen . . ." Gary stuttered, hardly able to echo the strange name.

Mickey saw the opening for a good taunt at his captor. "Call him Kelsey, lad," the leprechaun said with obvious enjoyment. "Everyone does."

"Sounds good to me," Gary said pointedly, realizing the elf's renewed glare. At that moment, anything that bothered the elf—the elf who had interrupted Gary's pleasure—would have sounded good to Gary. "Who invited you up the tree, Kelsey?" Gary asked evenly.

He realized at once that he was pushing his luck.

Kelsey said not a word; his hand didn't even go to the hilt of his exquisite sword. But the look he gave Gary silenced the young man as completely as that sword ever could.

Kelsey let the stare linger a bit longer, then turned about sharply and strode away.

"He's a good enough sort," Mickey explained to Gary. "Ye can get a bit o' fun outa that one, but be knowing, lad, that he saved your life."

Gary shot an incredulous look the leprechaun's way.

"She'd not ever have let ye go," Mickey went on. "Ye'd have died up there—a pleasing way to go, I'm not for arguing."

Gary did not seem convinced.

"Ye'd have been a goner," Mickey went on. "In the likes of Leshiye's clutches, ye'd have forgotten to eat or drink. Might that ye'd have forgotten to breathe, lad! Yer mind would've been set to one task only, until yer body died for the effort."

Gary slipped his sneaker on his foot and quickly tied it. "I can take care of myself," he declared.

"So have sayed a hundred men in that nymph's embrace," Mickey replied. "So have sayed a hundred dead men." The leprechaun chuckled and moved off after the elf, pulling out *The Hobbit* as he walked.

Gary stood for a while shaking his head and considering whether or not he should go back up the tree. Just to make things more difficult for him, Leshiye appeared again over the edge of the hollow, smiling coyly. But the nymph looked out towards Kelsey, not so far away and with his longbow in hand, and she did not call out to the human this time.

Gary saw Kelsey, too, and he figured that if he started up the tree, the elf would surely put an arrow into his wrist, or perhaps somewhere else, somewhere more vital. "Time to go," he prudently told himself, and, casting a quick glance Kelsey's way, he zipped up his shorts. He gave more than one lamenting glance back at the tree as he wandered away, back at Leshiye in her translucent gown reclining comfortably on the branch beside the hollow.

Even Kelsey didn't blame him.

The elf set a swift pace through the forest, following no trail at all as far as Gary could discern. But Kelsey seemed to know where he was going, and Gary thought the better of questioning him. Mickey proved to be little comfort on the journey. The leprechaun skipped along, his footsteps impossibly light, with his face buried in *The Hobbit*, laughing every now and then or muttering a "begorra." Gary was glad that the leprechaun was enjoying the book. Even though Mickey, by the leprechaun's own admission, had kidnapped him, Gary found that he liked the little guy.

Another laugh from Mickey sent Gary over to him. He peeked over the leprechaun's shoulder (not a difficult thing to do), trying to see what chapter Mickey was on.

"What?" Gary babbled when he saw the open book. What had once been ordinary typeset was now a flowing script, in a language totally unrecognizable to Gary. Great sweeping lines had replaced the block letters, forming runes that did not resemble any alphabet Gary had ever seen. "What did you do to it?" he demanded.

Mickey looked up, his gray eyes turned up happily at their edges. "Do to what?" he asked innocently.

"My book," Gary protested, reaching down to take back the copy. He flipped through the pages, each showing the same unintelligible script. "What did you do to my book?"

"I made it readable," Mickey explained.

"It was readable."

"For yerself," replied Mickey, yanking the book back. "But ye can read it anytime—who's knowing how long I've got with it? So I made it readable for meself, and quit yer fretting. Ye'll get it back when I'm done."

"Forget the book," said a voice up ahead. The two looked to see Kelsey, stern-faced as usual, standing by a fat elm. "The book does not matter," the elf went on, talking to Gary. "You have more important concerns than casual reading." Kelsey cast Mickey a suspicious glance. "Have you informed him of the quest?"

"I been meaning to," Mickey replied. "Truly I have. But I'm wanting to break the lad in slowly, let him get used to things one at a time."

"We have not the time for that," said Kelsey. "The arrangements have already been made in Dilnamarra. We will soon be there to collect the artifacts, and then the quest begins in full."

"Very well, then," Mickey conceded, closing *The Hobbit* and dropping it into an impossibly deep pocket in his gray jacket. "Lead on and I'll tell the lad as we go."

"We will break now," Kelsey replied. "You will tell him before we go."

Mickey and Kelsey eyed each other suspiciously for a few moments. The leprechaun knew that Kelsey had only ordered a break in the march so that he could better monitor the story that Mickey laid out to Gary. "Sure'n Tylwyth Teg's a trusting bunch," Mickey muttered quietly, but Kelsey's smile showed that he had heard clearly enough.

"I told ye that ye were bringed here to serve an elf," Mickey began to Gary. "And so ye've met the elf, Kelsenel . . ." He stumbled over the long name, looked at Kelsey in frustration, and said, "Kelsey," gaining a measure of satisfaction in the insulted elf's returned scowl.

"Kelsey catched me to catch yerself—that, too, ye know," Mickey continued. "He's got himself a life-quest—the Tylwyth Teg take that sort o' stuff seriously, ye must understand—and he's needing a human of the right size to see it through."

Gary looked over at Kelsey, standing impassive and proud, and truly felt used. He wanted to shout out against the treatment, but he reminded himself, somewhat unconvincingly, that it was only a dream, after all.

"Kelsey's to reforge the spear of Cedric Donigarten," Mickey explained. "No easy task, that."

"Shouldn't you have caught a blacksmith?" Gary asked sarcastically.

"Oh, ye're not here to forge . . ." Mickey started to explain.

"The blacksmith will be next," Kelsey interrupted, aiming his words at Mickey. They had some effect, Gary saw, for the leprechaun stuttered over his next few words.

"Ye're the holder," Mickey managed to say at last. "The spear must be in the hands of a human—one in the armor of Cedric Donigarten, which is why ye were measured—when it's melted back together."

Gary didn't see the point of all this. "Who is Cedric Donigarten?" he asked. "And why can't he just wear his own armor?"

"Who is Cedric Donigarten?" Kelsey echoed in disbelief. "Where did you get this one, leprechaun?" he growled at Mickey.

"Ye said ye needed a man that'd fit," Mickey snapped back. "Ye did not say anything more for requirements." He looked back to Gary, thinking he had properly put Kelsey in his place. "Sir Cedric was the greatest King of Faerie," he began reverently. "He brought all the goodly folks together for the goblin wars—wars the goblins would sure'n have won if not for Cedric. A human, too, if ye can imagine that! All the goodly folks of all the lands—sprites, elfs, men, and dwarfs—speak the legend of Cedric Donigarten, and speak it with respect and admiring, to their children. Sure'n 'tis a shame that men don't live longer lives."

"Some men," Kelsey corrected.

"Aye," Mickey agreed with a chuckle, but his voice was reverent again as he continued. "Cedric's been dead three hundred years now, killed by a dragon in the last battle o' the goblin wars. And now Kelsey's to honor the dead with his life-quest, by reforging the mighty spear broken in that last battle."

Gary nodded. "Fine, then" he agreed. "Take me to the armor, and to the smithy, and let's go honor the dead."

"Fine it is!" laughed Mickey. He looked to Kelsey and cried, "Lead on!" hoping his enthusiasm would satisfy the elf and relieve him of the unpleasant task of finishing the story.

Kelsey crossed his slender arms over his chest and stood his ground. "Tell him of the smithy," the elf commanded.

"Ah, yes," said Mickey, pretending that he overlooked that minor point. "The smithy. We'll be needing a dwarf for that. 'Greatest smithy in all the land,' commands the spear's legend, and the greatest smithy in all the land's ever been one o' the bearded folk."

Gary didn't appear the least bothered, so Mickey clapped his hands and started towards Kelsey again.

"Explain the problem," the elf said sternly. Mickey stopped abruptly and turned back to Gary.

"Ye see, lad," he said. "Elfs and dwarfs don't get on so well—not that dwarfs get on well with anyone. We'll have to catch the smithy we're needing."

"Catch?" Gary asked suspiciously.

"Steal," Mickey explained.

Gary nodded, then shook his head, then nearly laughed aloud, silently praising himself for a weird and wonderful imagination.

"Are ye contented?" Mickey asked Kelsey.

"Tell him of the forge," the elf replied.

Mickey sighed and spun back on Gary. This time the leprechaun's face was obviously grave. "The spear's a special one," Mickey explained. "No bellows could get a fire hot enough, even could we get two mountain trolls to pump it! So we're needing a bit of an unusual forge, so declared the legend." He looked at Kelsey and frowned. "I'm growing tired of that damned legend," he said.

"Tell him," Kelsey demanded sternly.

Mickey paused as if he couldn't get the explanation past his lips.

"An unusual forge," Gary prompted after a long silence.

"I told ye before that ye'll be playing with dragons," Mickey blurted.

Gary rocked back on his heels and spent a long moment of thought. "Let me get this straight," he said, wanting to play all of Mickey's meandering words in a straight line. "You mean that I have to hold some dead King's spear while a dragon breathes fire on it and some captured dwarven smithy puts it back together?"

"There!" Mickey cried triumphantly. "The lad's got it! On we go, Kelsey." Mickey started along again but stopped, seeing that Kelsey hadn't moved and sensing that Gary wasn't following.

"What now, lad?" asked the exasperated leprechaun.

Gary paid him no heed. He slapped himself softly on the cheek several times and pinched his arm once or twice. "Well, if this is a dream," he said to no one in particular, "then it's time to wake up."

Kelsey shook his head, not pleased, then glowered at Mickey. "Where did you get this one?" he demanded.

Mickey shrugged. "I told me friends to bring one that'd fit the armor, just as ye told me," he replied. "Are ye getting particular?"

Kelsey regarded Gary for a while. He was big and well muscled—bigger than any of the people in Dilnamarra and probably as big as Cedric Donigarten himself. Mickey had assured him that Gary would fit the armor and Kelsey didn't doubt it. And Mickey was right with the remark about "getting particular." The legends said nothing of the subject's demeanor, just that he be human and wearing the armor. Kelsey walked over to Gary.

"Come along," the elf ordered to both of them. "You are not dreaming, and we want you here as little as you apparently wish to be here. Complete the task and you shall return to your own place."

"And suppose that I refuse to go along?" Gary dared to ask, not appreciating the elf's superior tone.

"Uh-oh," Mickey muttered, his grave tone making Gary wonder again if he had overstepped the bounds.

Kelsey's golden eyes narrowed and his lips turned up in a perfectly wicked grin. "Then I will declare you an outlaw," the elf said evenly. "For breaking the rules of capture. And a coward, deserving a brand." He paused for a moment so that Gary could get the full effect. "Then I shall kill you."

Gary's eyes popped wide and he looked to Mickey.

"I told ye the Tylwyth Teg take their quests seriously," was all the comfort the leprechaun could offer.

"Do we go on?" Kelsey asked, putting a hand on the hilt of his fine sword.

Gary did not doubt the elf's grim promise for a minute. "Lead on, good elf," he said. "To Dilnamarra."

Kelsey nodded and turned away.

"Good that that's settled," Mickey said to the elf as he strode past "Ye've got yer man now. I'll be taking me leave."

Kelsey's sword came out in the blink of an eye. "No, you will not," the elf replied. "He is your responsibility and you will see this through for the time being."

Gary didn't appreciate the derisive way Kelsey had said "he," but he was glad that the leprechaun would apparently be sticking around for a bit longer. The thought of dealing with Kelsey alone, without Mickey to offer subtle advice and deflecting chatter, unnerved Gary more than a little.

"I caught you, Mickey McMickey," Kelsey declared. "And only I can release you."

"Ye made the terms and I've met them," Mickey argued.

"If you leave, I will go to all lengths to catch you again," Kelsey promised. "The next time—and I will indeed catch you again—I will have your pot of gold, and your word-twisting tongue for good measure."

"The Tylwyth Teg take their quests seriously," Gary snorted from behind.

"That they do," agreed Mickey. "Then lead on, me good elf, to Dilnamarra, though I'm sure to be ducking a hundred pairs of greedy hands in the human keep!"

Kelsey started away and Mickey took out *The Hobbit* again.

"Worried about the dragon?" Gary asked, coming up to walk beside the diminutive sprite.

"Forget the dragon," Mickey replied. "Ye ever met a dwarf, lad? Mighten be more trouble than any old wyrm, and with breath nearen as bad!

"But make the best of it, I always say," Mickey went on. "I've got me a good book for the road, if the company's a bit lacking.

Gary was too amused to take offense.

"I do not tolerate failure!" Ceridwen snarled. "You were given a task, and promised payment for that task, yet the stranger walks free."

The nymph giggled, embarrassed. Leshiye did not fear Ceridwen, not here in Tir na n'Og, the source of the nymph's power but a foreign place to the sorceress.

Ceridwen stopped talking and fixed an evil stare on Leshiye. Her icy-blue eyes narrowed and widened alternately, the only clue that she was calling upon her magical energies.

Dark clouds rolled in suddenly, the wind came howling to life.

Leshiye had a few tricks of her own. She let the sorceress fall deeper into her spellcasting, waited for Ceridwen's eyes to close altogether. Then Leshiye looked into her oak tree, followed its lead into the ground and along its long and deep roots. Other nearby oaks reached out their roots in welcome and the nymph easily glided through the plant door out of harm's way.

Ceridwen loosed her storm's fury anyway; several bolts of lightning belted the giant oak in rapid succession. But, furious though they were, they barely scarred the ancient and huge oak, still vital and with the strength of the earth coursing through its great limbs. Ceridwen's satisfied smile evaporated a moment later when she heard Leshiye's giggle from beyond the small field.

The witch did not send her storm in pursuit, realizing that she was over-matched and out of her place in Tir na n'Og. "You would be wise to ever remain in this wood," she warned the nymph, but Leshiye hardly cared for the threat; where else would she ever be?

The sorceress huffed and threw her black cloak high over her shoulder. As it descended, Ceridwen seemed to melt away beneath it, shrinking as the cloak moved closer to the ground. Then garment and sorceress blended as one and a large raven lifted off from where Ceridwen had stood.

She rose high over the enchanted wood, racing away towards Dilnamarra, scanning as she flew to see if she could discover the progress of the elf's party. Ceridwen wasn't overly disappointed by Leshiye's failure; she never really believed that stopping the life-quest of an elf-lord of Kelsenellenelvial Gil-Ravadry's high standing would be as easy as that.

But Ceridwen was a resourceful witch. She had other, if less subtle, plans set into motion, and even in light of her first failure, she would not have bet a copper coin on the success of Kelsey's quest.

FIVE

DILNAMARRA

As soon as they emerged from the wood, the land, even the air, seemed to change before them. Tir na n'Og had been bright and sunny and filled with springtime scents and chattering birds, but out here, beyond the forest, the land lay in perpetual gloom. Fog hung low on the dirt roads, human-crafted roads, and along the rolling farmlands and small unadorned stone-and-thatch cottages.

Fields, bordered by hedgerows and rock walls, rolled up and down the hilly region, thick with grass and thick with sheep and cattle. Copses of trees spotted the landscape, some standing in lines like silent sentinels, others huddled in thick but small groups, plotting privately. By all logical measures, it was a beautiful countryside, but it was shrouded in melancholy, as if the gloom was caused by more than the simple mist.

"Watch yer footing," the leprechaun offered to Gary.

Gary didn't seem to understand; the road ran straight and level.

"Ye're not wanting to step into the heeland coo left-behinds," Mickey explained.

"Heeland coo?" Gary asked.

"A great hairy and horned beast," Mickey replied. Gary glanced around nervously.

"All the farmers keep them," Mickey went on, trying to calm him. "They're not a dangerous sort—unless ye set to bothering them. Some o' the lads go in to tip them over when they're sleeping, and some o' the coos don't take well to that."

"Tip them?" Now Gary was starting to catch on, and he was not overly surprised when Mickey pointed up to a distant field, to a shaggy-haired brown cow grazing contentedly. Gary rolled Mickey's description over in his thoughts a few times.

"Highland cow," he said at length.

"Aye, that's what I said," answered Mickey. "Heeland coo. And ye've not seen a left-behind to match the droppings of a heeland coo!"

Gary couldn't bite back his chuckle. Mickey and Kelsey exchanged curious looks, and Kelsey led them off.

Whatever romantic thoughts remained to Gary of the forest Tir na n'Og or the melancholy countryside were washed away an hour later by the harsh reality of mud-filled Dilnamarra. To the unsuspecting visitor, the change came as dramatically as the shift that had brought him to the land of Faerie in the first place, as if his dream, or whatever it was, had taken a sidelong turn, an undoubtedly wrong turn.

A square stone tower set on a grassy hill dominated the settlement, with dozens of squat stone shacks, some barely more than open lean-tos clustered in the tower's shadow. Pigs and scrawny cows ran freely about the streets, their dung mixing with the cart-grooved mud and their stench just one more unpleasant ingredient in the overwhelming aroma.

People of all ages wandered about, hunched and as dirty and smelly as the animals.

"Pick me up, lad," Mickey said to Gary. Gary looked down to see not the leprechaun, but a small human toddler where Mickey had been standing. Gary studied the toddler curiously for a moment, for the youngster held his book.

"Look through it, I telled ye!" the toddler said somewhat angrily when Gary gave him a confused look. Gary peered closer, reminded himself who should be standing beside him and not to believe what his eyes were showing him. Then he saw Mickey again, behind the façade, and he nodded and scooped the leprechaun into his arms.

"I caught you," Gary whispered, smiling.

"Are ye to start with that nonsense again?" Mickey asked, and the leprechaun, too, was wearing a grin. "I'm yer brother, lad, for any what's asking. Ye just hope that none o' the folks see through me disguise as ye have done. Sure'n then Kelsey's sword'll be cutting man flesh this day."

Gary's smile disappeared. "Kelsey wouldn't," he said unconvincingly.

"The Tylwyth Teg have fallen out of favor with the men about," Mickey said. "Kelsey's here only for reasons of his life-quest; he has not a care, one way or th'other, for the wretches of Dilnamarra. Woe to any that get in Kelsey's way."

Gary looked back to Kelsey, worried that Mickey's prophecy would come true. Where would Gary stand in such a fight? he wondered. He owed no loyalty to Kelsey, or even to Mickey. If the elf took arms against people of Gary's own race . . .

Gary shook the dark thoughts away, reminding himself to play through this experience one step at a time.

Every pitiful inhabitant of Dilnamarra turned out to see the strange troupe as they passed along the dung-filled streets. In this town, Gary was no more akin to the wretches as was Kelsey, for he carried no scars of disease, no open sores, and his fingers were not blackened by years of muddy labors. Angry glares came at them from every corner of every hut, and beggars, some limping, but most crawling in the mud, moved to block their way with a tangle of trembling crooked fingers and skin-and-bone, dirt-covered arms.

Gary held his breath as Kelsey reached the first of this group, deciding at that moment that he wouldn't let the elf strike the pitiful man down; if Kelsey's sword came out, then Gary would tackle him, or punch him, or do whatever he could to prevent the massacre. Not that he gave himself any chance of surviving against the grim elf—he just could not sit back and watch helplessly.

It never came to that, though, for Mickey's estimate of Kelsey proved to be a bit exaggerated. The elf obviously didn't appreciate the interference, but his sword did not move an inch out of his scabbard. Kelsey simply slapped the reaching hands aside and continued straight ahead, never looking the beggars in the eye. The wave of wretches did not relent, though. They swept along behind the strangers, groaning and crawling to keep pace.

Mickey, too, avoided the pleading gazes, nestling deep in Gary's clutch and closing his eyes. It was a common sight to the leprechaun, one to which he had long ago numbed his sensibilities.

Gary saw the beggars, though, could not block them out, and their desperate state stung him in the heart. He had never seen such poverty; where he grew up, poor meant that your car was more than ten years old. And dirty was the term Gary used to describe his appearance after a day at the plastics shop. Somehow, looking at these people, his usage of that term now seemed very out of place.

If this, then, was Gary's fantasy, his "twilight fancy," as that Mr. Peter Beagle had described it in the introduction to *The Hobbit*, then in Gary's eyes, the light around reality was suddenly burning a bit brighter.

The crowd dispersed as Kelsey neared the stone keep. Two grim-faced guards stood at either side of its single, iron-bound door, and the glares they shot at the trailing lines of beggars were filled with utter contempt.

"The heights of royalty," Gary heard Mickey mutter softly.

Crossed pikes intercepted Kelsey as he neared the door. He stopped to regard the guards for a moment.

"I am Kelsenel . . ."

"We know who ye are, elf," one of the guards, a stout, bearded man, said roughly.

"Then let me pass," Kelsey replied. "I have business with your Baron."

"It's on 'is order that we're keepin' ye here," the guard answered. "Stand yer ground now, an' keep behind the spears."

Kelsey looked back at Gary and Mickey, his expression hinting at explosive anger.

"I'd thought the arrangements made," Gary said, or at least it appeared as though Gary had said it. In truth it was Mickey, using ventriloquism to keep up his toddler façade.

"As did I," Kelsey replied, understanding the leprechaun's trick. "I spoke with Baron Pwyll just a week ago. He was more than willing to agree, thinking that the reforging of Donigarten's spear during his reign would assure his name in the bard's tales."

"Then another has spoken with him," Mickey said through Gary, cutting off Gary's own forthcoming response. Gary gave Mickey a stern look to tell him that he didn't appreciate being used this way, but Mickey continued his conversation with Kelsey without missing a beat.

"Who wishes ye stopped?" the leprechaun asked.

Kelsey shook his head to dismiss the possibility, but he, too, was beginning to have his concerns. They hadn't even really yet begun their journey, and they had already run into two unforeseen obstacles.

The iron-bound door creaked open and a cleaner and better-dressed guard appeared. He whispered a short exchange with the other two, then beckoned for Kelsey and company to enter the keep.

The hazy sunlight disappeared altogether when the heavy door closed behind them, for the one window in the ground level of the squat tower was too tiny to admit more than a crack of light. Burning torches were set in the four corners, their shadowy flickers giving spooky dimension to the tapestries lining all the walls, morbid depictions of bloody, smoke-filled battles.

Across from the door, in a gem-studded throne, sat the Baron, wearing clothes that had once been expensive, but had worn through in several places. He was a big, robust man, with a bristling beard and an expressive mouth that could equally reflect jollity and outrage. Behind him stood two unremarkable guards and a lean figure carrying the mud of the road on his weathered cloak. This man's hood was up, but back enough for Gary to see his matted black hair and suspicious, darting eyes. He wore a dagger on his thick belt, and his hand rested on it as though that was where his hand always rested.

Gary followed Mickey's stare to the side of the throne, to an empty stone pedestal and an iron stand.

"So says King Kinnemore," Mickey said derisively under his breath, and Gary realized that the empty pedestal had probably been the resting place for the armor and spear. Kelsey, too, seemed less than pleased, focusing more on the pedestal and the road-worn figure behind the Baron than on Pywll himself.

The elf kept his composure, though. He walked proudly up to the throne and fell to one knee in a low respectful bow.

"My greetings, Baron Pwyll," Kelsey said. "As arranged in our previous meeting, I have returned."

Pwyll looked back, concerned, to the cloaked figure, then to Kelsey. "Things have changed since our last meeting," he said.

Kelsey stood up, fierce and unblinking.

"Our good Prince Geldion here—long live the King—" (there was something less than enthusiastic about the way Pwyll said those words) "has brought word that the armor and spear of Cedric Donigarten are not to leave my possession."

"I have your word," Kelsey argued.

Pwyll's eyes flashed with helpless anger. "My word has been overruled!" he retorted. The Baron's guards bristled behind him, as though expecting some sudden trouble.

Prince Geldion did not try to hide his superior smile.

"Are you a puppet to Kinnemore, then?" Kelsey dared to ask.

Pwyll's eyes flashed with anger.

"Oh, begorra," Gary heard himself moan.

Pwyll jumped up threateningly from his seat, but Kelsey did not blink and the blustery Baron soon settled back. Pwyll could not refute Kelsey's insult at that time, in these circumstances.

"Where is yer edict, good Baron," Mickey said through Gary. Gary looked down angrily, but the toddler appeared fast asleep and did not return his stare.

Pwyll's angry glare fell over Gary. "And who are you, who speaks unannounced and without my permission?" he demanded.

"Gar—" Gary started, but Mickey's thrown voice cut him short.

"The armor wearer, I be!" Gary heard himself proclaim, and he wondered why no one noticed that his lips were not moving in synch with the words. Or were they? It was all too confusing.

"He who will fulfill the prophecies, come from distant lands," Mickey's ventriloquism went on. "The spear carrier to look a dragon in the eye! A warrior who will not return until the legends and me task are complete. So where be yer edict, I say? And what King dares to stand against prophecies of Sir Cedric Donigarten's own wizards?"

Pwyll sat in absolute disbelief for a moment, his mouth hanging open, and Gary thought the man would surely kill him for his outburst. But then a great blast of laughter erupted from the large man's mouth. He held an open hand behind him, to the Prince, and was given a rolled parchment, tied with the purple ribbons that served as the exclusive seal of King Kinnemore.

"And your name, good Sir Warrior?" Pwyll inquired through a grin.

A long moment of silence passed and Mickey nudged his carrier. "Gary," Gary replied hesitantly, expecting to be interrupted at any moment. "Gary Leger."

Pwyll scratched his thick beard. "And where did you say you came from?"

"From Bretaigne, beyond Cancarron Mountains," Mickey's voice answered. Both the Baron and the Prince appeared to catch the abrupt change in accent, but the Prince seemed to care more about it than did Pwyll.

"Well, Gary Leger from Bretaigne," Pwyll said. "Here is my edict, from King Kinnemore himself." He untied and unrolled the parchment and cleared his throat.

"To Baron Pwyll of Dilnamarra Keep," he began regally, articulating carefully in the proper language of royalty. "Be it known that I, King Kinnemore, have heard on good authority that the armor and spear of Cedric Donigarten, our most esteemed hero, will soon go out from Dilnamarra Keep on an expedition that might surely bring its destruction. Therefore, by my word—and my word is law—you are not to release the artifacts from your possession." Pwyll blinked and smoothed the parchment suddenly, as though it had in it a crease he had not noticed before.

". . . unless you, in your esteemed judgment, determine that said artifacts are given into the proper hands as spoken of in the prophecies." Pwyll blinked again in amazement, and before he could react, Prince Geldion reached down to tear the parchment from his grasp.

Pwyll resisted, though, and he held the parchment up for the Prince to see. "Below the fold," he instructed, his voice reflecting confusion as profound as that marked on Geldion's face. "I did not see the fold before, nor the clause."

The Prince's lips moved as he read the words—words he, too, had not seen before.

"Right above your own father's signature," Pwyll said pointedly. "Well, that does put things in a different light, I say."

"What treachery is this?" Prince Geldion demanded, starting at Kelsey and Gary. He stopped before he ever rounded the throne, however, for though his hand remained on the hilt of his belted dagger, Kelsey's had now gone to his fine elven sword. Geldion had heard enough tales of the Tylwyth Teg to know better than continue his futile threat.

"What treachery?" he said again, this time spinning on the Baron.

Pwyll shrugged and laughed at him. "Get the armor," he instructed his guards. "Put it on Gary Leger of Bretaigne. Let us see how it fits."

"The armor is not to leave Dilnamarra Keep," Geldion protested.

"Except by my own judgment," Pwyll calmly replied. "So says your own father. You remember him, do you not?"

"There is some magic here!" Geldion protested. "That was not in the edict; I penned it myself . . . under my father's word," he added quickly, seeing the suspicious stares coming at him from all directions.

"Magic?" Mickey's voice, through Gary, quickly put in. "Me good Baron o' Dilnamarra. A stranger I am to yer lands, but was it not by yer own King's edict that magic be declared an impossible thing? A tool of traitors and devil-chasers, did yer King Kinnemore not say? It may be that I've heard wrong, but I came across the mountains thinking that I'd left all thoughts o' magic behind."

"No," answered Baron Pwyll, "you have not heard wrong. There is no magic in Dilnamarra, nor anywhere else in Kinnemore Kingdom, so proclaimed King Kinnemore." He looked wryly at Geldion. "Unless the Prince is privy to more than the rest of us."

"You tread along dangerous shores, Baron Pwyll!" Geldion roared, and he crumpled the parchment and stuck it in his cloak pocket. "Hold the armor, I say, until the King may address the situation."

"We have a deal," Kelsey interrupted, his golden eyes boring into Geldion's dark orbs. "I shall not delay my given quest in the week it will take a messenger to get to Connacht, and the week it will take him to return. You have the edict of your King," he said to Pwyll. "Do you find this Gary Leger fit to bear the weight of the prophecies?"

"The armor first," Pwyll said, giving Kelsey a wink. "Then I will give my decision."

Outraged beyond words, Prince Geldion kicked the empty pedestal, then limped out of the chamber.

"You really expect me to walk around in this suit?" Gary asked as the attendants fit the heavy, overlapping plates and links of metal onto his chest. His legs were already encumbered by the mail and he felt certain that when they were finished with him he would weigh half a ton.

"The weight is well distributed," Kelsey answered. "You will become comfortable in the suit soon enough—once your weak muscles grow strong under its burden."

Gary flashed an angry glare the elf's way but held his thoughts silent. He was twice Kelsey's weight and no doubt much stronger than the elf, and he didn't appreciate Kelsey's insults, particularly when the elf wore a finely crafted suit of thin chain links, much lighter and more flexible than the bulky armor of Cedric Donigarten.

"Cheer up, lad," Mickey offered. "Ye'll be glad enough o' the weight the first time the mail turns a goblin's sword or a troll's weighty punch!"

"How I am supposed to keep taking this off and putting it back on if we're going to be out on the road for days?" Gary reasoned. "You can't expect me to sleep in it."

"The first time is the most difficult for fitting the armor," Kelsey explained. "Once the attendants have properly designed the padded undersuit, you will be able to strip and don the armor much more quickly."

"Yeah," Mickey snickered. "Only an hour or two for the lot of it. Kelsey and meself will hold back any foes 'til ye're ready."

Gary was beginning to appreciate Mickey's sarcasm less and less.

"It is finished," one of the attendants announced. "Shield and helmet are over there." He pointed to the wall, where several shields and helmets lay in a pile. "You will have to see the Baron if you desire the spear."

It was not difficult to determine which items in the jumble matched the decorated armor, for only one shield bore the griffon-clutching-spear insignia of dead King Cedric, and only one helmet, edged in beaten gold and plumed with a single purple feather from some giant bird, could appropriately cap the decorated suit.

Mickey picked out the helmet right away, and as the attendants left the room, it came floating from the pile, hovering near Gary's face. Gary reached out to take it, but his attempt was lumbering at best and the leprechaun easily levitated the helmet up and out of his reach.

Again, Gary glared at the leprechaun, but it was Kelsey that put an end to Mickey's antics.

"You wear the guise of a human child, but still you act the fool," Kelsey growled. "If the Baron or the Prince were to enter now, how might we explain your trick? There is no magic here, they say, unless it is magic spawned in Hell. They burn witches in Dilnamarra."

Mickey snapped his fingers and the helmet dropped. Gary, his hands on hips and his arms weighted in metal, could not react quickly enough to get out of the way, or to block the descent. The helmet thumped onto his head and slipped down over his ears, settling backwards on the armor's steel collar. Gary teetered, dazed, and Mickey's voice sounded distant, hollow.

"Catch him, elf!" the leprechaun cried. "Sure'n if he falls we'll be needing six men to pick him up!"

Kelsey's slender fingers wrapped around Gary's wrist and he jerked the young man straight. Gary reached for the helmet, but Kelsey beat him to it, roughly turning it about so that the man might see. Gary felt as if he was sporting a stewing pot on his head, with a small slit cut out in front for viewing. The helmet was quite loose—Gary wondered just how big this Cedric Donigarten's head actually was!—but better loose than tight, he figured.

"You look the part of a king," Kelsey remarked. Gary took it as a compliment until the elf finished the thought. "But you, too, act the part of a fool." He handed Gary the huge and heavy shield and moved back to join the leprechaun. Gary slipped his arm into the shield's belt and, with some effort, lifted it from the floor. It was wide at the top, tapering to a rounded point at the bottom—to set it in the ground, Gary realized—and more than half Gary's height.

"Baron Pwyll will have to agree," Kelsey said to Mickey. "The suit fits properly in body if not in stature."

Tired of the insults and wanting to make a point (and also wanting to give his already weary arm a break), Gary dropped the shield tip to the floor. Unfortunately, instead of clanging defiantly on the stone, as Gary had planned, it came to rest on top of his foot.

Gary bit his lip to keep from screaming, glad for the masking helmet.

Kelsey just shook his head in disbelief and walked past the armored man and out of the room, back to see Baron Pwyll.

"Ye'll get used to it," Mickey offered hopefully, giving Gary a wink as he followed Kelsey.

"The Lady will gives usses gifts, eh?" a big goblin croaked in Geek's face.

"Many gifts," Geek replied, bobbing his head stupidly. "M'lady Ceridwen wantses usses not to hurts the elf, but stops them, we will!"

The big goblin joined in the head-bobbing, his overgrown canines curling grotesquely around his saliva-wetted lips. He looked around excitedly at the host behind him, and they began wagging their heads and slapping each other.

"No like," said another of the band. "Too far from mountains. Too much peoples here. No like."

"You no like, you goes back!" Geek growled, moving right up to the dissenter. The big, toothy goblin moved to support Geek and all the others fanned out around them, clutching their crude spears and clubs tightly.

"Did Lady send usses?" the dissenter asked bluntly. "Did Lady tells Geek to kill 'n' catch?"

Geek started to retort, but the big goblin rushed to Geek's defense, stepping in front of Geek and cutting his reply short.

"Geek know what Lady Ceridwen wantses!" the brute declared, and he curled up his crooked fist and punched the dissenter square in the mouth.

The smaller goblin fell over backwards but was caught by those closest to him and hoisted roughly back to his feet. He stood swaying, barely conscious, but, with typical goblin stubbornness and stupidity, managed to utter, "No like."

The words sent the already excited band into a sudden and vicious frenzy. The big goblin struck first, slamming his huge forearm straight down on the dissenter's head. This time, the smaller goblin did fall to the ground, and those around him, rather than support him, fell over him, jabbing with their spears and hammering with their clubs. The fallen goblin managed a few cries of protest, a few pitiful squeaks, which quickly turned to blood-choked gurgles.

The band continued to beat him long after he was dead.

"Geek know what Lady Ceridwen wantses!" the big goblin declared again, and this time, not a single voice spoke against him. The host respectfully circled Geek to hear his forthcoming commands.

"They goes in town," Geek explained. "But come out soon, they will. Lady says they goes to mountains. We catches them on road in trees; catches elf and killses humans."

The other goblins wagged their fat heads and hooted their agreement, banging their spears and clubs off trees and rocks, or the goblins standing beside them or against anything else they could find.

Convincing goblins to "kill 'n' catch" was never a very difficult thing to do.

* * *

Gary did find the armor growing more comfortable as he loped along beside Mickey on the road leading east out of Dilnamarra. The suit was also surprisingly quiet, considering that more than half of it was of metal and it hadn't been used in centuries.

They had set right out from the keep after Baron Pwyll had tentatively agreed, over Prince Geldion's vehement protests, that they could take the artifacts. The sunlight was fading fast even then, but Kelsey would not wait for the next morn, not with the Prince so determined to stop him and the Baron caught in a dilemma that ought soon lead him to second thoughts. Now the sun had dipped below the horizon, and the usual wafting mist off the southern moors had come up, drifting lazily across the road, obscuring their vision even further.

Kelsey would not relent his pace, though, despite Mickey's constant grumbling.

"We should've stayed the night in the keep," the leprechaun said repeatedly. "A warm bed and a fine meal would've done us all the good."

Gary remained silent through it all, sensing that Kelsey was on the verge of an explosion. Finally, after perhaps the hundredth such complaint from Mickey, the elf turned back on him sharply.

"We never would have gotten out of Dilnamarra Keep if we had stayed the night!" he scolded. "Geldion meant to stop us and he had more than one guard at his disposal."

"He'd not have gone against us openly," Mickey argued. "Not in Pwyll's own keep."

"Perhaps not," Kelsey conceded. "But he might have convinced Pwyll to hold us until the matter of the edict was properly settled. I applaud your actions in the audience chamber, leprechaun, but the illusionary script would not have fooled them forever."

"Don't ye be thinking too highly of humans," Mickey replied, then he cleared his throat, embarrassed, as the insulted Gary turned on him.

But the events in the keep had left Gary quite confused, and he had too many questions to worry about Mickey's unintentional affront. "What illusionary script?" he asked Kelsey.

"Ye see what I'm saying?" Mickey snickered, throwing a wink Kelsey's way.

Now even Kelsey managed a smile. "The Prince did pen the edict, by his own admission," the elf explained to Gary. "Mickey simply added a few words."

Gary turned his incredulous stare on the smug leprechaun.

"And that fact make us outlaws," Kelsey continued, more to Mickey than Gary. "The road is now our sanctuary, and the more distance we put between ourselves and Prince Geldion, the better our chances."

"*Yer* chances, ye mean," Mickey muttered.

Kelsey let it go. For all the leprechaun's complaining, the elf could not deny Mickey's value to the quest. Without Mickey's illusions, Kelsey would never have gotten the armor and spear out of Dilnamarra Keep.

"Three more hours, then we may rest," the elf said, picking up the leather case that held the ancient spear. The weapon had been broken almost exactly in half and the pieces were laid side by side, but the case was still nearly as tall as Kelsey.

Gary was more than a little curious to view the legendary weapon—only Kelsey had seen it back at the keep—but he did not press the elf at that time. He hoisted the heavy shield and unremarkable spear he had been given and trudged off after Kelsey.

Mickey stood alone for a few moments, kicking at a rock with one curly-toed shoe. "Ye landed yerself in it deep this time, Mickey McMickey," he said quietly, and then he shrugged helplessly and tagged along.

SIX

CROSSROADS

They set camp far from the road, fearing that the Prince and his men might be out looking for them. Kelsey took the watch, and said he would keep it for all the night, sitting grim-faced and stoic, his thin sword lying ready across his lap. No sense of chivalry bubbled up in Gary to argue. He was thoroughly exhausted from the weighted hiking and he was ready, too, after the mud-filled spectacle of Dilnamarra, to put this entire crazy fantasy behind him. Dilnamarra was unlike any town Gary had ever fantasized about, with so much suffering and true poverty, and after that sight, he figured he would never look upon Lancashire and upon his own existence in quite the same negative way.

But how to get back there? It seemed only logical, Gary tried to convince himself, that if he went to sleep in the middle of a dream, he would wake up in reality.

"Go to sleep," he whispered quietly to himself, "if you want to wake up."

Mickey heard the private conversation as Gary laid out the blankets and stripped off the bulkier parts of his armor. "As it always is and always will be with big folk from Real-earth," the leprechaun chuckled, and took a deep draw on his long pipe.

Gary knew that Mickey was laughing at him and his hopes of returning home, and he knew, too, that those hopes had no foundation in this situation. For all of his logical denial, Gary was beginning to catch on to the truth of his very real situation. Still, he turned sharply on Mickey and stubbornly held on to his previous perceptions of reality.

"You'll be gone soon," he assured the sprite.

Mickey chuckled again, conjured a small globe of light, and opened *The Hobbit*. Gary stared at him a moment longer, then dropped to the blankets and tried to put the leprechaun out of his thoughts.

Every time the mist thinned, Gary got a too-brief glimpse of the evening canopy. A million stars dotted the sky, an enchanting view, but Gary rarely got to see more than a fraction of it through the opaque veil. The mist was stubborn, hanging like a pall over the land, dulling the crisp and wonderful sights that would indeed have made this a world of twilight fancies.

It hadn't missed the mark by far. Tir na n'Og was bright and cheery and warm and song-filled, a fitting forest indeed. Such places of enchantment could not be found in Gary's world—at least, not as far as Gary knew. And the Faerie countryside, if a bit plain, was untainted and undeniably lush.

But the harshness of Dilnamarra overshadowed the wood and the fields, brought a grim reality to steal the harmony of the forest song and country road.

Gary washed it all from his thoughts. He focused on his Jeep and the cemetery and the stool by the grinder, and hoped that he would not wake up too late for at least a cold supper, that his parents weren't too worried.

Then he saw the mist again, silvery in the starlight, and Kelsey keeping silent watch, and Mickey busy reading. How many hours had he been here? Not broken and episodic but real hours, filled with experiences both exciting and mundane, with all the little details that he never considered a part of the realm of dreams.

Gary knew that this was no dream. Plain and simple. He wondered if he had died, or gone insane. Had his love of fantasy novels and daydreams consumed his mind? Had his disappointments with life's realities driven him mad? He thought of a Jack Nicholson movie, of psychotics wandering aimlessly, hopelessly lost, and he wondered if they, too, had entered their own land of Faerie.

And what now for him? What "realities" now awaited Gary Leger? Would he find a long line of dreary towns like Dilnamarra, or a world of enchantment, a world of Tir na n'Og and leprechauns and stern elfs and wood nymphs?

The mist cleared again and Gary got his best view yet of the twinkling stars. Then it faded as his physical exhaustion overcame the turmoil in his mind and he drifted off to sleep.

Gary knew as soon as he opened his eyes that he was outdoors. He thought—hoped—for a brief moment that he was in the familiar wood back home, between the school and the cemetery and the intruding houses, but that hope died as soon as he smelled the breakfast cooking and heard Mickey's flavored voice.

"Mushroom stew'll fill yer belly fine," the leprechaun said to Kelsey.

"Prepare it quickly," Kelsey replied. "We have many more miles to go this day, and it will be hot. I expect our friend will need to stop and rest every few minutes." Kelsey's tone was not complimentary.

"Ye're too hard on the lad," Mickey said. "Ye'd be wanting rest yerself if ye had to walk around in that man-sized bucket."

"I, too, wear metal mail," Kelsey reminded him.

"Chain crafted by the Tylwyth Teg?" Mickey balked. "Sure'n yer whole suit's weighing less than Donigarten's helmet alone!"

"Prepare the stew quickly," Kelsey ordered again, his snarling tones revealing that he had run out of arguments. "I wish to be on the road before the sun has come fully over the horizon."

"Ah, ye're up, then!" Mickey greeted Gary, seeing Gary sitting on the blankets and stretching. "Good for that; now ye'll get a fine meal in yer belly."

Gary looked all around in continued disbelief, his expression a mixture of confusion and budding anger.

"I told ye that ye can go home after ye finish the task," the leprechaun explained, honestly sympathetic, "I told ye that ye were not dreaming; I'd not be lying to ye."

Still unable to come to terms with all of this, Gary shook his head slowly and nibbled his upper lip.

"Call it a dream if it makes ye feel better," the leprechaun advised. "And whatever ye might call it, enjoy it!"

"I didn't find the town so enjoyable," Gary said grimly.

"Then think o' Leshiye in the wood," Mickey offered with a sly wink. "I know ye liked that part."

That notion did bring a smile to Gary's face, and the mushroom stew proved truly delicious and did fill his belly. They were back on the road soon after, Kelsey leading them at a swift pace and Gary struggling to keep the loose-fitting helmet on straight and the heavy shield from dragging its tip along the ground.

Soon, Gary didn't even try to keep the shield aloft. The day was hot and dreary, damp with the mist and painfully bright. Sweat soaked the underpadding of Gary's suit and stung his eyes. He kept stopping and poking his fingers through the eye slit of the helmet to wipe the moisture away, but it hardly helped, since his fingers were as wet as his face.

"Take the helmet off and hang it on yer spear," Mickey offered to him, seeing his distress. Kelsey, up ahead, spun about.

"Oh, let him!" the leprechaun spouted, cutting short the elf's forthcoming argument. "He'll drop dead in that suit in this heat, and what good'll he be to yer quest then?"

Kelsey turned back and started away and Mickey smiled smugly. He helped Gary get the cumbersome helmet in place on the spear and they set off again with Gary feeling much better.

His brightened mood sustained him through most of the morning, but near noon they came to a crossroads, two intercepting muddy trails in the otherwise unremarkable rolling fields. Four high poles had been set into the ground, one at each corner of the intersection.

Men were hanging from them, by the neck, long dead and bloated, twisting slowly in the gentle breeze.

Gary dropped his spear and shield and clutched at his turning stomach. Even Kelsey, halting his determined march to stare unblinking, seemed affected by the gruesome sight.

"Poor wretches," Mickey remarked. "Cut them down, will ye?" he asked Kelsey.

Kelsey's hand went to his sword hilt, but he stopped and shook his head.

"Cut them down!" Gary shouted suddenly, though he nearly lost his breakfast for the effort.

"I cannot!" Kelsey shouted back at him. "None in all of Faerie would dare to do so but the Tylwyth Teg, and if I cut them down now it would surely tell Prince Geldion that we passed this way. As surely as if I signed my name on the road. I do not want the Prince anywhere near to us."

Gary and Mickey couldn't really argue against the practical reasoning.

"What did they do?" Gary asked somberly. "Were they criminals? And why would they be hung out here, so far from the town?"

"Probably couldn't pay their taxes," Mickey spat in reply. "Or said something the Prince didn't like hearing. Or stole a piece o' bread for feeding their children. Get yerself used to the sight, lad. Ye'll be seeing it at many crossroads."

"They always hang them at crossroads," Kelsey explained. "That way, if a dead man's vengeful spirit comes back seeking justice, it will not know which way to go."

"Vengeful spirits," Mickey grumbled. "The poor wretches hadn't the strength to fight in life, never mind in death."

"Let us get far from this place," Kelsey offered, and the others did not disagree.

Long after they had put the crossroads behind them, Mickey noticed that Gary's visage had not softened.

"Don't ye let it trouble ye, lad," the leprechaun offered. "Sure'n 'twas a terrible sight, but it's behind us now."

Gary's expression did not change. "'Call it a dream,' you said," he replied evenly. "But should I call it a dream or a nightmare?"

For the first time, Gary's words had left the leprechaun without reply.

"You said that I had heard of this land of Faerie," Gary went on, trying to hold his voice steady and hide his rising anger. "And so I have, in old folktales—fairy tales. But according to those stories, the world of elfs and leprechauns was supposed to be an enchanted place, peaceful and beautiful, and not a place where a man is left hanging by the neck at a crossroads for stealing bread to feed his hungry children."

"Aye," Mickey agreed somberly. His gray eyes misted over sorrowfully and took on a faraway look. "And so it once was," he went on, "before him named Kinnemore found a seat on the throne . . ."

"Enough!" shouted Kelsey, who had come back to join them and had overheard their conversation. He glared at Mickey, then turned on Gary. "The politics and ways of the land are not your concern," he growled. "You were brought here to play a small part in a quest, and nothing more. Whether the sights of Faerie please you or turn your stomach is of no concern to me."

Gary accepted the elf's berating without question, understanding that his and Mickey's observations had struck a sensitive nerve in Kelsey. He could not help but notice Kelsey's helpless frustration. The sight of the hanging men had stung the elf as deeply as any, maybe more so, and Gary knew that such images as that and as the huddled wretches of Dilnamarra were not in agreement with Kelsey's high-browed views of how the world should be.

Mickey and Gary exchanged shrugs as Kelsey started off again and they said no more as the miles passed. For Gary, it was hot and lonely and dreadful. His thoughts drifted back to his own world, back to Tir na n'Og, or to nowhere at all, and in his blank trance, he didn't even notice that Kelsey had stopped, crouching low as though he was inspecting something in the road.

Fortunately Mickey managed to grab Gary before he walked right into the bending elf.

"What've ye found?" the leprechaun asked.

"Tracks," Kelsey replied quietly. He looked up at Mickey and Gary, his face grave. "Goblin tracks."

"Goblins here?" Mickey asked. He put a hand above his eyes and peered at the distant mountains. "Five days yet," he muttered. "Too far for goblins to be wandering." He looked to Gary as though he expected the inexperienced man to confirm his suspicions.

"Goblin tracks," Kelsey said again, this time with a tone of finality.

Mickey looked all around, to the mountains and back to Kelsey. Then he understood. "Ye're thinking it's no coincidence?" he asked.

Kelsey didn't immediately respond, though his expression revealed that he considered Mickey's guess right on target. They were barely into the second day of the quest, yet they had met interference at every turn. First the nymph, then the Prince, and now recent evidence of a band of goblins (and no small band, judging by the number of tracks) nearly a hundred miles from their mountain holes.

"We'll know soon enough," Kelsey replied, studying the westering sun. "If the goblins are still about, the night will likely reveal them."

"And with us sitting open in the middle of the plain," moaned Mickey.

"Not so," said Kelsey. "The wood, Cowtangle, is but a few miles down the road. We must hurry to get there before all the daylight is gone."

Gary didn't like the thought of hurrying, but he liked the thought of meeting goblins even less. He put his helmet back on and started off as quickly as he could go. Kelsey and Mickey helped him as much as possible; Kelsey even took turns with Gary carrying the heavy shield.

By the time they reached their destination, it was so late that the trees seemed no more than a darker silhouette against a deep gray background. With his keen eyes, Kelsey led them into the thicket easily, though, and soon found a clearing where they could set camp in relative safety.

"Set no fires," Kelsey ordered, then he looked pointedly at Mickey. "And light no enchanted globes." To Gary, he added, "Keep your armor on and your spear close. If we are forced to flee, do not forget a single piece of the ancient and priceless suit."

Kelsey seemed to be trying to convince himself as much as the others as he added quietly, "The wood will hide us."

Both Mickey and Gary couldn't help thinking that the thick trees of Cowtangle might be hiding other things as well.

From the shallow depths of a fitful sleep, Gary heard Kelsey's startled cry. He opened his eyes just in time to see a form go crashing back into the brush away from the elf.

A ghostly light encircled the area—Mickey's doing, Gary knew—and everything seemed to be moving too slowly.

"Run!" Kelsey yelled, turning back towards Gary, and Mickey added, "For all yer life, lad!"

Gary's mind was wide awake now and alert, but his body moved sluggishly as he tried to rise in the bulky armor. Kelsey ran over to him; there was movement and shouting now from every direction, wild hoots and croaks.

Gary accepted the elf's free hand and started to rise, pausing just long enough to notice that Kelsey's sword dripped of blood. As if sensing his horrified hesitation, Kelsey jerked him upright with surprising strength, plopped his helmet on his head, handed him both spear and shield, and pushed him off behind Mickey.

Gary knew that the elf had joined battle right behind him only a split second later. He tried to turn back and look over his shoulder, but the helmet was not properly strapped on and it did not turn with his head.

"This way!" Mickey yelled up ahead. "Don't ye be fearing for Kelsey!"

It was all a shadowy blur to Gary when they came out of the clearing and out of Mickey's magical light. He stumbled and crashed through many small branches, desperately trying to keep up with the nimble leprechaun. The fine armor easily deflected the weight of the blows, and Gary did finally catch up to Mickey, the leprechaun casually sitting on a low branch, peering back the way they had come.

Mickey absently waved Gary by, and the frightened man stumbled on blindly, not daring to slow. Every tree seemed an ominous form; he imagined branches as sword-wielding goblin arms, reaching out to cut him down. Every bush seemed a crouched demon, poised to leap up in his face and swallow him. He tried to reason through the terror, he tried to catch his breath.

He tried.

Mickey carefully considered his next moves. If Kelsey was too distracted to see through the deception, then the leprechaun might bring him harm. But goblins were everywhere, scrambling and shouting, and goblins could see in the dark.

Kelsey might escape, Mickey surely would, but unless Mickey took some prompt action, Gary Leger was doomed.

"Tisk, tisk, trees in the mist," the leprechaun chanted, waving his hands to create the most common trick used to deter would-be leprechaun hunters. A simple illusion but a nasty one.

Every tree between Mickey and the clearing appeared to move three feet to the left.

It didn't take Kelsey long to figure out what had happened. He saw a goblin darting to the side of him run face-first into a thick oak and drop in a dizzy heap. Another goblin, a big toothy one, came straight at Kelsey, but veered to the right at the last moment and got collared by a low branch. The creature's neck snapped with a horrible *crack!* and it lay quite still.

At that moment, Kelsey came to consider again that having a leprechaun around might not be such a bad thing. He started off on a circling route, but stopped as another goblin rebounded off yet another tree. The creature stood staring in confusion and scratching its head, and Kelsey, not worrying about fair play where goblins were concerned, promptly stuck it through the exposed ribs.

Then the elf slipped into the brush, carefully picking his way past Mickey's splendid illusion.

For the first time in his life, Gary Leger truly knew fear. He heard the goblins, many goblins; they seemed to be nipping right at his heels, and now he had lost his friends! What would he do if the goblins caught up with him? He didn't know how to fight with a spear and he could hardly move about in the armor.

Gary was far beyond the area of Mickey's deception, but that hardly mattered, for he could not see in the dark anyway, particularly with his loose helmet bouncing all about his shoulders, and could hardly think above his paralyzing terror. He hooked his shield on some brush and stumbled. He caught his balance quickly, but the jerk sent his helmet spinning right about, the eye slit facing behind him.

Gary realized that he was in trouble and tried to reach up and turn the thing back right, but the continuing goblin snorts and shouts overruled his rational decision to slow down. A root tripped him up and he lurched forward. Somehow, he kept his footing.

A rush of relief came over him as he stood up straight and finally maneuvered the helmet back aright, but his sigh lasted only the second it took him to register the low and thick branch directly crossing his path. Gary actually wished he hadn't turned the helmet; he would have preferred not to see it coming.

He heard the dull thud and felt the sudden jolt, and the next thing he knew, he was lying on his back thinking how pretty the stars were this night. Strangely he could still see the stars, a million stars, even though the jolt had turned his helmet back around to cover his eyes.

"Lie still and stay that way!" he heard Mickey say a few moments later. Gary managed to lift his head and tilt his enormous helmet back far enough to see the leprechaun running past, slowing to mutter a few soft chants and wave his small but plump hand Gary's way.

"Lie still and stay that way!" Mickey said again, more forcefully, and then he disappeared into the thick brush.

Gary hardly comprehended anything at that dazed moment—until he heard the croaks and hoots and floppy footfalls and remembered the monstrous pursuit. His first instinct was to jump up and flee, but he could tell from the proximity of the hoots that the closing goblins would surely catch him before he went very far, probably before he ever got to his feet. Mickey's words rang in his thoughts and Gary was wise enough to understand that he had no practical choice but to put his trust in the leprechaun. He lay back flat, very still.

The goblins, grouped together again, gained confidence with every step and every tree safely passed. They had gone beyond the area of Mickey's first illusion, though they had lost track of the nimble elf completely. It didn't trouble Geek and his surly friends, though, for they knew the general direction the fleeing human had taken—and there was just one footpath through the heavy brush in this area. Goblins could see in the dark, as could elfs, but humans were quite helpless in a thick and gloomy forest after sunset.

But it was that very night vision that betrayed the goblins again. Geek led them on wildly, hooting and beating at any hiding places in the bushes beside the trail. They skipped over roots and ducked under low branches, and scrambled across one unremarkable mound.

Gary, the unremarkable mound, tried hard to stifle his grunts as the goblin troupe thudded over him. One goblin hooked its foot between helmet and breastplate and crashed headlong onto Gary's legs. Gary thought he was surely doomed, but the creature simply got back up, brushed imaginary dirt off its filthy tunic, and continued down the path.

Then they were gone, their hoots trailing away in the distance. Gary didn't even try to stand. He lay quite still and helpless, his chest heaving as he tried futilely to calm himself. He had no idea what to do, where to go, and above everything else, he feared that his companions were surely dead or lost to him.

"Get up!" came a harsh cry a moment later. Gary recognized Kelsey's voice, then heard some light footsteps and sensed that the elf was bending over him.

Kelsey's sigh reflected as much anger as sorrow. "What mighty beast did this to you, poor soul?" Kelsey moaned, staring at Gary's backwards helmet. "Twisted your neck so completely . . ."

Gary reached up to straighten the great helm and the elf fell back in horror.

"I'm all right," Gary tried to explain, finally managing to turn the cumbersome thing.

"He's been stepped on, that's all," Mickey added, coming out of the underbrush to Kelsey's side. "Just a bump in the road to the stupid goblins' eyes."

"Then get up," Kelsey growled, embarrassed and angry. He reached down and roughly pulled Gary back to his feet.

"They'll not be gone long," Mickey remarked.

"Why were they here at all?" Kelsey replied grimly.

Mickey nodded, understanding where Kelsey's question was leading. Too many things seemed to be interrupting them to be explained away by coincidence. Alone, the nymph, the Prince, even the goblins, could be brushed aside as one of the many dangers of undertaking such a journey, but together, those ingredients added up to a conspiracy.

"And who might be talking to them all?" Mickey asked.

"To who?" Gary asked, trying to get included in the vague conversation.

"Who has the ear of kings and goblins alike?" Mickey went on, ignoring Gary. "And who in all the world might be making any suggestions to Leshiye?"

Kelsey didn't need to respond, for they both knew that there was only one possible solution to Mickey's questions.

"Then ye've got yet answers," Mickey snarled, suddenly gruff and dark. Gary looked at the leprechaun curiously, never having seen this side of the normally cheery sprite.

Still, Kelsey said nothing. He led them off silently to find a new place to camp.

They settled under the low-hanging boughs of a huge pine tree, quite removed from the forest outside. Despite the relative safety, though, neither Kelsey nor Mickey grew at ease. Mickey called up a tiny spot of light and took out the book, but Kelsey was on him in a blink.

"Dispel it!" the elf commanded in a soft but harsh whisper.

"It cannot be seen outside the branches," Mickey argued. "Ye mean to sit here in the dark?" He looked over to Gary. "Sure'n that one'd not get through the night without hurtin' himself."

Gary was more concerned with the tension in Kelsey's face than with Mickey's words. The elf seemed barely able to respond; the lines of his angular face creased under the strain of his clenched jaw. He looked at Gary and started to speak, but his golden eyes widened and he grinned weirdly, shaking his head.

"Just a bit o' reading?" Mickey asked, realizing what Kelsey had noticed and hoping the humorous sight—muddy goblin-sized footprints running down the front of Gary's armor—would bring some much-needed relief.

Kelsey moved to the natural wall, pushed aside some branches, and peered out through the tangle. Mickey took that as permission and he quickly popped his pipe in his mouth and found his place in the book.

Gary wanted to talk to the leprechaun or to Kelsey, to find out what they had decided concerning this unknown conspiracy, but he dared not say anything as the night deepened. He sat down against the tree trunk and tried to get as comfortable as possible, though he now knew better than to take off anything more than his helmet. He hoped that he would find sleep again and hoped that this time it would bring him back awake in his proper place.

He didn't believe it, though. Whatever this was—insanity, death, or perhaps a wild but very real journey—Gary was now fully convinced that it was not a dream.

He had just begun to nod off when Kelsey prodded him. Looking up into the elf's stern visage, Gary at first wondered what he had done wrong this time.

"You take this," Kelsey explained, handing Gary the long leather case that held the legendary spear. Kelsey untied it at one end and slid out the marvelous weapon. It was pitch-black, shaft and head, and even in the dim light, its polished tip gleamed as though it held some inner brooding light.

Gary couldn't pull his gaze from that crafted spearhead. Its basic shape was triangular, as long and nearly as thick as his forearm. Small barbs ran along the edges of the front tip, and the back two points were elongated and curled up towards the front. Runes, ancient and wonderfully crafted with swirling images of noble warriors and fearsome beasts, canvassed the black metal of the head and shaft.

"When it is forged whole, it will stand half again your height," Kelsey said. He gave the bared weapon to Gary to let the man feel the strength of its iron.

Gary grasped it tightly. It appeared as though it would weigh a hundred pounds, but when Kelsey let go, Gary found it to be surprisingly light.

And incredibly balanced—Gary felt as though he could heave the thing a hundred yards.

"The magic," Kelsey explained, understanding Gary's confused expression. For perhaps the first time since he had met Gary, the elf truly smiled. He took the weapon, slid it back into its case, and retied the end.

"You want me to carry it?" Gary asked him.

"Our trials are not ended," Kelsey replied. "Even if we elude the goblins, I know now that there will be other dangers along our path. I remain dedicated to my quest, but, on my word, I must keep safe the artifacts of King Cedric. If the goblins fall upon us, I will lead them away. You must then get the spear and armor back to Baron Pwyll." There was no compromise in Kelsey's tone.

"Give me your word of honor," he demanded.

Gary nodded and Kelsey walked away.

Gary was glad that Kelsey had entrusted him with so important a task, but the elf's uncharacteristic behavior only made him more uncomfortable with the events at hand. Something very dangerous was going on around him, something that even his new friends, who seemed so superior, greatly feared.

Mickey did not alleviate Gary's concerns a moment later, when the leprechaun threw *The Hobbit* off of Gary's chest and gave a resounding "Oh, pooh!"

"What's the matter?" Gary asked, scooping up the book.

"Calling himself an historian, is yer J.R.R. Tolkien fellow?" Mickey asked incredulously. "And what a pretentious sort to be calling himself by his initials like that! Afraid to use his whole name?"

"What?" was all that Gary could sputter.

"Read at the folded page!" Mickey replied. Gary found the mark easily enough, but he could hardly read the flowing runes that Mickey had placed where the typeset had once been.

"Sunlight turning trolls to stone?" Mickey spouted, seeing Gary at a loss. "Bag o' blarney! Every fool's knowing that to be a rumor started by the trolls alone. They're the ones carving troll statues, making people think it's trolls turned by sunlight. How many stupid travelers have turned back on the trolls chasing them, pointing a finger and laughing when the sun peeked over the rim? How many stupid travelers then found themselves stuffed into a troll's hungry mouth?"

"What the hell are you talking about?" Gary cried.

Kelsey jumped in between them, his flashing eyes reminding them that silence was their ally.

Mickey waved his hand furiously, his magic pulling *The Hobbit* from Gary's grasp and levitating it back to his waiting hand. "Mr. J.R.R. Tolkien, Historian," he muttered sarcastically. "How many stupid travelers will get eaten after reading yer bag o' blarney?"

Gary just looked at Kelsey and smiled sheepishly.

The nervous elf did not smile back.

SEVEN

WET WITH BLOOD

The three unlikely companions ate a meal of berries and bread and started off just before dawn, Kelsey leading them through the tangle of underbrush far from the main road. Both the elf and the leprechaun covered the rough ground with little trouble and not much more than an occasional rustle, but Gary, in his heavy armor, stumbled and crashed with every step, broke apart branches and committed wholesale slaughter on the many unfortunate plants in his path.

"We'd best get him to the road," Mickey said after only a short while.

"The goblins may be watching the road," Kelsey answered grimly.

"Better that the goblins kill him than he kills himself," Mickey retorted. "Besides, with the clamor that one's making, all the wood'll know of our passing!"

Kelsey gave Gary yet another of his increasingly common derisive stares. Gary wanted to argue back, to ensure the elf that he could make it through, but unfortunately he picked that moment to hook his toe on yet another snag. Down he went heavily and noisily, and the exasperated elf announced, before he even bothered to pick Gary up, that the road seemed the safer course.

For all of his wounded pride, Gary did have a better time with the flat road than the thicket, though the day grew hot, particularly so under the thick padding of the armor. Gary had thought that his body was getting used to the weight, that, except for the heat, he was actually beginning to feel somewhat comfortable in the stuff. But a short while later, he came to believe that the armor felt even heavier and less balanced than it had the day before. Gary didn't understand the change until Mickey abruptly appeared, comfortably perched on his shoulder.

"You've been sitting there all along," Gary accused him.

"Ye did not even notice," Mickey replied. "I weigh but a pittance next to that armor ye carry. If I'd stayed invisible, ye'd have carried me all the way to Dvergamal without a word o' complaint!"

"Dvergamal?" The strange word deflected Gary's ire.

"Voice o' the dwarf," Mickey explained. "A name given to the stony mountainsides where we'll find the buldrefolk, the dwarfs."

Gary considered the revelations for a moment, wondering if he had heard those curious names somewhere back in his own world. "Well, why didn't you stay invisible?" he scolded Mickey, half heartedly trying to push the bothersome leprechaun from his shoulder—a quite impossible feat given Mickey's uncanny agility and the restricting shoulder plates of Gary's armor.

"I've some reading to do," Mickey answered calmly, and he promptly produced *The Hobbit*. "Can't do that when me and the book are invisible, now can I?'

Gary was seriously considering diving sidelong to the ground, just to annoy the annoying leprechaun, but Kelsey turned back on them suddenly, ferociously.

"Silence!" the elf commanded in hushed but very firm tones. "We walk in dangerous . . ." Kelsey paused suddenly and Gary could see the elf's fine muscles tighten.

In a movement too swift for Gary to follow, Kelsey snapped his sword from its scabbard and leaped straight up, leading with his deadly blade. There came a squeak from a thick-leafed branch overhanging the road then a goblin tumbled from the thicket to land dead at Kelsey's feet.

Gary felt a jolt on his side and looked down to see a crude arrow lying on the ground, its tip snapped from the impact against his metal armor.

"Mickey," he started to say, but the leprechaun was not to be seen, nor to be felt.

Hoots and shouts went up all about the sides of the road and the goblins were upon them.

For all that he had been forewarned about Kelsey's battle prowess, Gary could not have imagined anything as precise and perfect as the elf-lord's movements. Kelsey danced a ballet, silent except for the swish of his fine sword and the screams of those enemies he encountered.

A large and fat goblin came upon the elf first, wrapping him in a bear hug from behind. As if he had anticipated the move, Kelsey stuck his sword arm far out in front, keeping it from the cumbersome creature's grasp. The sword dipped through the elf's legs and came slicing up between the goblin's legs.

The monster let go, right away.

From across the road, in front of the elf, two goblins charged out, holding a net between them. Kelsey crouched low and let them get right near to him, then leaped straight up, planting his feet atop the net and driving it down beneath him. The overbalanced goblins lurched helplessly and Kelsey's sword flashed left, then right. The gleaming silver blade appeared crimson now, and two more goblins crumpled.

So entranced by the spectacle in front of him, Gary hardly understood his own peril. He could not outrun the goblins, could not even hope to make it to the side of the road and hide in the underbrush.

An arrow bonked off the side of his helmet. He spun quickly to the side (though his loose-fitting helmet did not). Still, he saw enough to be afraid, for the goblin archer was now charging him, screaming wildly and holding a spiked club high above its gruesome head.

Something nicked Gary on the other side of the head, straightening his helmet as it flew by, and Gary registered the scene clearly as the heavy rock soared past him, crashing right into the charging goblin's face. The monster's head snapped back with a loud cracking noise and it dropped straight to the ground.

"Oh, good shootin'!" Gary heard Mickey congratulate himself from somewhere behind.

Three more goblins had surrounded Kelsey, coming at the skilled elf in measured, defensive strides. Time favored the goblins, for they had many allies lying in wait along this entire area, and hoots and cries echoed from every direction as more of the filthy creatures rushed to join the fight.

"Run!" Kelsey commanded Gary. "Back to Dilnamarra!" Then the elf charged his three opponents, quickly reversed direction, and broke free, scampering back towards Gary.

Gary turned and lumbered away, wondering what in the world he would do when Kelsey, and then the goblins, overtook him.

But Kelsey had other ideas. He had almost caught up to Gary, and had purposely allowed the goblins to keep pace, when he wheeled about suddenly and threw himself into the goblins' midst.

The startled creatures hadn't even leveled their spears, and they would never get the chance. A shield smash downed the one on Kelsey's left. He thrust out to the right with his sword, catching another monster cleanly in the throat, then buried the third in a tight embrace and bore it to the ground.

Other goblins were coming out of the brush, but they were all farther up ahead on the road—the trap had been sprung too quickly, before the companions had gotten past the first ranks of the creatures—leaving Gary a clear path back the way he and his companions had come.

And Gary did run, as best as he could, and it took him a long moment to wonder why Kelsey hadn't sprinted by. He dared to stop and turn, and he saw the elf struggling in the dirt with one foe, another dazed goblin nearby trying to pick himself up.

And a dozen more monsters charging down the road.

"Keep running!" Mickey cried from the brush to the side. "Ye can do nothing for him, lad, but to save the precious items!"

Gary cared nothing for the armor, or even for the legendary spear that seemed so valuable to the people of the land. His gaze focused only on Kelsey, not yet truly a friend, perhaps, but one who had selflessly thrown himself back on the goblins so that Gary could escape. Gary had never considered himself overly brave, and he most assuredly was scared to death at that brutal moment, but he could not leave Kelsey to such a fate. He hoisted his spear for a desperate throw.

"Do not throw it!" rang a voice in his head. *"What weapon will thee fight with when the spear is loosed?"*

Not about to take the time to argue, Gary leveled the spear and charged, a primal scream that was as much terror as anger erupting from his lips. The dazed goblin to Kelsey's left started for the struggling elf, then saw Gary coming and hooted in glee, abruptly changing its course.

"Now what?" Gary moaned, and he tried to veer to the side, but stumbled instead and crashed heavily against a thick tree. As soon as he righted himself, he hoisted the spear again, desperate to stop the charging monster.

"Do not throw it!" came that inner voice again.

"Then what?" Gary answered silently.

"Take it up and fight with it!" implored the voice.

Gary braced the spear against the side of his heavy shield and wondered how he might maneuver the weapon well enough with one hand to possibly defeat the goblin.

The monster was almost on him; Gary could see the saliva dripping over its thick bottom lip from between its pointy yellow teeth.

"Not like that!" screamed the inner voice.

Gary's helpless frustration apparently sufficed as an answer, for the voice quickly explained. *"Against the tree,"* it said calmly. *"Brace the spear's butt end against the tree."*

Gary considered the words. He was out of time; the goblin was upon him.

"Now!" cried the voice. Gary didn't even think about his movements as he followed the undeniable command.

The goblin foolishly barreled in, its own spear leading. Gary's weapon caught fast on the tree; his shield deflected the goblin's spear up high and to the side. Then the monster was up against him, its breath hot and smelly in his face, its bulbous, vein-streaked eyes boring into his.

Geek led the goblin charge down the road. The elf was gaining an upper hand in his struggles, but the goblin knew that even if the elf won, he could never recover in time to escape the approaching horde. The plan seemed so beautifully executed; wouldn't Lady Ceridwen be thrilled!

Suddenly the road was fully blocked by a huge spiderweb. Geek shrieked (even goblins are terrified of the merciless giant spiders), dropped his spear, and covered up, plunging headlong into the tangle. Those others up in front shared similar fates, and the trailing goblins halted their charge and looked about in confusion.

Kelsey finally got atop the goblin, pinning its spear with his shield. He pushed free of the creature's stubborn grasp, getting into a kneeling position, and put his sword in line.

The doomed goblin whined and frantically threw its arm across its face. Kelsey's fine sword dove right through the arm, and right through the face.

Kelsey looked up the road, expecting to be overwhelmed. What he saw instead brought a smile to his dirtied lips. A dozen goblins thrashed and rolled, caught fast by an illusionary web. A score more stood behind, jostling each other and scratching their fat heads.

Then Kelsey heard a horn, back behind him, and the thunder of hoofbeats rolling down the road.

"The web'll not fool them for long," Mickey whispered from the side. "We should be going."

The creature's mouth opened wide in a silent, agonized scream. Staring into its gaping, yellow-toothed maw, Gary feared that it meant to bite him. The goblin's features contorted weirdly; a few sudden convulsions brought some blood out of its mouth.

Then Gary truly understood. He still held his spear, out straight, and the goblin's heaving tummy was right against that hand.

"Oh my God," Gary muttered without thinking.

The goblin jerked, showering Gary in blood, then went limp. Gary let go of the spear, watching mesmerized as the dead thing toppled to the side, the front half of his spear protruding from the creature's back, covered in blood and gore and entrails.

The young man stood very still for a long moment, not even remembering to breathe.

"*Well done, goodly young sprout,*" congratulated that voice in his head, but Gary wanted no applause, didn't feel a hero, didn't feel anything except sick to his stomach.

He put his head in his sweaty hands and tried to find the strength to retrieve his stained weapon.

The sound of approaching riders brought him back to the situation at hand. A score of armored knights charged down the road, banners waving and lances leveled. Gary forgot his horror for a brief moment and thought their salvation at hand. He lifted his arm and hailed loudly through the growing tumult.

Something crashed heavily into his back and the surrounding brush seemed to rush up and catch him. His first thoughts were that a goblin had tackled him, but the hand that came up under his chin was not gnarly and scratchy, like a goblin's, but delicate, though strong.

"What?" he started to ask, but found his head jerked back roughly and a fine-edged, bloodstained sword came in against his exposed neck.

"Silence," Kelsey whispered into his ear, but the command seemed hardly necessary with the elf's blade scraping a clear warning against Gary's throat.

"Prince Geldion," Mickey added. "Me thinking's that it should be a fair fight." The leprechaun looked back down the road at the goblins and blinked his eyes. The creatures stopped their thrashing as the illusionary web disappeared, and they gave it no more thought as the new nemesis, Prince Geldion and his guard, charged into them.

The first moments of battle went all the knights' way. Lances struck home and horses trampled helpless, sprawling goblins. But many more of the monsters were still filtering out of the woods to join the battle, and soon the Prince and his company found themselves tangled in a mire of goblin flesh. One rider was borne down under the weight of a dozen creatures, and he and his horse were swallowed up before they even settled to the ground.

"We have to help them!" Gary cried, and he struggled against Kelsey's loosened grasp.

Kelsey slapped him on the back of the helmet and put his full weight over Gary to hold him down. "Whoever wins would indeed be pleased to see us so easily delivered," the elf said grimly.

"The riders came for us?"

"It would seem so, lad," Mickey answered. "What other business would Prince Geldion have on the eastern road? It's no secret in Dilnamarra that we meant to go to the mountains."

Out on the road, the goblin press continued, but the knights were skilled fighters and seemed to be more than holding their own.

"We should be on our way," Kelsey commented. "The goblins could flee at any time, and if the Prince fathoms that we are in the area, we'll not have an easy time escaping." He crawled off of Gary's back and, still crawling, led Gary deeper into the underbrush. Soon they were up and trotting at a cautious pace, heading east and paralleling the road, but deep within the concealing shadows of the thick woods.

"I'm thinking that yer chosen quest might take a bit o' doing," Mickey remarked after the sounds of the continuing battle at last faded far behind them. "Ye've got enemies coming at ye from both sides, it'd seem."

"Why would the Prince . . ." Gary started to ask, but Kelsey cut him short.

"Both seek similar results, I would agree," the elf answered Mickey. "But they do not work in unison—that is our hope."

"Aye," Mickey replied. "One hand tangled the other."

"What are you talking about?" Gary demanded. "And why would the Prince . . ."

"It is of no concern to you," Kelsey interrupted once again.

"If someone's trying to kill me, I consider it my business," Gary replied as forcefully as he had ever spoken to the grim elf.

Unexpectedly Kelsey did not scold him, or even flash him a threatening glare. "You did well in the battle," the elf said sincerely. "Your bravery surprised me, as did your skill in handling the spear."

Gary shrugged, a bit embarrassed. "Thank Mickey," he explained. "He talked me through the whole fight."

Kelsey's look to the leprechaun was no less confused than the leprechaun's own expression. "Did I, then?" Mickey asked curiously.

"Well, you helped anyway," Gary replied, but his own face twisted in confusion as he came to realize that his guess was not correct. "It's curious that your accent changed when you communicated telepathically," Gary went on, trying to resolve the situation logically. "I never thought about it before, but I guess it makes sense. We all think the same way, even if we talk differently, and I didn't really hear words. I heard thoughts, if that makes any sense."

Mickey took a long draw on his pipe and nodded to Kelsey. "It wasn't me in yer head," the leprechaun explained to Gary.

"When did these inner voices begin?" Kelsey asked.

"Only at the battle," Gary replied, now growing concerned.

"And what do you carry on your back?"

"Just the spe—" Gary fumbled around to grasp the leather case, pulling it in front of him. "This thing talks?" he asked, his voice only a whisper.

"*Thing?*" rang a perturbed voice in his head.

"Of course it cannot talk," Mickey explained. "But its magic is strong, among the strongest in all the land."

"Sentient?" Gary reasoned.

"Aye, to its possessor," answered Mickey. "And ye'd be wise to listen to it carefully—that spear's seen more battle than the rest of us."

Gary sent the leather pack swinging back around him as though he was afraid of the thing.

"Be glad," Kelsey said to him. "You have an ally now who will aid you greatly in the trials ahead." A horn blew back down the road, once and then again, and Kelsey spun about. "And the trials behind," the elf added grimly.

"The Prince has won," Mickey remarked. "No goblin'd blow a note so clear."

"Then we must hope that Geldion has suffered too many losses to continue his pursuit," said Kelsey. "Cowtangle will soon end and the land between the wood and the mountains is clear."

An image of running across hedge-lined fields came into Gary's thoughts, with himself stumbling and struggling to get over each barrier, while the great armored knights pursuing him easily jumped their steeds along. Surely this adventure had taken on the dressings of a nightmare, with Gary running slowly, too slowly, to outdistance his determined pursuers.

They came out of Cowtangle Wood a short time later, as Kelsey had predicted. The mountains towered much closer now, seeming far less than the five days away Kelsey had claimed them to be when he had first discovered the goblin tracks. But as the day moved on, Gary understood the illusion. The ground was uneven here, rolling up and down regularly, and often at a steep pitch, and after four hours of walking, the mountains seemed no closer than they had when Gary had first exited the woods.

Kelsey veered north from the road then, explaining that he had no desire to go near to the town of Braemar.

"Probably find more traps waiting for us there," Mickey readily agreed.

They came to the bank of a river, running swiftly westwards from the mountains, a short while later. "The River Oustle," Mickey explained. "It'll take us right near to Dvergamal, though we'll get away from it before we get there, I expect, to keep around the town of Drochit."

Kelsey nodded at the leprechaun's reasoning.

Though this was no road, they made good time, and no evident pursuit, goblin or knight, came down the trail behind them.

Geek stumbled out of Cowtangle Wood to the southwest, a region of thick mosses and steamy bogs. Not many of his band remained alive, the goblin knew; perhaps he was the only one. He plopped down on a patch of moss and put his pointy chin in his rough hands.

"Drat the luck," he muttered.

He hadn't even considered yet what he might tell Lady Ceridwen, who was sure to be none too pleased.

"Drat the luck," the goblin spat again. "Stupid princes."

He heard a rustle to the side and jumped to the ready, thinking the knights had found him. He saw nothing, though, and figured it to be just the wind in the birch trees.

When he turned back, he nearly swooned. A shimmering blue and white light hovered over the ground he had just been sitting upon, gradually taking shape. Geek gulped audibly, recognizing the spectacle.

Lady Ceridwen stood before him.

"Dear Geek," the sorceress began, her voice sounding as a cat's purr. "Do tell me what happened. Who has harmed my dear Geek?"

"Mens," Geek replied. "Many mens, Prince's mens. What does they be doing in wood?"

"Perhaps," Ceridwen replied, pursing her lips, her flashing eyes staring far away. "Perhaps they were working for me." Her glare fell with full force over the now-trembling Geek. "Perhaps they were doing as I instructed, instead of interfering!"

"Geek did it for Lady," the goblin whined, falling to his knees and slobbering wet kisses all over Ceridwen's delicate hand.

The sorceress pulled away, revolted. "Why were you here?" she asked calmly.

"Geek catches elf and killses man," the goblin sputtered. "For Lady. Geek take armor—for Lady!"

"Did Lady tell Geek to do this?" Ceridwen prompted calmly.

The goblin shook his head. "Geek thinks . . ."

"Did Lady tell Geek to think?" Ceridwen asked, her voice louder, revealing some of her anger.

The goblin found no reply.

Ceridwen stepped back and drew out a thin wand from her sleeve.

"Lady!" Geek pleaded, and then he said no more, for frogs have little command of the common language.

Ceridwen walked over and casually picked up the pitiful creature. She moved to toss him into a nearby pool, then reconsidered and started away, petting Geek and casually promising him all sorts of adventure.

The merciless sorceress carried the goblin-frog to the other side of the small swamp, to a place where she knew a fat snake made its home.

EIGHT

DVERGAMAL

They traveled easily over the next couple of days, though Kelsey set a swift pace and only stopped for camp long after sunset, and had them on the trail again before the dawn. After the battle of Cowtangle Wood, Gary offered no arguments against the elf's haste; Mickey, of course, kept up his steady stream of under-the-breath remarks every step of the way.

The journey to the foothills crossed rolling but not broken land, and after the initial soreness of the unfamiliar armor had worn off, Gary found that he could get along quite well in the bulky suit.

Then they came to Dvergamal.

Sheer and jagged, bare and bony-hard, the mountains seemed a barrier that no man could hope to pass. Cliffs rose up a thousand feet; gullies beyond them dropped a thousand more than that, and all the way seemed a confusing crisscross of narrow and perilous trails. Kelsey seemed confident enough of his steps as he found a path and started up. Mickey, just a leprechaun's stride behind, never even took his eyes off *The Hobbit*.

Truly Gary felt embarrassed at his own fears, and that gave him the courage to fall in line. Each step out, crossing deep ravines, winding along the sides of mountains, did little to bolster his confidence, though, and he continually found himself wondering how much a suit of mail might cushion so long a fall.

Where Kelsey skipped, Mickey rambled absently and Gary crawled. Short climbs which the elf took with a single leap, grab, and twist, and Mickey by simply floating up, Gary had to be threatened, then hauled and levitated, just to get over.

And all the while for poor Gary loomed death-promising drops, drops that grew ever deeper as the small troupe wound its way ever higher into Dvergamal. Sometimes their trail was open to both sides, sheer drops, left and right. Other times they disappeared into impossibly narrow crevices, twenty feet deep and barely a few feet wide and bordered by high walls of sharp stone.

That first night in the mountains, they camped out in the open (for lack of choice), on the side of a mountain where the ledge was at its widest, and this being only about five feet. The stiff wind bit at them, foiled any fire-making attempts, and threatened to push them over the edge if they did not take care.

When the sky mercifully lightened and Kelsey led them off, Gary's eyes showed the dark rings of a sleepless night.

"Set the pace a might slower this day," Mickey bade Kelsey, seeing Gary's condition. "Weary's not the way for crossing Dvergamal."

Kelsey looked back at Gary and huffed loudly. "The journey is hard," the elf scolded sternly. "Why did you not sleep?"

A helpless expression crossed Gary's face.

"He's not used to such heights," the leprechaun answered for him. "Be easy on the lad; ye've asked a lot of him these past days, and he's answered ye with little complaint."

Kelsey huffed again and started off, but he did keep the pace easier.

The large raven spotted the troupe later that day and marked their surprising progress with some concern. Leshiye, Geldion, and Geek had all failed her, and now Ceridwen, in her black-feathered form, had to find another obstacle to throw in Kelsey's path. She knew Kelsey's destination, and her growing respect for the resourceful elf only heightened her fears that he might get past the next expected barriers—dwarf echoes, hurled boulders, and water slicks.

"But how far will you get if the buldrefolk know that you mean to steal Geno?" the raven cackled. "And where will Kelsey turn if Geno is no more?" Several devious options crossed Ceridwen's thoughts as she sped along the mountain updrafts and began her own search for the reclusive dwarfs.

"We'll have no talking from here on in," Mickey whispered to Gary as they crossed one high and sharp ridge. "The mountains have ears all about us, more foe than friend." The leprechaun put a stubby finger over his pursed lips, gave Gary a wink, and skittered up ahead, back in line between Gary and Kelsey.

Long shadows marked the jagged mountains as scattered dark clouds swept along on the wind overhead, or sometimes below. Peaks disappeared in a veil of gray. Crevices and jutting outcroppings cut sharply from every angle, and rivulets of water, from the morning rains and morning mists, slipped down every mountainside, some dark under ominous clouds, others glittering in sunlight, skipping easily across the stones.

Gary wondered what power had shaped this region, what force had so blasted and torn the earth. He had viewed this scene in his imagination, and in the illustrations of imaginative artists, before, while reading books of prehistory, of the violent upheaval that split the continents and raised the mountains. The preternatural edge of stone before the eons of wind and water beat it down and tamed it.

And that primordial, majestic scene spread out all about him, coupled with the interspersed sunlight and Mickey's warning, added greatly to the out-of-place human's trepidation. How insignificant he seemed beside the cliffs of Dvergamal! Gary bent low to the rock along the narrow trail, feeling a strength in the land itself that could blot him out in the blink of his eye.

What creatures might call this land home? he wondered, imagining beasts of incredible might crouched behind every stone, or watching from nearby ledges.

His fears slowed him, and by the time he bothered to notice, Mickey and Kelsey were far ahead, turning a bend that would put them out of sight.

"Wait up!" Gary called, forgetting the leprechaun's words.

"Wait up!" came a response from the side.

"Up," replied another distant stone. "Up . . . up . . . up . . . up? . . . up!"

Gary looked all about, startled and confused by the suddenness of the echoes and the changes in their inflection.

"I told ye to hold yer words!" Mickey scolded, spinning about.

"Words . . . words . . . wo . . . wo . . . words . . . rds . . . rds," the echoes grumbled back, resonating through every valley.

Kelsey and Mickey scrambled back to join Gary. "What is it?" Gary whispered harshly, seeing from his companions' expressions that these were indeed more than ordinary echoes.

"It," the hidden voices replied. "It . . . itititit . . . it?"

"Dvergamal," Mickey said under his breath. "Voice o' the dwarfs. They're playing with us, as they do with all who speak in their mountains." His voice had risen as he talked and the echoes took up a responsive chant.

"Oh, shut yer mouths!" Mickey shouted.

"Shut yer mouths . . . yer mouths . . . shut them good! . . . yer mouths."

"Shut them good?" Gary asked incredulously.

"Dwarfs like to put their own thoughts in," Mickey explained dryly.

"Come along, then," Kelsey interjected. "And keep silent—or they will follow our every move."

"Yes, do come," answered the echoes that were not echoes. "And keep silent . . . silent . . . silent . . . ssssh!"

Gary's trepidations only increased, but this time he worked much harder to keep close behind Kelsey and Mickey.

Down a deep ravine, amidst a tumble of boulders, the dwarven mimickers congratulated themselves.

"A bit of fun, that," Dvalin, the chiseled dwarf with wild black hair atop his thick head, but not a bit of fuzz on his cheeks and chin, clucked to his brother Durin, an ancient specimen, gray-haired and with a beard long enough to tuck into his boots if he so chose. Both dwarfs were overjoyed to hear the passage of strangers in the mountains. It was their month to guard the passes, a normally tedious duty, and playing the echo game with a passing troupe came as a most welcomed diversion.

"If they keep to the high ridges, we will catch them again crossing the north side," Dvalin reasoned, rubbing his stony, stubby hands together (which produced a rocky, grating sound).

"And if they turn down low, their path will bring them right past us," added Durin, adjusting his wide belt to straighten his beard. "Perhaps we should gather some of the others . . ."

"Dogtail their every step!" Dvalin finished, thinking the idea positively grand. Dvalin turned to leave but stopped abruptly as a large raven flapped down to land on a rock only a foot from his prominent nose.

Both startled dwarfs hooted and rushed about, bumping into each other and into boulders—both types of collision making similar sounds—grabbing wildly for their belted weapons, mattock for Durin, axe for Dvalin.

"Boulders!" howled Durin a moment later, regaining his wits and adjusting his belt once more. "It is only a bird!"

"Only a bird indeed!" Ceridwen retorted sharply, sending the dwarfs into another bouncing dance.

"Brother," Dvalin began very slowly, fingering his small but wicked-looking axe, "did that bird speak to us?"

"You have never met a talking raven?" Ceridwen asked, cocking her little black head. "The memories of dwarfs are not so long as the tales tell!"

"Talking ravens!" the brothers howled at each other, and then the stones rumbled their cry again and again in a true echo.

"A thousand thousand pardons," Durin answered, dipping into a bow that dragged his long silver beard on the ground.

"None of your race has been seen in Dvergamal in a grandfather dwarf's memory," added Dvalin, similarly dipping impossibly low.

"Well, one has been seen now," Ceridwen said a bit more sharply than she intended. "One has come to tell you to ware the elf, the man, and the sprite you so gladly taunt. The elf most of all. His name is Kelsenellenelvial . . ."

"Elfs have such stupid names," Durin remarked dryly.

"And he has come in search of a smith," Ceridwen finished.

"No, no," replied Dvalin. "We cannot have that. Not for an elf; not at any price!"

"He does not mean to pay," Ceridwen explained. "He means to steal. And the smith he has in mind . . ."

"Geno!" the dwarfs hooted together, and they hopped about, rebounding around the boulder tumble until they finally popped free of it.

"We shall see!" insisted Dvalin.

"And thank you, O great speaking raven," added Durin, dipping another bow as he rolled away.

Ceridwen watched them disappear into the shadows, then flew off to further ensure her success.

Kelsey pulled up in a shallow cave a short while later, sheltered, he hoped, from the eyes and ears of the mountains.

"We are close," the elf announced when Mickey and Gary entered. "I have seen the dwarfsign."

"Dwarfsign?" Gary had to ask.

"Scrapings on the stone," Mickey explained. "I never did meet a dwarf who could pass a good piece o' stone without taking a taste of it."

This time, Gary kept his questions to himself.

"They know we are about," Kelsey went on, then he paused and looked at Gary as though he expected Gary to interrupt once again. "Since one of us chose to reveal our whereabouts," he finished a moment later, his golden eyes boring into the bumbling human. "But travelers are not uncommon in Dvergamal, and most go to all lengths to keep clear of the dwarfs."

"They'll not be expecting us," Mickey put in. "No wise folks'd go looking for them."

Kelsey's unrelenting glare settled on the leprechaun. He pulled a parchment, a map, from a pocket in his cloak and spread it on the floor. "We are here," he explained, pointing to one of many mountains on the scroll. They all seemed quite unremarkable to Gary, but he didn't question Kelsey's proclamation.

Kelsey moved his finger a short distance across the map. "Here lies the Firth of Buldre, the falls," he said. "And here, too, somewhere, we shall find Geno Hammerthrower."

"Somewhere?" Gary dared to ask. "How will you know for certain?"

Kelsey didn't blink for a long, long while. He replaced the map and headed toward the cave entrance. "Come," he bade his companions. "We must get to the smith and back out again before the shadows engulf the mountains. I do not wish to be in the region after sunset while holding a captive."

"What happens if we come across some dwarfs other than this Geno?" Gary asked Mickey before the leprechaun could scamper after Kelsey.

"I told ye before," Mickey replied grimly, "elfs and dwarfs don't get on well."

The three had barely gotten back on the open trail when a growling rumble shook the mountainside. It came from within the stony ground, yet it rolled as loudly as a thunderstroke. Kelsey and Mickey exchanged concerned glances, but the elf pressed ahead, picking up the pace. They were terribly exposed now, transversing the top ridge of a double-peaked mountain.

A second trail broke off from the first, diving down between the twin peaks. Kelsey considered the course for just a moment, then plunged ahead, thinking the lower trails safer. He had only gone a dozen long strides, though, when the ground opened up suddenly before his lead foot. Like an animal maw, the earth snapped shut. Kelsey's uncanny agility saved him, for though he was startled by the sudden break, he managed to twist around to the side to stay his momentum.

The earthen mouth opened again and snapped shut, like some hungry child straining to reach a morsel that had dropped to his chin.

"Might that they know why we're here?" Mickey asked.

Kelsey didn't answer. He rushed around the snapping maw and down the path, drawing his sword and muttering with every step.

"Come along, lad," Mickey coaxed. "And don't ye get too close to the mouth!"

Gary watched the snapping earth for some time before he mustered the courage to continue. He couldn't imagine any power that could bring the ground to life like that, and he suspected the maw to be an illusion. His suspicions, however, did not give him the courage to march across the opening and prove his theory.

As they continued on, Gary tried his best to keep up, but in the heavy armor he was no match for Kelsey's frantic strides. Worse than his fears of separation, Gary now heard his clanking and thumping echoing back at him from every direction.

And he was certain that those echoes were not from any natural formations. He thought he heard giggling from one side, but all that he saw there was a broken cluster of fallen boulders. He shook his head, telling himself that it was just his imagination.

Then one of the boulders rose off the ground.

"Mickey!"

Gary's yell came just in time. The boulder went soaring through the air, and would surely have smashed in the back of Kelsey's head, but the leprechaun spun about and pointed a finger at the approaching rock, countering the magic and holding it still in midair.

"Run on!" Kelsey ordered, and he rushed away. More boulders shuddered, as if to life, then rose up, and the three companions scrambled furiously to find some cover or simply to get out of range.

Gary felt better this time when Mickey appeared perched on his shoulder.

"Keep going, lad," the leprechaun prodded, waving one finger about in the air. "I'll catch any that's coming from behind!"

To Gary's dismay, they were soon back on an exposed ledge, with a deep gorge to their left. The ground sloped more gradually to Gary's right, and he considered running down that way. But Mickey, apparently understanding Gary's thoughts, told him to keep in line behind Kelsey and trust in the elf's judgment.

Soon they heard a dull, continuous roar, and then the perpetual mist from the towering waterfalls, the Firth of Buldre, came into sight, not so far to the left of the fairly straight trail. Gary didn't dare look behind him; he could tell from Mickey's grumbling and wild, jerking movements that flying rocks were still in pursuit.

Up ahead, Kelsey stopped suddenly and whacked his fine sword against a boulder on the side of the trail. Gary didn't understand until he got up close enough to see that the rock had reached out an arm to grab at the passing elf!

"Dwarf magic," Mickey muttered, then he yelled, "Duck, lad!"

Gary lurched forward and stumbled, unable to break his weighted momentum.

The boulder shot by him, a near miss, then continued on to slam heavily into the rock holding Kelsey. Both stones split apart and the shocking jolt sent the elf sprawling to the ground.

Gary lumbered by, fighting for his balance, reaching for the downed elf. Another rock skipped alongside him, clipping his shin. The earth roared and trembled, and Mickey tumbled from Gary's shoulder.

"Kelsey!" Gary called, and he finally skidded to a halt on the edge of the trail. He turned about to regard his elven companion, then found his own troubles as the rocks broke away under his feet.

"Catch him!" he heard Kelsey yell to Mickey, but the leprechaun, already holding two large stones motionless in the air, had no magic left for Gary.

The air rushed past him; his shield twisted painfully behind him, holding hostage his strapped arm. He felt the fine mist as he descended below the level of the waterfalls, several streams of water eagerly rushing and diving over the ledge.

That horrible moment did not feel like any dream to Gary Leger. The blur, the rush of air, was too real; he knew that he would not awaken safely in his own bed. The continuous thunder of the Firth of Buldre drowned out his pitiful screams.

And then he hit with force enough to rattle every bone in his body, in a pool protected from the tumult of the falls by a rock jetty. Everything seemed to move in slow motion as Gary floundered, not comprehending which way was up. His helmed head clanked against rocks; the current, the aches, and the weight of his armor fought against his every move. Then his foot hooked on a chunk of stone, and his momentum, as he rolled his body back over the leg, brought his head and shoulders clear of the cold water.

Gary gasped and sputtered as the water drained from his helmet. He kept enough wits about him to throw his shield arm over some nearby rocks, hooking the bulky item securely. He hung there for what seemed like many minutes, finally dragging himself half out of the pool, getting enough of his weight onto the rocks to keep him from sliding back in, at least.

He could hear nothing above the thunderous falls, could feel nothing beyond the hard stone and the chilling bite of the water, and his long wet hair hung in his eyes. Somehow he managed to get a numbed finger into the helmet's eye slit and brush the hair aside.

And then he glimpsed a wondrous sight indeed.

All about him, the water cascaded down the hundred-foot cliff face in dozens of separate falls, barely visible through the perpetual mist. Huge chunks of rock stuck up out of the basin pools, stubborn sentinels against the relentless onslaught, defying the pounding water. In this basin, many of the mountain streams created by the seasonal melt came together, collecting below the falls to form the birthplace of the River Oustle.

From the angle where he was lying, Gary could also see behind the largest of the falls. Instead of the expected stone wall, though, there loomed a cave, lighted within from the blazing fire of an open hearth. Gary struggled a bit to the side to get a better view. There was a table in the little room, with an empty platter and a large flagon atop it, and a bench filled with ironworking tools: tongs, hammers, and the like.

The single occupant, bandy-legged but broad-shouldered, stood before the hearth, swinging a huge hammer easily at the end of one of his lean, sinewy arms. His sandy-brown hair hung straight under a tall knitted cap and he continually flicked his head, as if to move some strands from in front of his face. The creature could not have been more than half Gary's height, half again taller than Mickey, but there was a solidness about this one, a powerful presence that Gary could sense clearly, even from this distance.

Gary knew it was a dwarf, though he couldn't be certain if it was *the* dwarf. But what if this was the famous Geno? Gary pondered. What might arrogant Kelsey say if Gary walked right in and captured the smithy? Gary realized then that he had lost his spear in the fall. He twisted about to look up the long cliff— was amazed that he had even survived such a dive—and realized, too, that he had lost all trace of his companions.

"He can't be that tough," Gary told himself, sluggishly dragging himself farther up onto the rocks. He meant to sneak in and make the capture bare-handed, but he stopped before he had even cleared the water, watching curiously as a large raven swooped in around the thunder of the waterfall and landed inside the little room, behind the oblivious dwarf.

Gary grew truly amazed as the raven shifted form, flattening out as it slipped down to the floor, transforming into a long black snake. It started for the dwarf, then seemed to change its mind and made for the table instead. It coiled and curled its way up the table's single central leg and slithered over the flat rim to the flagon.

"What the hell?" was all that the disbelieving Gary could mutter as the snake hooked its considerable fangs over the lip of the mug and began milking venom into the dwarf's drink.

Gary finally managed to get his legs under him. He tried to rise, but wound up crawling instead, knowing that he had to get behind the falls. He stumbled down with a loud clang and held very still. But neither the dwarf nor the snake apparently heard him—of course they didn't with the continual roar.

The snake had finished by then and it slithered back to the floor and across the room, disappearing into a crack in the wall.

The dwarf, too, had finished. He turned about—his face was clean-shaven and his eyes wide and blue-gray—and headed for the table.

Gary called out to him, but he didn't seem to notice.

"Can't let him drink that!" Gary growled at himself, and he picked up a stone and threw himself forward, scrambling and rolling the last few yards to the edge of the room, his fear for the dwarf overruling his sincere respect for the powerful falls.

The dwarf had hoisted the flagon by the time Gary got in range, but the man launched the large stone anyway, praying for luck. The missile bopped off the side of the dwarf's head, causing little damage, but it did manage to knock the poisoned flagon to the floor on the rebound.

"What?" the dwarf roared, and Gary, sheltered somewhat from the roar of the falls by the rim of the cave, heard him clearly. Gary got up to his feet, finally, and he fell back against the cave wall, bruised and exhausted, and knowing that he owed the diminutive smithy an explanation.

The dwarf, seeming not even dazed by the rock, turned on Gary and planted his stubby knuckles against his hips, against the leather sides of a wide and jeweled belt.

"Poisoned," Gary rasped helplessly against the growling echoes, and the steely-eyed creature didn't blink.

Gary started forward from the wall, figuring he couldn't be heard well enough to explain.

Then he learned how Geno Hammerthrower had earned his name.

"You spilled my mead!" the dwarf roared, and he launched the hammer so effortlessly that Gary didn't even realize it had been thrown—until it popped him square in the faceplate of his helm. He grunted and bounced back against the wall.

When his eyes stopped spinning, he saw a second hammer spinning end over end his way, and then a third and fourth, before the second even reached him.

"Wait!" Gary shrieked, trying futilely to get the heavy shield up to block. The hammers bonked in—one, two, three—again right between the eyes.

Waves of dizziness rolled over Gary, the clangs echoed over and over in his ears. Another hammer struck home, and then another—did this infernal dwarf have an endless supply?

Gary realized that he was sitting now. He looked out the helm's small slit— it wasn't running straight across anymore—and saw the diminutive dwarf hoisting an impossibly huge hammer. Even Cedric's magical helm wouldn't stop that one, Gary realized, but there was little the dazed man could do to stop the dwarf from finishing him off.

There came a splash from the side and Kelsey swung into the cave at the end of a rope. His momentum carried him right into the dwarf, sending both of them tumbling across the floor.

Mickey came into the room then, floating right through the falls at the end of an umbrella! The leprechaun landed easily, snapped his fingers to make the umbrella fold up again and disappear up his sleeve, and tossed Gary a casual wink.

Kelsey came up first, putting his sword in line with the dwarf's face. "I have you!" the elf declared. The dwarf, still kneeling, spat in Kelsey's eye. His gnarly hands seemed to actually grab hold of the floor and he jerked it as a maid might snap a carpet. The ground rolled under Kelsey, sending him head over heels backwards. He rolled right back to his feet, but without his precious sword, and then he crashed against a wall.

Gary felt a tug on his back. He watched curiously as a leather strap across his chest untied itself. The tug came again, and the case holding the spear of Cedric Donigarten slipped out from under him. Gary understood what was causing the strange events when he noticed Mickey holding his hand out towards the case, magically pulling it in.

Kelsey was still standing, leaning, against the wall, and Gary thought the stunned elf would surely be crushed as the wild dwarf dipped his rock-hard head and barreled in.

But Mickey was the next to strike. The spear case shot across the room, just a few inches from the floor, and cut in between the dwarf's pumping legs. The creature pitched in headlong, and Kelsey found a hold above his head and lifted his legs high and wide.

With a tremendous *crack!* the beardless dwarf hit the wall face-first. He bounced back several feet, but somehow managed to hold his balance.

"I have you, Geno Hammerthrower!" Kelsey cried again, and he jumped out, pulling a chain, shackles at its ends, from under his green cape. The stunned dwarf still did not move as Kelsey looped the chain over him and snapped the shackles around his wrists.

NINE

RULES IS RULES

"I have you," Kelsey said again. "And you must fulfill my wish before you shall regain your freedom."

The dwarf considered the shackles and the loosely looped chain for a moment. He had relative freedom of movement, for the chain dragged long on the floor behind him. He looked at Kelsey and smiled widely, showing one large hole where a tooth had once been.

Kelsey seemed to read his thoughts. "*Biellen*," the elf whispered, even as Geno's legs started to move. Geno had hardly taken a step before the magical chain suddenly shortened, pulling his arms tightly behind his back. His gap-toothed smile disappeared along with his balance, replaced by a wide-eyed look of disbelief as he pitched headlong to the floor.

"Now we are leaving," declared the victorious elf, scooping up his sword and laying its blade to the side of Geno's stubby neck. "By the lawful rules of capture, you are bound to me. I'll not tolerate any more resistance." He pulled the dwarf to his feet, while Mickey went to see about Gary.

"Nasty dents in the helm," the leprechaun remarked. "I'm hoping yer head isn't the same."

"Yes . . . er, no," Gary replied, somewhat absently. He had watched the capture from afar, his thoughts still filled with spinning hammers and pretty stars—there seemed to be so many stars in this wondrous land!

With Mickey's help, the young man managed to get unsteadily back to his feet, and once there, Gary realized just how sore he was, from the fall and the hammers, and just crawling across the jagged rocks. Every joint in his body seemed as if it had been pulled and stretched beyond its limits. There was not time for whining, though, not with Geno captured and many other crafty dwarfs nearby no doubt already spinning devious spells to block their escape.

Kelsey quickly collected Geno's hammers, and some heavy gloves the dwarf kept near the burning forge, and the troupe prepared to depart.

"I've lost my spear," Gary remarked as Mickey started away. Three sets of eyes turned to him.

"In the fall," he explained. "It's probably in the river, a mile away by now."

Mickey looked to Geno. "Spear?" he asked. The dwarf nodded to a cubby, barely a crack in the wall. Mickey cast him a suspicious glance, then wagged a finger the crack's way. A dozen different weapons came tumbling into the room to the leprechaun's magical call: swords, axes, a tall halberd, and one spear. "Better than the one ye lost," Mickey muttered and he floated the iron-shafted weapon into Gary's hands.

Feeling the balance of the dwarf-crafted weapon, Gary couldn't disagree.

"Now we must be on our way," Kelsey demanded. He looked straight into the dwarf's gray-blue eyes. "Which way?"

Geno nodded towards a narrow tunnel on the far side of the little chamber. Gary regarded it curiously for a second, mentally comparing this image to the one he had seen when first he gazed upon the hearth-lighted room.

"That opening wasn't there before," he started to protest, fearful of this newest trick, vividly recalling the biting maw in the earth up along the high trail.

Mickey looked to him, then nodded to Kelsey. Then, to Gary's disbelief, Kelsey continued straight ahead, leading the way to the tunnel.

The elf had barely crossed the threshold when the walls snapped shut, jagged stone teeth closing about the elf.

Geno Hammerthrower squealed with glee.

"No!" Gary shouted, and started forward.

Mickey intercepted him. "Haven't ye learned yet to look through the mist?" Gary didn't understand until the real Kelsey, still standing next to Geno, slapped him on the shoulder.

The dwarf's devious grin disappeared, replaced by a stone-face grimace.

"Rules is rules," Mickey scolded the dwarf.

"You reject the rules of capture?" Kelsey added angrily. "You disgrace your people and your trade? You are the finest smithy in all of Faerie, Geno Hammerthrower; you should understand your responsibilities in these matters."

"Not a fair capture!" the dwarf huffed. He stomped one heavy boot and tried to cross his arms over his thick chest, but of course, the shackles wouldn't allow for that.

"How so?" Kelsey and Mickey asked together.

"You caught me," Geno said to Kelsey. "But you were not the first attacker. Rules is rules!" he snarled, imitating Mickey's accent. "And by the rules, only the first attacker is entitled to make the capture!"

"Who . . ." Mickey started to ask, but then he realized the answer as he looked at Gary, the only one who had been in the chamber before Kelsey.

"You have ruined everything!" Kelsey roared at poor, confused Gary. "By what authority did you take it upon yourself . . ."

"I didn't do anything!" Gary protested.

"Stonebubbles!" Geno yelled, thrusting his chiseled chin Gary's way. "He hit me with a rock—right in the face!" The dwarf took a step to the side and kicked the same rock, lying conspicuously next to the fallen flagon in the middle of the floor.

"Explain your actions!" Kelsey demanded of Gary.

"I wasn't trying to catch him," Gary stammered.

"To kill me, then?" Geno huffed. "That, too, denies the elf the right of capture . . ."

"No!" cried Gary. He looked helplessly to Mickey, the only possible supporter in the room. "I just tried to stop him from drinking the mead."

"Worse than killing me!" Geno roared.

"It was poisoned," Gary explained,

"Poisoned?" Mickey balked. "Come now, lad. How might ye know such a thing?"

"I saw it," Gary replied, and now everyone, even the outraged dwarf, was listening intently. "The raven . . . I mean the snake. Well, it was a raven when it flew in, but it became a snake, and it crawled up the table to the mug. It had started for you," he said, pointing to the dwarf. "I don't know, maybe it didn't think it would like the taste of dwarf."

"That's believable enough," Mickey put in with a snicker.

"Then it went to the cup," Gary continued. "I saw it, I swear. The snake hooked its fangs on the top of the cup and pumped venom in. I swear it."

"Fairy tales!" Geno snarled.

"Look who's talking," Gary retorted.

Kelsey and Mickey stared long and hard at each other. If their suspicions about the source of their continuing problems were correct, Gary's story was not so unbelievable.

The issue became almost irrelevant a moment later, though, when the wall at the back of the small chamber split wide and a dozen bandy-legged dwarfs charged in, wielding all sorts of nasty-looking cudgels. They surrounded the companions in the blink of an eye, and one of them, a hunchbacked, gray-haired, and gray-bearded creature, asked Geno casually, "Which one shall we kill first?"

"Hold, Durin," Geno replied, not so quick to risk his reputation, though he hardly believed Gary's tale.

Kelsey clutched his sword hilt tightly, inching it closer to Geno's exposed neck. But Mickey, pulling out his long pipe, seemed well at ease.

"And tell me," the leprechaun bade, suddenly putting all the pieces of this puzzle together, "Who told ye that we were about?"

Durin and his black-haired brother exchanged curious glances. "We saw you ourselves," Dvalin replied honestly—and purposely dodging the question. "Crossing the high trails."

"And do ye always attack wandering travelers?" Mickey asked. "For, to be sure, me and me friends were attacked, and attacked by dwarfish magic."

"Thieves!" Dvalin snapped angrily.

"And how did ye know our intent?" Mickey replied, taking a deep draw, appearing not at all concerned. "Who told ye that we came for Geno?"

The dwarven brothers looked to each other again and shrugged, wondering what could be the harm. "It was a great speaking bird," Durin replied.

"A raven?" asked Mickey, and he looked to Gary and nodded.

Both the dwarfs bobbed their heads.

Mickey waggled a finger, retrieving the fallen flagon. "There's a bit o' mead left inside," the leprechaun explained, holding the flagon out to Geno. "Would ye care for a drink?"

Geno kicked the stone at his feet clear across the room. "Damn!" he spat.

"What is it, rock-kin?" Durin cried, and all the dwarfs took up their weapons. "Who must we kill?"

"None!" Geno growled back. "I am caught fairly, it would seem, indentured to this elf"—the word did not sound like a compliment—"and owing my life to this wretched human thing."

"No!" came several dwarven voices all at once, and the dwarfs took up their weapons and advanced another step towards the companions. But Geno knew well the rules of capture, a responsibility that the finest smithy in Faerie often found dropped upon his rock-hard shoulders.

They left the Firth of Buldre a short time later, accompanied by an armed guard of twenty none-too-happy dwarfs. The bandy-legged warriors did not try to hinder Kelsey's departure at all, though, even though the elf had Geno firmly in tow.

Gary did not quite understand it all, and his continued ignorance bothered him even after the other dwarfs had departed and the companions were once again out on the open trails.

"Why did they let us go?" he asked Mickey, who was perched comfortably on his shoulder again, reading *The Hobbit*.

"Why did this hobbit feel guilty about gaining the ring from the wretch in the cave?" Mickey answered without missing a beat. He held the open book Gary's way.

Gary thought about it for just a moment; he knew the tale as well as any. "Bilbo didn't play fairly at the riddle game," he replied. "He cheated, and his keeping the magic ring could have been considered stealing. Although," Gary quickly added, in defense of his favorite character, "if he had given it back, he would have been invited for supper, if you know what I mean."

"And there ye have it," Mickey said. "For still, he felt guilty. Faerie, too, is a land of ancient rules. And rules is rules, lad. To break them would bring ye dishonor in the eyes of all. What are ye without yer honor, I ask? Even the wretch, this Gollum thing, a murderer and thief a hundred times over and a heap bit worse than our Geno, thought twice about cheating in the riddle game."

Gary considered the answer, wondering how many people of his own world would have given in to the capture merely for the sake of an intangible thing such as their honor, as had Geno, with so obvious an advantage in the fight.

"Just one more question," he begged Mickey, who had gone back to his reading. The leprechaun looked up.

"You said that illusions wouldn't work on dwarfs, but in Geno's room, you fooled him completely with the image of Kelsey walking into the phony tunnel."

"Indeed, illusions do not work well on dwarfs," Mickey replied. "But I showed Geno just what Geno most wanted to see. Tricks work much the finer when they play on yer target's heart. Even if yer target's a dwarf."

Gary nodded; it seemed logical enough. "Where now?" he asked, looking ahead to Kelsey and the dwarf.

"Ye said one question," Mickey reminded him.

Gary gave him a pleading look.

"Straight through the mountains to the east," Mickey replied. "The trails are flat and not to be so tough with Geno talking to the stones. Then north to Gondabuggan, to buy a gnomish thief—second best thieves in all the world are the gnomes."

Gary suspected that he knew which race ranked above the gnomes, but he kept his thought to himself.

"Then back to the southern end of Dvergamal," Mickey went on. "And up the plain and the Crahgs to a place called Giant's Thumb." He dropped his voice to a mysterious whisper as he finished. "Where ye'll meet the worm."

Ceridwen looked across the few miles to Dvergamal, where she knew Kelsey's party was making fine progress. The sorceress had left the stronghold of the dwarfs soon after the companions had set out from the falls. With the dwarfs on their guard and in their mountain homeland, Ceridwen knew that she could do little against Kelsey. She had to somehow turn the party back, get them out on the plain west of the mountains, and buy herself some time.

She stood under a holly tree beside an unremarkable gray stone, surrounded by lifeless dirt, a spot she had marked well in ages past. "Come awake, Old Wife," the sorceress demanded softly. "I know your guise and need you now."

A long uneventful moment passed.

"Come awake, Old Wife!" Ceridwen called again, more loudly. She reached into a pocket of her black robes and took out a small bag, passing it quickly back and forth from hand to hand, for it was deathly cold.

"Summer has passed, autumn wanes," the sorceress lied, and she opened the bag over the stone, sprinkling icy magical crystals. The stone began to tremble almost immediately. Its hue shifted from dull gray to icy blue, and then it began to grow and re-form.

Soon it towered over the sorceress, twenty feet high and still growing. Its shape became that of an old woman, white-haired, one-eyed, and with skin as blue as winter ice on a clear day. Despite her height, the giantess appeared a meager thing, incredibly lean and wrapped in a tattered plaid.

"Cailleac," Ceridwen whispered, obviously impressed by the spectacle.

The giantess looked about curiously. "Allhallows has not passed," she said through her brown-stained teeth. "What trick is this?" She looked down then, and seemed to notice Ceridwen for the first time.

"Ah, sorceress," the Cailleac said, as if those words explained everything.

"I need you," Ceridwen explained.

"My time is not come," the Cailleac replied sternly.

"Just in Dvergamal," Ceridwen quickly added. "In the mountains where the chill wind blows even in the high days of summer. A small favor is all that I ask, and then you may return to your slumbers."

The Cailleac looked around at the new-blossomed flowers and the green summer canopy, feeling uncomfortable. Ceridwen tossed another handful of chilling dust at her and that seemed to comfort her.

"Do this for me and I will have your bed tended throughout the season," Ceridwen promised. "My minions will keep it cold for you and signal you when Allhallows is passed."

"Just in the mountains?" the Cailleac tentatively agreed.

Ceridwen smiled and nodded, confident that she had just bought herself the time she needed.

The companions camped on a flat stone in a gully between towering peaks. The wind was stiff this night, their second from the Firth of Buldre, and a bit chill, but it seemed refreshing to the weary troupe. Gary, Mickey, and Geno sat around the fire, with Gary glad for the break from wearing his cumbersome armor. Kelsey thought them safe enough in Dvergamal with a dwarven guide, and with the other dwarfs sworn to leave them be. The stones would tell Geno of the approach of any enemy long before the creature became a threat. The elf had even removed Geno's shackles, knowing that the bonds of responsibility would hold the dwarf tighter than any metal ever could.

Gary never took his gaze off the dwarf. Geno was much different from his kin (at least from those that Gary had seen), younger looking, almost boyish, despite his obvious strength. His unkempt hair was lustrous and his gray-blue eyes shone clear and bright and inquisitive. His missing tooth reminded Gary of a mischievous nephew back in that other world, a boy whose smile inevitably signaled trouble.

"How long have you been a smithy?" Gary asked, surprising even himself with the words. He had been silently trying to determine the curious dwarf's approximate age.

Geno snapped an unblinking glare upon him and did not respond. Mickey, too, paused in his reading to look up at Gary.

"I mean," Gary stammered, suddenly uncomfortable, "is that all you do?"

The dwarf rose and walked out of the firelight.

"What?" Gary asked, looking back to Mickey.

The leprechaun chuckled and went back to the book.

"What did I say to offend him?" Gary pressed, not willing to let this issue slip past.

"Ye think he'd be one for talking?" Mickey replied. "He's catched, lad."

"So were you, but you seemed friendly enough," Gary replied indignantly, brushing his black hair out of his eyes.

"I'm a leprechaun," Mickey answered. "I'm supposed to get catched. Makes everyone's life a bit more exciting, don't ye see?"

"Bull," said Gary. "You were as miserable as Geno—probably still are—but at least you had . . . have . . . the decency to talk to your companions." He said it loudly, purposely wanting Geno to overhear. "I'm a captive, too, when you get right down to it."

"Geno's owing to ye," Mickey explained. "It's not something he's comfortable over."

Gary didn't understand.

"Ye saved his life," Mickey went on, chuckling softly at Gary's continuing confusion. The young man couldn't quite seem to catch on to anything in Faerie. "Rules is rules," Mickey explained. "And, sure enough, there be rules for saving lives, too."

"He's coming with us; I thought that was my repayment," Gary replied.

"He's come to answer for Kelsey's capture, not for yerself," Mickey explained. "This is the elf's quest, and not yer own."

Geno walked back into the firelight then, still staring unblinkingly at Gary.

"I don't want any favors!" Gary snapped suddenly, sick of that stare.

Geno hooted and charged right through the dancing flames. He was on top of Gary in an instant, easily pinning the young man flat on his back.

"Ye shouldn't've said that," Mickey remarked, and he went back to his book.

Gary couldn't believe the strength of the dwarf's iron-like grip. He struggled and wiggled to no avail, and all the while, Geno leered at him, showing the gap in his shiny teeth.

"Let me . . ." Gary started to say, but Geno head-butted him and shut him up.

"What is going on here?" Kelsey demanded, storming into the camp, his sword drawn.

"The boy insulted the dwarf," Mickey replied absently.

Geno hopped off Gary, growled at Kelsey, and went back to his place opposite the fire, again walking straight through the glowing embers. He spun about and plopped down, dropping his accusing, threatening stare fully over Gary once again.

He kept it up interminably; Gary fell asleep with that uncomfortable image full in his thoughts.

Gary awoke sometime before dawn, shivering, for the wind had grown wickedly chill. Mickey and the others were also up and about, trying to get the fire back to life in the whipping breeze.

"Are we that high up?" Gary asked, moving to join them.

Geno and Kelsey ignored him, as usual, and as usual, Mickey tried to explain.

"Not so high," the leprechaun replied. "And a bit cold for the season even if we were among the tallest peaks of Dvergamal. But not to fear; we'll get the fire up in a bit, and a bit after that we'll find the morning sun."

Dawn did come soon after, but it was a gray and unwarming one, shrouded by a heavy overcast. The wind relented somewhat, but the air hung cold about the companions, their breath coming out in visible puffs.

"It smells like snow," Mickey remarked. Kelsey seemed not to appreciate the grim observation. He led them off without even a breakfast.

The first flakes drifted down around them less than an hour later.

Kelsey looked to Geno—this was the dwarf's homeland, after all—for some explanation, but the smithy offered nothing and seemed as confused as the rest of them.

"Do we go on or go back?" Mickey asked. "We've a week o' walking before us, but just two days behind."

"The weather cannot continue," Kelsey insisted. "Summer is upon us—even Dvergamal warms under its gentle breath."

As if in response, the wind groaned loudly throughout the mountain valleys.

By noon, snow was beginning to collect and many rocks grew dangerously slick with nearly invisible ice. It was then that the companions found their answers.

Geno bolted straight upright, as though some unknown voice had spoken to him. He rushed back to a high point the party had just passed and peered through the still-gathering storm into the far distance.

"Cailleac Bheur!" the dwarf cried, the first words he had spoken since they had left his waterfall home.

Mickey and Kelsey nearly fell over at the unexpected revelation. When they finally recovered, they rushed to join the dwarf, with Gary right on their heels.

Gary peered through the storm to the distant peaks. He thought he saw something, but simply couldn't bring himself to believe it.

"Cailleac Bheur!" Geno cried again.

"The Old Wife," Mickey translated for Gary.

Gary looked harder, beginning to understand that his vision was no trick of the weather. Drifting on the wind from mountaintop to mountaintop, barely visible through the snowy veil, was a huge woman, leaning on a giant staff and trailed by several large herons.

"Sure'n ye've heard of the Blue Hag," Mickey said to Gary. "'Tis she that brings the winter, withers the crops, and freezes the ground. Her touch is death, lad, to men and to the land."

"It is months before her time," Kelsey argued.

But the elf's words rang hollow, for the Blue Hag drifted on towards them, leaving in her deathly wake snowcapped peaks where there had been, only moments before, bare stone.

TEN

WINTER FROLICS

"We shall stay to the lower trails," Kelsey insisted, leading them on stubbornly against the gathering storm.

Mickey and Geno exchanged looks that did not comfort Gary Leger. He thought he had heard of the Blue Hag before, in a fairy tale, perhaps, and he vaguely remembered that what he had heard had not been pleasant.

The temperature continued to plummet. Kelsey took them down to the lower trails, but even there, the snow was fast piling. They plodded and struggled, slipped on ice-covered stones, and fought hard against the stiff and freezing wind. Finally even the elf realized that he could not keep to his determined course.

"We're getting deeper into her storm," Mickey remarked. "Even if the Cailleac is out on a confused wander, ye're taking us right to her killing feet!"

"And, Kelsey," the leprechaun added ominously, "we're both knowing that she's not out on any confused wander."

Kelsey turned to Geno. "Get us back to the west," he instructed. "Through the swiftest trails you know."

"You go beyond the bounds of my indenture," the dwarf replied, somewhat hiding his relief.

"To save us is to save yourself," Kelsey promptly reminded him. "Dwarfs fare no better than elves in the Cailleac's wake."

Geno's grunt was filled with hatred, but the dwarf rushed back to the end of the line and turned them about. Geno moved along at a tremendous, rolling pace, and once again, poor Gary found himself hard-pressed to keep up. Mickey perched upon his shoulder and whispered grim reminders of what would happen to him if he lagged too far behind.

At first, the small party seemed to be outrunning the storm, for the trails were flat and smooth. But then as they began to tire and cross rougher ground, the winds caught up to them, nipping at their backsides, howling like a pack of hungry wolves, and promising doom. Snow swirled all about them, limiting their vision to only a few feet. At one point, they came sliding and slipping down a steep and narrow decline, the stones slick with ice and a sheer drop to their right.

Kelsey shouted warnings, Gary screamed, and the leprechaun, holding on for all his life, nearly choked the young man, as they neared the bottom, for the trail took a sharp right turn that seemed as if it would leave them flying headlong over the drop.

Geno knew the area well, though, and he listened to the promises of the stones rather than depending on his vision. The dwarf called to the mountain, and a curving and smooth slab rose up from the lip at the turn, blocking the fall and deflecting the out-of-control companions safely along the trail. Every time the trail wound sharply, dwarven magic lifted a stone banking to guide them along.

Their pace continued to slow, though, as the snow deepened. Gary's feet and legs went numb and many times he thought he would simply fall down and wait for the blizzard to bury him.

Then Geno made a most welcomed announcement.

"Cave!" the dwarf shouted, and he slipped around a boulder and into a narrow opening.

"We can only rest for a moment," Kelsey said.

"My legs are numb," Gary retorted. "I won't make it if we go back out there."

"I, too, would prefer to rest," the elf replied. "To build a fire and sit in here until the storm abates." He looked at Mickey, who nodded his agreement. "But the Cailleac is out with a purpose, I fear. The trails this deep in the mountains will be blocked before nightfall and then we will have nowhere to go."

"We cannot stay and wait," Mickey agreed.

"Who said we would?" Geno, who had been sniffing around the back of the cave, huffed. "But I'll not go back out there," he declared, pointing to the whiteness beyond the cave entrance.

All three looked at him curiously.

"Get a fire going," Geno commanded. He walked to the back of the shallow cave again, braced his shoulder against a rocky spur, and heaved with all his strength. To the amazement, and relief, of his companions, the rock slid away, revealing a dark tunnel winding down into the west. "You might as well warm yourselves while we rest," Geno said nonchalantly.

Kelsey always kept some kindling in his pack, and he soon had a small fire burning. It wouldn't last long, they all knew, so they huddled about it, stealing every bit of warmth they possibly could.

"How far does the tunnel go?" Kelsey asked. With the immediate danger passed, the elf was more concerned with what the future might hold. This would be a temporary stay indeed if they came out still many miles from the edge of Dvergamal with the Cailleac's storm deep about them.

"Long way," Geno replied.

"You saved us all," Gary remarked honestly.

"Shut your mouth!" the dwarf snapped back. "I saved myself."

"We just happened to be along to get saved with ye," Mickey added, understanding the dwarf's feelings.

Geno briskly rubbed his thick hands together, brushed his hair from in front of his face, and stormed away from the fire.

"Keep quiet, lad," the leprechaun whispered to Gary. "Ye'll find no friendship with that one, and if ye anger him too much, he'll sure'n leave us lost in the dark."

"Time to go," Kelsey said, realizing before the others that Geno had already disappeared into the tunnel. The elf considered the dying fire, wondering if he might salvage a brand large enough to use as a torch. There wasn't much left, though, so Kelsey gave an uncomfortable grimace and a helpless shrug.

"Just keep close to the dwarf," Mickey reassured him.

Kelsey looked to his longbow and to the glowing embers.

"It'd only burn for a few minutes," Mickey quickly reminded him. "Then ye'd be without light and without yer bow."

Kelsey shrugged, obviously uncomfortable, and rushed into the darkness.

"Elfs aren't overly fond of caves," Mickey explained to Gary as he floated to his regular position atop the young man's shoulder.

"I knew that," Gary replied quietly.

Deep and dark, so dark that Gary couldn't see his hand if he waggled it just inches in front of his face. Not even a shadow of it.

Deep and dark.

Gary's sigh was audible when Mickey, perched upon his shoulder, conjured some light to read by.

"Put it out!" Geno roared from up ahead.

"We're not all dwarfs, ye know," Mickey retaliated. "Our eyes don't show us much through the dark. If ye want . . ."

Geno stormed back, nearly toppling Kelsey, and hopped up on his toes to put his face right up to Mickey's knees. "Put it out," the dwarf growled.

Kelsey, also very glad for the light, started to interrupt, but Geno would hear none of it.

"There are dark things sleeping down here," the dwarf warned. "Big and dark. Would you want to wake them?"

Mickey and Gary looked to Kelsey, who was sweating and obviously uncomfortable in the tunnel. To Gary, this hardly seemed the imposing elf he had come to know. When Geno, too, turned about and snapped a glare on the elf, Kelsey only shrugged and turned away.

Reluctantly Mickey extinguished his light.

"Good enough," grumbled Geno. "Now keep close to my back; if you get lost down here, you will never find your way out."

They trudged on slowly, Gary, even agile Kelsey, stumbling often. Gary thought that Geno must surely be enjoying all of this. On one occasion, Gary came down an abrupt decline and slammed his helmet into a low-hanging stone. Mickey squeaked and dropped heavily from his shoulder.

"Duck your head near the bottom," Geno said, a bit late with the warning. Mickey lit another globe, just long enough to find his way back to Gary, and the dwarf, too amused to even scold him, continued on, hardly hiding his snickers.

Gary had never been this far underground before. He had never suffered claustrophobia of any kind, but every step now came hesitantly to him as he became conscious of the thousands of tons of stone above his head. The air grew comfortably warm again—that was something, at least—but Gary's breathing came in terror-filled gasps; he felt he would just scream out, or plunge blindly into the darkness.

"Are ye all right, lad?" Mickey asked, hearing the labored breaths.

When Gary didn't even respond, Mickey lit a globe of light.

"Put it out!" came the expected roar from up front.

"Wait," said Kelsey, who had also seen—or felt—enough of the blackness, "Hold the enchantment." He turned to Geno. "I would rather awaken a horde of demons than continue on blindly. I do not care much for your dwarven realm, good smithy."

"Good enough for you, then," Geno growled back. "And when we do awaken the dark things, I'll gladly step aside that you alone might battle them!"

"Hold the enchantment," Kelsey said again to Mickey, and the leprechaun shrugged and pulled out *The Hobbit*, thinking, as usual, to make the best of the situation.

As they at last continued on, Gary wasn't certain if he liked the light better or not. Whenever the walls and ceiling came tight about them, he felt as though they would surely be smothered, and whenever the passage opened up wide and high, stalactites leered down at him, and stalagmite mounds resembled those demons that Kelsey had made mention of.

They made better progress, though, not having to shuffle blindly, not stubbing their toes every other step. Even Geno grew more at ease, particularly when the tunnel at last began to slope upwards once more.

How many miles they walked as the hours slipped by only the dwarf knew for certain, but the passage was almost arrow-straight and all of them, except for Geno, were quite surprised when they finally saw the waning light of day up ahead and came out on the western fringes of Dvergamal, not too far from the foothills.

"We've covered near to two days of trail walking in half a day," Mickey remarked with obvious admiration.

The leprechaun's claims proved true enough, but the danger was not completely behind them. The leading edge of the Blue Hag's storm had passed even this point and the snow lay deep about the tunnel exit, and still more tumbled down from the thick gray sky.

"We'll gain nothing by waiting," Kelsey said. "Move ahead and quickly, before the cold weakens us once more." Unfamiliar with their exact location, the elf let Geno continue in the lead.

The new-fallen snow was no match for the heavy footsteps of Geno Hammerthrower. The dwarf put a hammer in each hand and plowed ahead wildly, bursting through drifts more than twice his height and smashing away patches of ice wherever he found them. In his wake, the others had an easier time of it, though the blizzard grew stronger and the wind bit at them and forced lithe Kelsey to take a step to the side for every one he took forward. Mickey prudently put the book away (the pages would have gotten soaked anyway) and clamped both his hands around Gary's helmet.

With the lower foothills in sight and Geno cutting a path for them, the group made great progress and their hopes soared. Perhaps it was that strong pace and budding confidence that made Gary a bit less cautious, and on one slick descending trail, disaster struck.

Sheltered by a high mountain wall from the brunt of the wind, the trail was not so deep with snow. The companions trotted along anxiously, Geno leading, then Kelsey, then Gary, with Mickey more relaxed on his shoulder.

The leprechaun regretted loosening his grip when Gary slipped to his back and skidded down the slope, gaining momentum. Like a turtle on its shell, the young armored man flailed helplessly. Kelsey nimbly hopped out of harm's way; Geno, busily calling up a blocking stone, as he had done on the earlier winding trails, noticed Gary only at the last moment.

The dwarf swung about and braced himself, his muscles snapping taut as Gary barreled into him. The force of the impact sent Mickey head over heels. They all came to a skidding stop, Mickey atop Geno now, and Geno's heels hanging out over a deep ravine.

"You nearly killed us both!" the dwarf roared at Gary.

"All three, ye mean," Mickey quickly added. He started to say something else, but his words turned into a shriek as a gust of wind slammed him and knocked him from Geno's back.

"Mickey!" Gary cried, rolling about to get his head over the lip of the ravine. He saw the leprechaun spinning down, his tam-o'-shanter flying away, and then an umbrella opened, offering some hope.

But the wind whipped and swirled in the narrow ravine, and Mickey's umbrella twisted and turned, then folded up on itself. The sound of a renewed shriek and the image of plummeting Mickey died away, buried in the wind-whipped, deadening snow.

"Mickey," Gary whispered again.

"The leprechaun has many tricks," Kelsey offered, though there was little confidence in his tone.

Gary just continued to stare blankly into the chasm.

"How can we get down there?" Kelsey asked Geno.

The dwarf pointed across the narrow ravine. The path continued on after the ten-foot expanse; the ravine was really just a sharp crack where the ancient mountain had split apart.

Without saying a word, the dwarf coiled his bowed legs under his boulder-like torso and leaped out. He slammed face-first into the cliff across the way, but found a solid grip with his powerful hands and easily scrambled back up to the path.

Kelsey went next—two short strides and a graceful leap that cleared the ravine with several feet to spare.

Gary looked at them in wonderment, then turned his gaze back to the deep fall. He knew that the expanse was barely ten feet across, but he was amazed at how far that distance appeared with a drop of several hundred feet between the ledges. Without the snow, and without the armor, he probably could have made the jump—if he could have summoned the courage to even make the attempt.

"You must come across," Kelsey yelled to him, the voice seeming distant through the blizzard, "If we are delayed, the Cailleac's storm will bury us."

"You forget what I'm wearing," Gary shouted back. "I wouldn't make it halfway!" He heard Geno and Kelsey conversing, though he couldn't make out the words.

"I will throw you a rope," Kelsey said after what seemed to Gary to be a long, long while. "Tie it about you securely."

Gary didn't really see how that would be of much help; if he leaped and came up short, he would just swing down into the side of the cliff, probably breaking every bone in his body.

"Wait for the wave!" came Geno's gravelly voice.

"Wave?" The tone of Gary's question did not reflect an abundance of confidence.

"You will know when to leap!" the dwarf promised, and then Gary heard him chanting softly, as softly as Geno could with his grating, thunder-rumbling voice. The ground came alive under Gary's feet, swaying and rolling like an ocean.

Gary felt the momentum building, each surge stronger than the last, the ice cracking and sliding away. The stone groaned for the effort and Gary blinked in amazement as he watched one tall wave speeding at him from behind. Understanding now the dwarf's instructions, he waited until it bucked the ground behind him, then, knowing that it would surely toss him into the ravine if he did not act, he summoned his courage and leaped with all his strength.

His timing was perfect; he sailed high and far, easily clearing the expanse, even clearing Kelsey and Geno. So relieved to be over the chasm, Gary didn't even consider his new problem.

Landing.

He came down stumbling and scrambling. Realizing that he could not stay on his feet, he quickly veered for a pillowy-looking snowbank. Appearances can indeed be deceiving, as Gary learned when he crashed through the scant inch of snow covering the boulder.

He lay very still on the hard ground, not noticing the cold, or even the whiteness of the snow-filled sky.

Just the stars again.

After what seemed like an hour, he felt a small hand roughly clasp his arm and he was flying again, back up to his feet. He had no choice but to fight away the dizziness, for by the time he even realized that he was standing, Kelsey and Geno had already started away.

The three charged along for just a few minutes, then Geno stopped suddenly and put an ear to the mountain wall. The dwarf stepped back, as though he was considering what the mountain had told him. He reached for a loose slab of stone, somewhat bowl-shaped, and hoisted it from its position beside the wall. Gary shook his head at the feat, for though the slab must have weighed several hundred pounds, powerful Geno handled it easily.

"Get on," the dwarf ordered, laying the slab out before him. "The trail is ice-covered from here on down."

Kelsey jumped right aboard, but Gary wasn't so certain about tobogganing down a narrow mountain trail, especially not with a sheer drop looming on one side.

"Stay if you choose," Geno said, and he started to kick the sled away. "I will not promise that I'll come and retrieve your frozen body when the storm abates."

Gary caught him three strides down, diving to the sled and holding on for dear life. They had gone a hundred feet by the time Gary managed to get his whole body on the slab, taking a tight seat between Kelsey and the dwarf.

Geno remained in the back, hardly able to see over Gary. Since Gary considered the dwarf their pilot, he wasn't too confident of that arrangement, but the dwarf had his eyes closed anyway, concentrating and calling to the mountain to guide them.

They gained speed with every passing foot, plummeting along the steepening winding trail. They climbed several feet up the mountainside for every right-hand turn, and the trail conveniently (purposefully?) banked upwards to keep them from flying out on the left bends.

The wind roared inside Gary's loose helmet, and the eye slit did not offer enough protection to stop the windblown tears from flying freely. All the world became a surrealistic blur, mountain peaks blending together and rushing past. Sometimes the trail cut in from the ledge, sending the sledders rushing into darkness between towering walls of stone. Then the light returned in the blink of an eye as the sled zipped back out the other side.

As they flew through one tumble of boulders, Gary could only imagine that someone had turned a strobe upon them. The light flashed and flickered as they weaved in and out, under a small arching natural bridge and through a short and narrow tunnel.

"Hold tight!" Geno cried, a perfectly unnecessary order, as they came up on another ravine. Then they were flying in open air; the mountain seemed to disappear behind them. Gary hadn't yet found his stomach when they bounced back to earth, now speeding along an open and smooth rock face. The wind buffeted them fiercely, threatening to flip them right over.

"Lean!" Geno roared, and together they put the slab right up on one edge, letting their angled weight fight back against the stubborn wind.

All the world rushed back up around them as the trail dropped suddenly. With the counterbalancing wind suddenly blocked, their lean sent them along sideways, spinning out of control. Gary slid free, saw Kelsey jump clear, and watched in terror as Geno and the bouncing slab whipped down toward an empty stone wall.

The dwarf curled and kicked out ferociously, launching the slab into the air. *Crack!*

The slab hit the wall and broke apart into a thousand pieces. Geno skidded in after it, but hit feetfirst and was back up before Gary or Kelsey had even recovered.

"A fine ride," Kelsey commented.

Gary gave him a disbelieving look.

"How long would it have taken us to walk those icy trails?" the elf asked in reply. "We are near to the bottom now, and soon to be out of Dvergamal."

"What about Mickey?" Gary asked, looking at both his companions.

"The trail doubles back on itself," Geno answered. "We will soon go near to where the leprechaun fell."

Kelsey looked up at the gloomy sky and his doubting expression told Gary that he did not think they would have an easy time finding their lost friend. The sun did not set early this time of the year, but so thick was the overcast that the light in late afternoon was growing meager.

The snow was deeper down here, but the trails were fairly even, and with Geno chopping out a path, the companions made good time. Kelsey found Mickey's tam-o'-shanter after an hour or so, but they saw no other sign of the leprechaun, and their calls were hopelessly buried by the storm.

A dark twilight fell over them; Gary had almost lost hope. And then they saw a bright glow to the side of the trail—not the flicker of a fire, but the steady glow of a magical light. They rushed over and found a snowdrift—a glowing snowbank with a leprechaun-shaped depression in its side.

"Mickey!" Gary yelled, and he and Kelsey, though their hands were again numb, began digging furiously at the snow. More than two hours had passed since the leprechaun's fall and they didn't need to voice their concerns that Mickey could not have survived engulfed in snow.

"Ye think I'd stay in there?" came a voice behind them. In a shallow cubby on the wind-protected side of the mountain wall, the leprechaun came back from invisibility into view. "Sure'n I'd be a month in the thawing!" He dropped his gaze to Kelsey's belt and smiled widely. "Ah, good, ye found me hat!"

"Unbelievable" was all that Gary could mutter, and his remark was the only response at all forthcoming from the three amazed companions.

They soon realized that they had put the worst of the storm behind them. They came out of the foothills a short while later, walking from winter into summer, it seemed, for even the Cailleac had little power over the lowlands in this season. Gary could only equate it to the time he had flown from Boston to Los Angeles on a December day.

They set a comfortable camp and Kelsey went off with his bow, returning a short time later with several coneys.

"You saved me up there," Gary mentioned to Geno, looking back to towering Dvergamal.

Anger flashed in Geno's blue-gray eyes. "I saved myself," the dwarf insisted.

"No," Gary corrected. "Not at the ravine where Mickey fell. I had no way across, and you could have gone on without me. But you didn't. You used your magic to help me across."

Geno mulled over the words for a moment, then spat on Gary's sneaker and stalked away.

Kelsey came up and glowered at the confused young man. "Take care that you do not release him from too many bonds!" the elf growled right in Gary's face, the words sounding clearly as a threat. And then Kelsey, too, charged off.

Gary looked helplessly to Mickey, who sat with arms crossed and not looking too pleased.

"Now ye got yer wish," the leprechaun scolded. "Ye released the dwarf from yer responsibility and he's owing ye nothing. I wouldn't be talking with Geno overly much, lad—he'll likely rip yer tongue from yer mouth."

"Why is he so miserable?" Gary snapped back.

"He's a dwarf," Mickey was quick to answer, as though that explained everything. "Dwarfs don't like peoples who aren't dwarfs!" the leprechaun added, seeing that Gary still did not understand. "Besides, he's been catched, and that's not an agreeable state."

Gary silently denied Mickey's claims. For whatever reason, Geno had taken the trouble to save him, to save them all, and the "he's a dwarf" argument simply didn't hold up against that fact.

ELEVEN

TROLLS

The snake's muscles rippled, slowly drawing the helpless frog deeper into its mouth. The frog struggled pitifully, but it was just a harmless, weak thing and no match for the great black serpent. This was the natural way of things, but to Geek, the goblin-turned-frog, it did not seem natural at all.

He knew that soon the unhinged jaw would slip beyond his bulbous eyes, and then all the world would be darkness. He had seen engorged snakes before and knew that it would be a long time before he was fully digested. How long would he live in that awful state?

"Dear Geek," he heard someone—was it Lady Ceridwen?—say. "We have no time for such play!"

"Play!" he wanted to scream back at the wicked sorceress, but his cry came out as no more than a breathless croak as the snake clamped down on its fairly won quarry.

Then Geek saw the tip of a wand dip down before his bulging eyes. The snake started to wriggle away, dragging the helpless frog with it. Ceridwen uttered a few words and there came a *pop!* and a ripping sound, and Geek was a goblin again, lying facedown on the swampy ground.

"Bless you, me lady!" he groveled, trying to crawl to Ceridwen's feet. He found himself encumbered by the body of the ten-foot snake, its head and upper torso torn apart by the transformation, but still stubbornly clinging to Geek's waist and legs. The goblin whimpered and thrashed to get free, thoroughly disgusted.

"Will you please stop playing with that snake?" Ceridwen said calmly. "We have much business to attend. And get up out of that mud! You are the personal attendant of Lady Ceridwen! Do try to look the part!"

Geek bit back the curses he wanted to spout at the sorceress and instead resumed his groveling, slobbering kisses all over Ceridwen's muddy feet. She kicked him in the face and he thanked her over and over.

"I have turned them back from Dvergamal," the sorceress explained. "We must catch them on the plain, before they get south around the mountains, heading up towards the Crahgs." Her deadly, icy gaze fell fully over the goblin. "You must catch them."

Geek nearly toppled, realizing the price of failure. He looked back to the shredded remains of the black snake and knew that many more such creatures, and even worse creatures, lived in the swamp.

"Geek go get goblins for help," he stammered.

"Goblins?" Ceridwen laughed. "You would be defeated, as you were defeated on the road." Those icy-blue death-promising eyes flashed again. "We'll need bigger things than goblins to stop Kelsenellenelvial and his friends—and they have a dwarf with them now."

"Bigger?" Geek dared to ask, though he truly feared to hear the answer.

"You will go into Dvergamal for me," Ceridwen explained. "To a northern valley feared by travelers and even by the dwarfs."

Geek paled, beginning to understand why he was saved.

"I have some friends there which you must enlist," the witch said calmly, as though it was all no more than a minor task.

"Lady . . ." Geek began, thinking then that he preferred being a frog.

"They are big enough to catch the likes of that troublesome elf," Ceridwen went on, totally ignoring the whining goblin. "And cunning enough to resist the foolery of that leprechaun." Her description was unnecessary at that moment; Geek knew that she was talking of trolls. Horrid trolls, which even mighty Ceridwen did not wish to face.

"Lady . . ." he gasped again.

"Promise them a hundred gold pieces and a dozen fat sheep," Ceridwen went on. "A purse and mutton, that should bring them running. Two hundred gold pieces and two dozen sheep if they do not kill the elf or any of his friends. Just catch them and bring them to me."

"Trolls will eats me!" Geek cried.

"Oh, Geek," Ceridwen laughed. "You are always thinking of play! You will not be eaten, not if you promise them enough."

"Geek bring gold?" the goblin asked hopefully.

Ceridwen laughed again, louder. "Bring gold?" she echoed incredulously. "*Promise* gold, dear Geek.

"Oh, very well," Ceridwen said after Geek did not relinquish his pouting expression. Geek smiled hopefully, a grin that dissipated as soon as Ceridwen handed him a single gold piece.

"Give them this," the sorceress explained. "Promise them the rest."

Geek looked to the west, to the towering, snow-covered mountains, then back to the torn snake behind him, honestly wondering which fate he preferred. It wasn't his choice to make.

Ceridwen uttered a few words and made a hand gesture or two, and in the blink of the astonished goblin's eye, Geek found himself far from the swamp and the plain. Jagged snow-packed mountains surrounded him, stretching as high up as he could see.

"No, lady, no," he whined through chattering teeth, though he realized that Ceridwen couldn't hear him, and wouldn't care anyway.

He inched along the trail in a secluded dell on the southern side of

Dvergamal. The Cailleac Bheur's storm had diminished and the temperature had grown more seasonable, but still the paths remained deep with snow. Poor Geek's progress slowed even further with each step, hindered as much by valid fears as by the icy trails. Somehow, Geek almost found himself homesick for the snake's unhinged jaw. He rarely dealt with trolls, especially huge and nasty mountain trolls who were always hungry and not particular about what, or who, they stuffed into their yellow-fanged mouths.

The pitiful goblin came around a ridge, trying to be as stealthy as possible. He heard the trolls grumbling and arguing (trolls were always grumbling and arguing) in the distance and saw the flickering light of their campfire. Then the world went dark for poor Geek as a sack dropped over his head. In a second, he was hoisted feet-up and slung over a huge shoulder.

"Ten thousand golds and a million sheep!" Geek cried in terror, smelling disgusting troll breath right through the dirty sack. He managed to poke one hand out of the sack, presenting the troll with a single gold piece, the coin Ceridwen had enchanted with promises of splendid riches.

The companions broke camp early the next day. An uncomfortable stillness engulfed them, fed by silent fears of their powerful nemesis and by the heightened surliness of the gruff dwarf. No one dared to ask Geno to help in breaking down the camp, and the dwarf did not offer.

Stern-faced and without saying a word, Kelsey led them off. The elf had barely gone a dozen feet when Mickey trotted up ahead of him and turned back sharply.

"Where're ye going, then?" the leprechaun asked. "Ye're needing a gnome, and Gondabuggan, the gnome burrows, are to the north, not the south."

Kelsey stared unblinkingly at the sprite.

"Gnomes're the second best of thieves," Mickey went on, somewhat hesitantly, for he was beginning to catch on.

"Second best will not suffice," Kelsey replied evenly.

Mickey's sparkling gray eyes narrowed to dart-throwing slits. "Ye're beyond the bounds," he muttered.

"Then run," Kelsey offered, his tone unyielding and his stare promising that he could make Mickey's life much more unpleasant.

Mickey wasn't overly surprised. He had suspected that Kelsey would force him along from the very beginning. Elfs were usually cheerful folk, especially towards sprites, but life-quests had a way of stealing their mirth.

The leprechaun pulled a long drag on his pipe and let Kelsey pass him by. He fell into line beside Gary without saying a word and a short time later had resumed his perch on the young man's shoulder, book in hand.

Gary didn't mind the leprechaun's familiarity. After his mistakes of the previous night and the anger both Kelsey and Geno had shown him, he was glad for the company.

They trudged on through that day with few words being exchanged. Kelsey kept the point position, far out in front, his hand often resting on his sword hilt, with the others following in no particular order. Geno grumbled every now and again, and spat often, usually in Gary's general direction. It all seemed unremarkable and quite boring to Gary, except that on several occasions, he noticed Mickey put something resembling a whistle up to his lips. No sound, at least none that Gary could hear, emanated from the little silver instrument when Mickey blew into it, though, so Gary did not question the leprechaun about it and let it fall from his thoughts.

He tried to concentrate on his own predicament instead. He had no remaining thoughts whatsoever that this might be a dream. But what, then? The only answer that came into Gary's mind, the only possible solution, he decided, was that he had gone quite insane. Several times, he tried to look through the guises of his companions, to see them as people from his own world.

He gave that up quickly enough, seeing no hint that anything was any different. If he had gone insane, then he obviously could not consciously push that insanity away.

So he decided to continue to play it out and made a vow to at least try to enjoy the adventure.

He kept thinking of his parents, though, and of the distress he was no doubt causing them.

Gary suspected that something out of the ordinary was up as soon as he saw Mickey slip out of camp later that night, that curious silver whistle in hand. He followed the leprechaun in a roundabout way, not wanting to be noticed but not wanting the elusive Mickey to get out of his sight. Mickey did, though, as usual, and, Gary suspected, without too much difficulty. The young man found himself out alone, peering helplessly into the dark tangles of a tree copse.

Gary was about to give up and head back to camp when he heard a curious buzzing noise followed by the leprechaun's voice. He crept slowly in the direction of the noise, and his eyes grew wider when he saw, under the light of a full moon, Mickey's companion—the same sprite who had stuck Gary with the poisoned arrow and started this whole adventure.

"Ye know what's to be done," he heard Mickey whisper. The sprite's high-pitched reply came too fast for Gary to decipher any of the words.

"A loss it is," Mickey agreed. "But I've no way to get out of it without angering the likes o' the Tylwyth Teg, and I've no desire to walk into Robert's lair without having a few scoring cards tucked up me sleeve."

Gary silently mouthed the name Robert thinking that Mickey couldn't be referring to the dragon.

Again the sprite buzzed a response that Gary couldn't understand.

"I'll be getting it back, don't ye doubt!" Mickey insisted as forcefully as Gary had ever heard him. "But me first concern's getting meself back with me skin still on."

The sprite buzzed and bowed, and disappeared into the brush. Mickey stared ahead for a few moments, then sighed loudly and took out his pipe.

Gary thought it best not to question Mickey about the strange encounter, so he said nothing later that evening when Mickey strolled back into camp, nor all the next day, hiking along the roiling hills east of the mountains.

The weather was fine, if the company was not, and they continued to make steady progress that day, and then the next. When the southern edge of Dvergamal at last came into view, Kelsey picked up the pace.

But then Geno stopped suddenly and sniffed the air. Mickey uncrossed his ankles and looked up from his book; even Kelsey spun about curiously on the dwarf. Geno didn't seem to notice either of them. He stood very still, head back and nose up, sniffing at the air.

"What is it?" Kelsey asked, drawing his sword.

Gary could feel the tension growing.

"Uh-oh," he heard Mickey whisper.

Geno glanced right, then left, then spun right around, his wide and round blue-gray eyes darting every which way.

Kelsey's golden orbs flashed with mounting anxiety. "What is it?" the elf demanded again.

Geno met his stare head-on. "Trolls," the dwarf announced.

"Uh-oh," Mickey said again.

Gary turned on the leprechaun. "That's enough," he growled. "Ever since we left Dilnamarra, I've had the feeling that you and Kelsey know more than you're telling me. What's going on? Who's after us, and why?"

"Ye wouldn't understand," Mickey replied." 'Tis of no concern . . ."

"You tell me now or I'm done with this adventure and you can send me right back to my own world," Gary snapped. He threw his spear to the ground, looped the case with Donigarten's spear over his shoulder and let that fall, too, and crossed his armored arms defiantly over his chest.

"Tell him as we run," Kelsey bade Mickey. Geno was still standing, sniffing the air, his expression growing more and more alarmed,

Seeing even the steady dwarf so obviously unnerved, Gary lost the momentum for his argument. He scooped up his belongings and off they went, Geno leading them away from the mountains.

"'Tis Ceridwen, we're thinking," Mickey started to explain to Gary, the leprechaun taking his usual seat.

"You have angered the sorceress?" Geno cried, overhearing. He skidded to a stop and spun around, eyes flashing and his jaw clenched tight. "And it was she who roused the Cailleac," he said angrily.

Mickey nodded gravely.

Geno turned on Kelsey. "You said nothing about battling the likes of Ceridwen!" he roared. "You did not mention the witch at all!"

Gary listened to the conversation distantly, his thoughts tied around the name of the witch. So many names in this enchanted land seemed somehow familiar to him, and he was certain that he had heard of Ceridwen before, back in his own world.

"I did not know that the witch was involved," Kelsey answered honestly. "Only when I spied the Cailleac drifting across the peaks of Dvergamal did I come to truly believe that the dangers we have encountered have not been random chances."

"For only she could rouse the Cailleac," Geno reasoned grimly.

"And the trolls?" Mickey put in, prodding them all to the realization that this might not be the best opportunity to sit and discuss the matter.

The reminder sobered Geno. He spun all about, sniffing anxiously at every direction. "Trolls," he replied. "And not too far."

As if on cue, the others suddenly caught the disgusting scent.

"Run!" Kelsey cried, and he and Geno led them on wildly, Kelsey stopping every few feet to encourage Gary to keep up. Now more comfortable with the armor, Gary was up to the great pace, but still the stench of trolls deepened around them, from every side.

Geno led them up a small, bare hillock. "They are all about!" the dwarf declared, taking up his two favorite throwing hammers and arranging the others for easy grabbing off his wide belt. "Set for defense!"

Kelsey pulled his longbow off his shoulder and quickly strung it, while Mickey hopped down from his perch and surveyed the area, wondering what tricks he might play. Gary tried hard to appear busy, though he had little idea of what to do. He clasped his spear tightly in both hands, feeling the balance, and foolishly ran a finger along (instead of across) its metal tip, drawing a line of blood. With Kelsey, Geno, and even Mickey so worried about the trolls, Gary could only pray that the enchanted weapon on his back would aid him when the fighting started.

And then Gary watched and waited, wondering what a troll looked like.

It wasn't long before he found out. A huge, humanoid shape appeared over the rolling hills behind, lumbering towards them on legs as thick as the trunk of a mature oak. Another troll appeared behind it, and a third behind that.

"Three of them to the north," Gary remarked, squinting through the eye slit on his helmet.

"Three that way," Mickey corrected. Following the leprechaun's motion, Gary turned left and saw another troll, this one close enough for him to get a better view. The creature stood fully ten feet tall, maybe more, and wore filthy hides over its green, wart-covered skin. While its legs and torso were unbelievably thick, its arms were long and lean, made for snatching fleeing prey with long curling fingernails. Scraggly hair, yellow eyes, and even yellower teeth completed the gruesome picture. When he was finally able to pull himself from the approaching spectacle, Gary completed his visual circuit. Two more trolls had gotten ahead of the companions and now came in from the front, the south, and a seventh creature, accompanied by a smaller form, approached the hillock from the east.

"Have ye noticed the sunlight?" Mickey asked sarcastically. "When ye get back to yer own world, ye go and tell yer Mr. Tolkien that ye seen trolls moving about in the sunlight!"

"No regular hunting band," Geno remarked, regarding the engulfing formation. "This group is skilled in catching quarry."

"As part o' that quarry, I'm not pleased to be hearing ye," Mickey put in.

"They have not caught us yet," Kelsey declared, shooting the sarcastic leprechaun a dangerous glare. He took a bead on the closest troll, the one to the west, and his great bow twanged in rapid succession, sending a line of arrows at the monster.

If Gary had been impressed with the elf's swordsmanship against the goblin raiders, he was even more amazed now. Kelsey had his fifth arrow in the air before the first hit the approaching troll.

The elf's aim was near perfect, though the thin darts seemed to have little effect. One snapped in half against the troll's shoulder; another nicked the creature's neck, drawing a bit of blood. But the troll slapped it and the others away as though they were but a minor inconvenience, showing them no more heed than Gary might show a few stinging gnats.

But then Kelsey went from near perfect to perfect, driving an arrow into the troll's eye. The creature howled in agony, swerved to the side, and went down in a heap, screaming and thrashing, its clawing hands and kicking feet digging wide holes on the grassy plain.

Geno went to work on the two trolls charging in from the north. Hammers spun in, bonking against the attackers with tremendous force.

"Ow!" cried the first, catching a hammer squarely on the tip of its stubby thumb.

"Me nose!" snuffled the other. "'E breaked me nose!" Even twenty yards away, Gary could hear the cartilage cracking as the monster grabbed its prominent proboscis in both hands and twisted it back trying to stem the flow of gushing blood.

Both of those trolls ducked and dodged, suddenly more concerned with keeping away from the continuing stream of hammers than with attacking the hillock.

Gary looked at his spear and at the trolls closing from behind and from the east. The three behind were not an immediate threat, having taken up a zigzag route around a wide crack that had suddenly appeared in the ground between them and the hillock. Gary had just crossed that same ground, running in an unhindered straight line. He didn't have to spy out the concentrating leprechaun to know that Mickey's illusions had caused the crack.

The troll from the east, having left its smaller companion (which Gary now recognized as a goblin) far behind, was not deterred, though, and with Kelsey and Geno deep in their own fights and Mickey busy with his illusion, only Gary stood to block the monster's way.

He looked again at his spear.

"*Do not even think of throwing it,*" came the voice in his head.

"I wasn't!" Gary retorted aloud.

"*A thousand pardons,*" answered the silent voice. "*Take heart, now, young warrior. I will guide thee.*"

Gary was glad for the help, but hardly taking heart. The troll hadn't even started up the side of the hillock, but its evil yellow eyes were even with Gary's. Up, up, came the monster, holding a huge club at its side.

"*Strike before it finds even footing!*" the spear of Cedric Donigarten implored, and Gary did, thrusting straight out, driving the point of his dwarf-forged spear against the troll's massive chest. The weapon dug in just an inch, then its long tip bent over to the side.

"Blimey!" screamed the troll, stopping its ascent and looking down in surprise.

Gary didn't hesitate. On his own instincts, he curled his legs under him and leaped out, slamming his heavy shield into the troll's face and chest.

The foolish young man bounced back, stunned, without his breath, and with every metal plate of his armor singing a vibrating tune.

"*Never shield-rush a mountain troll!*" scolded Cedric's spear.

Down to his knees, Gary hardly comprehended the call. He noticed his spear lying beside him, and then noticed impossibly huge feet and impossibly thick ankles on either side of him. He understood, somewhere in the back of his spinning mind, that the troll straddling him held its club up, ready to squash him.

"*Up! Up!*" cried the sentient spear on his back.

The call could have meant several things, Gary noted, but he again went with his instincts, grabbing his dwarven spear in both hands and thrusting it straight up above his head. He heard a sickly squishy sound and watched the monster hop up to its tippy-toes. The troll groaned weakly, then toppled, pulling the spear from Gary's grasp as it went.

A relieved Gary knew that he had done well, but when he looked around for applause, he realized that he could hardly afford to stop and congratulate himself.

Geno had run out of throwing hammers and now met the two trolls head-on. A larger hammer in each hand, the dwarf scooted every which way, between the trolls' legs, around to the side, slapping and smacking wherever he found an opening.

Kelsey hadn't joined the dwarf, though, for two of the trolls from behind had found their way through Mickey's maze and pressed in on the elf.

"Two trolls?" Gary muttered. "Only two?" He got a terrible feeling and spun about, bringing his shield up more as a matter of reflex than conscious thought.

There, right behind him, he found the missing troll, and saw, too, its arcing club. The heavy weapon slammed the top of Gary's shield, snapping the straps and nearly breaking Gary's arm, then clipped the young man on the side of the head. Gary's helmet spun about several times, finally coming to a stop facing backwards.

Donigarten's spear implored him to action, crying for him to dive and roll, or fall back and tumble down the hillock.

None of it mattered, for Gary wasn't seeing anything or hearing anything at that moment. The ground rushed up to catch him, but he didn't know it.

Kelsey's sword spun and swirled, cut teasingly wide arcs, then darted straight ahead at troll hands or troll faces, or whatever target the elf could find. The two trolls trying to get at Kelsey had a dozen wounds each, but these were minor nicks, for the elf's sword was a slender weapon, more designed for battling smaller, less mountain-like foes.

Still, Kelsey, fighting in a purely defensive manner, managed to keep them at bay for many minutes, though he knew that something dramatic had to happen if he and his companions were to prevail. Two trolls were down—the one Kelsey had blinded with an arrow and the one Gary had pierced through the groin—but five others remained. One was busy now, wrapping Gary in a crude net; Geno had the remaining two fully engaged.

The time had come for Kelsey to strike hard.

"Circle 'im!" one of his opponents cried, slipping around to Kelsey's side. The other, after a moment's consideration, moved the other way, getting opposite the elf from his companion. Kelsey worked hard to keep them on his sides, where he could watch their every movement. They stepped towards him and back out, lifted their clubs and waved them about menacingly, looking for an opening.

Kelsey dipped under a clumsy club swing, but instead of backing away to keep his defensive posture, he leaned forward under the blow and charged straight in. The surprised troll had no way to get its club back in line for any semblance of defense. It waved its free arm frantically, trying to keep Kelsey at bay.

The elf drove in fiercely. His crafted sword bent nearly double as he thrust it into the rock-like troll's chest, but it was a magical blade and it did not break.

He heard the troll wheeze as the blade slipped through its ribs, then it fell back, grabbing at its chest.

The doomed creature's companion bellowed and hurled his club, but Kelsey, hearing the roar, was not caught unawares. He tucked his head and rolled to the side, barely dodging the heavy missile. The troll came on, diving after Kelsey and grabbing him by the leg in one huge hand. Quickly the troll scrambled back to its knees and tugged with all its strength, meaning to spin Kelsey around and around.

The elf did come off the ground under the troll's incredibly powerful pull, but Kelsey, veteran of a hundred battles, kept his composure and bent over double against the momentum, hacking at the troll's hand with all his might. Troll fingers fell to the ground and Kelsey, free of the grasp, went spinning through the air. Agile as any cat, he landed easily and started right back in for the fight.

But then a boot fell over his back and he was flattened to the grass. Kelsey felt as if a mountain had fallen on him; he couldn't even squirm about under the tremendous weight.

"Squish 'im, Earl!" yelled the troll that had thrown him. "He cut off me fingers!"

Geno Hammerthrower was no novice to troll fighting. The trolls were the very worst enemy of the dwarfs of Dvergamal, and every time one of their hunting parties went anywhere near the thunderous spray of the Firth of Buldre, Geno had personally led the charge.

The odds had always been better than this, however. For the first time, Geno found himself outnumbered by trolls two to one, and outweighed by at least twenty to one. Undaunted, the dwarf growled and spat, and used every trick he had ever been taught about fighting giant-kin.

"I'll puts ye in a sandwi—" one of the beasts started to say, but it stopped abruptly when Geno's hurled hammer put out two of its teeth. The troll spit the hammer out, and Geno was quick to reclaim it, preferring to fight with both hands.

The other troll, seeing Geno going for the hammer, went for Geno, both its hands outstretched.

"Stupid!" Geno laughed, spinning about, and he laughed even louder as he realized that the troll's reaching fingers were straight out and rigid.

"This will hurt!" Geno promised, and he smashed both his hammers, one after the other, straight into the tips of the monster's fingers. Suddenly the troll had little desire to grab at the dwarf—or grab anything at all.

Geno wasn't quite finished, though. He scooted through the troll's widespread legs, but reversed his direction and came right back out the front. His ploy worked perfectly and the stupid monster was still looking over its shoulder as Geno cracked a hammer into its kneecap.

* * *

Kelsey stared blankly as his own arms became writhing tentacles, horribly tipped by barbed claws. The troll standing over him jerked back in surprise, its foot coming up enough to allow the elf to draw breath.

Then Kelsey noticed Mickey standing beside the massive body of the troll that Gary had downed. The elf mouthed a silent thank-you, then started to cry out an alarm as he noticed a goblin creeping up behind the leprechaun, sack in hand.

But Kelsey had his own problems. The sack went over Mickey and the tentacle illusion was no more. The troll growled and pressed down again, even more forcefully.

"Squish 'im, Earl!" screamed its wounded companion, and Kelsey surely thought that his life was at an end. But then Earl reached down and grabbed him in both hands, plucked his sword away, and tossed him into the same net that held Gary.

"I gots him, I gots him!" Geek squealed in glee, holding up the leprechaun-filled sack by its drawstring. But then the bag went limp, giving the illusion that the leprechaun had somehow vanished. Stunned, the goblin grabbed at the sack, stupidly pulling it open.

A long-stemmed pipe whipped out and cracked into Geek's eyes, and the sack fell free.

Mickey thought himself quite clever—until a huge hand plucked him out of midair.

"No, ye don'ts, ye trickster!" growled the nearby troll, holding its sliced groin in one hand and wrapping the other about the leprechaun. The troll gave an uncomfortable squeeze.

"Any more o' yer tricks, and I'll squash ye good!" it warned, and Mickey didn't have to be told twice.

The troll clutched its busted knee and hopped up and down on its good leg. Every time it came down, though, Geno slammed a hammer onto its toes.

The gap-toothed troll crept up behind the dwarf, club in hand.

"Quiet as a thunderstorm!" Geno chided, rolling out of harm's way just as the sneaking troll launched its swing. The swinging club took the troll's hopping companion on the side of the good leg and sent the poor monster tumbling down the hillock like an avalanche.

The gap-toothed troll flew into a rage, swatting and clubbing frantically, putting huge dents in the soft ground, but never, for all its fury, getting anywhere near to hitting Geno. The dwarf scrambled and dove, appearing desperate, but using each maneuver to better his position for counterstrikes.

He came up alongside the club one time and smacked the troll's hand; another time, he used the down-cutting club to great advantage, tossing a hammer right over it as it descended. The stupid troll never even saw the missile until it rebounded away from its face, taking another tooth with it. Geno was upon the weapon in a split second, coming back up, both hands ready to continue.

Then the troll got more cautious. It bent low to the dwarf, keeping its club raised defensively between its face and Geno.

Geno shrugged and hurled a hammer into the club, which in turn smacked the troll in the face. The monster roared and lifted its weapon high, just as the dwarf had anticipated. Geno leaped right into its face, grabbing a handful of scraggly hair and flailing away furiously with his remaining weapon. Geno understood and even anticipated the stupid creature's every move, and he leaped away just as the heavy club came swatting in.

The troll's head snapped over backwards; the club fell to the ground. The monster stood very still for a long moment, regarding Geno through crossed eyes, then fell like a cut tree.

But now Earl came stomping over, followed by his seven-fingered companion, and by a gingerly walking troll holding a small sack.

"Sorry to leave you," Geno called to his captured companions. "But fair is fair!" The dwarf figured his indenture to be at an end; he had never agreed to die beside the elf. When Geno turned to go, though, he found that retreat would not be so easy a feat. Another troll, with a broken arrow protruding from one eye and a murderous look in its other eye, had come around behind the dwarf, and the first troll Geno had felled was also back up, limping and still holding its knee, but blocking that route.

The chase and fight went on for several minutes. Geno whipped a hammer here, smacked a hammer there, and put each of the trolls down more than once. But there were too many enemies, and finally Earl put a bag over the stubborn dwarf's head.

TWELVE

YNIS GWYDRIN

It was a long time before Gary Leger opened his eyes again. He was tangled up with Kelsey, hanging in a net supported by poles slung over the shoulders of two trolls. The first thing that struck Gary, aside from the throbs of a terrible headache, was the condition of his captors, for the trolls, though victorious, had not come away unscathed. There were six of them now, not seven, and each one of these showed fresh and vicious battle scars. The one carrying the net up front was missing fingers on its right hand; the one behind Gary had a bandage wrapped about his head, angled to cover one eye.

Trolls flanked the net on either side. Gary recognized the one to his left, walking gingerly, as the one who had caught his spear between the legs. The troll across on the right sported an even more pronounced limp and it reached down often to clutch its kneecap. The remaining two monsters walked up front, along with a scrawny goblin. From his tangled position, Gary couldn't see this group very well, but he noticed that one of the trolls carried a large sack, which it banged against a tree whenever they passed one along the side of the road. From the sputtering, cursing, and thrashing that inevitably erupted from inside the sack after each hit, Gary soon understood that Geno's ride was even less pleasant than his own.

"We didn't win, huh?" he groaned as soon as he felt able to speak. His mouth felt as though it had been stuffed with cotton and his throat was sorely parched. How long had he been out?

Kelsey twisted about, which turned Gary's leg in a very uncomfortable way.

"We fared better than most against the likes of trolls!" the proud elf growled angrily.

"'Ere, shut yer mouth!" snarled the troll behind and it shook the poles roughly, jostling the net. Scratchy cords dug at Gary from every angle, finding creases in his armor and cutting at his skin.

"At least Mickey got away," Gary whispered hopefully after a few minutes had passed.

Kelsey shook his head. "He did not," the elf explained. "The large troll up front has him."

"Earl's got 'im!" snarled the troll on the right, having overheard. "In his pocket. Even the little trickster won't get outa Earl's pocket!"

The troll behind gave another rough shake on the poles and Gary fell silent, feeling thoroughly miserable. Was he to be cooked in a large pot? And what would death in this land of Faerie mean back in the real world? Gary had heard that people who died in their dreams really did die, from the shock. He had never believed that, but he wasn't anxious to try out the theory.

And worse still, Gary absolutely did not believe this adventure to be a dream. The little details, like the rope now digging at the back of his knee, were too complete and too real—and how long could a dream last anyway? Were these trolls, then, hospital attendants, the proverbial "men in white coats"?

Gary shook the absurd thoughts away, replaced them with his heartfelt belief that all of this was as it seemed, that he was actually in this magical land of Faerie.

Talk about your absurd thoughts!

The trolls bumped along at a great pace—even wounded trolls could cover wide expanses with their long-legged strides—across the rolling plain region, through a small wood, and then over many more miles of open lands. They set no camp, ran right through the night, and the next morning, they went up into yet another mountain region. Gary, lost though he was, was certain that these peaks were not part of Dvergamal, though. They were less jagged and foreboding, though rugged enough.

"Penllyn," Kelsey muttered grimly, and the name meant something to Gary, though he couldn't exactly place it. Kelsey fell silent as the trolls lumbered on, through tight passes, through a tunnel once, and over ridges that Gary would have spent half an hour climbing, but that the trolls merely stepped across. Poor Geno continued to get the worst of it. At one point, the troll carrying him dropped the sack to the ground and jerked and dragged it along with a lead rope, purposely bouncing it among the sharpest stones while the troll and its companions shared a wicked laugh.

Geno kept up his muffled stream of stubborn curses throughout the ordeal, promising retribution and revealing no pain.

"Gwydrin! Gwydrin!" Geek the goblin squealed a short while later. The trolls got noticeably nervous at the proclamation, but it was Kelsey, up tight against Gary, who seemed the most afraid, more afraid than Gary had ever seen him.

"What is Gwydrin?" Gary whispered, but the elf offered no reply.

The troupe came around a jutting stone then, and a wide mountain lake spread before them, reflecting the surrounding peaks on its crystalline surface. In the middle, far away and barely visible, loomed an island that, despite its tiny size, filled Gary with dread. Somehow he knew that to be their destination, as though the island itself was emanating some evil, beckoning energies.

"Gwydrin!" Geek squealed again. He rushed down to the shoreline and led the trolls to several small craft hidden in tall weeds.

"Puts them in the boatses," Geek squeaked. "We takes them to the Lady."

"Where's me pay, goblin thing?" croaked Earl, casting a not-so-fond stare at the rowboats—small boats indeed by a troll's estimation!

"Lady pays," Geek promised.

"Goblin pays!" Earl corrected. "Or Earl eats goblin!"

"Two hundreds?" Geek replied squeamishly.

"Ten thousands, ye says!" howled the seven-fingered troll, dropping its end of the net with a thump. Geek shied away from the brute but had nowhere to run.

"Yeah," added Earl, poking the goblin in the back hard enough to send him flat to his face. "An' a millions sheeps!" Earl reached down and grabbed poor Geek up by the head, giving him just a little shake for the fun of it. "Where's me sheeps?"

The goblin didn't even try to fight back. Earl's hand fully covered Geek's head and he knew well that one little squeeze from the mighty troll would pop his skull.

There came a shriek from far out on the lake, the cry of a large bird. Trolls and captives alike watched a black speck soaring high into the clear sky, growing larger as it sped towards them. The great black bird went into a curl-winged stoop, plummeting for the glassy surface of the minor lake. At the last second, it leveled out and let its momentum carry it quickly to the shore, where it landed right before Earl and his captive.

"What's . . ." Earl started to say, but he was interrupted by a sudden and blinding flash of light. When the big troll's vision returned, Lady Ceridwen stood before him, cold and stern and incredibly beautiful in her shimmering black gown.

"What's . . ." Earl started to say again, but truly the troll forgot what it wanted to ask and the words stuck in its throat.

"Good," purred Ceridwen. "You have brought them alive." She looked more closely at Kelsey and Gary, trying to fathom if any more forms were caught up in that tangle of ropes and limbs. Then she looked to the large sack and the blood staining its side.

As if on cue, the troll holding the bag gave a quick shake and Geno set into bitching again.

"And the leprechaun is in there as well?" Ceridwen asked.

"'E's in me pocket," grumbled Earl, growing more suspicious and less impressed by the moment.

"Alive?"

"Fer me to know," Earl retorted. "And fer yous to find out when ye pays me me gold and sheeps!"

"Two hundred gold and two dozen sheep," Ceridwen offered.

"Ten thousands, 'e says!" Earl corrected, poking Geek hard.

"An' a millions shee—" the seven-fingered troll started to assert, but Ceridwen's icy gaze froze the words in its mouth.

Ceridwen looked sternly at her goblin slave. "A hundred gold and a dozen sheep was my bargain," she explained, as much to the terrified goblin as to the trolls. "Twice that if they are all alive. That was my offer; that remains my offer."

The trolls blustered and grumbled, each looking to the other to make the first move against the impertinent witch. Ceridwen's reputation was not something to be taken lightly, though, not even for a group of mountain trolls.

"Ten thousands!" one of the monsters, the one Gary had stuck, growled finally. "Or we eats yous all!" The troll took one step towards Ceridwen, but the witch uttered a simple phrase, and the troll found itself hopping instead of walking.

"She turned 'im into a rabbit!" the seven-fingered blusterer peeped. Indeed, where a moment before had stood a twelve-foot-tall mountain troll now sat a lop-eared bunny-troll, no bigger than Earl's fat thumb.

Gary blinked in sheer amazement as the trolls grumbled and milled about in confusion. The monsters were not amused.

But neither were they making any moves towards the raven-haired witch.

"Is the leprechaun alive?" Ceridwen asked Earl again.

Earl shoved his hand into a pocket and pulled out a very shook-up, but very alive, Mickey McMickey. Earl held the stunned leprechaun high between his thumb and index finger and gave Mickey a rough shake, telling him to "Squeak out."

Mickey couldn't find the words to respond and Earl went to shake him again, but Ceridwen stopped the troll with an outstretched palm. "Two hundred pieces of gold and two dozen plump sheep," the witch agreed.

"Ten . . ." the seven-fingered troll started to complain, but a look from Earl and its three other remaining companions put an end to that.

"We gets to keep the dwarf?" Earl asked. "Me friends be wantin' a pie."

"Keep the dwarf," Ceridwen replied, and Earl smiled wide. Nothing tasted better than dwarf pie, after all, not even two dozen plump sheep.

But then the witch abruptly changed her mind, considering the benefits of having the finest smithy in all the world at her disposal, a prisoner on her island. "I take the dwarf," she insisted.

Gary knew what was coming, but he cringed anyway when Earl begged on, "We keeps the man?"

"Oh, no," Ceridwen said. "Not the man, nor the elf, nor the leprechaun, I am afraid."

"What about me pie?" Earl grumbled.

Ceridwen thought for a moment, cast a look at Geek that made the goblin faint dead away, then came up with a solution. "Rabbits make fine pies," she offered.

With typical troll loyalty, the four monsters behind Earl fell murderously over the lop-eared troll-bunny.

"Not big enough!" grumbled the seven-fingered troll, and a moment later, it, too, found itself hopping along the ground zigging and zagging desperately to get away from greedy troll hands.

"Big enough now?" Ceridwen asked Earl when the second troll-bunny was at last scooped up by its floppy ears, kicking wildly.

Earl blanched, managed a smile, and nodded stupidly.

Ceridwen snapped her fingers and two boats drifted out from the weeds. "Put the prisoners in the square one," she instructed. The trolls looked all around, waiting again for another to take the lead.

"Now!" Ceridwen cried, and the monsters fell all over themselves getting to the prisoners. Geno went flying in first with a crash, followed by Gary and Kelsey, and finally Mickey, who managed to produce an umbrella at the last second to slow his descent.

Ceridwen waved her hand, and lines of blue light, a magical cage, shot up around the boat's perimeter.

"And put their equipment in the other boat," Ceridwen said.

Earl shrugged, quite a heave for the square-shouldered giant, as if he did not understand. "Equip—?" the troll stuttered, hoping to get away with the precious items.

"Hop, hop," Ceridwen promised. A sword, two shields, a spear, a leather case, assorted packs, and a dozen hammers went flying into the boat.

"And be throwin' in the trickster's hat!" Ceridwen heard herself say, though it was neither her thought nor her voice. Before she could say anything, Earl flipped Mickey's tam-o'-shanter into the boat.

Ceridwen's icy-blue eyes flashed in Mickey's direction, but the sprite only shrugged in reply and the witch's visage softened, revealing almost admiration for the clever trick.

The companions didn't even try to get out of their boat prison as Geek towed them far out on the lake.

"Caught again," Geno grumbled. "And now I am working for that wretched witch."

"The burdens of fame," Mickey put in, drawing a scowl from the dwarf.

"We'll not be long on Ceridwen's isle," Kelsey vowed.

Gary let them ramble on without him, more interested in the island. A castle sat upon it, walls glistening in the sunlight as though they were made of glass. Gary sat and stared at the magnificent structure for a long while, mesmerized by the beauty.

"The Isle of Glass," Mickey explained, shifting beside him.

"Ynis Gwydrin," Gary replied off handedly. Only Mickey's sudden startled movement reminded the young man that his knowledge of the place was unexpected.

"Where'd ye hear of it?" the leprechaun asked.

"Folktale," Gary replied. "I must have read it in some book. It's like many of the things and places around here, yourself included." Gary's brow crinkled as he tried to sort it all out, his green eyes reflecting the sparkle of the glistening waters of Loch Gwydrin.

"The names are strange to me," he explained after some time, "but I know that I've heard them before." He looked to Mickey for answers. "Does that make any sense?"

"Aye," Mickey replied, to Gary's relief. "Many from yer own world have crossed to Faerie and returned with 'folktales,' as ye call them."

"And Penllyn," Gary went on. "That name, too, is familiar, but I think it is an actual place in my world."

"Not to doubt," replied the leprechaun. "Many are the places that share borders, and many more that share names, between Faerie and yer own world, though not nearly as many as there used to be. 'Tis a sad thing."

"And what have you heard of Ynis Gwydrin?" Kelsey asked, hearing the conversation.

"Just the name, that I can recall," Gary answered. "And that it was an enchanted place."

"*Is* an enchanted place," Mickey corrected. "But not as it used to be. The isle is Ceridwen's now, and that's not a good thing for the likes o' me and yerself."

"We'll not be long on Ceridwen's isle!" Kelsey said again, more forcefully, but the vow seemed lost on all of them at that moment, for Geek's boat had already scraped bottom and the dreary beach loomed just a dozen feet away.

Ceridwen met them as they landed. With a wave of her delicate hand, both boats climbed right up on the sand. A second wave brought down the cage of blue light, and the companions filtered out onto the shore.

"Welcome to Ynis Gwydrin, Kelsenellenelvial Gil-Ravadry," the witch said with a polite curtsy. "You may retrieve your belongings; the isle is yours to enjoy."

"You would give me my sword?" the elf asked suspiciously.

"It won't be bringing her harm," Mickey explained, "No weapon forged by mortal hands, even elvish hands, can wound Lady Ceridwen."

"How true," purred the witch. "And how convenient for me!"

Kelsey said nothing, but thought of the many ways in which he might cause havoc on Ynis Gwydrin and escape the island. Ceridwen smiled as though she had read the elf's thoughts. In a burst of movement, she twirled about and waved her arms, her voice crackling as she cried:

"Elf and dwarf and man and sprite
By any day and any night
If you swim the water blue
As acid it will be to you.

And any boat you seek to take
Upon the waters of my lake
Will fall apart and splinter thin
And in the acid drop you in!
And if you find a way to fly
Across the lake up in the sky
Let a wind come rushing down
And push you in to burn and drown!"

"Not very good," Mickey commented dryly.

Ceridwen stopped laughing and shot a glare at the impertinent leprechaun. "But effective, do not doubt!" she promised, and none of them, not even Geno, wanted to go and try the water.

"How long are we to be held here?" the dwarf growled. "I have work to do, many contracts to fulfill."

"A hundred years," Ceridwen replied. "Or until that one"—she pointed to Gary—"has died. Ynis Gwydrin is your home now. Do make yourselves comfortable. There are caves, which should please you, good dwarf, and my resourceful slaves have even managed to construct some small huts. With your fighting skills, mighty elf-lord, you should be able to claim one or two structures as your own."

"Why have you interfered?" Kelsey demanded. "This was no business of yours, witch Ceridwen!"

"But it was," Ceridwen replied. "I cannot allow you to reforge the spear and stir up thoughts of ancient heroes."

"Yer puppet strings're not so tight on Kinnemore?" Mickey asked slyly.

"On the King, yes," Kelsey reasoned, remembering Prince Geldion's interference. "But not on the common people. She fears that they will look back to find their heritage and their way out of the mire."

"You are a fool, Kelsenellenelvial Gil-Ravadry," Ceridwen spat.

"Call him Kelsey," Mickey offered, but the witch paid the leprechaun no heed.

"Ever were the elf-lords of Faerie fools!" Ceridwen went on. "You sing old songs and play with legends while I . . ." She stopped suddenly, realizing that she might be revealing too much—even to prisoners.

"Come along, Geek!" Ceridwen growled, and she grabbed up the case containing Cedric's spear and rushed away, the cowering goblin close behind.

There was really very little that the companions could do. Geno retrieved a hammer from the goblin's boat and hurled it Ceridwen's way, but it turned into a crow long before it ever reached the witch and simply flew off into the sky.

So the weary companions set a camp and sat down in the sand, and stared glumly at the shore. It did not seem so far, with the mountains rising up sharply beyond the water's edge, but the trip in the boat had taken many minutes, covering a half mile, at least. Given Ceridwen's spell, the shore might as well have been a world away.

The break gave Gary time to consider his fate, and the consequences of this strange adventure. He slid over to sit by Mickey, who was just about done with *The Hobbit*.

"Too bad I don't have the rest of the series," he offered. "You'd have a way to spend the next week or two."

"Fine with the words, is yer Mr. Tolkien," the leprechaun agreed, never looking up from the book.

"Mickey," Gary started again somberly, and he put a hand on the leprechaun's shoulder. Mickey looked up and knew at once that something was deeply troubling his captured man.

"How many days . . . I mean, I've been here a while . . ."

Mickey's sudden burst of laughter put Gary a bit at rest. "Not to worry, lad," the leprechaun explained. "Time's running different in Faerie. When the sprites danced about ye, they danced against the turn o' the clock."

"Against the turn?" Gary did not understand.

"If they go against the turn, then the time in Faerie runs quicker than time in yer own world," Mickey explained. "If they go with the clock, then the other runs true. A day here'd see a dozen years pass in yer own world. But they went against the clock in bringing ye; ye'll not be missed in yer home for a long, long time."

"But what happens . . ." Gary stuttered on, searching for the right words. "I mean, if I die here, do I wake up there? I hadn't really thought about it before . . . well . . . maybe in the goblin fight, and just for the moment when I fell over the cliff. But what happens?"

Mickey's comforting smile faded. "No, lad," he replied quietly. "If ye die here, then die ye do. They'd not find yer body—unless I can think of a way to bring ye back to the woods where me pixie took ye. This is no dream, I telled ye before."

Gary spent a few minutes considering the grim possibility that he would die here, and the pain it would bring to his parents. He imagined them looking over his sword-hacked body in the woods out back, totally perplexed, and with half the Lancashire police force standing right beside them, having no explanations.

How many unexplained deaths. . . ? Gary dismissed the seemingly limitless possibilities of the confusing notion, preferring to concentrate on his own predicament.

"Suppose Ceridwen keeps us, for a year or ten years," Gary reasoned, "and then you get me back?"

"As I said, in yer world, ye'll have been gone just a short time, even though ye been ten years in Faerie."

"But will I have aged?" Now Gary thought he saw some intriguing possibil- ities here concerning immortality. Mickey dashed them immediately.

"Aye," the leprechaun replied, and he chuckled as he thought about it. "Ye'd be showing the ten years. Many's the ones who've gone back to yer world after long years in Faerie, trying to explain how their hair turned all gray overnight."

"But it won't be ten years, or a hundred," Gary prompted, looking over to Kelsey, sitting a short distance away and staring into the darkening sky. "You'll get me out of here."

"Ceridwen's a mighty foe," Mickey began, not at all convinced. It wasn't hard to see, though, that Gary needed some comforting. "Aye, lad," the leprechaun finished as cheerfully as he could. "Kelsey'll find a way to beat the witch."

Gary smiled and motioned for Mickey to go back to his book, then joined Kelsey in the silent stare to the twilight sky.

THIRTEEN

ISLAND BOSS

They spent a quiet night—almost. Sometime before dawn, Gary awakened from a fitful sleep to find yellow eyes staring at the camp from every direction. Kelsey and Geno were already up; Gary could make out their dark forms nearby in the gloom.

The yellow eyes slowly advanced.

"Give us some light," Kelsey whispered, and with a snap of a leprechaun's fingers, the whole area was bathed in a soft glow. The grubby slaves of Ceridwen's island jumped back, startled, then began thumping crooked clubs against their makeshift shields and throwing sand into the air. Not even Kelsey or Mickey had ever seen such a mixture of rabble. Dirty humans, goblins, a troll, and even a dwarf stood shoulder-to-shoulder (or shoulder-to-hip) in the threatening ring about the camp. Gary wasn't sure whether they wanted a fight, or if they had come to enlist the newest slaves in their ragtag army, and he wasn't certain which of those choices he would prefer.

The rabble calmed and quieted as the initial surprise of the light wore off and once again they tightened their ranks. They looked around to each other, hesitatingly, and finally one ugly, powerfully built man, fully armored (though his armor was quite rusty), strode out boldly from the ranks.

"Jacek," he proclaimed, thumbing his barrel-like chest. In a proclamation of superiority, the large man chopped his heavy sword against the soft ground. "This is Jacek's island."

"Seems this one's for Kelsey," Mickey mentioned, and the grim elf nodded his agreement. Without the slightest trepidation showing in his determined strides, Kelsey stepped out to meet Jacek squarely.

"I had been told that this was Ceridwen's island," the elf replied to the boast.

"Castle is Ceridwen's," Jacek retorted without a second's hesitation. "Island belongs to Jacek."

The grubby dwarf stepped out of the ranks then, eyeing Geno fiercely and stroking his thick blue beard.

"Ye know him?" Mickey asked.

"Not of my clan," Geno replied, never taking his eyes from his counterpart. Like Geno, the stranger had several hammers hanging from his wide belt. Deliberately Geno pulled two hammers out and sent them spinning into the air above him. After just a few catches, he added a third. The other dwarf did

likewise, and added a fourth as soon as Geno had, then put a fifth up before
Geno could respond.

"Dwarfs have their own types o' challenges," Mickey explained to Gary.

"Well, Jacek," Kelsey said evenly, "it seems that you must now share your
island, for Ceridwen has trapped us here."

"You join with Jacek!" the ugly man roared. "You serve Jacek and Jacek lets
you live."

Kelsey looked at Mickey and Gary and the two could tell from his smirk
that Jacek was about to get a lesson.

"I think not," Kelsey replied. Jacek started to turn towards his own troops,
but Kelsey's sword flashed up and nicked him on the ear. The ugly man spun
back and wetted his finger in his own blood, his face contorted in budding
outrage.

Gary realized that Kelsey could have killed the man as he had turned away,
but he understood the elf's caution, and his plan. Kelsey didn't want the whole
rabble force, particularly the troll, to get into the fight, and the elf was betting
that defeating Jacek fairly would put an end to it all.

The nick on the ear had worked. Too angry to care about his allies, Jacek
roared and launched a mighty swing Kelsey's way.

Kelsey was too nimble for the heavy weapon. He easily stepped back, then
came in with a straightforward thrust that cut a strap on Jacek's crude breastplate, leaving a vulnerable hollow. Kelsey couldn't finish the move, though, for
Jacek, incredibly strong, reversed the lumbering swing and came across again,
driving the elf backwards.

Jacek advanced, holding his sword by both hands straight out in front of
him. Kelsey moved to the side and Jacek turned to follow, wisely keeping the
swift elf out at sword's length.

A fierce thrust had Kelsey spinning to the side. He slipped down to one
knee and Jacek roared in, cutting an overhand chop. Gary screamed, thinking
Kelsey doomed, but the elf dove and rolled towards Jacek, inside the angle of
the blow, and came up beside and then beyond the man, slashing him in the
leg as he passed.

Jacek growled, but seemed not to care about the wound. From his scars,
Gary could see that he had suffered many worse hits in his fighting days.

To the side of the main action, Geno and the grubby dwarf continued their
five-hammer juggling. In the blink of an eye, the grubby dwarf, seeing his
leader in trouble, launched one of his weapons Kelsey's way. Fully engaged,
Kelsey never saw it coming.

But Geno did. He, too, hurled a hammer, his catching the grubby dwarf's
missile in midflight and deflecting it harmlessly away from Kelsey.

Gary and Mickey, even Kelsey and Jacek, turned to regard the dwarfs. In
a flurry of movement that none of them could truly follow, the half-sized

opponents whipped their hammers at each other. Sparks flew as hammers connected in midair; Geno grunted as he took one off his chest; the grubby dwarf grunted as one of Geno's connected.

Then from the midst of the confusion there came a sharp *crack!* and both dwarfs stood facing each other for a long, silent moment, each holding his last remaining hammer. Gary wasn't sure what had happened, but he came to understand when he noticed the line of blood rolling down the grubby dwarf's forehead. Without a sound, the little creature fell facedown on the sand.

A goblin started out from the ranks, but Geno waved his hammer the creature's way and it promptly retreated. Gary knew the rabble forces, wouldn't hold back for long, though; all of them began shifting uncomfortably and looking about.

"Get ready for a fight," Mickey said at Gary's side.

"I will kill you and kill your dwarf next!" Jacek promised. He launched a series of wild, straight-across cuts that kept Kelsey up on his toes and backing, but in no serious trouble. Jacek continued the vicious assault, swinging and slashing and muttering curses. Soon, though, Kelsey tired of the game. The heavy sword came across a bit low and the nimble elf hopped right above it, coming back down and charging ahead, slamming his shield into the side of Jacek's head before the man could possibly recover.

Kelsey went right by the man, just ahead of Jacek's fast-approaching backhand sword cut. The elf fell low to his knees, reversing his grip on his sword as he dropped. Jacek's heavy sword waved dangerously close above Kelsey's head, but Kelsey expected it, and knew it would miss, and didn't even flinch. He doubled his own weapon back under one arm and thrust it straight out behind him, driving it deep into the self-proclaimed island boss's lung.

Jacek heaved for air and started to bring his sword back in. Kelsey came up and about, throwing his shield against Jacek's arms to stop the dangerous weapon from coming back around. Kelsey was face-to-face with the man now, barely an inch apart, close enough to smell Jacek's hot breath.

Kelsey grimaced and pulled straight up on his sword hilt, further tearing the man's insides.

"Kill you," the big man promised, but his threat was lost in a breathless wheeze and a spout of blood. He shook violently a couple of times, then Kelsey unceremoniously pushed him back to the ground, where he lay quite still.

"Are there any others who claim ownership of the island?" Kelsey asked evenly. The goblin reappeared from the ranks, looking the troll's way, and started to mutter something. Geno had seen enough of that one. The dwarf's hammer went spinning, catching the ugly goblin on the side of the head and cleanly snapping its neck.

"Pretend ye got more," Mickey whispered to Geno, and the dwarf laughed in reply and began pumping his (empty) arms. Illusionary hammers spun out at the rabble. They dove and ducked, and turned and fled, the hammers chasing them out impossibly far into the night.

Soon the whole force was in wild flight, running with all speed to the south. Geno kept up his laughing, Mickey joined in, and Kelsey flashed a satisfied smile as he wiped the blood from his sword on Jacek's pants.

"Shut up," Gary demanded, his green eyes narrowed as he regarded the wildly amused dwarf. Geno turned on him sharply.

"You got a real one?" the dwarf growled at Mickey, holding one hand out as though he expected the leprechaun to give him a real hammer to heave at Gary.

"They're dead," Gary replied, thinking that those words explained everything.

"They asked to die," Kelsey cut in. "Would you feel better if it were my own body and Geno's lying in the sand?"

"You don't have to enjoy it so much," Gary protested.

"He was just a human," Kelsey spat. "If you care so much for him, then give him to the lake, or bury him." Never releasing Gary from his golden-eyed gaze, the elf walked away, Geno in tow. Gary looked to Mickey, but the leprechaun had no answers for him this time.

So Gary did bury Jacek, and the dead dwarf and goblin as well. He thought of his parents throughout the task and wondered what pain they would suffer if he never returned to them. He imagined his picture on telephone poles and milk cartons, fliers handed out at malls, as his parents sought desperately some information about what had happened to him.

When he got back to the others the next morning, Gary's eyes were bloodshot. None of them asked him about it, though, and he was beginning to believe that they didn't even care.

The day passed without incident, without anything but the small, wind-driven waves lapping on the forlorn beach and the mountains hovering just out of reach. The next night, too, showed no excitement, no noises in the dark or yellow eyes staring at the encampment.

By the morning after that, Gary came to realize that boredom would be their biggest enemy, boredom that led to ambivalence, ambivalence that would lead the companions to the same state as Jacek and his wretched band.

Gary feared that many, many days and nights would pass quietly. He had seen Kelsey in dire straits, outnumbered by goblins and by trolls, but the elf had fought with fire in his golden eyes, slashing and battling fiercely even when all seemed lost. Now, though, Kelsey truly appeared defeated. He sat on the beach, staring.

Just staring.

Mickey finished *The Hobbit* that day. "Fine tale," he muttered as he handed it back to Gary, but when Gary tried to respond, tried to get the leprechaun to elaborate, Mickey only walked away.

Geno was the noisiest of the group, stomping and cursing, throwing hammers at any target that presented itself. But the dwarf would not talk directly to Gary, or to Kelsey or Mickey, and every time Gary went anywhere near him, he lifted a hammer threateningly.

Gary snorted at him and spun away, angry and afraid. He felt as though a cage had been built around him. He almost wanted to test Ceridwen's spell and jump in the water, but he couldn't find the courage. "Can't I go for a walk?" he asked Mickey some time later.

"Go north," the leprechaun advised. "And ye might want to put yer armor back on." The leprechaun nodded to the pile, lying on the beach.

Something odd struck Gary Leger then. Ceridwen had pointedly taken the broken spear from him, though she cared nothing for his dwarf-forged spear and allowed the others to keep their weapons as well. Why hadn't she taken the armor? It certainly was as valuable as the spear.

"Ceridwen's got slaves all about, and most're nasty things like the ones we fought, would be me guess," Mickey went on, not noticing Gary's perplexed expression.

Gary nodded but started away, leaving the armor in a pile on the beach.

"And keep from the castle!" Mickey shouted a warning. "It's warded, don't ye doubt!"

Though the glassy-sided castle did intrigue Gary, he had no intention of going anywhere near the place at that time. He stayed along the beach, studying the shore, looking for some solution to Ceridwen's riddle, and thinking, too, of the mystery surrounding the missing spear. The distance across the lake was much less north and west of the island, but Gary saw no chances for escape in those directions. Sheer mountain walls ran down right into the lake, and even if Gary and his friends managed to get across the shorter expanse of the water, they'd have an impossible time trying to get up from the lake. The only way out was back in the same direction they had come, Gary knew, but he had no idea of how they might get across.

An hour later, Gary found himself scrambling over the sharp rocks of a jutting jetty, dangerously close to the water. Too frustrated to really care, he just spat at the lake that would burn like acid and continued on, stubbornly inching ever closer to the edge. Then Gary dropped flat to his belly, suddenly, wide-eyed and staring ahead to the lagoon beyond the rocks. Many yards from shore, but only waist-deep in the water, stood a monster that would have towered above the mountain trolls, a giant three times Gary's height.

It was lean, though still huge, and apparently fishing for a meal, slapping its thick hands into the water but coming up empty each time.

Gary watched for several minutes, filled with a combination of amazement and terror, then dared to get back to his knees and began backtracking the way he had come. He knew it was only a matter of time before the behemoth looked his way, and he felt naked indeed out on the rocks without his spear and armor (though he didn't know what good the puny weapon, dwarven-forged or not, would do against the likes of this monster!).

He had almost made it to the sand, and was thinking that it was a good thing that he did not have the bulky armor on, when the giant saw him.

"Duh, hey!" it cried, a booming baritone voice.

Gary didn't stop to reply. He scrambled and kicked his way across the remaining stones of the jetty, jumped down to the sand, and sprinted away, spurred on by the approaching splashes as the behemoth lumbered its way across the lagoon.

Sand dragged at Gary's legs, slowing him—again he felt as if he was in that dream state unable to outrun his pursuer. An image of his parents flashed in his mind, the two of them staring down in disbelief at their son, squashed in the blueberry bushes in the woods out back.

Then the sound of splashing stopped and Gary dared to look back, hoping that the monster had changed its course. But the giant hadn't given up its pursuit; to Gary's surprise and dismay, the huge thing had already made it to the beach and was almost across the rock jetty.

"Stupid to come out here," Gary berated himself. He put his head down and ran on, knowing that the giant's long strides would surely overtake him before too long.

His breath came in labored gasps. He veered to the water, then prudently remembered the curse and realized he would find no escape that way. Now his weary feet dragged even deeper in the sand. He heard the heavy footsteps closing, inevitably closing.

They were right at his back!

Gary swung about to meet his doom. The giant towered over him but made no immediate moves, its heaving breaths coming nearly as labored as Gary's. "Duh, you run fast," the monster commented.

"Not fast enough," Gary muttered under his breath as he glanced all about for some possible escape. He pointed suddenly back to the water, cried out, "A whale!" and took off as soon as the dim-witted monster turned about.

"Where?" the giant asked, oblivious to the trick. By the time it turned back, Gary was way ahead. "Hey, wait!" the monster called, and the chase was on once more.

Gary knew that his only hope was to find some cover, so he veered away from the water's edge, heading for the bare stones farther inland.

The giant plodded behind, its wide feet unhindered by the soft sand. "Duh, hey!" it called out several times.

The first of the huge stones was barely twenty feet away.

Out in front of Gary stepped Kelsey, sword in hand. Geno came around the other side of the rock, juggling three hammers. Gary nearly fainted in sheer relief. He turned back to consider the giant. It still approached, but at a walk, more cautiously.

"Duh, hey," it said again.

Geno whipped a hammer off its shin.

"Du . . . ow!" the behemoth roared, grabbing at the leg. Another hammer bounced off its shoulder, and both Kelsey and Geno circled to opposite sides and steadily advanced.

Great birds shrieked and rushed down from the skies to peck at the giant's head; huge-clawed crabs dug themselves out of the sand and snapped at its bare toes. The monster squealed and cried, kicking and slapping.

Gary was only confused for the second it took him to realize that Mickey must also be in the area. "Where are you, Mickey?" he demanded.

The leprechaun materialized, perched upon a stone off to Gary's right. "This kind's bigger than trolls," he remarked. "But not so hard to fool. Ye're lucky we came out to get ye, lad."

Gary wasn't so sure about the leprechaun's assessment. Another hammer bounced off the giant's head and it howled again. Behind it, Kelsey stood with leveled sword, lining up a vital area for a critical strike. The pitiful giant was too engaged and confused by Mickey's illusions and Geno's missiles to even know that the elf was behind it.

"Stop it!" Gary yelled at Mickey. The leprechaun shot him a curious glance.

"What're ye about?"

Again Gary found himself without the words to answer. The giant hadn't harmed him; he had the feeling now that he was not so vulnerable, that maybe the giant hadn't meant to harm him at all. "Just stop it!" he screamed in Mickey's face, loud enough to get Kelsey and Geno's attention as well, and he swung around and rushed towards the combatants. Gary silently congratulated himself as Mickey's illusions disappeared, but the giant wasn't out of danger yet.

"Behind you!" Gary heard himself yell, to his own disbelief, as Kelsey again leveled the sword and started his thrust. The giant spun about and Kelsey reversed his attack and hopped back defensively, turning a murderous stare upon Gary.

Gary didn't care. He ran right up to the giant and skidded to a stop in the sand, standing with his arms out wide. Geno raised yet another hammer for a throw, but Gary poked a finger the dwarf's way and warned, "Don't!" Amazingly the gruff dwarf lowered the weapon and scratched at his hairless chin.

Gary and the giant regarded one another for the second time.

"What are you doing?" Kelsey demanded of Gary.

"I don't think he meant to hurt me," Gary replied. "He was just fishing when I found him. He's a prisoner, too, isn't he?"

"But a dangerous one, don't ye doubt," Mickey answered, strolling up to a position a few cautious feet behind Gary. "Giants been known to make meals of ones such as yerself."

"Duh, eat him?" the giant balked, a disgusted look crossing his thick but almost boyish features: dimpled cheeks, thick lips, and bright eyes the color of a crisp and clear winter sky.

"I thought so," Gary said, noting the expression and relaxing visibly.

"How come I have not seen you before?" the giant asked in its slow, deliberate voice. "Elf and dwarf?" The giant scratched at its wild black hair.

"We haven't been here for very long," Gary replied. "I'm Gary Leger and these are . . ."

"Enough!" Kelsey demanded. Then to the giant, he said, "Your life has been spared. Now be gone, before you feel the sting of my blade."

"I've more hammers yet!" Geno added, putting three more up in a juggling routine.

"Forget them!" Gary growled, commanding the behemoth's attention. "What's your name?"

"Duh, Tommy," the giant replied, glancing around nervously from elf to dwarf. He held up his huge hands, showing a missing digit on one. "Tommy One-Thumb."

"Well, Duh Tommy," Geno muttered sarcastically, "I believe that you should be leaving now."

"Greetings, Tommy One-Thumb," Gary said, more at the obstinate dwarf than at the giant. "I'm sorry for the fight."

"He's a giant, lad," Mickey warned. "A rogue, a killer, don't ye doubt. Giants aren't evil like the trolls, but they can be a nasty lot and a mighty enemy. Let him go and come along—for everyone's good fortune."

When Gary looked upon Mickey, he saw only sincere concern in the leprechaun's gray eyes.

"Maybe ye should go back to yer fishing, Tommy One-Thumb," Mickey offered.

"Where is whale?" Tommy asked Gary. "Tommy did not see any whale."

"There wasn't any whale," Gary apologized. "I was just trying to trick you. I was afraid."

"Duh, oh," mumbled Tommy. "Most people are afraid of Tommy."

"Well, can ye blame them?" Mickey asked.

The giant shrugged and turned, and started slowly away. Gary began to protest, but Geno and Kelsey rushed up to stand right before him, Geno purposely stomping his heavy boots down on the tops of Gary's sneakers.

"You ask him along, and my next hammer kisses you good!" Geno promised, poking a stubby finger against Gary's nose to accentuate his point. Gary tried to push the dwarf away, but Geno shoved off first, and Gary, his feet hooked under the dwarf's boots, fell down to the sand. He jerked aside to avoid a stream of Geno's spittle.

Kelsey said nothing, but the elf's narrow-eyed stare revealed similar sentiments and, as with the fight of the previous day, Mickey had no answers for Gary.

Ceridwen was waiting for them, or more particularly, for Kelsey, when they arrived back at the camp.

"So you have defeated Jacek," she purred at Kelsey, placing her hand familiarly on the elf's shoulder. Kelsey brushed her away but would not look her in the eye.

"I had hoped that would happen," Ceridwen went on. "Jacek was such a brutish beast. The slaves will perform better with you leading them."

"I'll not lead your wretched slaves," Kelsey replied.

"We shall see," Ceridwen said calmly. Her hand went back to Kelsey's shoulder and she stroked the long strands of his sparkling golden hair back from his face.

"And I'll not serve you in any capacity!" the elf screamed at her, verily running away from her undeniably alluring touch.

"I could not let you complete your quest," Ceridwen explained, and it seemed to Gary that the witch was almost apologizing. "You understand that, of course."

"I understand more than you believe," Kelsey countered slyly.

"Not so," Ceridwen retorted, stubbornly walking back to stand beside the elf. "You have no idea of how long a hundred years can be on an empty island, Kelsenellenelvial Gil-Ravadry. Your people will not come for you— not here. You have only me." Ceridwen's hand went back to Kelsey's golden locks, petting delicately. Kelsey tried to pull away again, but this time the witch grabbed tightly to his hair and pulled him to her as easily as if he had been made of paper.

Gary was horrified at Ceridwen's bared power; Kelsey seemed so insignificant against her. Both Mickey and Geno had turned away, but Gary could not avert his eyes.

Ceridwen had Kelsey's head bent at an awkward angle, as though she meant to snap his neck. "Draw your sword and strike me down!" the evil witch hissed in Kelsey's face.

Kelsey's hand went for his sword hilt, but he backed it off immediately, his whole body slumping in despair.

"You are my slave," Ceridwen growled, a voice that seemed unearthly, demonic. "My plaything. I will do with you as I please, and when I please!" With just the one hand, Ceridwen tossed Kelsey into the air, towards the shore. He landed in the sand, dangerously close to water's edge, and as he rolled about, his elbow touched the lake.

Kelsey howled and rolled back, clutching at his burning arm. If Gary or any of the others had doubted Ceridwen's spell, they knew better now, for Kelsey's sleeve and fine armor were burned right through at the elbow from barely brushing the deadly water.

"I will have some work for you soon," the witch said to Geno, paying no heed to the wounded elf.

"As you wish, my lady," the brown-haired dwarf replied with a low bow. Ceridwen cackled and threw her black cape high about her shoulders. As it descended, her form shifted and she was again a raven, soaring back to her castle of glass.

FOURTEEN

TOMMY ONE-THUMB

The meals were tasteless, the sun hot, the days long, and the nights empty.

Every day that went by deepened the feeling of solitude for Gary. He couldn't remember the last joke Mickey had cracked, or even the last time the leprechaun had spoken to him without first being asked a direct question. Even beyond their obvious dilemma, something seemed to be bothering Mickey. Gary could only think back to the first night after they had left Dvergamal, when he had seen Mickey making some secret deal with the pixie. Whatever it was, Mickey wasn't talking.

And Kelsey. When Gary had first met the golden-haired elf, in Leshiye's tree, he had looked upon Kelsey with awe, a sincere admiration that had only grown throughout their first few ordeals. But now Kelsey seemed quite an ordinary being to Gary, helpless and forlorn, accepting defeat. Kelsey sat and watched the water and the sky, sat and did nothing to facilitate their escape. Also, Gary couldn't forget, would never forget, the carefree manner in which Kelsey had killed Jacek, had killed a human being without the slightest hint of remorse.

Of all his companions over those next few days, Gary found that he actually preferred Geno's company. The gruff dwarf more often responded with spit than words to Gary's questions, and once Geno had even launched a hammer Gary's way (though Gary had seen enough of the dwarf's hammer-throwing proficiency to know that if Geno had really meant to hit him, he surely would have been smacked). But Geno, at least, was not complacent about their situation, not willing to surrender. Despite his feigned subservience to the witch a few days before, the dwarf promised that he would somehow find a way to pay Ceridwen back.

Gary didn't doubt him for a minute.

Finally one gray but uncomfortably hot day, Gary Leger had seen enough. "What's our plan?" he asked Kelsey, sitting in his usual position on the shore.

The elf looked up at him blankly. Gary noticed how pallid Kelsey appeared, and how thin and dirty. Kelsey had been barely eating enough to keep himself alive.

"What's our plan?" Gary asked again.

"Our plan for what?" Kelsey replied absently, going back to his distant stare.

"Our plan to get off of this island!" Gary retorted, more sharply than he had intended.

"Ye don't understand the nature of our enemy," Mickey, sitting to the side, put in. "Ceridwen's got us, lad. We'll no find a way through her tight clutches."

"That's it, then?" Gary balked. "You're all giving up? We're just going to sit here until we die?" Gary considered his own words for a moment, then remarked, even more pointedly, "Or should I say, until I die? You'll all live longer than me, right? So you can wait the hundred years . . ."

"I've no desire to sit here a hundred years, lad," Mickey offered halfheartedly.

"Nor do I!" Geno roared. The dwarf stood with his bowed legs wide apart, gnarly hands on his wide belt (which sported five more hammers now, taken from the grubby dwarf), and his blue-gray eyes narrowed dangerously. "I'll give it back to that witch!"

"Ah, save yer bluster," Mickey scolded. "Ye cannot do anything against the likes o' Ceridwen, and ye know it well enough."

"I won't accept that," Gary growled, and he poked a finger Kelsey's way. "You owe me!" he declared.

"I owe you nothing." The elf's tone showed more resignation than anger, and that, too, made Gary want to reach down and choke him.

"It was by your command that I was brought here," Gary fumed. "And by your deed," he added, snapping his accusing finger Mickey's way. "You both share the responsibility of taking care of me, of getting me back safely to where I belong."

Kelsey came up in Gary's face, suddenly showing more fire in his golden eyes than he had in many days.

"Strike me down," Gary invited him, and he honestly wasn't sure that Kelsey wouldn't. "That's how you work, isn't it? Brave Kelsey," he spat sarcastically. "But brave only when he knows that he can defeat his foe."

"You are bound by the rules of cap—" Kelsey began, but Gary didn't want to hear that again.

"Save it," he snapped. "I am bound to you by nothing!"

"Calm ye, lad," Mickey said quietly, obviously stunned by Gary's outburst and fearing that Kelsey would surely kill him.

"You strike him down and the witch might let the rest of us go," Geno reasoned logically.

"You kidnapped me—that's all it can be called," Gary went on, ignoring the leprechaun's condescension and the dwarf's frightening logic. "You can put all the pretty names on it that you want, but you stole me from my world and from my home. So strike me now, Kelsenellene . . . whatever the hell your name is. Strike me down and compound your crime!"

Kelsey's golden eyes flashed, his jaw clenched tight, and his hand slipped slowly towards his sword hilt. But Gary had faced him down, for the elf did indeed feel responsible for their dilemma. Kelsey turned back to the lake and sat on the sand.

"I expected as much," Gary mumbled, and he walked away. Mickey was quick to catch up with him.

"Don't be too hard on the elf," the leprechaun explained when they were some distance away. "Ceridwen's given him a bitter pill."

"We have to fight back," Gary replied.

"If ye think it's that easy, then ye're reading too many of these books," Mickey said, patting Gary's pocket, which held *The Hobbit*. "Not all in Faerie's got such a happy ending; not all the dragons go belly-up to a well-aimed arrow."

"So we don't even try?" came Gary's sarcastic response.

Mickey had no answer.

"I'm taking the armor and my spear," Gary announced. "I've earned that much and you won't need it anyway."

"Ye going somewhere?" Now Mickey seemed truly concerned.

"Away from here," Gary answered. "Maybe Tommy will help me."

"Don't ye be bringing that giant around," Mickey warned. "Forget Kelsey and be worrying about Geno—dwarfs and giants don't get on well."

"Dwarfs don't get on well with anything," Gary reminded the leprechaun, and for the first time in many days they shared a smile.

Gary found the giant in the same lagoon, fishing contentedly, but using a pole this time instead of his monstrous hands.

"Catch anything?" Gary called, and Tommy's huge face lit up as soon as he noticed the man.

"Come and fish with me," the giant offered happily. Gary moved to the water's edge and almost hopped in—until he fortunately remembered the curse. He wondered why Ceridwen hadn't similarly cursed the giant. He couldn't imagine one as gentle as Tommy being a willing accomplice to the evil witch.

Gary moved down the rocks towards the beach, and met Tommy there, coming out of the water with an armful of fish.

"Tommy does better now," the giant announced. "Uses a sticky stick!"

"Sticky stick?" Gary echoed, examining the giant's fishing pole. It was thin and hollow, nearly eight feet long, and Gary understood Tommy's description when he saw that its end was covered in a gooey substance.

Tommy smiled and poked the stick down on a nearby rock. When the giant lifted the stick, the rock came up with it, firmly secured to the goo.

"Where did you find that?" Gary inquired, thinking that he might somehow find some use for the substance.

Tommy pointed down the beach to a thick patch of reeds and weeds on the far side of the lagoon. Gary immediately started around the beach and the giant followed. There were two main types of reeds: green ones filled with the sticky substance, and brown hollow ones, like the one Tommy was using to catch fish.

"Tommy will make one for you," the giant offered. "Then we can fish together."

Gary smiled and shook his head. "I can't go in the water," he explained.

"It is not cold."

Gary just smiled again and did not even try to explain.

They spent the rest of the day talking, with Tommy showing Gary all the secrets of the lagoon region he had come to claim as his home. Gary felt quite safe, even before Tommy assured him that no others would dare to come around and bother them.

The talkative giant came as a welcome distraction for Gary, and Gary as even more of one for lonely Tommy. Tommy eagerly told Gary everything he could remember about himself. He told of life as a giant in the world beyond the lake, of how both his parents had been hunted by scared farmers and killed. Tommy had escaped, after losing one of his thumbs, but had nowhere to go, for he was just a young giant at the time. Lost and alone, Tommy had stumbled upon Ceridwen, and she had taken him to the island, where she told him he would be safe.

At first Gary didn't know what to make of the witch's uncharacteristic mercy, but when Tommy continued, recalling the first "soldiers" Ceridwen had asked him to fight beside, Gary came to understand that Tommy was merely meant to be another addition to the witch's slave collection.

"Then Ceridwen gave Tommy a new boss, a man named Jacek and a dwarf—smelly—named Gomer," Tommy continued, his big-featured face souring.

"Not nice people," the giant explained. "Jacek is mean. He hurts things."

"Not anymore," Gary assured him, confident that Tommy bore no friendship at all for the rogues. "He tried to hurt Kelsey, my elf friend, but Kelsey killed him in a sword fight."

Tommy considered the news for a long time, then decided that it was a good thing.

"Now you live all alone," Gary reasoned. "How long has it been?"

Tommy started counting on his nine fingers, but ran out of digits. "Ten years," he decided, though his face crinkled in confusion. "No, twenty." He shrugged helplessly. "Long time."

"Don't you get bored?"

Again the giant only shrugged.

"Then why have you stayed?" Gary asked. "There must be other giants like you out in the mountains beyond the lake."

The giant thought that a ridiculous question. "Tommy can't swim," he explained. "And no boats are big enough for Tommy."

"How convenient for dear Ceridwen," Gary muttered under his breath. Tommy didn't hear him. The giant looked around, as though expecting someone to be eavesdropping, then he put his face right up to Gary's.

"Tommy walked off island once," he whispered, as much as a giant can whisper. "Water go over Tommy's head, but Tommy jumped up real high and breathed, jump up and breathe."

"You made it all the way?" Now Gary was starting to get some ideas.

The giant looked over his shoulder again, then turned back, his grin from ear to ear. "Yes!" he replied. "But Tommy came right back—did not want to make the Lady mad!"

"Of course not," Gary readily agreed, but what the young man was thinking at that time would certainly not have pleased Ceridwen.

Gary slept in Tommy's cave that night, or at least he stayed there, for he hardly closed his eyes. He had learned quite a few things in his single day with Tommy One-Thumb, and he believed in his heart that he could somehow turn that knowledge into escape. When he had heard of Tommy's lake crossing, he had almost asked the giant to pick him up and carry him over. But that wouldn't work. Even if he could get Tommy to agree, which he doubted, the giant's descriptions of jumping "real high" just to get his head above the water didn't bode well for passengers, not when splashes from the lake would burn Gary's skin away!

But the answer was before him, Gary knew. Like pieces of a puzzle, just waiting to be put into proper order.

Gary finally fell asleep, long into the night, with those thoughts in mind.

When he opened his eyes, he found not Tommy, but Ceridwen, waiting for him. Gary's first thought was that the witch had somehow read his mind and that he was about to be turned into a rabbit or some other benign little creature. He realized a moment later, though, that the witch was as surprised to see him as he was to see her. She called to Tommy, who came bouncing back in the cave entrance.

"What is he doing here?" Ceridwen asked the giant sharply.

"I came to visit Tommy," Gary answered before Tommy could blurt anything out. "I've never known a giant before—I was curious."

Ceridwen thought it over, then flashed her disarming smile Gary's way. "It is good that you have made a new friend," she said, that same throaty voice she had tried on Kelsey a few days earlier. "You will be here for a long time—all of your life, in fact. You may as well enjoy your stay."

Gary didn't like the subtle inferences of that last statement, especially not with Ceridwen standing so very close to him. His disdain for her apparently showed in his face, for the witch's expression went from smile to scowl and she pointedly turned away from Gary.

"There is a wall to be fixed at the castle," she mentioned to Tommy. "See to it."

"Tommy will fix it," the giant assured her.

"And get the dwarf," Ceridwen said after a moment. "Let him help you. I want to see if Geno Hammerthrower lives up to his considerable reputation before I give him any of the more important tasks I have in mind."

Tommy started to object, not wanting anything to do with fiery Geno, but Gary motioned for the giant to remain silent. Ceridwen saw the confusion on the giant's face and guessed easily enough that Gary, standing behind her, was the cause.

"Good," she purred, turning back to Gary. "You play the role of ambassador, and make things easier for everyone."

"I do what I can," Gary said evenly.

"A long time," Ceridwen reminded him in her throaty voice, her perfect, lush lips curling up in a lascivious smile. She let her gaze linger on the sturdy young man for a long while, then turned back on Tommy. "I will be away for a few days. I expect that wall to be repaired by the time I return.

"And when I return," she continued, looking coyly over her shoulder at Gary, "perhaps you and I can become better friends."

An old saying about snowballs and hell crossed Gary's mind, but he wisely held his thoughts silent. Again he worried that the witch could read his mind, but then she was gone, in the blink of an eye, a large raven soaring out over the smooth lake.

It took some convincing, but Gary finally had Tommy willing to go with him to get Geno. The giant really didn't want to face the volatile dwarf, or the surly elf, again, but Tommy, desperately in need of some companionship, had already come to trust in Gary, and Gary promised him that nothing bad would happen.

Gary almost wished he hadn't made that promise when they came in sight of the camp, for the first things he and Tommy noticed were Kelsey, bow in hand, and Geno, juggling his hammers and eyeing Tommy with open hatred.

"You'd better wait here," Gary offered, and Tommy didn't have to be asked twice. Even though Gary went the rest of the way alone, Kelsey did not lower his drawn bow.

"Ceridwen wants Geno to go and help the giant fix a wall," Gary explained as he came into the camp.

Geno snorted and spat. "Cold day in a dwarf's forge," he muttered.

Gary blinked and paused a moment to consider the similarities of that curious phrase to one he had been thinking of earlier. He wondered how many sayings from his world had variations in Faerie. How many sayings in his world had actually come from Faerie, and were just adapted to make better sense in his world?

"I think you should go," Gary said at length, reminding himself not to get sidetracked. Mickey moved up, suspicious of Gary's smug tone, and Kelsey finally lowered his bow.

"In fact," Gary continued, "I think that we should all go."

"To the castle?" Mickey asked incredulously.

"That's where Cedric's spear is located," Gary replied, as though the answer should have been obvious. "We wouldn't want to leave Ynis Gwydrin without Cedric's spear."

"What're ye talking about?" Now Mickey's tone was more curious than incredulous.

"If you know of something, then speak it clearly," Kelsey demanded. "What riddles do you offer?"

"I know a way that we can get off the island," Gary said bluntly.

Even Geno moved up then, to better hear. All three—dwarf, leprechaun, and elf—looked to each other and to Gary, waiting impatiently for the young man to elaborate.

"I haven't worked out all the details," Gary said, not wanting to reveal his as yet uncompleted scheme. "But I can get us out of here—I'm sure of it."

Mickey seemed intrigued, but Kelsey and Geno frowned and turned away.

"Cold day in a dwarf's forge," Gary heard Geno say again. Gary growled and rushed around them, cutting off their retreat.

"Do either of you have a better idea?" he demanded angrily. "Have you thought of something wonderful during the hours you have wasted staring at the water?"

Knowing the Tylwyth Teg better than anyone who wasn't of the Tylwyth Teg, Mickey cringed at Gary's bold sarcasm. But Kelsey didn't retaliate, physically or verbally. Both he and Geno stood staring at Gary, neither of them blinking.

"I can get us out of here," Gary said evenly.

Kelsey looked to Geno, who just shrugged.

"We'll go to the castle," the elf agreed.

"And if we manage to steal back the spear," Mickey put in, "and then we don't get off the island, who's going to face Ceridwen?"

"It's my plan," Gary offered.

"I will claim responsibility," Kelsey declared suddenly. "What can she do to me that would be worse than exile on this forsaken island?"

Mickey looked at the elf in blank amazement. "Ye always were a hard one to figure," the leprechaun commented.

For the first time in many days, Kelsey flashed one of his rare smiles. "I am of the Tylwyth Teg," he explained to Mickey. "Am I not expected to be difficult?"

"I always expected that out o' ye," Mickey readily agreed.

FIFTEEN

CERIDWEN'S PLACE

The castle proved to be even more splendid up close than it had appeared from the beach. High crystalline walls gave way to even higher crystalline turrets, spiraling up into the sky, every inch of them glistening and sparkling in the morning sunlight. Intricate angles and many-faceted stones threw the light off in a hundred directions, making Gary and his companions squint their eyes from the stinging brilliance.

This was a castle for a goodly, king, Gary decided then, and not the appropriate palace for an evil witch. How sad for the land of Faerie that Ceridwen had come to call Ynis Gwydrin her home.

Geek met the companions at the front gate, eyeing them suspiciously and casting particularly uncomfortable glances at Kelsey's sheathed sword.

"Lady said to meet Tommy and a dwarf," the goblin asserted. "Just Tommy and a dwarf."

"She asked . . . she told . . . us all to help," Gary replied.

Geek's yellow eyes narrowed doubtfully.

"We refused, except for the dwarf," Gary bluffed. "So Ceridwen probably didn't tell you to expect us. But we thought it over and figured that repairing a wall would be a better thing than facing the Lady's wrath when she returns from her trip."

"And if I don't lets yous in, Ceridwen will punish you?" the goblin asked, and the weaselly little creature seemed to like that idea.

"In that event, we might as well kill you, since we would be doomed anyway," Kelsey reasoned evenly. "At least I might know some enjoyment before Ceridwen's wrath descends over me." The elf's hand inched towards his belted sword.

Geek's face crinkled for a moment, then he nodded stupidly and told them to follow.

"Well done," Kelsey congratulated Gary, but it was Mickey's expression towards the young man, both amused and amazed, that Gary took as the highest compliment.

They moved across a gigantic audience hall and along a maze of mirror-walled corridors. The ceilings were quite high, but Tommy had to stoop anyway, and even crawl in some places, just to get through. Gary went up front for some small talk with the goblin, trying to gain Geek's confidence, but Geek said little, and commented more than once that he hated the smell of humans.

The maze continued, down a stairway, through a few irregular-shaped rooms, up a stairway, and along several corridors. Gary suspected, and he knew that he wasn't the only one with the feeling, that Geek was purposely leading them in a roundabout manner, as if trying to prevent them from getting any bearings about their location in the castle. It made sense—they were certainly less likely to try any mischief if they couldn't even find their way back out.

Finally they came into a room, similarly mirrored as the corridors except for one wall where the glass had all been broken away. The companions were somewhat amazed to see stonework behind the shattered section; from every angle, the castle appeared almost translucent, though undeniably solid. In one area, the stones, too, were broken away—this was undoubtedly what Ceridwen wanted repaired, for the dwarf was no glassworker.

Beyond the hole in the wall lay another room, this one set with braziers and a pentagram design on the floor. Even Gary knew enough about legends of magic to guess this second chamber to be a room for summoning. He couldn't contain a shudder, wondering what beast Ceridwen might have conjured, wondering what hellish beast might have blasted the wall.

"Right there," Geek explained. "Fix the stones. The Lady will put new glass over them." Gary started to ask the goblin something, but Geek spun about and left immediately, giving the distinct impression that he was uncomfortable in this place.

"She brought in a big one," Mickey commented, looking at the blasted wall.

"A big what?" Gary dared to ask.

"Demon, lad," the leprechaun replied. "Ceridwen's always playing with demons."

Gary wanted to claim that he didn't believe in demons, but it seemed a silly thing to say to a leprechaun, since he didn't believe in leprechauns, either.

"So we are in the castle," Kelsey remarked. "Now we must find the spear and be gone. And quickly . . ." He stopped, seeing Gary with a finger over pursed lips, his other hand subtly pointing in Tommy's direction.

Tommy was oblivious to the conversation, though. The giant had already started clearing aside the rubble, while Geno measured the break and pondered the best way to patch it.

Kelsey called Gary and Mickey over to the far side of the room for a private conference.

"Do we let them work on it?" the elf asked. "I fear that the goblin will return to check on our progress."

"I can make the poor thing think he's seeing us fixing it," Mickey replied. "But I'd have to stay here."

"Could you then find your way out?" Kelsey asked. "I would like to have the dwarf, at least, accompany me on the search for the spear."

"I'll go with you," Gary offered. Kelsey gave him a sidelong smirk.

"I will need another fighter," the elf continued to Mickey, "if, as I expect, Ceridwen has the spear guarded."

Gary accepted the insult without comment, thinking that having two friendly—or at least nonenemy—fighters around him might not be such a bad thing.

"Take him," Mickey replied, looking to Geno. "The giant'll think the dwarf's here working, and the goblin'll think so, too, if the stupid creature returns.

"I'll give ye just an hour, though," Mickey went on. "If ye get into trouble or get found out, I've no desire to get catched in this castle!"

"Two hours," Kelsey bargained. "It is a big place."

Mickey agreed.

"The door's locked," Gary reminded them.

Mickey laughed and waved a hand, then called to Tommy. "Ye'd find patching easier if ye used this slab leaning against the wall over here," the leprechaun reasoned. Tommy and the others followed Mickey's leading gaze to the door, or at least, to where the door had been. Now the portal appeared as leaning beams and cross sections, the perfect infrastructure for a wall.

"Yeah, get it," Geno agreed, and Gary wasn't sure if the dwarf understood the illusion or was just happy to see that much of the work was already done.

Gary feared that Tommy would figure out the dupe—they had just come through that same door, after all. But the giant, not a powerful thinker, moved right up to the illusionary beams and searched for handholds along their sides. He tugged, but the illusion didn't move. Tommy set his feet wide apart and pulled mightily, then turned back to the wall holding his prize between his huge hands.

"Door's not locked anymore," Mickey said smugly. Gary looked through the illusion to the gaping hole in the wall; Tommy had yanked out the door, jamb and all.

A moment later, Geno came over to join Gary and Kelsey, though when Gary looked back, he saw Geno working hard beside Tommy, tying to fit the door, which still appeared as beams and planks, into the original hole in the wall. Mickey moved over to the side, plopped down, and popped his pipe in his mouth, folding his chubby little hands behind his head.

"Is dealing with leprechauns always this confusing?" Gary asked helplessly to Kelsey.

"Aye, lad," snickered the real Mickey, standing invisibly behind the elf. "Ye should try catching one sometime."

Gary blinked and looked back to the side, where the illusionary Mickey sat contentedly drawing on his pipe.

"Now off with ye," the real Mickey told them. "Ye got two hours and not a minute more!" He grabbed Gary as the man started away, and shoved something into his hand. "Take this," the leprechaun explained. "It'll get ye back to me and bring ye luck on yer hunt."

When Gary opened his hand, he found a four-leaf clover. He wasn't surprised.

Once again, Gary, Kelsey, and Geno found themselves in the maze, but this time they had no goblin to guide them. Kelsey took up the lead, alternating his turns, left and right, to prevent them from walking in circles. The elf tried to appear assured of his steps, but Gary figured that he was simply guessing.

"I would find our way if this was underground," Geno grumbled more than once. And more than once, the dwarf turned a corner and smacked a hammer into his own reflection, thinking, in his startlement, that the enemy had found them. "Stupid mirrors!" Geno just grumbled as he continued on his way, leaving a spider's web of broken glass behind him every time.

When they did actually come across one of Ceridwen's guards, an unfortunate goblin, it took them a long moment to even realize that it was not some manifestation of the tricky mirrors. The goblin squeaked once and turned to flee, but Kelsey's sword and Geno's hammer sliced and pounded it down before it got two steps away.

Then on they went, blindly, turning corners and crossing identical rooms with identical furnishings. Kelsey's confidence seemed to waver; they came to one four-way intersection and the elf hesitated and glanced one way and then another, before finally deciding to go straight ahead.

"No, left," Gary corrected suddenly. Kelsey and Geno turned on him in surprise.

Gary had no definite answers to their questioning stares; he just, for some reason he could not explain, believed that they had to go left at that point. Kelsey shot him an incredulous look and started straight ahead again, but Gary was certain of his mysterious insight.

"Left," he said again, more forcefully.

"What do you know?" Kelsey demanded. Gary shook his head.

"I know only that we have to go to the left," he answered honestly.

"We have wasted half an hour going your way," Geno reminded the elf.

They went left, and at the next intersection, when Geno and Kelsey looked to Gary for guidance, he quickly replied, "Straight ahead." At each corner, Gary's feelings grew more definite—he only feared that the sensations might be some trick of Ceridwen's to lure them into a trap.

But then, with a profound sigh of relief, he figured it out.

"It is the spear," he announced unexpectedly. "Cedric's spear is calling to me!"

"Good spear," Geno mumbled, and Kelsey did not argue the point, nor did the elf any longer doubt Gary's instincts.

They knew a few turns later that they were nearing Ceridwen's private quarters. No longer did mirrors line the walls, and the furnishings were much richer in this section. There were many more guards, though, marching in tight, well-ordered formations.

The companions came through a set of large double doors, into a spacious room filled with comfortable chairs and a long oaken table. Across from them stood another set of double doors, even more ornate than the ones they had just come through, and corridors ran off both sides of the wide room.

"Meeting hall," Geno reasoned.

"And Ceridwen's chamber beyond," added Kelsey. He looked to Gary for confirmation. Gary closed his eyes and heard the cry of the spear. Very close, straight ahead.

"That's it," Gary announced. He started forward, but Kelsey pulled him suddenly around the door and back into the previous corridor. Geno, too, slipped out of the room, and before Gary could begin to argue, he heard the marching stomp of many boots.

Peeking through the slightly cracked door, they saw two nervous goblins rush into the meeting room from the left corridor, quickly straightening their armor and helmets and taking positions on either side of the ornate double doors. A moment later, the troupe arrived, in ranks three abreast and five deep, marching from right to left through the meeting room and led by one burly goblin and a troll he commanded to keep his ragtag troops in line. The burly goblin paused to consider the two guards, eyeing them suspiciously for some time before he two-stepped to catch up to his still-marching troops.

"We have to take them out quickly," Kelsey whispered, lamenting that he had left his bow back on the beach. In answer, Geno flipped two hammers up into the air.

Kelsey grabbed the door handle and mouthed, "One . . . two . . . three," then yanked the door open and Geno let fly.

The first hammer caught the goblin on the left square in the faceplate of its helmet, hurling the creature back into the wall. The second goblin, breaking into a run, caught the next hammer on the shoulder, a glancing but wicked blow. Still, the goblin managed to keep on going.

Kelsey charged in; Geno readied another hammer. But Gary beat them to it, hurling his spear at the fleeing monster. He got the goblin on the hip and it went down squealing.

The first goblin had recovered by then, but found Kelsey, or more pointedly, Kelsey's sword, dancing right in its face. The creature yanked out its own weapon desperately, then lost all sense of reality. It felt no pain, but saw the floor rush up and the room spin about wildly. The goblin realized its horrid fate in the last instant of its life, as it looked back to its headless body still leaning upright against the door.

The other goblin stopped squealing almost immediately as Geno fired hammer after hammer into its head. Gary figured that the thing was dead after the second hit, but the dwarf hurled three more hammers into it, then rushed up and konked it a few more times just for good measure.

"Fine throw," Geno commented, tearing out Gary's bloodied spear and handing it back to the man. Gary knew that the dwarf wouldn't give him an unconditional compliment, and sure enough, Geno lived up to his reputation.

"Next time, hit it in the lungs so it cannot yell out," Geno growled. "Its screaming will probably bring the whole force back upon us!"

"Next time, you try to hit it right with the first throw," Gary snapped back. Geno shrugged and "accidentally" dropped a hammer on Gary's toe. Gary grimaced and bit his lip, but would not give the dwarf the satisfaction of seeing his pain.

"The door is trapped, no doubt," Kelsey said to them, reminding them that they had little time to waste.

Still fuming, Geno stomped over and inspected the portal. He grunted and scratched his hairless chin, then moved to the other end; grunted and scratched his chin again. He pulled a chisel from his endlessly pocketed belt and went to work, tapping here and tapping there, popping a hinge pin on one side and then the other. Then he walked back three steps, bowed to Kelsey (eyeing Gary all the while), and tossed a hammer into the center of the doors. They fell in like a cut tree, hitting the floor with a tremendous *whoosh!*

"Stealthy," Gary remarked sarcastically, and he prudently hopped away before Geno could have any more accidents concerning hammers and toes.

Ceridwen's room, for this was indeed the witch's private chamber, was among the most remarkable places Gary Leger had ever seen. A huge desk lined one wall, covered with parchments and inkwells, quills and books, some opened and some tightly bound with leather straps. Metal sconces, gracefully designed, though somehow discordant or unbalanced, or something else that made Gary uncomfortable to look at them, were evenly spaced around the room, each holding a torch that burned with a different-colored flame. The witch's bed was centered along the back wall, huge and canopied in purple silk. All three companions breathed a little easier when Kelsey went over and moved the curtain aside, showing the bed to be made up and empty.

The elf spotted the spear case, set on the wall beside a changing screen opposite the desk. He sheathed his sword and went for it immediately, reaching with hungry hands.

"*Trap!*" came a call in Gary's head.

"That's not it!" Gary cried.

The warning came too late. As Kelsey grabbed the case, it broke apart in his hands and an egg fell from a concealed cubby in the wall behind it. The three companions froze, staring at the cracked egg curiously, and with a shared sense of dread.

The egg split in half and a cloud of black smoke burst forth. Kelsey threw his hand over his mouth; Geno dove away; and Gary, too, assumed the vapors to be toxic. But the trap was nothing that simple; as the cloud rose up, it took a definite shape. Glowing red eyes appeared and a huge, gaping maw opened wide, hungrily. Black mist still hung about, obscuring the monster's form, but it seemed to have no absolute form anyway, shifting, growing limbs, almost on a whim, a writhing mass of blackness. Whatever its shape, it was huge and mighty, exuding a horrible power.

And for all his denials and all his logic, Gary Leger would never again make the claim that he did not believe in demons.

A thick black arm shot out at Kelsey from the still-forming cloud. The elf got his shield up to block, though his arm went numb under the sheer weight of the blow, and countered with his sword, the magical blade sizzling and hissing as it struck demon flesh. The demon howled—it might have been a laugh— and another arm appeared, and then a third arm, and a fourth beside that.

"Tylwyth Teg!" the monster bellowed in a voice that Gary could only compare to the grating of a diesel truck. "I have not killed one of the Tylwyth Teg in centuries! Is elf flesh still as tasty as I remember?"

A hammer whipped past Kelsey into the mist, but seemed to float to the floor, finding nothing tangible to smash against.

In an instant, Kelsey was pressed hard, fending against all four demon arms. The elf's shield and sword worked in perfect harmony, parrying and blocking. Kelsey dodged and dove, coming right back up to catch another blow with his fine shield. For all his brilliance, though, Kelsey couldn't hope to slow the attacks enough to get in any more solid hits of his own.

Gary knew that he must go to his companion, his friend, but he found his feet rooted to the floor in terror. He lifted his spear halfheartedly in both hands as if to rush in, but then changed his mind and took aim, thinking it wiser to throw the weapon instead. The demon's red eyes fell over him, and, caught in their hellish gaze, Gary felt as though his weapon weighed a hundred pounds.

The monster continued to stare at him, and continued to battle Kelsey, as though its mind could work easily in different directions at once. Gary noticed Geno dash ahead and slide down to the floor, the cunning dwarf's hammer going to work furiously on the eggshell, smashing it to little bits. For the first time, the demon seemed wounded; its ensuing cry was obviously founded in pain. A huge, clawed foot appeared from the mist and stomped down on Geno, but the diminutive and stubborn dwarf kept on smashing at the bits of egg.

The demon roared again, in pain and outrage, and twin lines of fire shot out from its eyes towards Gary. Gary managed to get a blocking forearm up in front of his face in time, but the searing jets burned into him and their sheer force hurled him backwards across the room. He found himself sitting against something hard, alternately clutching at his arm and at the twin holes burned into the armplate of Cedric Donigarten's fine armor.

Despite the distractions of both Gary and Geno, there was no letup at all in the demon's attacks against Kelsey. A heavy arm thumped against the elf's shield, and another battering limb came in the other way at the same time, forcing Kelsey to throw his sword out wide in a desperate parry. A third arm came in between sword and shield, with long horrid claws reaching for Kelsey's heart.

Kelsey threw himself straight backwards into a roll, but the arms, stretching impossibly long, followed him every inch of the way.

Geno was made of the stuff of mountains, but even that dwarfish trait seemed puny under the weight of the demon's huge foot. The dwarf smashed away, and when the pieces of egg were too small to hit anymore, he stuffed as many as he could grab into his mouth and swallowed them. He felt the weight on his back diminish, as though his actions had actually lessened the substance of the monster. Spurred by his success, the dwarf dropped his hammer aside and reached out with both hands, trying to find every last bit of eggshell.

But then the weight returned, crushing him down, pinning him helplessly. In one hand, Geno held a fair-sized chunk of the shell, but he couldn't hope to get that hand anywhere near his mouth.

He bit the foot instead, but that seemed to have little effect. And even Geno, who had eaten more unconventional meals than a billy goat in a junkyard, had to admit that demon flesh was among the most horrid things he had ever tasted.

The demonic gaze fell over Kelsey, and the elf slumped, knowing he was surely doomed.

Propped against Ceridwen's desk one arm hanging useless by his side, Gary thought again of his parents. Where would he run when Kelsey was gone and Geno crushed? Where could he hide from this hell-spawned monster?

A temporary reprieve came to them as the goblin patrol unwittingly rushed into the room. The demon's head shot up and the creature sent its flaming beams out at the newest intruders. The burly goblin, in the lead, threw its arm up as Gary had done, but it was not wearing armor nearly as fine as Cedric's. The fire bored right through the goblin's arm and then right through its head, and it fell, smoldering and quite dead, to the floor.

Flashes of fire continued throughout the goblin ranks, felling several others. Goblins rushed all about, banging into each other, hacking at each other to get free and get away. The one troll bravely, stupidly, charged ahead, not understanding its foe. A demon arm caught it by the throat and lifted it from the ground before it ever got close to the misty cloud. The great, clawed hand clenched down—Gary heard a resounding *snap*—and the troll suddenly stopped thrashing.

The demon shook the huge form a few times, then hurled it into the midst of the scrambling goblins, crushing one. And then the demon, too, came on, suddenly just a billowing cloud once more. It overtook the goblins in the meeting room and passed right through their ranks. One cloud became three and a monster stood to block every exit.

Hearing the screams from that meeting room, cries of sheer terror and sheer agony, Gary hugged tight to the desk leg and even Kelsey, bravely in pursuit of the monster, stopped in his tracks and backpedaled.

In a moment, the cries diminished and three goblins came rushing back into the room. Jets of flame cut two of them down; the third ran right by Kelsey, hooking the stunned elf's arm and holding tight behind him.

"Pleases! Pleases!" the goblin sputtered. "Kills it! Oh, kills it!"

Kelsey shrugged the goblin away and stood firm to meet his foe. Geno stuffed that last hunk of eggshell into his mouth, retrieved his favorite hammer, and moved beside the elf.

Gary, too, knew that he must go and join his friends, go and die beside his friends. Determinedly he hooked his arm over the desktop and pulled himself to his feet. He meant to turn and go straight over but found himself held suddenly by the images in an open book on Ceridwen's desk.

Gary blinked several times, glancing over his shoulder and then back to those strange images. In the book, he saw Kelsey and Geno, standing as they were now standing in the middle of the room! Cowering in the corner behind them was the goblin.

"It has been an honor to fight beside you," Kelsey said to the dwarf, and Gary blinked again as the spoken words became a flowing script (though in a language he could not read) at the top of the page!

"A journal?" Gary breathed in disbelief.

He continued to stare dumbfounded as the page turned of its own accord. The next scene showed him the demon in the door, advancing on his friends.

Gary grabbed a nearby quill and poked it at the image of the demon, but the instrument snapped apart as it struck the magical book. Desperately Gary grabbed at the pages and flipped them back, hoping beyond reason that he might turn back time.

But the demon came on and the book fought back against Gary's actions, its pages trying to catch up with the events at hand. Gary put all his weight on one side of the book to hold it open where it was, at the two pages depicting Kelsey reaching for the spear case, and the egg coming apart on the floor.

Gary couldn't see the renewed fighting behind him, but he heard a crash by the canopied bed and heard Geno grunt and groan from that direction.

Without even thinking of the possible consequences, the desperate man grabbed at the page with the intact demon egg and pulled with all his strength.

Suddenly Gary was in darkness, floating in space, it seemed, but there were no stars and no sun to light the way.

SIXTEEN

TIME UNGLUED

Gary floated in the dim grayness, searching for some bearing, for some reference point in this unremarkable universe. He saw a seam before him, far in the distance, a line, perhaps, in the fabric of existence.

Gary willed himself towards that seam, understood then that this was not some physical place he had been dropped into, but an extra dimension, a place of the mind. He reached for the seam with prying fingers, tried to push himself through it, figuring that anything beyond it could only be an improvement.

One finger slipped through. Suddenly Gary was not so sure of his actions. What if he was at the gates of Hell? Or what if his tearing of this seam unraveled the fabric of the physical universe. But he decided at last that he couldn't just hover in the grayness and wait. Determinedly he drove his hand through the barrier, and then his other hand, and with all his strength began pulling the gray walls apart.

His blood pounded in his head—he could feel that distinctly, the pressure growing, though he was sure that his consciousness was somehow detached from this physical form. Gary steeled his mind and pulled. He feared he wouldn't be strong enough, and indeed, the sides of the curtain, for that is what he now believed it to be, barely moved apart. Through the crack came a blinding light, stinging Gary's eyes and all his sensibilities.

He thought he would surely collapse. He thought all the world would be destroyed if he persisted. He thought that his tear might loose a thousand other demons upon the land of Faerie. He thought . . .

But while he thought, Gary continued to pull, stubbornly held on to his course, and gradually the curtains did begin to move apart.

The light overwhelmed him.

And then he was back in Ceridwen's room, holding a torn page from the magical book. Kelsey and Geno stood side by side in the center of the room beside the burned and broken corpses of several goblins and the troll; the lone living goblin cowered in the corner. The demon was gone, but above the goblin's head, another egg (or was it the same egg?) teetered on the edge of a cubby much too shallow to hold it.

"Egg!" was all that desperate Gary managed to cry out, pointing to the cubby. Kelsey seemed to understand. The elf spun around just in time to see the egg drop.

It landed on the goblin's stooped shoulder. It did not break, though, but started to roll. The stupid creature reflexively caught it. Kelsey rushed in; the goblin squealed and threw the egg at him.

Kelsey's sword and shield went flying to the sides. The elf fell to his knees, juggling the precious egg, his hands moving in a blur to soften the impact until he finally managed to get control of it. Quickly Kelsey inspected the delicate shell, then breathed a sigh of relief to see that it had no visible cracks.

The companions' troubles were not ended, though. The troll body rose up suddenly and flew back through the air to the spot where the demon had thrown it. It shook a few times and dropped to land on its feet, very much alive. One of Geno's hammers, lying on the floor, came spinning back at the dwarf, who kept the presence of mind to catch it. Fire crackled and shot out of the bodies of the dead goblins, and some of them began to stir once more.

"What is happening?" Gary cried, but he had a better guess at the answer than either of his stunned companions. He had torn the fabric of time, at least as far as Ceridwen's magical journal was concerned. He felt himself falling away again, into the grayness, into the void.

He reached over and closed the book.

The dead goblins fell dead again, the troll crashed down in a heavy, broken lump, and the fires died away. And Kelsey, still on his knees, held the fragile egg.

"What have you done?" Geno asked Gary breathlessly.

Gary had no answer, had never seen the tough dwarf so unnerved.

"Pleases! Pleases!" the lone living goblin begged, groveling on the floor before Kelsey. Geno, frustrated and confused, started for it, hammer raised, but Gary stopped him.

"The goblin can show us the way out," he blurted.

"But we have not found the spear," replied Kelsey.

Gary fell within himself, consciously tried to reach his thought out to the spear. He knew that it was in here, that it had been the one who had warned him when Kelsey had reached for the phony case.

"*Up high, above the room,*" came an answer. Gary looked up to the unremarkable ceiling, thinking there must be a concealed trapdoor somewhere. Then his gaze settled on the high canopy of Ceridwen's silk-covered bed.

"The canopy," he explained. "The spear is on top of the canopy."

One of the bottom bedposts was already down, having taken a hit during the fight. Geno made short work of the other bottom post, flinging a hammer through it. The canopy fell diagonally to the floor and the precious spear case rolled off it, coming to a stop just a few feet from Kelsey.

The elf reached for it, but this time, Gary's warning came quickly enough to stop him.

"No!" Gary shrieked. He grabbed a blue-glowing torch from a sconce beside him and rushed over, and to Kelsey's horror, he put the flames to the case. The leather erupted in a sizzling display, sickly green fumes rushing up from the white-hot fires.

"What are you doing?" Kelsey demanded, and he pushed Gary aside. The elf hopped about the blaze, blowing at it, kicking at it, frantically trying to save the legendary spear—though, if Kelsey had not been so badly shaken, if he had taken the moment to calm himself and consider things, he would have realized that no simple torch fire could have possibly harmed the legendary spear.

The fire was gone an instant later, the leather case completely consumed. The spear remained, though, unscathed, and Kelsey thought himself foolish for his fears.

"The case was poisoned," Gary explained. "Contact poison. If you had touched it . . ." Gary let the thought hang in the air as he tentatively moved to pick up the spear. He found it surprisingly cool to his touch.

"Hello again," he said, and then, though he didn't really know why, he added, "I have missed you."

"*My greetings as well, young warrior*," came the spear's telepathic reply. Gary considered that title and smiled, obviously pleased.

"What are you planning to do with the egg?" Geno asked Kelsey. "I do not believe that we would take it along."

Kelsey paled at that suggestion.

"Give it to me," Gary said, nearly laughing aloud at his plan. Kelsey hesitated for a moment, but then, apparently realizing that Gary had earned his trust, handed it over.

Gary moved to Ceridwen's desk again and took one of the side drawers right out of its perch. With all caution, he placed the egg deep inside the hole, then replaced the drawer, easing it halfway in, but taking care not to crush the fragile egg.

"Ceridwen will have a bit of a surprise waiting for her when she closes that drawer," Gary snickered, letting them in on the joke.

"Again you have proven more valuable than I would have believed," Kelsey remarked, his tone brightened, almost lighthearted. He looked to the book on Ceridwen's desk. "Against the demon, with the spear, and in this matter. Not many, I would guess, could look into one of Ceridwen's tomes and find the strength . . ."

"My thanks," Gary interrupted, reverently sliding the spear through a loop on the side of his belt. "But can you tell me later? Right now, I just want to get the hell out of here."

"That is a curious way to put it," Geno piped in, though the dwarf wholeheartedly agreed. "Do you know the way out?" he barked at the goblin.

The goblin thought it over for a moment, then answered, "No know."

"Kill him," Geno said evenly to Kelsey, and not a person in the room had any doubts about the dwarf's sincerity.

"Knows the way out?" the goblin cried, as though it had misunderstood the original question. "Yesses, oh yesses. Jesper shows you out, oh yesses!"

"I guess you have to know how to talk to them," Gary remarked, and Geno nodded and grinned, his missing tooth again reminding Gary of his mischievous nephew. Their smiles abruptly disappeared, though, and Geno whirled towards the bed and whipped a hammer. Following the hammer's flight, Gary and Kelsey both saw a flash of black dart back under the bed.

"A cat," Gary said, hearing the creature's ensuing cry.

"Witch's familiar!" Kelsey corrected, and he dove down flat to his belly and poked his sword under the bed. But then the cat's meow became a lion's roar and a huge paw shot out, hooking Kelsey under the shoulder blade. A split second later, the elf disappeared under the bed, only his feet sticking out.

Geno roared and charged right into the bed, his cord-like muscles heaving wildly. The bed came up, and so did the lion, bowling over Geno and bearing down on Gary.

The sentient spear cried a hundred different telepathic commands in that one terrible instant, but Gary heard none of them. He fell backwards—he had nowhere else to go—bringing his dwarven spear up defensively as he toppled. Unable to break its momentum, the lion came on, catching the spear in the chest. The dwarf-forged shaft bowed but did not break as the lion's full five-hundred-pound weight fell over Gary. The beast thrashed and roared as it impaled itself.

Unlike the goblin Gary had impaled many days before, though, this enemy kept thrashing, and with its huge claws getting closer and closer to Gary as it slid down the spear pole, the young man thought he was surely doomed. One paw raked at his chest, claws squealing against the metallic armor.

Geno roared again and ran headfirst into the flank of the impaled cat, knocking it over to the side. The lion continued to thrash, but no one was in its range then, the dwarf having gone right over and continued his rolling and Gary quick to scramble the other way.

Kelsey helped Gary to his feet. The elf didn't seem too badly hurt, though one of his sleeves had been torn off and his bare arm showed several fairly deep scratches.

"The spear will finish it," Kelsey said uneasily, obviously shaken from the second or two he had spent under the bed with the lion.

"How many pets does Ceridwen keep?" Gary asked.

"Too many," came Geno's reply.

A moment later, the cat lay still. A gray mist surrounded it and it seemed to melt away. To the friends' surprise, the black house cat sprang out of the mist and zipped into the cubby formed by the overturned bed. Geno started for it, then changed his mind.

"I am thinking that we should be leaving," the dwarf offered, and he found no arguments, not even from the still-cowering goblin.

They had barely gone through the adjacent meeting room, pointedly closing the door behind them, when there came another lion's roar from Ceridwen's chambers.

"Stubborn cat," the dwarf remarked dryly.

SEVENTEEN

READING BETWEEN THE LINES

They found Mickey some time later, after a dozen wrong turns and close brushes with goblin guards. The leprechaun was sitting against the wall as he—or at least, as his illusion—had been doing when they left him. Tommy was still hard at work on the wall beside the illusionary dwarf.

"Time to go," Kelsey said to the leprechaun. "Has our goblin friend returned?"

"Twice," Mickey replied, drawing deeply on his pipe. "He's thinking everything's as it should be."

From somewhere down the halls, there came the roar of a lion.

"Time to go," Kelsey said again, pulling the frightened goblin prisoner into the room beside him. "We have a guide."

Gary nodded from Mickey to the giant, who was still oblivious to the fact that the missing group had even entered the room. "He won't go unless he thinks he's finished," Gary explained.

"Then let him stay," whispered Geno. "Who wants a giant around?"

"We need him," Gary said firmly, and he feared that he would have to go into a long and detailed explanation of his tentative escape plans, an explanation that he was sure would make little sense to his companions.

Mickey trusted him, though. The leprechaun winked Gary's way and the illusionary dwarf went into a whirlwind of activity that had the hole patched in mere seconds. Tommy blinked at the sight, not quite knowing what to make of it.

"Ye must leave now!" the goblin prisoner heard himself command, though he hadn't moved his lips. He looked questioningly around the room, but Kelsey's sword came up beside him in a flash.

"If you make any more noise than drawing your breath, I will cut off your head," the elf promised.

"Duh, is the wall fixed?" Tommy asked helplessly. He felt around as though he didn't believe his eyes. "The wall is not fixed."

"Now!" cried the goblin with a leprechaun's voice. "The Lady wants ye out o' the house!"

The illusionary dwarf walked over and seemed to blend right in with Geno. "The wall is fixed," Geno answered Tommy, taking the cue, though he gave Gary an angry sidelong glance as he addressed the giant.

"Come on, Tommy," Gary added. "I'll show you something else that will please the Lady." That got the giant's attention, and he shrugged at the somehow-fixed wall, scratched his huge head one final time, and fell into line behind Gary.

"One wrong turn costs you your head," Kelsey promised, whispering into the goblin's ear so that the giant would not hear. But the terrified goblin needed no prodding. It had seen quite too much of the powerful companions already to offer any resistance. It led them on at a great pace, pausing every now and then at an intersection to check its bearings.

They came unexpectedly upon one group of guards, bursting in through open doors before they even noticed that the room was not empty.

"I have to get these wretches outa the castle," Mickey's voice explained from the goblin's mouth, before Kelsey could set his sword into action. Mickey wanted no fights here, not with Ceridwen's pet in pursuit and a tentative and unpredictable giant by his side.

A roar erupted from somewhere behind them and the eyes of the goblin guards went wide.

"The Lady's cat's not too pleased that they're still around," Mickey went on.

"Then gets them out of here!" screamed one of the goblins, and it, and the others, darted out a side passage, scrambling away with all speed from the pursuing cat.

"That is Alice," Tommy said. The others looked at him curiously. "The Lady's cat," the giant explained. "Alice. The Lady lets me play with her sometimes."

"Go and play with Alice now," Geno offered.

"Shut up!" Gary snapped at the dwarf, and he thought himself incredibly stupid for talking that way to the volatile Geno. But Kelsey backed him this time.

"We have no time for bickering," the elf said, and he prodded the goblin along once more. "Let us discuss our differences when we are safely outside."

They ran down one long hallway, the outer doors in sight, but then Geek the goblin turned into the hall behind them. "Where is yous going?" the spindly-limbed goblin demanded. "You comes back here!"

Tommy spun about, confused, but Mickey was quicker, putting up an illusion of an empty hallway behind them.

"Come on, Tommy," Gary prodded, grabbing the giant's thumb in his hand and pulling with all his might.

"Duh," was all that Tommy replied, giving in to Gary's tug.

The distant goblin began shouting again, until a roar silenced his further tirade. "No, Alice," they heard Geek cry as they continued through the doors. "Nice kitty, Alice!"

And then they were outside. Geno closed the doors behind them and popped a spike into the ground at their base for good measure.

"If they have any way of contacting Ceridwen . . ." Kelsey warned, but he did not finish the thought, seeing Tommy overly interested in his words. He pulled Gary and Mickey aside, and the goblin prisoner, seeing a chance, wasted no time. As soon as Kelsey let go of it, with Geno busy at the doors, the creature ran off.

"How do we get off the island?" Kelsey asked bluntly, paying no heed to the fleeing goblin.

Gary still hadn't actually figured out exactly how they should proceed at that point; retrieving the magical spear and getting out of the castle had come in such a wild rush. Whatever details were yet to be worked out, though, Gary knew what role his companions had to play. "Get back to the camp and retrieve all of our belongings," he instructed. "And bring one boat along. Go north along the beach until you find a rocky jetty. I'll meet you there."

"And what of the giant?"

"He comes with me," Gary replied. He looked to Mickey, trying to think things through, trying to figure out what coaxing Tommy might need. "You had better come with me, too," he said.

Gary had little trouble convincing Tommy to go with him to the lagoon. Thrilled at preparing another surprise for the Lady, the giant even picked Gary and Mickey up and carried them along. Once again, Gary was amazed at the giant's strength, and glad, for he knew that Tommy would need all of it to carry out the plan.

When they got back to the lagoon, Gary instructed Tommy to retrieve weeds, both brown and green. The giant shrugged and did as he was asked, though he had no idea what the man had in mind. Mickey's amused smile showed that the leprechaun was beginning to catch on, though.

Gary found the widest hollow tubes of the bunch and glued them together with the sticky goo from the green reeds.

"Okay, Tommy," he said confidently, "put this in your mouth."

"I do not like to eat the water plants," Tommy explained.

"No, don't eat them," Gary explained. "Breathe through them." Off to the side, Mickey whistled and couldn't contain a chuckle.

Tommy scratched his huge head. "Duh?"

"Don't you understand?" Gary asked, as though things should have been obvious. He had to continue to appear confident, he knew, if he was to have any chance of convincing the giant. "With these, you can walk all the way across the lake."

"That will not please the Lady," Tommy reasoned.

"Oh, but it will!" Gary replied immediately. "If you can go back and forth without having to jump and scramble, you'll be able to carry things for Ceri . . . the Lady."

Tommy scratched his head.

"When the Lady has things to bring across to the island, she will no longer have to go back and forth with puny boats," Gary went on, revealing his sincere excitement. "She will have you to simply carry the things across for her."

"Duh, I do not . . ." the giant began slowly.

"Just try it," Gary pleaded. "Go across once, and then come back."

Tommy looked at the reed tube sourly and shook his head. Gary knew that his time was running out. And with all the damage they had done back in the castle, and with the spear back in their possession, he had no desire to be on the island when Ceridwen returned.

"You already went across once," Gary said grimly, his tone an obvious warning. "If the Lady finds out, she'll be mad."

"You will not tell her?" Tommy begged.

Gary shrugged his shoulders noncommittally. "If this works, though, you can explain to the Lady that you went across only because you wanted to find some way you could help her. Won't that make her happy?"

Tommy thought for a moment, then took the reed tube.

"Just put the tube in your mouth and your face in the water," Gary explained. "Keep calm and breathe easy."

Tommy walked into the lagoon and did as Gary asked, but brought the whole tube underwater with him and came up a few seconds later, coughing wildly.

"It does not work," he complained as soon as the fit had ended.

"We're in trouble, lad," Mickey remarked.

Gary motioned for Tommy to come back to him, then showed the giant how to keep one end of the tube above the lake, so that the air could go into him. The giant shrugged and went back into the water, ducking his head. Again, he came up in mere seconds, panicked and spitting water.

"We're in trouble," Mickey said again.

Gary realized that Tommy's mouth was simply too big for the tube. He called Tommy back to the shore, then refitted the reeds, this time smearing goo all around them to secure them in the giant's mouth. Using both hands, he pinched Tommy's nostrils to show the giant that he could indeed breathe through the tube.

Tommy shrugged, went back and tried again, and again, and each time he stayed underwater a little longer and came up looking less afraid.

"Long way to the shore," Mickey remarked. "Ye're thinking that the giant can keep calm enough to stay underwater all the way, carrying us besides?"

"Would you rather stay here and take your chances with Ceridwen?" Gary replied dryly.

"Good point, lad," agreed the leprechaun. He looked down the beach past the jetty and saw Kelsey and Geno approaching, Kelsey laden with their belongings and Geno carrying the heavy boat up over his head.

"How does he do that?" Gary remarked, amazed at the diminutive dwarf's incredible power.

"Comes from eating rocks," Mickey replied, and Gary couldn't tell from the leprechaun's tone if he was kidding or not.

Tommy came back to Gary and Mickey at about the same time as their other companions joined them. Tommy eyed the boat suspiciously, wondering what Gary had in mind, what this whole business was about.

"For the test," Gary explained, reading the giant's thoughts (not a difficult task). "You carry the boat high above your head; take care that it does not touch the water!"

"Duh, why are they here?" Tommy asked, pointing particularly at Geno. "The Lady does not want you to leave the island. You should not have a boat."

Tommy stood motionless, perplexed, trying to remember all that he had learned of his companions' dilemma. The giant was slow to catch on, but not nearly as stupid as some people assumed.

"You want Tommy to carry you past the water," he reasoned, his big eyes growing bigger.

"Carry us? Don't be silly!" Gary lied, flashing a disarming smile. "Kelsey and Geno will help me to pile rocks in the boat as you walk underwater past the end of the jetty. We have to see how strong you are, how much you can carry, before you go and tell the Lady your surprise."

"I am strong!" the giant asserted, an obvious fact that none of the companions were about to argue against.

Gary bobbed his head. "But we should know exactly how much you can carry before you tell the Lady about your surprise. The water's deep enough by the jetty's end to get the boat down near our level." Gary could only hope that the slow-to-catch-on giant wouldn't simply reason that it would be easier to fill the boat before he even started out. Tommy stood scratching his head, and looking at the lake and mountains beyond, then at the boat, and then, suspiciously, at Geno and Kelsey. Finally, to Gary's relief, Tommy popped his reed pipe in his mouth and hoisted the boat overhead.

Gary clapped his hands together and beamed at his friends, but Geno and Kelsey didn't seem to share his enthusiasm.

"You want us to climb in the boat as the giant walks past us?" the dwarf balked as soon as the giant moved far enough away. "I have lived too long—and hope to live too long again—for such a stupid trick!"

"You forget that the lake is acid to us," Kelsey added sourly.

Gary motioned to Mickey to give the answer, thinking that the leprechaun's backing might not be such a bad thing at that time.

"Would ye rather stay here and take yer chances with Ceridwen?" Mickey asked.

They were all in place on the end of the jagged jetty as Tommy came walking past, still holding the boat high. This was the trickiest part of the whole plan, for Gary couldn't be sure that the water was deep enough to get over the giant's head and keep him blinded to their real intentions.

It was, but just barely, and the giant's long arms had the boat high up above them, with Gary having no way to instruct Tommy to lower it. They tossed their bundles into the boat, then Gary jumped up and caught the side. He was going to tell his companions to climb up over him, but they hardly needed an invitation. Kelsey verily ran up his back. Mickey, boosted by Geno, barely touched Gary's shoulders as he flew past, and the dwarf came last—Gary was amazed at how much weight was packed into that little body!

They pulled Gary in, and then they all sat tight, fearful that the water, which Ceridwen had promised would burn them as acid, was only about six or seven feet below them. Looking over the edge of the boat, when any of them mustered the nerve to look over the edge, they could see the top of Tommy's head, bobbing along steadily.

As the giant continued deeper into the lake, his head disappeared altogether, and they grew even more afraid, for the dangerous water came closer and closer.

"If he bends his arms, we're done for," Mickey commented, and none of them appreciated the remark.

"Stupid plan," Geno muttered. "And I am a stupid dwarf for going along with it!"

Fifteen minutes later, Tommy was still walking. They were much closer to the mountainous shoreline than the island, and resting a bit easier. Tommy's iron-hard arms did not quiver, and the boat was steadily, if gradually, coming up again, for the giant had passed the lake's deepest point.

"Clever lad, to find a way through Ceridwen's spell," Mickey commented, aiming the remark more at Kelsey and Geno than at Gary. "I feared that the giant'd panic long before he reached the shore, but he's soon to be breathing without help o' yer . . . what did ye call it again?"

"Snorkel," Gary replied, peeking over the side. "When Tommy's head clears the water, stay still in the middle of the boat," Gary warned, "I don't know how he'll react when he finds out we've tricked him."

The lake grew more shallow with each giant step, and soon, not only Tommy's head but the top half of his body were clear of the water. He paused and looked back towards the island, as amazed as anyone that he had come this far.

The boat shifted suddenly as Tommy let go with one hand. It did not tip too far, though, so strong was the giant's remaining grip. The companions didn't know what the giant was up to, but then they heard Tommy pull the snorkel from his mouth.

"Duh, the Lady will be happy with me," the companions heard him say, to their absolute relief. But then, to their surprise and dismay, Tommy grabbed the boat in both hands again, turned around, and headed back towards the island.

"Stop him!" Kelsey mouthed silently at Gary, the elf's face contorted with frustration.

Gary looked around desperately. There was no escape; the land was simply too far away for them to even attempt a jump. Gary took a deep breath and leaned far over the edge of the boat. "No, Tommy," he called. "Get to the shore first, then we can go back."

Tommy spit out his snorkel in surprise. "Duh, what are you doing in my boat?" asked the confused giant.

"I . . . we," Gary stammered.

Mickey started a spell, but before he could get it off, Tommy lowered the boat down by his chest and looked less than thrilled to see the four companions inside. "Hey!" he cried.

"You held the boat up too high when you passed us on the jetty," Gary blurted suddenly. "We couldn't get the rocks inside, so we climbed in instead. The weight is about . . ."

"You tricked Tommy!" the giant roared. "The Lady wants you to stay on the island!" He started to turn back, but Geno, horrified at the thought of going back to face the witch, whipped a hammer into his chest. The weapon bounced off without doing any serious damage, and, as a pointed reminder to the companions, it dropped into the water and dissolved before their eyes.

Kelsey rushed up beside the giant, his sword bared and point aimed in towards Tommy's heart. "To the shore!" the elf demanded.

He almost got his wish. With a great growl, Tommy heaved the boat towards the shore, but it didn't quite make it, landing with a tremendous splash a few feet from the beach. Ceridwen's spell began its wicked work immediately—the boat started to sizzle and sputter, white smoke rising up from its timbers.

Kelsey and Geno went into action, grabbing bundles and hurling them to shore. Geno picked up Mickey and flung him to the beach, then grabbed Gary and, before the stunned man could protest, put him up above his head, spun him about twice to gain momentum, and launched him as well.

Gary landed heavily on the rocky shore. He rolled to a sitting position, spat sand from his mouth, and regarded Mickey, sitting next to him. "From eating rocks, huh?" Gary remarked.

Kelsey leaped across the ten-foot gap with no trouble, but the dwarf did not follow. Geno considered the jump and considered the consequences of not getting out of the fast-breaking boat, but the dwarf knew that his bandy legs couldn't possibly propel his body all the way to the shore.

"Who is the next best smithy in the world?" Kelsey, ever the pragmatist, inquired of Geno.

Geno couldn't jump the ten feet but his spit made it across easily enough.

"Help him, Tommy!" Gary cried. "The water will kill him!"

The giant regarded the boat curiously, scratching his head. Geno couldn't wait for him to make up his mind.

"Come and play, blockhead!" the dwarf roared, and he twirled another hammer Tommy's way.

Of all the insults one might throw at a giant, none could stir such a creature more than "blockhead." Tommy growled and charged and Geno got up on the very lip of the boat closest to shore. When Tommy crashed over the back of the splintering boat, the other end, Geno's end, went high into the air. The dwarf timed his leap perfectly, using the momentum of the tilting boat to send him high and far. As Gary had done with the stone wave back in Dvergamal, Geno easily cleared his friends. He soared past and came down headfirst into a huge chunk of stone, laughing wildly all the way, even after he had bounced off.

Their troubles were far from over, though, for Tommy bounded up onto the shore, his big fists clenched in rage. "You told Tommy that it would please the Lady!" the giant sputtered.

"I'm sorry, Tommy," Gary replied sincerely, making no move to either run or defend himself "But we had to get off that island. Ceridwen would have killed us all."

"She will be mad at me."

"Then go back in the lake and drown," Geno offered. Tommy's next words came out as undecipherable, guttural snarls and he advanced upon the dwarf. For the first time since he had met Geno, Gary sensed that the dwarf was afraid.

"Why, Tommy?" Gary asked simply, leaping up to catch hold of the giant's fist.

Tommy looked down at him. "Why?"

"You're free now," Gary explained. "You don't have to go back to the island, or if you do go back, you don't have to tell Ceridwen how we got off the island."

"She will be mad at me," the giant said again.

"No, she won't," Gary insisted. "Not unless she finds out what happened." He and the giant stared at each other for a long while, Gary finally slipping from Tommy's fist back to the ground. Tommy had no further designs on Geno. He went over to the water's edge and sat down, putting his chin in his huge hands.

Kelsey intercepted Gary before he could get near his forlorn friend.

"Leave him, lad," said Mickey, agreeing with the elf. "We cannot wait here, and if we're found near the giant, then all the worse for him."

Gary hated to go, but he couldn't disagree. They scooped up their bundles and set off along the mountain trail, leaving the giant to his staring and his thinking.

EIGHTEEN

SMORGASBORD

"We have come too far to the south," Kelsey explained when they entered a valley that allowed them to look out beyond Penllyn's peaks. The elf pointed back to the north, to the distant towering mountains of Dvergamal. "But we are closer to Giant's Thumb now than before the trolls captured us, and the ground between here and the mountain should be easier traveling once we have broken free of these mountains."

"Not so easy in the Crahgs," Geno remarked, but no one seemed to hear.

"Giant's Thumb?" Gary asked Mickey.

"That's where Robert makes his lair," the leprechaun explained. "Not too big a mountain—not as big as those in Dvergamal—but flat-topped and big enough to keep the dragon comfortable."

"Robert?" Gary asked. "Who is this Robert?" It was the second time Gary had heard the leprechaun speak the name, but he thought it wise not to mention his previous eavesdropping.

Mickey gave him an incredulous stare. "The dragon," he answered. "Have ye not been listening?"

"A dragon named Robert?" Gary had to remind himself of the gravity of their situation, of all that they had come through and could expect to yet face, to keep from bursting out in laughter.

"Robert the Righteous, he calls himself," Kelsey put in.

"Though most others peg him as 'Robert the Wretched,'" Mickey added with a snicker. "It's not his real name, of course, not a name for a dragon. But that's a hard one, harder than Kelsenellelll . . . oh, well, ye get me meaning."

"Only thing harder to pronounce than the name of an elf is the true name of a dragon," Geno clarified grumpily. He gave Kelsey a derisive stare. "At least dragons have the courtesy to give themselves an easier title that people can use when addressing them."

"Afore they're eaten," Mickey had to add.

Gary looked from one of his companions to the other, as lost in the conversation, and all the innuendo he instinctively knew was flying about, as he was in this strange world. For the first time, Gary gave careful consideration to this upcoming beast. When Mickey had first mentioned the quest, and the dragon, Gary had thought this whole adventure a dream and had not given it too much thought. Between then and now, the young man had simply been too busy just keeping himself out of trouble to think about what lay at the end of his road. Now, though, with Ceridwen's island behind them and Kelsey promising a clear road to Giant's Thumb, the dragon—Robert the Righteous, or Wretched, or whatever title best fit the beast—inevitably hovered about Gary's thoughts.

"How big is this dragon?" Gary asked a short while later. Mickey was back on his shoulder, the leprechaun having no chance of matching the elf's eager pace with his tiny legs.

"Read your Mr. Tolkien, lad," the leprechaun replied. "Seems he got the dragon part right, at least. Aye, he's been to Faerie, that one. Not a secondhand account o' that Smaug creature. I'm just a bit surprised that since he seen it, he got back to yer own world to write about it!"

Gary started to say, "You're kidding," but changed his mind, realizing that the leprechaun spoke with all seriousness. And given his own unbelievable situation, how could Gary say with certainty that Tolkien had not visited Faerie? Or so many other of the fantasy writers he loved to read? And what about the common folktales of a dozen different countries, particularly Ireland and Scotland? Might those legends of elfs and sprites, dragons and bandy-legged dwarfs, be based on the actual experiences of simple farmers?

"What're ye thinking?" the leprechaun asked him, seeing his face crinkled in confusion.

"I don't even know," Gary replied honestly, for the notion had over-whelmed him.

"Well, if ye're thinking of old Robert, then don't ye bother," Mickey said, and Gary couldn't help but notice that the leprechaun's tone had taken on a grim edge. "Ye cannot imagine a dragon, lad. Nothing yer mind'd conjure could come close to the truth.

"Read yer Mr. Tolkien again, lad," Mickey went on. "Read and be afraid. Ceridwen's made the day dark for us, but Robert will make it darker still!"

Gary took out *The Hobbit* and considered opening to Bilbo's first encounter with the dreaded dragon. Then he thought the better of it and put the book back into his pocket. No sense in scaring himself, he figured.

Robert would do it for him.

"I told ye they'd come walkin' back from the witch's island," one troll boasted to another, seeing the companions crossing the lower trails near to the edge of Penllyn. "We gots to go tell Earl!"

"Meat fer the table," the other agreed. "Them bunnies was good, but a dwarf pie'll taste better!"

"An' manflesh and elf-on-a-stick!" said the first. "And the little trickster's goin' in me mouth before Earl gets 'is fat paws on 'im!"

The other troll punched him in the eye. "In *me* mouth, ye ogre baby," the troll protested. "I seen 'im first."

"*I* seen him first!" the first troll argued back, but he didn't move to retaliate physically, more concerned with dinner than with fighting at that moment. "But I'll split the trickster with ye—right down the middle!"

The other troll smacked his lips with his big fat tongue and rubbed his greedy hands together. "Let's go get Earl," he offered. "Me belly's growlin' awrful."

The companions ran on long past sunset, none of them complaining about putting the miles between them and Ceridwen's island and all of them anxious to be out of the dark mountains. When they finally set camp, on a high flat rock with the empty plain in sight and the scattered bumps that were the Crahgs beyond it, they agreed, again without protest (except a squeak from Mickey—and Kelsey said that didn't count because Mickey was always complaining), that they wouldn't start a fire. The night was chilly for the season, with a cold wind blowing down across the empty miles from Dvergamal—the last remnants of the Cailleac Bheur's summer storm, Mickey reasoned. A full moon made its way up above them, bathing all the land in silvery light.

Gary got up often, rubbing his arms and walking briskly in circles to keep his circulation going. He knew that he would get little sleep that night, but he didn't care. They had come to the last stage of their journey, for better or worse, and he knew that a little weariness wouldn't slow him down.

He felt better, too, about having the sentient spear back on his belt. He sensed that the weapon was communicating with him almost constantly, though not on a level that he could consciously respond to. It was just a feeling he got, a subconscious bonding. Whatever was happening, Gary carried his normal spear with growing confidence, thinking that if it came to blows again, he would know what to do.

Still, he wasn't pleased to find out if his instincts were correct quite so soon.

Kelsey saw the dark silhouettes shortly after midnight, circling the camp at a wide radius, cutting in and out of the shadows of jagged boulders and rocky outcroppings. The elf and dwarf agreed that the big shapes were trolls, and the fact that there were four of them led them all to believe that they had met this particular band before.

"Four against four," Gary whispered, crouching beside Kelsey and Mickey and popping his loose-fitting helmet onto his head. "Even odds."

"Anyone who's ever fought trolls'd tell ye that even numbers don't make for even odds," Mickey was quick to point out.

"We nearly beat them before!" Geno growled. "And there were seven of them then!" As if to further his point, the dwarf sent a hammer spinning out into the darkness, heard a thump, and grunted in pleasure as a troll groaned.

"You see?" the beaming dwarf asked, looking so much again like a disreputable youngster with his one tooth missing and his cat-ate-the-canary smile.

Things didn't follow the exact course that Geno expected. Kelsey cocked back his bow, Geno readied another hammer, but before they began their assaults, several large rocks came bouncing into the small camp. One caught Gary in the chest and blew the air from his lungs, sending him flying over backwards. Kelsey managed to dive around a second throw, but his evasive action took him right into the path of a third. He twisted and rolled, but the rock caught him squarely in the knee and sent him spiraling down to the ground.

Mickey threw up one of his umbrellas. Lying next to the leprechaun, Gary wondered what good it would do, but amazingly a rock heading straight for the sprite hit the umbrella and bounced harmlessly away.

"You got one of those for me?" Gary asked weakly, struggling to get back to his feet.

Geno launched a hammer and scored another hit (at least another troll groaned as though it had been hit), but a second volley of rocks thundered in. The dwarf was the main target this time, and he was struck twice, though the missiles appeared to do little damage and hardly moved him. One soared past Geno, though, and scored another hit on Kelsey, knocking him flat.

And then the trolls were upon them.

Mickey lit up the area with an eye-stinging flash of light.

"Go to Kelsey!" Gary instructed Mickey. The leprechaun seemed hesitant to leave the inexperienced human, but Kelsey, out cold on the ground, seemed in more dire peril. Mickey leaped over to the prone elf and conjured an illusion to make Kelsey appear as a part of the flat rock. Then the leprechaun prudently faded into invisibility, hoping that no trolls had noticed his actions.

Geno went into his customary troll-battle maneuvers, darting between legs, stomping his hammers down on troll toes, and generally making life miserable for the two attacking him.

One of the trolls—Gary recognized him as Earl—went over towards where Kelsey had been lying, sniffing the air and prodding the ground suspiciously. Out of the illusion came Kelsey, sword leading, and Earl got a good cut on the arm for his efforts.

Gary squared off against the fourth of the group. He held his spear and shield in front of him, feeling their balance. The troll came straight in, unafraid, swinging its heavy club for Gary's head.

Gary went down low beneath the blow and countered with a sharp spear jab that poked the troll in the belly and sent it hopping back onto its tiptoes. Gary used the break to circle to the side opposite the troll's weapon hand. The monster turned with him, more apprehensive now.

A second swing from the troll fell harmlessly short. Gary started to counter, then thought the better of it, for the troll was recovering much more quickly this time.

The monster tensed; Gary knew another swing was coming. As the troll's arm came about, Gary dropped forward to his knees, braced his shield against his shoulder, and angled it to deflect the club harmlessly high. At the same time, he got his spear in line with the troll's hand, angled so that the weapon's butt end remained tight against the ground.

The troll howled in pain and its club went flying as it drove its hand deep onto Gary's spear tip. Gary's own clever actions amazed him, but he knew that this was not the time to gloat, nor to pause and consider his fortunes. He came up from his knees, bowling straight ahead, and got two or three good spear pokes in on the troll before it recovered enough so that he was forced to back off.

The creature stood staring at Gary dumbfounded, clutching its wounded hand, and with several trickles of blood running down its filthy shirt.

The two trolls fighting Geno were growing dizzy indeed as the dwarf, slapping and cursing every step of the way, continued his wild darting. Always, the trolls' counters seemed one step behind Geno, coming crashing down onto the hard rock at the dwarf's heels as he slipped between the monsters or between their widespread legs.

"'Ere, watch where ye're swingin'!" one of the trolls warned the other, having had the misfortune to have battled the cunning dwarf in the previous fight as well. "He's lookin' to get ye to hit me!"

The dwarf charged in on it as it spoke, and the troll, thinking it had its diminutive opponent's tactics figured out, quickly pulled its legs together. Geno's hammer led the way, smashing the inside of the troll's left knee. The legs went back apart and the dwarf darted through, smacking the inside of the right knee as he passed.

The other troll had come around to intercept, and the dwarf spun about, but slipped on the flat stone and skidded down.

Two trolls hovered over him, clubs raised and yellow-toothed smiles wide.

Kelsey fought valiantly for many seconds, spinning his sword about and in too quickly for Earl to launch any counterstrikes. The elf was hurt, though, bleeding from the side of his head and unable to use his legs to keep him out of Earl's reach.

Earl recognized this advantage immediately and tossed the club to the ground, reaching in with both hands. Kelsey nicked one, then the other, then cut a third time at the first arm. Earl seemed not to notice, and wrapped a huge hand about Kelsey's waist.

A dart appeared from nowhere, arcing through the air to find a resting place on Earl's big nose. Kelsey was free again as Earl tried to pull the stinger out.

"Won me championships three years in a row," Mickey boasted, coming visible again and putting another dart into Earl's face. Kelsey smiled and joined in the fun, more than willing to take advantage of the distraction. He stepped right in and drove his sword in and down above Earl's kneecap.

"Ye cut me hand," the monster whined.

"More than that," Gary promised. He pumped his arm as if to throw, then leaped ahead instead, dropping his heavy and pointy-tipped shield onto the troll's toe. He knew that he was vulnerable right beneath the towering giant, but knew, too, that quickness was on his side. The troll, after a howl, had just begun to bend low to grab at him, when the spear came rushing up, blasting out a troll tooth and widening the creature's smile.

The troll fell back, staggered, and for some reason, Gary had no doubt at all that he would win this fight. Still, he was surprised when the troll's eyes went wide and the creature turned suddenly and sped away.

If he had not been so self-congratulatory at that point, Gary might have realized that the suddenly terrified troll had looked right past him.

Geno hoped that one of the trolls would pick him up and try to put him in a sack. At least that way, he'd have the satisfaction of getting a few more good strikes in before going out of the fight.

The trolls weren't intent on capturing the companions this time, the dwarf soon realized, and he realized, too, that he had no way of getting away from the great clubs.

But then one of the trolls rose up from the ground and went flying away into the darkness. The other troll stared ahead blankly, its eyes going up, up, up, until it met the gaze of Tommy One-Thumb.

On a troll's list of things to avoid, giants ranked just below dragons, and the terror was obvious in this troll's scream as it whipped its club across at Tommy.

The giant did wince, a little bit, as the club rebounded off his massive chest, but he did not fall back. Tommy came with a backhand response that caught the troll on the side of the head and sent it flying head over heels.

Gary had seen many wondrous things since coming to Faerie, but none of them outdid the spectacle of a twelve-foot-tall troll spinning through the air. He heard the resounding thump as the creature landed, and then heavy footsteps pounding away into the night.

"He's got me darts!" Gary heard Mickey yell, and then Earl loped past him. Strictly on instinct, Gary dropped to the ground, hooking his foot in front of Earl's huge ankle. Without even considering the move, Gary came across with a vicious spear swipe that caught the fleeing troll in the back on the knee (his one remaining good knee) and sent him crashing facedown to the stone. Without the slightest hesitation, Gary ran up the monster's back and dove headlong. His spear caught Earl on the back of the neck and drove up under the troll's thick skull bone.

Earl slumped back to the ground, shuddered once or twice, and expired.

Gary lay on the troll's back for a long time, holding tightly to his spear, hardly believing he had so efficiently dispatched such a powerful creature. When he finally looked back over his shoulder, he saw that Mickey and Kelsey shared his disbelief.

"When did ye learn to fight like that?" the leprechaun asked.

Gary had no answers for him—until a voice rang out in his mind. "*Thou has done well.*"

"You taught me," Gary replied out loud, looking down to the broken weapon on his belt.

"I did no such a thing," Mickey replied.

"Not you," Gary explained.

"The spear led ye through the fight?" Mickey asked.

Gary thought for a moment, then shrugged, unsure of exactly what had happened. In the previous fights, the spear's communications had been obvious, but if the spear had instructed him during this battle, he had not noticed. Still, Gary realized that he could not have fought so well on his own instincts. He wondered how closely he and the sentient spear had bonded, and which one had been in charge during the battle.

"Whatever it was, lad, ye did a fine job," Mickey went on, and Kelsey, wincing in pain again, nodded his head slowly in agreement.

"And Tommy saved us," Gary replied, speaking directly at Geno. The dwarf said nothing, just walked by Gary and spat on his sneaker.

"I'll take that as a thank-you," Gary said, a smile finding his face. He moved quickly (wisely) away from the dwarf and over to Tommy.

"You have our thanks, Tommy," he offered, reaching up to grab ahold of the giant's huge hand. "But why did you follow us?"

"He probably means to take us back to that stupid witch," Geno fumed.

"Tommy had nowhere else to go," the giant answered simply.

An idea came to Gary, but Mickey, seeing his face light up, was quick to squelch it.

"The giant's not coming to Robert's lair," the leprechaun insisted. "And better off he is for not coming!"

"He's a great fighter," Gary replied, confident that he would win this debate. "We might need . . ."

"Not so great against the likes o' Robert," Mickey was fast to interrupt. "If it comes to a fight, lad, he'd go down as quick as the rest."

"What are you talking about?" Gary yelled in reply. "We're going off happily to battle some dragon and you refuse allies? If it's that hopeless, they why are we going? How can we think that we might win?"

"You'll not be fighting the dragon," Kelsey replied evenly. "I will."

"You can hardly stand up," Gary shot back, more harshly than he had intended.

"I must fight the dragon in single combat," Kelsey explained. "And subdue the creature. If we brought the giant—if we brought an army—and killed the beast, what good would it be to us? No, we must get Robert's cooperation, and that can only be achieved in a challenge of honor."

"Then why can't Tommy go along?" Gary asked.

"Because dragons fear giants," Kelsey replied. "And if Robert is afraid, then he will fight us all and kill us before I even offer my challenge." The elf turned to Tommy. "You do indeed have our thanks, noble giant. And you may come with us across the brown plain and the Crahgs as far as the Giant's Thumb, if you are not afraid. But when we go up to the dragon's lair, we go alone."

Tommy just looked at Gary and shrugged again. When they broke camp the next dawn and began their run across the rolling hills, they were five, not four.

NINETEEN

THE CRAHGS

The companions passed through the rolling farmlands between Dvergamal and Penllyn without incident, taking shelter at night in ancient stone farmhouses, long deserted and with nothing left at all of their thatched roofs. In better times, when Ynis Gwydrin had been the seat of goodly power and not in the possession of evil Ceridwen, these farms were among the finest in all of Faerie, Mickey explained grimly to Gary.

Gary detected that faraway look in the leprechaun's gray eyes, that distant longing for times long past. Suddenly Gary found himself wishing that he could see Faerie at its magical glory, that he could walk in the land of twilight fancies and walking fairy tales.

This wasn't it, and if Gary doubted that fact for one moment, all he had to do was conjure an image of mud-filled Dilnamarra or of the poor souls hanging at the crossroads, turning slowly in the stench-filled breeze.

As the companions continued east the rolling hills and rock walls gave way to taller, more imposing mounds.

"The Crahgs," Mickey mentioned, obviously not at all pleased by the sight. The mountains appeared as great balled lumps of green grasses, interspersed with stone and plopped down randomly on the rolling fields. They rose up two or three thousand feet, with the tops of many shrouded by low-riding clouds, thick and gray and mysterious. Small but tightly packed groupings of trees sat on the sides of many of the Crahgs, usually huddled in sheltered dells from the unending winds, and every mountainside sported streams of crystalline water, dancing down in trenches of bare stone, leaping over rocky breaks in the otherwise smooth decline.

Gary didn't at first know what to make of this place. It seemed a land of paradoxes, both imposing and inviting, magnificently beautiful yet strangely eerie and untamed. Even the light came in uneven, unexpected bursts. One steep side of two joined mounds disappeared into mist at the top, while only a hundred feet down, the wet grass gleamed and rivulets sparkled in a distinct line of sunny brightness. Just a short distance below the sunshine loomed the shadow of another cloud, dark and foreboding.

Full of life, yet full of melancholy. The paradox of existence itself, Gary thought, of vital life and quiet death.

The companions spoke little as they hiked their way into the Crahgs, for the wind carried away all but the loudest shouts, and none of them felt secure enough to yell out. Silently they climbed and descended, under rushing clouds, in rain showers that lasted but a few minutes and sunshine that shared a similar, brief life.

The first day hadn't been so bad, and Gary had thought that the second would be easier, on his emotions if not on his body. But the Crahgs were no less eerie that second day, and Gary had the distinct feeling that he and his friends were being watched, every step, by eyes that were not friendly.

"Loch Devenshere," Mickey explained on the afternoon of the third day, when the group rounded a rocky outcropping and came in view of a long and narrow lake. The waters continued on beyond sight in the east, cutting between poised and ominous lines of crahgs. All the world seemed a patchwork quilt of green and gray to Gary as he looked out over the sun-speckled landscape. Below him, the waters of Loch Devenshere bristled under the wind, deep and dark—and cold, he could tell from the sudden chilly and moist bite of the breeze.

"Do we feel safe enough to cross?" Mickey asked Kelsey. The elf looked up to the sky, then back to the loch, finally settling his gaze upon Tommy. "The waters of the loch are far too deep for a giant to walk them," Kelsey quickly explained, seeing Tommy taking out his makeshift snorkel.

"We'll save days of walking by going across," Mickey reasoned, and he didn't have to add that all of them, that all of their weary feet, could use a break from the difficult hike.

"So spend a day in strapping a raft that will hold the giant," Geno put in, casting a none-too-happy glance Tommy's way. "Or leave him here—we already decided that he will not go all the way to the Giant's Thumb."

Gary grew alarmed at the resigned looks Kelsey and Mickey exchanged, fearing that Geno's blustery suggestion might actually be accepted. "You can't just leave him," Gary protested.

"There's not much wood to be found, lad," Mickey explained grimly. "I'm not for thinking that we'll get together a boat big enough to hold that one's weight."

Gary really couldn't argue against that reasoning, and he, too, had no desire to continue the brutal hike if it could in any way be avoided. But neither did Gary want to leave Tommy behind, alone in this strange and eerie place. "Compromise," Gary said at length. "Build the boat for us and keep it close to the shore. Tommy will keep up and keep in sight. He can get around these hills faster than us."

Mickey nodded, as did Kelsey, in acceptance of the compromise. Tommy had gotten them over obstacles that would have otherwise turned their path to the side many times in the last two days, and no doubt the giant could have crossed on an even straighter path unencumbered by his diminutive companions.

"Are ye up for it?" Mickey asked the giant. "The ground's sure to be hard going."

"Tommy likes mountains," came the giant's even-toned reply.

Kelsey nodded; he would not so quickly abandon their valuable companion. Even Geno did not seem too upset that the giant would parallel them on the shore, and the dwarf returned Kelsey's nod with an uncomplaining shrug of his broad shoulders.

With Tommy's powerful assistance, the group soon had two huge logs snapped together and in place on the waters of Devenshere. Gary and Kelsey worked to flatten the top of the raft and lessen its weight while Geno fashioned oarlocks and a rudder of stone. Thinner logs were soon shaped as oars, and the companions even managed to get a sail up, using Kelsey's forest-green cloak.

Tommy gave them a huge push for a start, and off they cruised, Gary working the sail (which didn't prove too effective) and Geno pulling tirelessly and mightily at the oars (which kept the raft rushing along at a great pace). Their path was smooth and straight, unlike Tommy's, but the giant, striding across sharp ravines and stepping over huge boulders, had no trouble keeping pace.

Gary worried when Kelsey flatly denied his request that they anchor for the night, allowing Tommy some rest. "The giant will keep pace with us," the elf declared, and he would hear no more of Gary's arguments. He didn't have to remind Gary of what they had left behind them, of the pursuit that would surely soon come.

They floated on easily through the night, putting many miles behind them. When the sun came back up, a lighter blur through the gray clouds, Gary was quite relieved to see that tireless Tommy had indeed kept pace with them through the hours of darkness. The giant moved easily, incredibly gracefully, across the trails and rocks lining the shore. There loomed no weary shadows on Tommy's face and he was even singing to himself, Gary noted with some amusement.

With his fears for Tommy eased, Gary's thoughts became as calm and smooth as the cold, dark water below them on the serene loch. He munched his morning meal and purposely kept any thoughts of Robert the dragon from his mind. Instead, the young man from that faraway world concentrated on nothing at all, allowed himself to bathe in the melancholy and majesty of the beautiful land about him. Whatever this adventure might be—even insanity— Gary did not want to lose these incredible images, wanted to engrain them indelibly on his mind and carry them with him for all of his life.

A ripple far to the side of the raft caught his attention away from the drifting mountains. Gary blinked many times, his trance dispelled, as a serpentine head appeared above the waters of the loch, rising up five to ten feet, followed in its meandering course by a dark hump and then a second.

Gary's mouth drooped open; his biscuit fell from his hand and rolled into the water.

"Don't ye be feeding her!" Mickey barked at him suddenly. The leprechaun darted to the edge of the raft and scooped the biscuit from the water. "Sure'n then she'd follow us all the way across!"

"She?" Gary barely managed to stammer. Continuing their course towards the center of the loch, away from the raft, the neck and humps slipped gently under the surface.

Wide-eyed still, Gary looked to Mickey. "Nessie?"

The leprechaun didn't seem to understand. Mickey's cherubic, bearded face crinkled profoundly.

Gary didn't press the point. He turned back to the open loch, its waters calm again save the bristles from the breeze, and watched, fearful yet intrigued. Too many questions came at him; too many possibilities. Out there, vulnerable on the makeshift raft, Gary desired the predictable days of home.

And yet, there remained in the young man that nagging yearn for adventure, that flickering flame of spirit that sent tingles along his spine as he held his gaze steady on the dark waters, searching for a monster on a deep and dark loch in a remote and untamed land.

He saw no more of the mysterious "she," but the tingles along his spine did not diminish for a long, long while.

As they rounded one bend in the loch, near twilight of that second day, the Crahgs seemed to part before them and Gary was treated to his first sight of the distant, dreaded mountain.

It seemed more akin to an obelisk than a mountain, a great cylinder of rock heaved up from the plain by long-past volcanic pressures. From this distance, Gary couldn't begin to guess how high the Giant's Thumb truly was, but that didn't make the spectacle any less imposing. Suddenly Gary found himself wanting to yell out at Kelsey and Mickey for bringing him along, to shake them good and tell them that there was simply no way they could hope to even get up the sides of that gigantic tower of stone. But he said nothing, and the view disappeared as abruptly as it had come when an opaque veil of gray mist floated past in the distant plain.

None of the companions, except for Tommy, was thrilled when they came to the eastern shore of Loch Devenshere. Reluctantly Gary pulled his sneakers back on his sore and swollen feet and tightened the many belts of Donigarten's armor. They camped before sunset, not far from the loch, and set off before sunrise with just a hasty breakfast.

Up and down, along winding trails, over boulder ridges and cold, dancing streams. Only the knowledge that they were nearing the end of the Crahgs enabled Gary to continue placing one foot in front of the other. Seeing his weariness, gentle Tommy offered to carry him, but Gary declined, thinking that the giant, without even the short reprieve of floating comfortably on the loch, had gotten the worst of this trip so far.

Unexpectedly the ground flattened out soon after, running along the lush and level base of a valley—Glen Druitch, Mickey called the place—for nearly a mile before rising up to form one final barrier to the plains beyond.

"The witch is modest this day," Mickey said grimly to Kelsey.

"Ceridwen?" Gary asked, overhearing.

"Not that witch," Mickey explained. The leprechaun pointed ahead to the visible end of the valley, and the end of the Crahgs: twin conical peaks shrouded halfway up to the top by a thick layer of fog. "The Witch's Teats," said the leprechaun. "She's wearing her veil, and that means trouble for wanderers in Glen Druitch, and in all the Crahgs."

"Can't we go around it . . . them?" Gary asked, suddenly not liking the look of that last obstacle.

"Too steep," Geno answered. "And too mean. There is just the one trail out from this point. Right through the cleft of the Teats."

"Or at least tight to their base," Mickey added grimly.

Kelsey suggested they pause and eat their lunch there in Glen Druitch before continuing, though the morning was barely half over. None disagreed, and so more than an hour passed before they at last came to the steep-sided twin mountains, sheets of rising green disappearing into low clouds, dotted by bare chunks of stone poking through the grass, and lined by several rushing and chattering streams. Kelsey spent a long moment staring up the Crahg, his gaze curious and, it seemed to Gary, just a bit fearful. Gary really didn't see anything different about this mound than the hundreds they had left behind, but he could not ignore the sense of dread that had obviously descended over his more knowledgeable companions.

Still, Gary was quite surprised when Kelsey announced that they would skirt the bottom of both Crahgs instead of clambering up through their cleft.

"That course will cost us two hours," Geno grumbled, considering the wide girth of the Witch's Teats.

"Skirt them," Kelsey said again, casting a sidelong, uncomfortable glance to the concealing cloud high up the slope. Mickey and Geno exchanged worried looks and Geno veered a bit to the side, heading for one small waterfall dancing through a tumble of boulders, as the others started off.

Gary spent more time looking behind, to Geno, than ahead, and he inadvertently kicked his foot against a jut of stone and fell headlong to the ground. Kelsey was upon him in an instant, roughly pulling him back to his feet.

"We have no time for blunders," the elf said in hushed tones, more sharply than Gary expected.

"I didn't mean . . ."

"What you meant does not matter," Kelsey argued as loudly as he dared. "Not here. Here, all that matters is what you did."

Gary's confusion only heightened a moment later when Geno grunted loudly. He and Kelsey turned back and saw the dwarf with his ear pressed against the stone behind the waterfall, a grim expression on his face. Finally Geno came out and looked at his companions, shaking his head resignedly and drawing out two hammers.

The moment seemed impossibly silent; not even the wind could disturb the calm.

Their emergence from the cloud veil was prefaced by a series of bone-chilling shrieks that stole the strength from Gary Leger's body.

"Crahg wolves!" he heard Mickey and Kelsey cry in unison, and he never had to ask what the two were talking about. Down the mountainside charged more than a dozen canine creatures. They resembled hyenas, though were much more slender, with dark gray, bristling fur and long and thick snouts. Their howls were part wolf, part human baby, it seemed, and part something else, something unnatural and evil.

They came down the steep slope at full speed, with front legs twice as long as their hind legs, allowing them to run downhill with complete balance. Long before they reached the companions, small groups of the cunning pack fanned out, left and right, flanking and surrounding their prey.

Geno darted out from the boulders around the waterfall and ran to another slab of rock set into the sloping side of the Crahg. One edge of this rock stuck out from the earth, allowing the dwarf to squeeze in behind it.

Watching the dwarf's movements, Gary at first thought that Geno had gone into hiding. But he dismissed that notion quickly, reminding himself that cowardice was not a part of the sturdy dwarf's makeup. Geno would fight any foe fearlessly, no matter the odds. While he took comfort in that knowledge, Gary had to wonder from the concerned looks on the faces of his other two visible companions (Mickey, of course, was nowhere to be found) just how bad these Crahg wolves might be.

Kelsey wasted no time in setting his bow to its deadly work. Arrow after arrow zipped up the hill, the elf concentrating his fire on the wolves that had circled to the right. One took a solid hit in the shoulder and began a yelping tumble; another caught an arrow right in the head and dropped straight down to the ground, skidding to an abrupt stop.

More shrieks echoed from above and another group of wolves came rushing out of the gray mist.

Gary heard a loud crack behind him and turned to see Tommy holding an uprooted tree. The giant shrugged, almost apologetically, and rubbed his foot across the ground where he had torn out the tree, trying to smooth the great divot.

It struck Gary then that part of Tommy's thick black hair was standing up straight, a curious cowlick, and he soon understood where the invisible, and opportunistic, Mickey had made his perch.

Kelsey continued to pepper the flanking wolf pack, each arrow finding a mark. The more immediate danger would come from straight ahead, Gary soon discerned, from the advance of the main pack.

The largest grouping of Crahg wolves came on fiercely, howling and drooling, eager for flesh. They hopped rocks and dropped over short abutments with ease, hardly slowing, hardly turning from the straight line to their intended victims.

The leading wolves came to one large and flat boulder, pressed against the grassy hillside with a sheer seven-foot drop beyond. On the wolves charged, taking no notice of the diminutive form wedged in the narrow opening between the rock slab and the ground behind it.

Geno, his back set firmly against the stone, let the first few wolves get past, then tightened his powerful legs and pushed with all his strength. The slab shifted out from the hillside so quickly that those wolves coming next could not adjust the angle of their charge.

Long forepaws dropped into the newly created ravine as the first wolf crashed in, slamming the bottom of its neck against the edged lip of stone. The creature's momentum carried it onward, bending it right over backwards as it rolled across the stone lip and down the hill beyond. Three trailing wolves were able to turn enough or duck enough to avoid a similar fate, but they slammed against the back side of the rock heavily and fell into the opened gully right beside the furious dwarf.

Gary shook his head in disbelief at the howl and yelps that came from behind that stone. One wolf clambered over the rock, trying to flee, but a stubby, gnarly hand appeared behind it, grabbing it by the tail and pulling it right back into the fray. Mud flew wildly; hammer-tops came up from behind the lip of the stone, then dove back down ferociously; a wolf paw appeared, sticking out one side of the rock, a wolf tail out the other. One wolf went flying up right above the stone, turning a complete somersault and then dropping back down into the dwarf's playroom.

But even with those four Crahg wolves dead or engaged, and with the pack of four to the right decimated by Kelsey's arrows, the fight was far from won. The third group of the first wave, also numbering four, rushed in from the left, and the ten more of the second wave came at the companions from above, prudently veering to avoid Geno's ravine.

Tommy hoisted his uprooted tree and rushed out to meet the closest attackers.

Up above, ten became nine as Kelsey fired one last arrow before dropping his bow and taking up his sword. The elf looked to Gary and nodded grimly.

"These are not stupid beasts—they will work together to separate us," Kelsey explained. "And then they will work to get at you from behind. Keep on the move, and turn often as you do."

Kelsey's predictions rang painfully true as the first wolf rushed in, heading straight for Gary, but then veering at the last moment to leap right between the young man and Kelsey. The creature took a severe hit from Kelsey's swift sword for its efforts, but its maneuver did the intended work, pushing the companions farther apart.

Then the wolves swarmed all about them, four to each, circling and nipping, looking for openings.

"*Thou must take the beasts one . . .*" the magical spear began to instruct Gary.

"I know how to fight them," Gary heard himself asserting, with a surprising (even to Gary) tone of confidence.

The spear imparted just one more thought before ending the communication altogether. "*Indeed.*"

In the tight quarters of the tiny ravine, the stiff-legged Crahg wolves found themselves at a serious disadvantage. The dwarf could not wind up very far with his hammers, but Geno didn't need to, popping the wolves with short and powerful chopping strokes. He had one wolf upside down and wedged low in the stone and earth gully, the creature kicking and howling pitifully. Whenever Geno found the opportunity, he smacked a hammer down on its back side, driving it deeper into the wedge.

One wolf managed to twist about and snap its jaws over Geno's forearm, drawing droplets of blood on the dwarf's stone-like skin. Geno clenched his hand as tightly as he could, flexing his smithy-hardened muscles so forcefully that the wolf's bite could not continue its penetration; the creature might as well have tried to tear through solid stone!

Geno whacked and hammered with his free arm to keep the remaining attacker off of him, then, when the opening presented itself, he used the wolves' own tactic, biting the nozzle of the wolf that was clamped onto his arm.

The beast yipped and thrashed, and let go of Geno's arm.

But Geno, growling every second, held firm his bite, even lifted the creature up before him with his teeth and pressed it against the stone wall, leaning against it with his heavy frame to smother its clawing kicks.

Thinking the dangerous dwarf fully engaged, the last wolf came back in.

Geno's hammer was waiting.

Tommy One-Thumb was not so fortunate. The giant's lumbering swipes with the uprooted tree could not match the speed and quickness of the darting wolves. They nipped at Tommy's heels, rushed between his legs, and kept him spinning and turning so fully that the giant soon found himself thoroughly dizzy.

Tommy leaned one way and then the other. A wolf threw its body against his thigh, trying to topple him; another leaped up high and bit Tommy on the hand.

Tommy knew that he must not fall. The wolves might cause him pain, but could do no serious damage against his massive legs. If he fell, though, more vital areas would surely be exposed.

He felt a pain in his calf, but ignored it, concentrating instead on simply keeping his balance, on stopping the world about him from turning. Gradually he began to reorient himself. The leaper came up again, snapping at Tommy's palm.

Stupid thing.

Tommy clamped his hand shut around the wolf's nozzle. He spun about and heaved with all his might, pitching the wolf head over heels back up the mountainside. It narrowly missed a rock, though that hardly mattered, for it crashed headlong into the slope, contorted weirdly with its tail end coming right up over the back of its head.

Tommy had no time to congratulate himself, though. There came again the pain in his calf, and then another bite, inside his thigh. The giant frantically tried to catch up with his attackers, but this only sent him spinning about again, and sent the whole world spinning around in Tommy's big eyes.

Gary wheeled and threw up his shield just in time to deflect a wolf charge from his back side. The young man could not take the time to calculate any maneuvers. He had to trust fully in his instincts now, and so far they had not let him down. Turning, thrusting, feinting, Gary continued to keep the four wolves at bay, but likewise, he did no real damage to them.

He knew that time would work against him, that he would tire long before his ravenous attackers.

A shriek turned him momentarily to the side, where a wolf lay dead, its head nearly severed. Now Kelsey, too, faced only four, and one of these was not so mobile, having taken a hit on its flank in its initial charge between the elf and Gary.

But Gary pushed away any hopes that Kelsey might soon come to his aid. Even if the elf managed to win out against the difficult odds, Gary doubted that Kelsey could get to him before the Crahg wolves tugged at his lifeless limbs.

Furthermore, Gary Leger was tired of being the extra baggage on this adventure. For his salvation this time, he would look no further than the end of his own spear.

A wolf snapped in low, but Gary dropped to one knee and dipped his shield sidelong to put it in line with the approaching foe. Sensing the creature's sudden reversal, Gary lifted the shield back upright and thrust straight out under its edge with his spear. The startled wolf, its head up, for it intended to leap over the dipped shield, caught the spear right through the base of its neck and down into its chest.

The creature issued a wheezing sound as Gary, realizing that every hit he made left him vulnerable to the other wolves, ripped the weapon out and frantically tried to rise and spin.

His clumsy shield hooked on the ground, slowing him, and only the fine armor saved his life, for a wolf leaped onto his back and bit at his neck.

Wolf jaws rushed in; Geno punched straight out, driving his hammer right down the creature's throat. The dwarf smiled grimly as he heard the canine jawbones crack and break. He let the wolf pull itself back from the hammer, but let the weapon fly to follow the creature's retreat.

It popped off the wolf's head, blinding it in one eye.

Geno slammed his heavy hand against the wolf he still pressed against the stone, pinning it by the throat. He finally pulled his face away, tearing off a chunk of the wolf's nose in his rock-munching teeth.

"Farewell, little doggie," the dwarf laughed, and, after just a moment to inspect his bitten arm, he nodded his satisfaction that the wound was not too serious and pounded home his second hammer, crushing the creature's skull.

Free again, Geno pulled another hammer from his belt and advanced on the half-blinded wolf. Its jaw broken, the creature had no desire to stick around and it had nearly scrambled over the blocking stone wall before Geno clamped his teeth onto its tail and held it in place. The wolf kicked with its short hind legs and tugged mightily, but then the dwarf's hammers went to work, pounding alternately against its exposed flanks. Wolf bones turned to sand under that brutal beating, and very soon the thrashing stopped.

Geno turned on the lone remaining wolf, still helplessly wedged upside down at the base of the stone.

"I would not want to be you right now," the dwarf said evenly, and, steady, too, was his determined advance.

Gary threw himself completely over, throwing his armor-enhanced weight right down on his attacker. The creature yelped briefly—for the split second it had any breath in its lungs—and Gary rolled over it, somehow managing to find his footing before the other two wolves overwhelmed him.

The wolf on the ground kicked and wriggled, but couldn't seem to right itself, indicating that Gary's crunching fall had snapped a vital bone or two.

The other wolves rushed at Gary from opposite sides, though. He flung his shield out to stop one, then tried to turn quickly enough to deflect the second. But again, the heavy shield hooked the ground, leaving Gary vulnerable.

He dove forward instead, narrowly dodging the flying creature's snapping maw.

"How did Cedric ever fight with a spear and this damned shield!" Gary screamed mentally.

"*He did not,*" the sentient spear on Gary's belt answered. "*King Cedric fought with spear alone. The shield was for ceremony, and for those times when Cedric chose to wield his sword.*"

Gary blinked and shook his head. He shook his arm, too, glad to be rid of the cumbersome shield. "Thanks for telling me," came his sarcastic thoughts.

"*I am here to serve,*" the spear answered sincerely, taking no offense.

Crahg wolves were not overly large creatures, nor were their jaws as powerful as those of normal wolves. Crahg wolves relied on numerical advantage, and also on their speed—jerky movements enhanced by the strange proportions of their legs.

In their fight with Kelsey, though, the Crahg wolves held no advantage at all.

Whenever a wolf came in at the elf's heels, it was met by a blinding backhand of Kelsey's fine sword. And unlike Tommy, Kelsey could spin and twirl endlessly, experiencing not the least bit of dizziness. He kept his balance perfectly, shifting his weight from foot to foot, and always with his sword poised to strike—at whatever angle necessary to turn back the closest wolf.

But Kelsey, too, knew that he could not hold a defensive posture for very long. While the elf did not fear that he would quickly tire, he knew that his less skilled and less agile companions would not likely hold out. And if either Geno or Gary was killed, killed, too, would be Kelsey's quest.

A wolf circled to Kelsey's right. Kelsey spun on it and took one step ahead, but backed off immediately as the creature hopped out of range.

A second wolf came in past the first, circling even farther to the elf's right. This time, Kelsey noticed something that the wolf did not.

He spun and charged, and the wolf hopped away. But Kelsey did not halt. Another bold step sent the wolf hopping backwards again, and this time it crashed into its wounded companion, the one Kelsey had first hit when it dove between him and Gary.

The wounded wolf faltered as it tried to get out of its comrade's way, for its sliced hip did not allow it much maneuverability. The healthy wolf scrambled and kicked but could not get away.

Kelsey's sword came thrusting in, once and then again.

Knowing two more creatures to be closing from behind, Kelsey rushed past his fresh kill, chopping down the wounded wolf as he passed. He spun about just beyond the bodies, lifting his sword in line for the closest attacker. The wolf veered, but too late; Kelsey hacked its long foreleg clean in half.

One against one, the remaining wolf had no heart to continue. It barked an impotent protest, turned, and fled. Kelsey started towards the limping, three-legged beast, but changed his mind and went for his dropped longbow instead.

Tommy stopped spinning, but the world did not. Nor did the pain in the giant's leg relent as the stubborn wolf held on. The giant started to bend low, thinking to grab hold of the wolf and launch it away.

The world spun too fast; the ground leaped up at Tommy.

Then he was lying on his back, looking curiously at the spinning clouds.

A dark form descended over him. Instinctively Tommy punched out with both hands, connecting solidly enough to knock the Crahg wolf aside. But his arms were out helplessly wide when a second dark form hurtled in at his exposed neck.

The wolf's snapping maw would have surely found a murderous hold had not a dwarven-hurled hammer intercepted its flight, spinning the creature right about in midair. The giant let out a muffled cry of surprise as the gray-furred beast flopped onto his face.

Instinctively again, Tommy's hands came back in together, wrapping the beast in a bear-like hug. The wolf bit at the giant's thick limb; Tommy's great arms squeezed in response. In such tight quarters, it was no contest.

Tommy won.

Without the encumbering shield, Gary became a whirlwind of movement, spinning, thrusting, and slapping with the butt end of his dwarven-forged spear so effectively that the remaining two wolves never got close to biting him.

He didn't think of tiring, didn't wonder if these movements were sentient-spear-guided or not. Gary didn't think of anything at all at that critical moment, reacting on pure instinct, letting his heart guide his movements more quickly than his mind ever could.

He almost stumbled but caught himself. The helm hid Gary's wry smile, for he continued to lean, purposely, and did not show his opponents that he had regained his balance, that he had his legs squarely under him. He even kept his spear out wide, appearing defenseless.

Expectedly a Crahg wolf rushed right at him.

Gary waited for the very last moment, then jumped straight up in the air, folding his legs under him. The startled wolf stopped abruptly and Gary crashed back down atop its back. The creature's legs buckled and flew out wide—was that snapping noise its backbone? Gary wondered.

Gary didn't wait to find out. He brought the spear in close and jabbed it straight down, straight through the wolf's back, with all his weight behind it.

The second wolf wasn't far behind the first. Gary ripped his spear free and reversed his grip on it as he fell over, away from the threat. Like Alice the lion in Ceridwen's chamber, the wolf's momentum carried it on, and in its helpless charge, it impaled itself upon Gary's deadly spear.

Gary kept the presence of mind to force the spear over and down to the side as the wolf slipped down its shaft, the doomed creature's jaws snapping frantically. It thrashed for a few moments longer, then lay very still.

Exhausted, his burst of energy spent, Gary dragged himself to his feet. To his right, Kelsey took careful aim and loosed an arrow, dropping the lone fleeing wolf.

Worried for the lying giant, Gary stumbled over to Tommy and Geno. Tommy held one squashed Crahg wolf close to his chest while the dwarf's hammers worked furiously on the wolf that was still stubbornly clamped onto Tommy's calf.

"It's dead," Gary remarked as he passed by the dwarf. Geno paused long enough to confirm the words.

"And stubborn," the dwarf replied, noting that death had down nothing to loosen the beast's tight jaws. Geno shrugged, put one of his hammers back into a loop on his belt, reached into a pouch, and took out a chisel instead.

"Are you all right?" Gary asked Tommy.

The giant nodded.

Geno's hammer smacked home on the chisel.

Tommy screamed and reflexively kicked, sending Geno soaring straight up into the air.

Thoughts of the Doppler effect flashed in Gary's mind as the flying dwarf, too, let out a rapidly diminishing howl. Gary wisely looked up as the dwarf cry again intensified, and he wisely dove to the side, flat to the ground alongside Tommy's head, as Geno the dwarven cannonball crashed in for a three-bounce landing.

Geno hopped right back up to his feet, glancing all about as though he was confused. Gary stayed on the ground, wondering if the dwarf would launch an explosive tirade.

"Hey, giant," Geno said instead, excitedly, after he spit out a clump of grass and dirt. "Remember that trick." He looked up again and scratched his brown hair, marveling at how high he had flown. "We might be using that one in our next fight!"

Tommy's reply echoed Gary's thoughts perfectly. "Duh?"

Gary started to pull himself back up to his feet, but stopped when he realized that something was odd about Tommy's prone posture. The giant's head was not flat to the ground, though the grass under it was certainly flattened and lying to the side.

Gary remembered then that someone was missing.

Mickey faded into view a moment later, looking thoroughly miserable pinned under Tommy's massive skull.

"Ye'd never guess how much a giant's head might weigh," the leprechaun remarked dryly.

Hearing the sprite, Tommy promptly lifted his head and Mickey slithered out.

"Run on!" Kelsey called to them suddenly, and his warning was surrounded by the distant howls of many more Crahg wolves.

Gary didn't know what to make of it all. The wolves had been formidable opponents, but no more so than many other creatures the companions had faced—and defeated. Why, then, did Kelsey and Mickey, and even gruff Geno, once again wear expressions of such profound fear?

"EEE YA YIP YIP YIP!"

The cry split the air like a chorus of a hundred sirens and a hundred cannons all at once. Gary's backbone seemed to melt away under that blast and he nearly fell to the ground.

"What the heck was that?" he gasped, after he had somewhat recovered.

"Run on, lad," Mickey said to him. "It's better that ye do not know."

TWENTY

CITADEL OF THE ROCK

"EEE YA YIP YIP YIP!"

It resounded off of every stone, coming at the companions from every direction.

"What is it?" Gary cried again, more frantically. He pulled and tugged at his spear, but it wouldn't come free from the impaled wolf.

Geno rushed over and pounded on the spear's butt end, pushing it nearly all the way through the gory mass. The dwarf ripped it out of the creature's body the rest of the way and tossed it, covered in blood, to Gary. Gary caught it tentatively and started to bend, to wipe the bloodied shaft on the wet grass, but then Tommy scooped him up and flew off in pursuit of Kelsey.

"EEE YA YIP YIP YIP!"

"What is it?" Gary demanded of Mickey, sitting atop Tommy's massive shoulder just above him.

The leprechaun, his face ashen and his expression more grave than Gary had ever seen it, ignored him and whispered something into Tommy's ear. Without slowing, the giant reached down as he passed Geno and scooped the dwarf into his other arm. Even carrying all three, the giant had no trouble in keeping pace with Kelsey, who was sprinting at a dead run.

Having no time for their original route around the base of both Crahgs, Kelsey scrambled for the pass between the Witch's Teats. The going was rough and the ground broken, but every time Kelsey got to a shelf or sharp ravine that would have slowed him, Tommy came up behind and hoisted him, or even tossed him, across.

"Crahg wolves!" Geno called, peering around the giant's wide girth to look behind.

"Run on!" Kelsey replied. "They cannot climb very well!"

Gary looked back and saw the truth of the elf's claims. The wolves were indeed in pursuit, but were lower down on the mountainside than the companions. With their long front legs, their progress was severely limited; some of them had even taken to trotting backwards up the slope, possibly the most curious thing Gary Leger had ever seen.

Despite their gains ahead of the wolf pack, none of Gary's companions breathed easier. They were not fleeing from mere Crahg wolves, the young man realized, but from something much more powerful.

Something much more terrible.

Up and down, around boulders and across sharp cracks in the weathered stone, they ran and they jumped. They came to the lip of a drop, perhaps fifty feet, above a brown pool of muddy water—or was it just mud? Gary couldn't be sure.

The path wound down to the side, steep and treacherous, and terribly narrow, promising slow going indeed.

"EEE YA YIP YIP YIP!" It came from every rock; the creature sounding that terrible call was behind them, beside them, in front of them—they just did not know!

Kelsey cried out and jumped. Still holding tight to Gary and Geno, and with Mickey holding tight to him, Tommy blindly followed.

They hit in a rush of mud and muck. Filthy water burst right under the lip of Gary's too-big helmet, splattering his face and flushing up his nose. He fumbled out of the helmet and saw Mickey gently descending below an umbrella, tilting the unorthodox parachute to catch the crosswinds and float him clear of the murky pool.

Gary shook his head at the leprechaun, always amazed. But not complaining, for he, too, wasn't really very wet. Nor was Geno, for Tommy continued to hold them up high, out of the muddy pool. Tommy had sunk in deeply, though, with just his head and shoulders up above the water level, and Kelsey, though he had managed to quickly scramble out of the water, was brown from head to foot.

"Keep moving," the elf instructed them. "We are still near to the Crahgs and can afford no delays."

Geno and Gary waited for a moment, then the dwarf looked curiously at Tommy. "Are you going to follow or not?"

Their gigantic friend seemed truly perplexed. "Tommy cannot move," the giant admitted after a brief struggle with the gripping mud.

Without a moment's thought, Gary slipped down from Tommy's arm into the pool. The water was only shoulder-deep to him, which should have put it somewhere around Tommy's knees. Yet, here Gary was, staring the giant directly in the eye.

"Oh, begorra," Mickey moaned, coming to the pool's edge and immediately comprehending their newest dilemma.

"He's ten feet into the mud," Gary reasoned gloomily. "At least."

"Oh, begorra," Mickey moaned again.

Kelsey looked fearfully back up towards the pass, then turned and considered the brown plains looming in the east.

"Not to worry," Geno asserted as Tommy carefully lifted him over to the edge of the water. The dwarf hopped around to the back side of the pool, inspecting the rock wall that formed its western border. "I can get him out," Geno claimed, nodding confidently at Tommy.

With that assurance, Tommy smiled widely as he hoisted Gary to the water's edge.

"Ye'll not pull him from that mire," Mickey replied to the dwarf. "Not if ye had a dozen ropes and a hundred dwarfs."

Geno agreed with the leprechaun's assessment wholeheartedly, but he had no intention of trying to pull Tommy out—not yet. The dwarf grabbed his largest hammer and began pounding furiously on the rock wall behind the pool. Kelsey grimaced at each resounding smack, glancing nervously up to the higher passes.

"The beast'll not come out o' the Crahgs," Mickey said to calm the elf. "The Witch's Teats marks the end of its domain."

"What beast?" Gary demanded.

"Ye heard it," Mickey replied casually.

"Heard what?" Gary shot back, frustration evident in his near-frantic tone.

"The haggis," Kelsey whispered softly.

"Wild hairy haggis," Mickey added grimly.

"Haggis?" Gary echoed incredulously. "Haggis?" The name was not new to Gary. In his bureau back home, he even had a sweatshirt depicting three small caricatures of Scotsmen and proclaiming them to be "Haggis Hunters Unlimited."

"You mean the little hairy creatures that run around the Scottish Highlands?" Gary asked.

"Not so little," Kelsey remarked.

"But more than a little hairy," added Mickey. "And mean, lad. Ye've never seen anything so mean as a wild hairy haggis."

Gary's incredulous stare did not diminish. Several times, he pinched himself on the arm and muttered, "Wake up.

Geno's victorious grunt turned them about. The dwarf had cracked a hole in the rock wall, and the water of the muddy pool was fast draining, leaving behind a quagmire, with the giant buried to the hips.

Kelsey produced some fine cord, while Geno began laying stones around the giant, giving Tommy something solid to use for leverage and giving the industrious dwarf a firm base from which he could begin to dig out the mud trapping his giant companion.

Gary could hardly believe the sight: the taciturn dwarf working frantically and determinedly to free a giant—a giant that Geno not so long ago had considered an enemy. And more than simple pragmatism was guiding Geno's actions, Gary knew, though none in the group would deny that Tommy was a valuable companion. Geno's determination now went beyond what the dwarf would do for a pack mule. Something wonderful had just happened back in dangerous Crahgs and here, now, in the muddy pool.

An undeniable bond of friendship.

Even with the teamwork, it took them more than an hour to get Tommy out of the mud. No more chilling cries came from the Crahgs, though, and no visible pursuit, of Crahg wolf or haggis.

Glad to leave the Crahgs behind, the companions cleaned themselves and their supplies as best they could and set out across the brown and blasted plain, with the Giant's Thumb, the lair of Robert, clearly in sight every step of the way.

In all his life, Gary had never seen such total desolation. The land was scarred, brutally and completely. They passed one long and wide patch of charred tree skeletons, once a teeming forest, and they came down into a flat region, a clay bed dotted with long puddles and small clumps of scraggly grass and weeds poking through at uneven intervals.

Many bleached bones lined the clay bed, fish bones, and before long, Gary realized that this area had once been a huge lake, as wide as Loch Devenshere, perhaps, though not as long.

"Aye, and so it was," Mickey confirmed when Gary asked him about it. "Loch Tullamore, she was called. Full of fish and full of beauty."

"But Robert, he did not like it," Mickey went on, his tone a combination of anger and sadness. The leprechaun paused and again came that faraway longing look in his gray eyes.

"What did he do?" Gary prompted after a while, honestly intrigued. After all, what could any beast, dragon or not, possibly do to a lake?

"He hissed it, lad," Mickey explained. "Breathed his fiery breath upon the waters until they were no more. Day after day, Robert the Wretched came here, steaming the waters of Tullamore away."

Gary had no comment to offer in response. The sheer scope of what Mickey claimed the dragon had done overwhelmed him, and his sense of dread only heightened when he looked up again at the distant obelisk-shaped mountain. Every step came harder to him then, every step towards the lair of Robert the Wretched. Fortunately for Gary's rattled emotions, the sight of the mountain was soon lost, for Kelsey led the troupe into a long and narrow crevice, a great crack in the clay-like ground. The walls, tight about Tommy's shoulders, rose up twenty feet on either side of his companions, and the trail wound on for many miles.

They camped that night on the plains above the crevice, the sheer stillness of the region serving as a testament to the dragon's ultimate desolation. Not a cricket chirped, and the fog came in early and thick, defeating any starlight offered by the evening sky. The next day, like the first, came hot and dreary, and unnervingly quiet. The mountain loomed much larger when the group gazed upon it before descending again into the crevice walkway, but Gary paid it as little heed as he could, preferring to keep his thoughts far away from the dragon and the dangers that lay ahead.

He could not ignore the sight late that afternoon, though, when the group emerged from the crevice, turning a final bend that again put them in direct line with the Giant's Thumb. Directly before them lay a small vale, cluttered by the charred remains of long-dead trees and a few patches of weeds and grass. And beyond the vale loomed the mountain.

Gary had to remind himself to breathe as he scanned up, up, up the side of that obelisk. And if the almost sheer cliffs of jutting and angular stones were not imposing enough, atop the mountain loomed a castle, its stonework walls and towers seeming as if they had grown right out of the natural stones as extensions of the mountainsides.

"We're going up that?" the stunned young man asked to anybody who could give him a rational answer.

"There is a more gradual road around the mountain's other side," Kelsey answered. "But we would find it crossing between the barracks of Robert's slave soldiers. This is our path."

"It must be five hundred feet," Gary protested.

Mickey lifted his tiny foot before him, comparing it to the scale of the enormous cliff. "Oh, five hundred feet at least," the leprechaun remarked. "Twice that'd be me own guess.

"Or just a hundred of his," Mickey added with a wink, casting a glance Tommy's way.

"We can't climb that," Gary asserted, his mood not improved at all by Mickey's attempted humor. "And what if there are guards on those castle walls?" Gary imagined buckets of hot oil rolling down at him, or a storm of arrows plucking him from a cliff that he had no desire to climb even if Kelsey could assure him that no monsters waited atop it. "And what kind of a dragon needs a castle anyway?" Gary protested.

"Our path is up," Kelsey announced, having no time for Gary's obviously terror-inspired rambling. "And the daylight is fast waning." The elf led them on, asking Geno to see what the stones would tell him concerning the swiftest and easiest path.

Tommy stood perplexed at the edge of the small vale. As soon as Gary looked at the pitiful giant, he understood, for Tommy had no chance of scaling the cliff all the way up to the dragon's castle. Even if he did manage to find giant-sized handholds, a climbing Tommy would certainly present an easy and obvious target for any castle guards. With the huge giant hanging out so many feet from the stone, guards up above could hardly miss him, even under the cover of night.

"Come along!" Kelsey instructed Gary sharply.

"Tommy cannot follow," Gary argued.

"Tommy was never meant to follow," Kelsey retorted. "We allowed him to come to the base of the mountain—that is all."

"Kelsey's right, lad," Mickey put in. "We've told ye already why the giant should not be going near to Robert's lair. It'd make the dragon uneasy and dangerous."

"We can't just leave him out here," said Gary.

"He'll be safer than the rest of us," Mickey reasoned.

Looking up at the imposing cliff and knowing what waited atop it, Gary couldn't honestly argue against the logic. He stared at his huge friend for a long moment.

"Tommy will wait," the giant assured him. He scratched his huge head, then pointed back to the crevice. "In there."

Gary nodded, managed a weak smile, and rushed to catch up to the others.

Kelsey led them through all the cover he could find in the vale. There wasn't much, actually, but the elf was not too worried, for if there were any guards along this side of the castle, the elf's sharp eyes couldn't spot them.

Without incident, the companions, now four again, made the base of the rock wall and started up. They discovered that the wall, which had looked so sheer from across the vale, was lined by many small ledges and walkways, but all of these seemed to lead nowhere and after a half hour of stretching up to reach the next handhold and inching their way along impossibly narrow ledges, they found that they had really made very little progress.

"Do the rocks tell you anything?" Kelsey whispered to the dwarf in frustration. "Is there no way up?"

Geno grunted and put his ear to the stone. He took out a small hammer and gave a series of light taps, which sounded to Gary like some strange code. The dwarf listened for a moment, then tapped again, then listened some more.

"Hmmm," the dwarf grunted, looking up at the distant castle walls and then back to his friends.

"The rock is not solid," he said evenly, though too loudly for Gary's or Mickey's liking. Both glanced nervously upwards to the castle, expecting a shower of arrows to come whizzing down at them.

"It seems sturdy enough to me," Kelsey replied quietly.

"Of course it is," Geno huffed, and he banged his forehead against the stone to accentuate that obvious point. "What I mean is that the mountain is not a solid block. It is honeycombed by caverns and tunnels."

"That would make sense," Gary concurred, his unexpected reasoning turning both Mickey and Kelsey to him.

"From the same volcanic pressures that formed the mountain," Gary explained. "From the steam and the pressure of the hot lava." Mickey and Kelsey looked to each other and shrugged incredulously, then turned back to Geno for an explanation.

"He speaks the truth," the dwarf said, giving Gary a sidelong glance. "I knew that there were caves before we ever started up, but I did not believe that they would aid us much. Now, though, I believe that some of them probably climb fairly high within the mountain. That might be a better path than out here—in the open."

Those words again inevitably turned their attention to the castle. A lamp was burning in one of the towers up above, and even Kelsey had to honestly admit that he felt vulnerable out on the ledge. While the elf was not fond of caverns, he had to admit as well that the climb would be long and handholds would not be easily found in the coming darkness.

"Ye're leading, elf," Mickey said. "But I'm thinking that the dawn will find us hanging halfway up the mountainside."

"Where will we find an entrance?" Kelsey asked Geno.

Geno put his ear to the wall and tap-tapped again, ever so lightly. "Down and around to the south," he announced a moment later.

They had spent the next few minutes clambering back to the ground and working their way along the mountain's base. After crossing one rocky outcropping of tree-like pillars of broken stones, they found themselves on the edge of yet another pool, this one wide and steamy and crimson red, even in the fast-fading light.

Geno and Kelsey, at the lead, did not dare to touch the water.

"Red from the blood of Robert's victims, no doubt," Mickey reasoned, and Gary suspected that a legend had just been born. He knew, too, that there was probably a quite natural explanation for the coloring of the water, an excess of iron oxide, or something like that, but after the looks he had received during his "volcanic pressures" lecture, he decided to keep the thoughts private. Besides, Gary thought, Mickey's explanation seemed more romantic and more fitting for the land of Faerie.

"We have a bit of a problem, elf," Geno said, pointing diagonally across the pool to the mountain wall behind it. "There is your cave entrance."

Kelsey determinedly knelt down and dipped a hand in the ominous water. "It is warm, but not too hot," he said, as though he meant to hop right in and cross over.

"But how deep?" Mickey was quick to ask.

Gingerly Kelsey turned about and lowered one leg into the pool. Up to the hip, he had still not touched bottom.

"We're to have a rough time getting through that," the diminutive leprechaun remarked, aiming his voice mostly Geno's way.

"Tommy could cross it!" Gary piped in, somewhat loudly.

"Hush!" Kelsey scolded him, but the elf's ire faded away as Gary's idea rang true to him. "Go get your giant friend," he bade Gary, and the smiling man didn't have to be asked twice.

Tommy had little trouble carrying the four across the warm-watered pool. He kept his snorkel handy on his wide belt, but he found no need for it, for the

water never got deeper than the middle of his chest. Still, the other companions were genuinely appreciative of the giant at that time—Geno even patted
Tommy on the head once (when the dwarf thought that no one was looking).

They were at the tunnel entrance in just a few short minutes, and there, a
few feet above the level of the pool, they had to say goodbye to the giant once
more. Again, Tommy promised to wait back in the crevice. He turned about in
the crimson water and strolled away, leaving great ripples in his wake.

The companions watched him for just a moment before he was lost in the
gathering gloom, then they turned to their own path, the winding cave.

Already Kelsey, more accustomed to dancing under an open sky, seemed
unnerved. He produced a tinderbox from his pack and a torch and quickly lit
it, despite Geno's warnings that the light would "bring in every critter in the
whole damn mountain!"

Kelsey ignored him and pressed in. The cave was a curious formation, its
arcing walls scalloped and winding.

"Like the inside of a worm," Gary muttered under his breath, not wanting
the others to hear that rather uncomfortable, though accurate, description.

The light bounced back at them from a dozen angles, flickering ominously,
and Gary held his breath around every corner, imagining that a great dragon's
treasure hoard, complete with a great dragon, awaited. When he took the time
to remind himself that they were still in the outer and lower chambers, not far
at all from the cave entrance, Gary thought himself incredibly foolish.

Until he realized that his companions were holding their breath, too.

Still not so far in, the group came upon some bones lying scattered in the
corridor.

"Just fish bones," Kelsey assured them on closer inspection.

"But what brought them here?" Gary had to ask, and his answer came not
from any of his companions, but from the gigantic crab that rushed at them
suddenly from around the next bend.

Tommy plodded slowly back across the crimson pond, paying little heed to his
surroundings and thinking of nothing at all (Tommy was good at that).

Even if he had been alert, though, the giant would have had a difficult
time in distinguishing the red-shelled crab moving effortlessly under the red-
colored water.

A great vice-like pincer locked around Tommy's waist; another found a
stubborn hold on his shoulder. The giant tried to scream out in the hope
that his companions were not so far into the tunnel, but before Tommy
hardly knew what had happened, he was pulled under the suddenly not-so-
tranquil crimson waters.

TWENTY-ONE

FLIES ON THE WALL

It was surely the stuff of 1950s sci-fi B movies, its clacking hard-shelled legs scampering to keep it balanced in the scalloped, curving walls of the tunnel—a tunnel that the giant crab easily filled. Great jagged-edged pincers swayed and snapped ominously.

Kelsey reacted first, slicing his sword in at the closest menacing claw. The weapon, fine though it was, bounced harmlessly aside and the monster claw came around more quickly than Kelsey had anticipated, opening wide enough to envelop the elf.

Geno saved him. The dwarf slammed into Kelsey, knocking the elf safely aside, then, unexpectedly, rushed straight ahead, into the grip of the snapping claw. The dwarf lifted his arms up high as he wedged in tightly, keeping his hammer-holding hands free to punish the crab even as it tried to crush him.

Gary and Mickey gasped in unison, but the tough dwarf understood his rock-hard makeup better than they. The gigantic crab claw squeezed relentlessly, but it hardly seemed to bother Geno, singing a song now and drumming his hammers against the monster's stubborn shell.

Kelsey, seeing that the dwarf was in no immediate peril, scrambled over the clawing arm to get in close to the crab's face. His fine sword swiped across at a stalk, and a crab eyeball dropped to the tunnel floor.

Any thoughts of quick and easy victory blew away, though, as the wounded monster went into a frenzy, whipping its engaged claw up behind the elf and knocking Kelsey across the way, into the reach of the other deadly appendage. Kelsey skittered down to the floor, rolled to his back, and slashed wildly with his sword, struggling to keep the second claw up above him. He tried to scramble out, but the press of the monstrous limb was too great, and the crab too quick.

"*Now is the time for courage, young sprout,*" came a call in Gary's head. Gary hardly needed the encouragement, and about the only thing in the communication that he took note of was the sentient spear's continuing reference to him as a "young sprout."

He took up his dwarven spear in both hands, leveling its iron tip before him, and as soon as he found the opening, let out a roar and charged straight ahead, between the deadly claws.

* * *

Many minutes passed with the giant crab holding tight to Tommy. Tommy fought against his building panic, forced himself to remain patient. He had popped the snorkel into his mouth soon after the crab had pulled him under, and though the instrument's seal wasn't tight without the extra goo around it, the giant found that he could breathe readily enough.

Tommy wasn't the most powerful of thinkers, but he was cunning enough in battle, having taken care of himself in the wild mountains since his childhood days. He knew now that he could not break the crab's hold, not with one of his arms so tightly pinned, but guessed that the creature would likely loosen its grip when it believed Tommy to be drowned.

Another crab, a much smaller one, pinched hard on Tommy's toe right through his heavy boot. The giant grimaced and sublimated the pain, knowing that to move now would only convince his captor that much more time was needed to finish the drowning. And Tommy was running short on patience. In the trapped and terrified giant's thoughts, the water was beginning to hug him nearly as tightly as the crab.

When the claw finally loosened around Tommy's arm, the giant exploded into action. He pulled his limb free, punched and kicked, and scrambled for the shore. He got free for just a second, but then the relentless crab's claw caught him again, by the ankle. Tommy grimaced and tugged. He lost his snorkel and had to fight, not only to get to the shore but to keep his head above the water.

He nearly turned the wrong way in the sudden confusion, thought for certain that the crab's wicked pincer would tear his foot right off, but somehow, he got within arm's reach of the outcropping of tree-like pillars along the shoreline. When the powerful giant clasped his hands around a tangible support, the crab had no chance of holding him back. The monster came right with Tommy out of the pool, snapping at the fleeing giant's legs every step of the way.

Tommy roared and turned about, grabbing one of the huge claws. Spinning around and around, he soon had the crab up in the air, and then he sent it soaring far out over the small pond. It hit the mountain wall with a resounding crack and splashed heavily into the crimson waters.

Far up above, Tommy heard shouts from the castle guards. He turned to run but found that his wounded ankle would not support his weight. So the terrified giant hopped and crawled, pulled himself any way he could back to the safety of the distant crevice.

The spear tip, still a bit bent over from Gary's fight with the mountain troll, ricocheted off crab shell, but then hit a fleshy spot near the creature's mouth. Determinedly Gary drove on, throwing all his weight behind the weapon. He smiled grimly as the head of the spear disappeared into the monster's flesh.

Crab claws flew about wildly—one holding Geno and slamming the dwarf off the ceiling, wall, and floor. The creature bucked and thrashed, kicking all of its legs, spinning a complete circle in the corridor, even trying to roll back over itself. The claw waving over Kelsey retreated, focusing on Gary, the more immediate danger. He felt its pinch about his waist, but told himself to hold onto the spear and trust in his armor and in his companions. Gary knew that he had committed himself to the charge; there could be no retreat.

Flecks of shell flew about the corridor as the relentless dwarf continued to batter the claw that was squeezing him. Chunks of flesh followed and soon the claw's iron grip relaxed.

Kelsey came up in an instant, knowing that Gary had helped him, literally, out of a tight pinch, and knowing, too, that now Gary was the one needing the help. The elf thought nothing of his prized quest as he leaped in to fight right beside the human, thought only of aiding a companion, of aiding this man who, unbelievably, had somehow become Kelsey's friend.

His first target was the crab's remaining eye, and in the flash of an elf's magical sword, it, too, bounced to the floor.

The remaining claw let go of Gary's waist immediately, but the crab's thrashing only intensified. Gary's helmet rolled about on his shoulders, blinding him as completely as the eyeless crab; his elbow slammed hard into a wall, sending waves of pain through him, followed by a tingling numbness.

He held on. For all his life, Gary Leger held on.

He was on the floor, a great weight atop him. Something battered the side of his head, but his spear slipped deeper into the monster, and still he held on.

Then it was over, suddenly. Gary couldn't see, didn't know how badly he was injured, but he heard Kelsey and Geno congratulating each other and felt the weight lessening as his friends worked to pull the giant crab off of him.

After what seemed like many minutes, Geno hoisted Gary to his feet and Kelsey straightened his helmet. Gary blinked in disbelief at the toppled monster, and managed a weak smile when he heard Geno smacking his lips and describing a hundred different ways to cook the thing.

"Sure'n the three of ye have come to fight well together," Mickey said from back down the corridor.

Gary's smile disappeared.

He spun towards the leprechaun, his green eyes narrowed. "And where were you?" he demanded. "That's twice now, two fights in which Mickey McMickey played no part and didn't even try to play a part!"

For the first time since he had met the leprechaun, Gary believed that his anger truly wounded Mickey.

"Tommy almost died against the Crahg wolves," Gary fumed on, holding to his ire. "And you would have let him die—as long as you could keep your hiding spot behind his head!"

"Crahg wolves pay no heed to illusions," the leprechaun explained meekly.

"Be easy, friend," Kelsey said to Gary, putting a calming hand on the young man's shoulder. The elf's words and the gesture struck Gary profoundly, an action he would never have expected from grim and aloof Kelsey.

"And what can I do against the likes of a crab?" Mickey asked, gaining strength from Kelsey's intervention. "Just an animal, and a stupid one at that! I've no weapons . . ."

"Enough!" Kelsey commanded, ending the pointless debate. "We are alive, and we have come far, but our greatest trial yet awaits us."

"Do you think we could stop and have a bit of supper before running off to face that trial?" Geno asked hopefully, smacking his lips again and staring at an exposed area of juicy crab meat.

Kelsey smiled—another action that struck Gary as curious, given their situation and their impending meeting with Robert—and started making his way over the fallen crab to the tunnel beyond. After he had passed the tangle of legs, he motioned for Geno and the others to follow.

"The meat will stay good for a few hours," the dwarf mumbled as he passed beside Gary. "So let us get to Robert and get our business finished quickly."

Mickey strolled by as Gary worked to free his spear. The leprechaun did not even look Gary's way, and Gary, though he now realized his previous ranting about Mickey's contributions to be ridiculous, couldn't find the words for an apology.

The scalloped tunnel wound in and up the mountain, climbing gradually mostly, but so steeply at some points that even Kelsey had a difficult time in climbing. The passage forked only once, and Kelsey led them to the left, deeper into the mountain. Fortunately for the companions, they met no more monsters and no guards, and a short while later they came to a small and square opening, covered by an iron grate.

Kelsey looked out to a flat gravel bed, lined by sheer walls fifteen feet high.

"Dry moat," the elf whispered.

"I can get the grate out," Geno remarked, but Kelsey stopped him as he reached for his hammer.

"Guards outside, no doubt," the elf remarked softly. They waited in the quiet and soon heard the scrape of many marching soldiers on the wall above them.

Geno shrugged and put his tool away.

"We will go back the other way," Kelsey instructed in a whisper, and he swung the group around and headed back for the fork.

When they came to the end of the other passage, they were not so certain that they were any better off. This exit had no iron grate covering, but it came out on the exposed side of the treacherous cliff, still more than twenty feet below the base of the castle wall and several hundred feet from the ground. Kelsey sighed as he looked down, way down, to the tops of tall trees.

"Back to the grate?" Geno asked him when he came back in, the dwarf's gravelly voice diminished by the wind's howl as it entered the tunnel.

Kelsey leaned out again, looking for some path up to the castle walls.

"This way is the better," the elf decided. He unbelted his sword and handed it to Gary, then removed his pack.

Gary leaned out to regard the cliff. Agile Kelsey might make it, he decided, but he wasn't so certain about himself, wasn't so certain that he would even willingly follow. He had never been afraid of heights, but this was insane, with sheer walls and a strong wind and the tops of trees waiting like feathered spikes down below.

Kelsey never hesitated. Sometimes holding on by no more than two fingers, the strong and agile elf picked his careful way up the mountain cliff. The difficulty only increased when Kelsey made the base of the wall, for the castle stones were tightly fitted and wind-beaten smooth. Still, the wall was not that high—no more than fifteen or twenty feet—and Kelsey only needed two well-spaced handholds to get his fingers on top of the parapet.

He heard a commotion, the rasping voices of several guards, not too far to the side just as he was about to pull himself up over the wall. He waited a moment to ensure that he was not the cause of that commotion, then gingerly peeked over the wall.

A group of three guards, scaly humanoids as much lizard as human (Kelsey knew them to be lava newts), huddled together along the wall a short distance from Kelsey. They apparently had no idea that there was an elf nearby, for they continued to peer down to the region of the crimson-colored pond.

Kelsey held his place and held his breath.

The lava newts' excitement soon ebbed, and two of them wandered away, back to their distant posts, while the third began a slow, meandering course back towards where Kelsey was hiding.

Kelsey had nowhere to run, nowhere to hide. He produced a slender dagger from his boot and put it between his teeth, then hung low, just his fingers on the wall.

The barely alert creature passed right by the hanging elf, taking no notice whatsoever. In the blink of an eye Kelsey came up behind it, slapping one hand around its snout and driving his dagger into its throat. The creature, much stronger than Kelsey, struggled back powerfully, bending forward to lift the elf's feet right from the ground and nearly breaking free of Kelsey's stubborn grasp.

Kelsey's dagger ripped in again and again, and finally the creature slumped heavily in Kelsey's arms. The elf glanced around nervously, praying that no other guards had seen.

The night was dark, though, and all the castle remained quiet.

Kelsey carefully rolled the heavy creature onto and then over the wall, letting it drop, to be swallowed up by the darkness and the mournful wind. The elf quickly secured a rope on the parapet above the cave exit, dropping one end down to his waiting companions, then took up a defensive position, hiding tight against the wall, but with his stained dagger drawn and ready.

Gary looked doubtfully at the dangling rope, and even more doubtfully at the deep drop below. This should be easy, he argued against all his instincts. He had seen dozens of adventure movies where the hero simply leaped out onto a rope and scaled hand over hand up impossible distances.

This wasn't easy.

In fact, Gary decided, as he leaned out and gingerly took the rope in his hands, this was damned impossible. He fell back into the tunnel, shaking his head helplessly.

"Ye have to go, lad," Mickey said to him. "Kelsey cannot wait for long."

Again, Gary shook his head.

"Get out of my way!" Geno fumed, roughly shoving Gary aside. The dwarf scrambled out to the edge of the tunnel, and, without the slightest hesitation or any look below, hopped out to the rope and began pumping arm over arm, powerfully and methodically, just like one of those adventure-movie heroes.

"Ye see?" Mickey coaxed. "It is not so hard a thing."

"I can't do it," Gary replied. "Especially not in this armor!"

Mickey saw the excuse for what it was. "Ye've gotten used to the fit," the leprechaun reasoned. "And it's not so heavy now, is it?

"Ah, go on, lad," Mickey continued. "Ye cannot fall with me below ye. Ye remember the rocks in Dvergamal? I catched them good, and held them up in the air. Ye think I'd let ye fall?" Mickey held a pointed finger up before him and motioned for Gary to go on.

Gary considered the words for a long moment, then moved again to the tunnel exit, taking the rocking rope in his hands. He couldn't see the top of the castle wall from this distance, but suddenly the rope stopped bobbing and Gary knew that Geno had already made it up.

"I've got to start eating rocks," Gary muttered dryly, and he checked once to make sure that both his spears were secure on his belt, then hoisted himself out onto the rope.

His arms ached every foot of the way; only the knowledge that Mickey was below him, ready to levitate him should he fall, gave Gary Leger the courage to continue.

He heard a sharp hiss from above, followed by a crunch that he knew instinctively to be the result of a dwarf-wielded hammer. Sure enough, just a moment later, another lizard-skinned humanoid form came tumbling over the wall.

"Quickly!" came Kelsey's hushed call from above. Gary tried to respond, but his already weary arms simply did not answer his mental call to pick up the pace. Finally, after what seemed like many minutes, Gary put his first hand onto the parapet. Geno grabbed it up in an instant and hauled the tired man over.

"I wish Mickey could have given me more of a magical push," Gary rasped. "With the leprechaun's magic, I don't even know why we needed that stupid rope anyway."

"The leprechaun's telekinetic powers are limited with regard to living beings," Kelsey replied. "Mickey can lift a rock easily enough, but would have a difficult time in levitating even a frog."

"What's that now?" Mickey asked, umbrella in hand as he floated easily over the wall.

Gary considered the deep drop one more time, then shot the leprechaun a dangerous glare.

Mickey shrugged innocently. "Call it a lie, lad," he said. "But it worked, now didn't it?"

They had crossed the castle's outer wall, but that signaled only the first obstacle in the two-tiered structure. Just a few feet down from the companions lay an open courtyard, encircling a higher cluster of stone buildings. The castle had been built around the natural formations of the mountain, and in many places, bricked walls blended harmoniously with natural jutting stone.

Fortunately the courtyard was not overly busy. The main bustle seemed to be to the companions' right, down a road that went beyond a portcullis out of the castle proper, and through many buildings tightly packed together.

"The side gate," Kelsey explained in a whisper, "Leading to the barracks. And up there"—he gazed at the walls of the structures looming above them—"is where we will find Robert."

Gary didn't like the prospects—even forgetting that a dragon waited at the end of their road. There were but two ways up from this level as far as they could see: a steep stair around the left-hand side of the massive structure directly before them, and a sloping cobblestone path circling up around the same building's right side that forked from the main road, which led out of the castle's side gate.

"The stairs?" Mickey asked softly.

Kelsey nodded. "The gates up the road will likely be closed—and guarded in any event." Kelsey motioned for them to wait, then took his sword from Gary and slipped across the courtyard to the base of the stairway. He didn't go up immediately; rather, he moved along the wall running down the left-hand side of the stair, around the base of the structure and out of sight of his companions.

The elf reappeared almost immediately, waving frantically for the others to run and join him, and Gary knew that trouble was brewing.

Sure enough, several sword-wielding lava newt soldiers intercepted them before they reached the stairs.

At the sight of Geno, leading Gary and Mickey, the monsters howled wildly (like so many of the races of Faerie, good and bad, lava newts hated dwarfs), and charged ahead, taking no note of Kelsey, lying in wait behind the solid handrail a few steps up the stairs behind them.

Three flying hammers preceded the dwarf's answering charge, dropping two of the seven newts. A third tumbled heavily at the end of Gary's hurled spear.

"Didst thou throw it?" the sentient weapon on Gary's belt screamed incredulously in Gary's head.

Confident of his actions, Gary didn't bother to answer. He was certain that Kelsey and Geno would make short work of the remaining four, and knew that even if he still held his weapon, he probably would never get close enough to an enemy to use it.

As he figured, Kelsey leaped down into the midst of the remaining group of monsters, his brilliant sword glowing fiercely as it flashed every which way. Geno barreled into the throng a moment later from in front of the group, and in mere seconds of whipping hammers and a slashing sword, all the guard lay dead.

Gary went for his spear but never got there. Around the side of the stair came a host of soldiers, and the blare of horns went up all around the trapped companions.

Gary felt a strong hand—he knew it to be Geno's—grab him by the arm and tug him along. "My spear . . ." he started to protest, but stopped almost immediately when he heard Kelsey, up ahead on the slightly curving stair, engaged in battle once again. Geno released Gary and charged up to join the elf, and Gary reluctantly reached for his belt and took out the tipped half of Cedric's magical weapon. Unbalanced and unwieldy, Gary could only hope that he could find some way to utilize it in battle.

"Fear not, young sprout," came a comforting thought. *"Thou art not alone."*

Kelsey slashed and fought savagely to gain each subsequent step, but a line of lava newts packed above him, blocking his progress every step of the way. At the back of the party, Geno faced similar unfavorable odds.

Gary trusted in his two warrior companions, and facing the newts one or two at a time on the narrow stair certainly made the situation less catastrophic. But the lines of newt soldiers were long indeed, and were only going to get longer, Gary knew.

Another lizard-like form went over the outside wall of the stair, at the end of Kelsey's sword.

Gary blinked once, even moved to rub his eyes, when he looked back to Kelsey, for he saw not an elf, but a great mountain troll in the place where

Kelsey had been. The lava newts up above apparently noticed the change as well, for no longer did they press the attack. Indeed, many of them turned about and fled back up the stairs; others even scrambled over the low wall of the handrail and dropped the fifteen to twenty feet to the outer courtyard.

Guessing the source of the apparent transformation, Gary turned to regard Mickey, standing at his side.

"I do what I can," the leprechaun remarked smugly, reminding Gary once more of how ridiculous his earlier remarks concerning Mickey's value had been.

They made great progress then, the illusionary troll Kelsey leading the charge all the way up to the upper courtyard. This area was more squared than the lower bailey, with a cobble-stoned base laid flat around many lumpy natural stone breaks, and lined by several buildings, some tall and towering, others low and long.

Still, the newts retreated from the troll figure, but many more poured out into the courtyard, threatening to surround the small band.

Kelsey gazed diagonally across the courtyard, to a distant door at the far end of a low-roofed but obviously sturdy structure. If the elf meant to go there, though, he quickly changed his mind as dozens of lava newts rushed out that very door. For lack of a better choice, Kelsey led his companions to his left instead, to the tallest structure. He burst through a door, neatly slicing the throat of the surprised newt standing just inside, and rambled up a narrow spiral stair.

Hearing the continuing battle behind him, Gary was glad that Geno had taken up the rear. The walls of the stair pressed in tightly against Gary's broad shoulders and he did not believe that he could manage to fight in here at all.

Geno, too, was tightly pressed, but the dwarf, with his chopping hammers, did not need much room to maneuver. One newt lunged in boldly, lizard maw snapping, and Geno promptly crushed its skull. Other monsters came on bravely, though, clambering right over their dead companion.

The room at the top of the stairs would have proven disastrous for the companions if the newts up there had been better prepared. Apparently oblivious to what had transpired outside, the undisciplined rabble hadn't even taken the effort to arm themselves.

Kelsey came in first, appearing as an elf again (Mickey's troll illusion wouldn't have been very convincing, given that a troll wouldn't even have fit in this low room!), hacking and slashing at the wildly rushing monsters. He nicked one but didn't bring it down, as it made its way for a magnificently ornamented dagger hanging on the far wall. A single glance revealed to Gary the magic of that ancient, gem-encrusted weapon and he knew that he must not allow the newt to retrieve it. He leaped forward past Kelsey, shoulder-blocked one newt aside, and closed on the one reaching for the dagger.

The evil soldier grasped the weapon and swung about, but Gary got his strike in first as it blindly turned, catching the newt on the shoulder.

It was not a deep wound, nor did the spear hit a vital area, and Gary threw up his arm and ducked aside, expecting a retaliation. The lava newt did not swing or throw the ornamental dagger, though, did not make any move at all, save to open its toothy maw in a silent scream.

"*Taste of blood!*" came an emphatic thought in Gary's head. He felt the power thrumming through Cedric's spear, a power long dormant. Horrified, Gary tried to pull the spear out, but the barbed weapon resisted, holding stubbornly to its enemy's wound. When Gary finally did extract the tip, he felt compelled beyond his control to thrust it right back into the dying newt, this time blasting the creature through the heart.

Telepathic waves of intense satisfaction rolled through Gary's mind and body. Gary couldn't stop and consider them, though, for Kelsey came to him, prodding him towards the small room's other door.

Gary managed to reach out and pluck the dagger from the fallen newt before Kelsey had pulled him too far, and Kelsey, intent on escape, did not even notice the ancient weapon. Hardly giving the dagger a further thought, Gary slid it under the folds of his wide belt.

Then they were out of the room, going down a staircase quite similar to the one that had taken them up the tower. A hallway ran off its side at the ground level and the companions heard lava newts stirring down there. Kelsey took the group right by the corridor, and moving through a door, they came back into the courtyard of the upper bailey just a short distance from the door that had first brought them into the tower.

That short distance gave the companions all the opening they needed to get across the way, for the pursuing newts were still stupidly gathered at the other door.

Mickey scrambled up to perch on Gary's shoulder. Gary started to protest, fearing that he would soon be fighting once again, but then he realized that the leprechaun needed the position to work some more of his magic. Soon Gary, Kelsey, and Geno all appeared as mountain trolls, their footsteps even sounding like the thunder of a troll charge. The newts scrambled furiously to keep out of their way as Kelsey led the charge across the courtyard towards the desired door in the low-roofed and sturdy structure.

Again the elf burst right through, sending two not-so-surprised lava newts fleeing down a small and dark passage directly ahead. Kelsey didn't pursue them. A few steps inside the building, beyond a hanging tapestry, he turned a corner and came into a huge and ornate hall.

Just a few lava newts stood in the hall, and these made no move to intercept the companions. They remained at their posts, spaced in regular intervals along the decorated walls. And those newts outside that had found the courage to pursue the group did not even enter the low-roofed building. Gary had the uncomfortable feeling that this had all been arranged, that he and his friends had been purposely herded to this very chamber.

Hammers ready for more play, Geno started for the closest newt, but Kelsey held him back. To the dwarf's—and to Gary's—amazement, the elf then sheathed his sword and nodded to Mickey.

The troll illusion disappeared. The group was just an elf, a dwarf, a man, and a leprechaun once more.

As if on cue, a huge man, red-haired and red-bearded, with thick and corded muscles, stepped out from behind a suit of plated armor at the far end of the hall. Even from this distance, Gary could tell that the man stood at least a foot taller than he, and a hundred pounds heavier.

"Kelsenellenelvial, how good of you to finally arrive," the red-haired man cried out in a bellowing voice that reverberated off of every wall.

Kelsey's return greeting confirmed what Gary somehow suspected, what Gary feared, though he couldn't sort out the obvious discrepancy in this strange man's appearance.

"My greetings, Robert."

TWENTY-TWO

IN SHEEP'S CLOTHING

Gary blinked many times in amazement as he scanned the huge torchlit hall. Suits of intricate and decorated armor, both metal and leather, stood at silent attention—why weren't the lava newt soldiers wearing them?—gleaming with new polish. Swords, spears, pole arms, weapons of so many shapes and sizes, lined the walls, joining the many rich-colored tapestries. One group of spears in particular caught Gary's eye. Identical in build, they were lashed halfway up the wall with their butt ends touching at evenly spaced angles, giving the whole ensemble a harmonious semicircular design, like the top half of the sun cresting the eastern horizon.

And one sword in particular held Gary in absolute awe, both for its obviously magnificent craftsmanship and for its sheer size. Unlike the other weapons in the room, this sword was not fitted to any wall or held by empty, decorative armor. It leaned easily against the far wall, as if waiting for a wielder, waiting for battle. Gary couldn't imagine anyone actually lifting the monstrous thing, let alone wielding it in a fight.

Beyond the armor and weapons and tapestries, and all the other fabulous decorations, the room itself seemed a spectacular thing. Thick stone walls ran up straight and smooth, giving way to a dark-wooded ceiling of great inter-locking beams. How high were those walls? Gary wondered. Twenty feet? Fifty? Dimensions seemed out of kilter in here—a room more suited to a giant than a man—and no matter how high it actually was, the sheer mass of that ceiling awed Gary and made him feel very small indeed.

"Your friend approves of my meeting hall," the huge red-haired man bellowed, looking from Kelsey to Gary. "Is he the one to fulfill the prophecies?" Robert walked a few steps closer, studying Gary as he came. His face brightened suddenly, as if in revelation, and, to Gary's sincere relief, he stopped his advance.

"Yes," Robert answered his own question. "I see that he wears the armor of Cedric Donigarten, though not as well as dead Cedric once wore it!" He roared out a laugh that came straight from his belly.

"Is there no one who does not know of your quest?" Geno, obviously not similarly amused, asked Kelsey snidely.

Kelsey turned on the dwarf sharply, and Gary could see true pain in the elf's golden eyes. Geno's sarcasm had stung; apparently Kelsey had not expected Robert to be so well informed.

"I could kill you all right now, you realize," the red-haired man said suddenly, and from the strength of his voice alone, Gary held no doubts about his claim.

"There's the boasts of a true dragon," Mickey replied dryly, and Robert's ensuing laughter shook the hall like the rumble of thunder.

By this time, Gary was even more confused. When he had first heard the man referred to as Robert, he had assumed that this was a different Robert, a human counterpart to the dreaded dragon, perhaps. Or Gary had hoped that this Robert was different, he realized, for in his heart he had known the truth all along. Gary could not deny the aura of power surrounding this being, a strength much greater than any mere human could contain.

But if this was really Robert the dreaded dragon, he certainly did not fit the description of the dragon in Gary's book, or, for that matter, any description of any dragon that Gary had ever heard of. Yet Mickey had told Gary to read those passages concerning the dragon in his book to get an idea of what Robert would be like.

"Well, I know why you are here," Robert said. "Or at least part of the reason. No doubt you have come to steal from me as well—I see that you have brought a dwarf along."

Geno ground his teeth at the insult, but, to Gary's amazement, did not offer any retort.

"We have come for one reason alone, great wyrm," Kelsey said firmly, stepping out in front of his companions and slapping his hand to his belted sword.

"Wyrm?" Gary whispered to Mickey, but the leprechaun motioned for him to keep silent.

Robert, appearing unimpressed by Kelsey's bravado, stalked the rest of the distance across the room to stand right before the elf.

Gary blew a silent whistle. The red-haired man was seven feet tall if he was an inch, with shoulders broad and strong, and corded arms that could tear Kelsey right in half with a simple twist and tug. If Geno got his strength from eating rocks, Gary decided, then this Robert ate mountains—whole.

"In accordance with the rules of our ancestors," Kelsey said, his voice not quivering in the least, "as was done by Ten-Temmera of Tir na n'Og against the dragon Rehir, as was done by Gilford of Drochit against the dragon Wobegone, as was done by . . ." The list went on for many minutes, with Kelsey naming ancient heroes in legendary duels against Faerie's most fearsome dragons.

"The Tylwyth Teg never could get by the formalities," Mickey whispered to Gary, and Geno, standing right beside the leprechaun, snorted his whole-hearted agreement.

"Thus, with these precedents in mind and in accordance with all of the stated rules," Kelsey finally finished, "I do challenge you to a fight of honor!"

Through the entirety of Kelsey's prepared speech, Robert did not blink.

"Again, in accordance with precedent and established rules," Kelsey added, "if you are defeated, you must perform one small service to me. And you know the task well, dragon Robert—you must furnish the fire to reforge the ancient spear of Cedric Donigarten."

Robert nodded as though he had fully anticipated that price.

"No fires wrought by mortals could soften its metal," he replied, as if reciting a portion of some ancient verse.

"And you must," Kelsey continued with a nod, "adhere to the rules of banishment and remain in your fortress for a hundred years."

Again Robert nodded casually. What was a hundred years to a dragon, after all?

"And if victorious?" the red-haired giant asked, too nonchalantly, his sincerely calm confidence sending shudders up Gary's spine.

"There are precedents for that possibility . . ." Kelsey began.

"Damn your precedents, elf!" Robert roared suddenly, and Kelsey, for all his nerve, retreated a step. "You wish me to do battle against you, a battle full of rules that eliminate my obvious advantages." He looked around at his lava newt guards, his smile reminding the companions that he could call in a hundred more loyal soldiers with a snap of his fingers.

"And you have told me of my price," Robert went on. "Irrelevant drivel! Do you truly believe that you have any chance of defeating me?"

Kelsey firmed his angular jaw, narrowed his golden eyes.

"So do not speak of precedents, elf," the dragon went on, nearly chuckling at the spectacle. "Tell me what I gain by accepting your challenge of honor; tell me why I should exert the effort against so pitiful a foe."

"Not so pitiful that ye did not take the trouble to gather his name," Mickey remarked, and Gary nodded, thinking it wise for the leprechaun to lend Kelsey some much needed support at that time.

Robert smirked but did not answer.

"If you win, my life is forfeited to you," Kelsey said at once.

"You state the obvious," Robert replied. "You will not survive the battle."

Kelsey drew out his magnificent sword. "And this," he said. "Forged by the Tylwyth Teg, it can only serve one so designated by its wielder. If you win and my life is forfeit, then I give to you my sword!"

"A pittance." Robert replied, and Kelsey frowned so gravely at the insult that Gary thought that the elf would surely strike out at Robert then and there. Robert turned his head, leading Kelsey's gaze across the room, to the gigantic and magnificent sword leaning against the far wall.

"But I will accept your pittance," Robert said suddenly, turning back on the elf. "Your life and your sword, elf, and the lives of your friends."

Mickey and Geno started to protest, with Gary startled too numb to even utter a single word, but Kelsey simply spoke above them. "According to precedent," he said. "And so we are agreed."

"Don't ye think that we've a word or two to say about it?" Mickey asked.

"No," was Robert's simple and straightforward reply, and while Kelsey did not openly vocalize his agreement, it seemed obvious to the others that he considered the dragon's demands quite reasonable.

The huge man walked easily across the room and casually lifted the massive sword.

"A strong one," Mickey remarked, seeing Gary's gawk, for not only had Robert lifted a sword that Gary thought more appropriate for a Tommy-sized giant, but he had lifted it, so very easily, with just one hand!

"You choose swords?" Kelsey asked, seeming confused. "I had thought . . ."

"I choose my weapons as I choose," Robert replied with an ironic chuckle. "The sword will do nicely—for a start." He moved to the hearth on the back wall. Bending low, the red-haired man, without the slightest hesitation or wince of pain, used his bare hands to push aside the glowing embers.

"Are you coming along?" he asked, and he tugged on one of the hearth's pokers, a concealed lever, which drew open a secret trapdoor. "And I warn you only once," he added, "if you steal a single coin or trinket from my gathered hoard, then the rules are no more, and your lives are surely forfeit! I have not come forth for many decades; perhaps it will be time again for Robert the Righteous to feast upon the flesh of men!"

Gary could hardly find his breath as he looked to Mickey. The leprechaun nodded gravely, not doubting the dragon's threats in the least.

The four companions, Kelsey determinedly at their lead, followed Robert down a long and winding set of stairs, ending in a series of vast and empty chambers. Mickey paused as they passed by one archway, low and covered by a hanging tapestry, the only man-made article they had seen down here under the castle.

"Treasure room," the leprechaun remarked to Gary's inquisitive stare. Gary knew from Mickey's expression that the leprechaun had no intention of trying to steal anything, nor did any of the companions, in light of Robert's warning. But there was a profound and obvious sadness in Mickey's eye as he continued to gaze back at the blocked archway. Gary studied the leprechaun closely, not understanding.

He didn't question the leprechaun about it, though, too concerned with what lay ahead to worry about what might lie behind.

The smell of sulphur continued to grow until it fully filled Gary's nostrils. At first he thought the aroma a relic from the ancient volcano that had raised the Giant's Thumb, but as Robert moved into one room and lit the torches lining the chamber's walls, Gary noticed many scarred and blasted areas, along every wall, the ceiling, and the floor.

Dragon fire?

Gary also noticed many scratches in the stone floor, deep and wide. If a dragon's claws had caused those . . .

That undeniable shudder ran its path again along Gary's spine.

"How did Robert know of our coming?" Kelsey whispered to Mickey as Robert moved far across the room to finish lighting up all of the torches.

"Maybe the witch told him," Gary offered, what he thought to be a logical conclusion. Three skeptical stares showed him differently, though.

"No, lad," Mickey explained. "Ceridwen would not be talking to the likes of Robert. Nor would any of her minions. They don't get on well; it'd be as likely for the witch to side with Kelsey in the coming battle as to side with Robert."

"She doesn't want the spear forged," Gary reminded him.

"Nor does she desire to see the spear and Cedric's armor fall into the dragon's clutches," Geno reasoned. "I would guess that Ceridwen would prefer to deal with Kelsey holding the repaired spear than to deal with Robert at all."

"The two do take pains to keep away from each other," Mickey said with an amused expression. That the leprechaun could find any mirth at all in their dire situation told Gary just how profoundly Ceridwen and Robert hated each other—to the delight of many of Faerie's inhabitants, no doubt.

Kelsey went back to his original question. "How did Robert know?" he asked again, and this time, it seemed to Gary, the elf cast more than a curious stare the leprechaun's way.

Mickey just shrugged and popped his pipe into his mouth. "Ye'd better take the lad's shield," the leprechaun remarked, deflecting the question. "It'd block a dragon's fire, so say the legends."

Kelsey looked again to Robert, now making his deliberate way back across the vast chamber, and knew that his question would have to wait.

He turned to Gary for the shield, but Gary, staring at approaching Robert, did not notice him. The image of this red-haired man spouting flames did not add up to Gary—and who ever heard of a dragon fighting with a sword?

"Well?" Kelsey's impatient tone pulled Gary from his private deliberations. He looked around curiously for a moment, confused, then realized what Kelsey was after and fumbled to get Cedric's great shield off of his back.

"Some of the straps have come loose," Gary explained. "When a troll hit it . . ."

A wave of Kelsey's hand stopped him. "I'll not use it in the battle," the elf said, to Gary's further confusion. "It is too cumbersome for swordplay, and little defense against that mighty sword, especially in the hands of Robert. The dragon would drive his blade right through this shield even if I were quick enough to raise it for a block." Kelsey took the shield then and turned away to begin his challenge, to meet his destiny.

"Then why did he take it?" Gary asked Mickey.

"As I said, the shield'll turn even a dragon's fire," Mickey replied casually, lighting up his pipe. "If Robert decides to loose his breath, then Kelsey'll be quick to pick it up."

"But he's not a dragon!" Gary cried in frustration, more loudly than he had intended.

Geno's laughter mocked him.

"Just watch, lad," Mickey replied. "Just watch."

Kelsey and Robert squared off near to the center of the huge chamber, Kelsey laying the magical shield on the floor beside one decapitated stalagmite and taking up his sword in both hands.

Robert, too, hoisted his weapon in both hands, bringing it into an easy, circular swing above his head. "Do not die too quickly, elf," the great man growled. "I have not enjoyed the excitement of battle for many years. A dozen lava newts fall too quickly for me to take pleasure in those jousts!" The monstrous sword whipped around suddenly, an exclamation point for Robert's boasts, and Kelsey barely fell back out of its nearly seven-foot reach.

Despite the momentum of the swing, Robert easily halted the sword's progress and brought it back in the other way. Wisely Kelsey never slowed his backpedaling, even rolling to his back and then to the right to come up facing his enemy, but far out of Robert's reach.

"Ah, very good!" Robert roared. "Hard to catch, if not so hard to kill!"

On came the red-haired monster in a frightening wild rush.

"Get out of there!" Gary heard himself cry out, but Kelsey had other ideas. As Robert charged, so did he, diving to his knees at the last moment and sliding right by the lumbering giant.

Kelsey's sword drove home once and then again into Robert's thick thigh as they passed, and Kelsey came back up before Robert could even spin about to regard him.

The red-haired man looked down to his injured leg, astonishment clear upon his face.

Gary's smile widened at Kelsey's brilliant move but it faded immediately when he looked upon Mickey, who seemed not so confident.

"Ah," Robert roared again. "Very good!" And then he laughed, so loudly and profoundly that it echoed again and again off of every stone in the chamber, sounding as if the dragon had brought along his own invisible cheering section. Giving no more heed to the wounds at all, he advanced upon Kelsey once again, this time slowly, deliberately, his great sword waving out before him.

"At least I'll get to see the damned elf die before it's my turn to face the wyrm," Geno muttered grimly.

TWENTY-THREE

THE FIGHTER AND THE WYRM

The great sword swiped about, then again, and a third time, the momentum of each swing bringing raging Robert just a bit closer to his prey. Kelsey didn't even try to parry the mighty blows, knowing that unless his sword angle was exactly perfect, Robert's powerful cuts would surely blast right through his meager defenses.

Normally in such a fight against a larger foe, the elf would hold a wide advantage of quickness, especially with his opponent wielding so heavy and unwieldy a sword. But not this time; Robert swung the blade as easily as Kelsey maneuvered his slender elven sword, and the giant man proved deceptively quick and always balanced.

Again came a mighty swing, and this time, the elf barely managed to get back out of harm's way. Robert's widening smile mocked Kelsey's continuing retreat.

Kelsey was far from ready to surrender, though—not that vicious Robert would have accepted it anyway. He had gone through many trials to get to this point, and now, so close to realizing his quest, the one great task appointed him for his life, his elven blood coursed through his slender limbs with renewed vigor. Besides, the elf reminded himself as the red-haired giant continued to stalk in, he had known all along that the fight against Robert would be the greatest trial of all his life.

Robert's sword whipped across yet again, and once more Kelsey slipped backwards out of reach. The huge man came on fiercely, suddenly, turning his wrists to send his weapon up high, then reversing his grip to angle the sword for a mighty downwards chop.

Kelsey threw his sword up above him, angled diagonally. In typical combat, the cunning elf would have turned his sword horizontal as the blow came in, catching his opponent's weapon on his own blade to fully stop his attacker's momentum chop. From there, a simple twist would throw the attacking sword harmlessly aside and leave Kelsey's foe vulnerable for a counter.

Wisely Kelsey did not try his usual tactics against the inhumanly strong Robert. As Robert's sword crashed in, the elf, instead of turning his sword to the horizontal plane, twisted it vertically and immediately stepped to his left, away from the deflected blow. Robert was quick to recover, but not quick enough to defeat Kelsey's obvious advantage. With Robert's sword far to the other side, Kelsey rushed by the red-haired man's right flank, launching a rapid series of stinging slashes and pokes as he passed.

"Oh, grand move!" Mickey blurted out around the edges of his long-stemmed pipe, clapping his chubby little hands together.

Every onlooker, and Robert as well, thought that Kelsey would then simply run out of range again, putting the fight back on even ground.

None of them, particularly not the dragon, truly understood the fires that burned in the veins of the noble elf.

As Robert spun to catch up with the passing elf, Kelsey cut around in a tight circle, keeping ahead of Robert's blade and keeping Robert's right flank open and vulnerable. The elf's sword hit home perhaps a dozen times in the next frenzied moments before Robert wisely stopped his futile chasing and retreated a few steps instead.

"Oh, grander move!" Mickey called, adding another series of claps. Robert turned an angry glare upon the leprechaun, silencing Mickey immediately, except for a profound gulp.

Gary thought that the huge man would surely run over and slaughter Mickey—and Gary didn't trust that the monstrous red-haired man would stop at that. The weight of doom suddenly heavy around his shoulders, Gary looked to Geno for support. He was not comforted by what he saw, though, for the dwarf had prudently moved a dozen long steps away from Mickey's other side.

But fears of the attack proved unfounded. Robert was too busy in his battle to take any actions against the others at that time. He turned his glower upon Kelsey, then looked disdainfully at his wounded side. His right arm had been opened in several places—one gash had the brute's corded muscles hanging out right beyond his thick skin.

"I had thought to spare you," Robert spat at Kelsey.

"A lie," Kelsey muttered in reply.

"But now you die!" Robert roared, and he came on wildly, sword slashing back and forth.

Despite Kelsey's previous moments of brilliance, Gary found that he absolutely believed Robert's prediction as the next furious assault began. How could anyone—especially one as slender and delicate as Kelsey—fend off or escape the crushing power of Robert's mighty swings? And even if Kelsey managed to stay away, how could he hope to win? He had nailed Robert with many direct hits—strikes that would have killed, or at least stopped, any real human opponent—to no avail, and Robert showed not the slightest signs of tiring.

Kelsey dropped behind one of the few stalagmite mounds in the room, hoping to diminish the intensity of the attack.

Robert didn't slow, didn't hold back his ringing sword at all. Sparks flew as the great weapon slammed against the stone, and when they cleared, the stalagmite mound stood but half its original height.

To the companions' dismay, Robert's sword had not broken, had not even visibly chipped. On came the red-haired monster, his face contorted with rage, his sword humming as it again began its death-promising sidelong cuts through the empty air.

Kelsey did not fear his constant retreating in the vast room, but neither did he believe that he was gaining any advantage, that the great Robert would tire. The elf knew that he would have to continue his brilliance and his daring, and that one mistake would surely cost him his life.

Kelsey nearly laughed at that thought. His life mattered not when weighed against the successful completion of his life-quest.

Kelsey backed and watched, watched closely the subtle movements of Robert's fingers clenched about the huge sword's leather-strapped hilt.

Gary tried to look away, not wanting to see his friend share a similar fate with the halved stalagmite. He found that he could not avoid the remarkable spectacle, though, and his mouth drooped open in confusion when he looked back to the combatants, back to Kelsey, unexpectedly smiling with apparently sincere confidence.

Gary couldn't know it then, but the elf had found his advantage. For all of Robert's sheer power and uncanny quickness, the dragon was not a swordsman—at least not by the elf's high standards. Robert's attacks were straightforward, his movements, even his feints, becoming more and more predictable to the seasoned warrior of Tylwyth Teg.

Kelsey continued to watch those gnarly, huge fingers, waiting for the telltale turn. A few strides, a few swings later, Robert twisted and sent his sword flying up high—and Kelsey was ready for him.

Just like the first time he had attempted the downwards chop, three quick strides brought the red-haired man rushing towards the elf.

Kelsey, though, did not offer a defense similar to the previous one. He, too, came rushing forward, sword leading, desperate to beat Robert to the quick.

Robert's great sword was still up high over his head when the fine tip of Kelsey's elven blade came in tight against Robert's throat.

"You lose!" the elf cried.

Robert roared and drove his sword down at the elf.

Kelsey could have thrust his sword right through Robert's throat—his instincts almost made him do it. But what good to him would be a slain dragon? He dove aside instead, rolling to his feet and pointing an accusing finger Robert's way.

"Treachery!" he yelled, looking to his companions, the witnesses, for support. "I had you bested."

"I am not down!" Robert roared back. "You had nothing!"

"What fairness is this?" Kelsey cried, pleading his case to Mickey and the others, to the stones of the cavern, to anyone and anything that could hear his voice. He turned back on Robert. "Must I kill you to win? What is my gain, then, in this challenge of honor?"

"You had nothing!" Robert roared back, and it seemed to Gary as if his voice had changed somewhat, taken on a more throaty call.

"My sword was at your throat!"

"And mine at your head," Robert quickly added. "To finish your move would have allowed me to finish mine." Robert poked his finger against his own throat. "Small hole," he spat sarcastically. "Perhaps fatal, but not so surely fatal as an elf cut down the middle!"

Kelsey knew Robert's estimate of the fight was far from accurate. He could have driven his sword right through Robert's neck and still dodged the downwards chop. But Robert's argument was convincing, Kelsey knew, convincing enough for the dragon to avoid the mark of dishonor in the general retelling of the fight.

"He's playing Bilbo's game," Gary muttered under his breath. Mickey looked up at him curiously, remembering the story, then nodded his accord.

"Half-truths," Gary went on. "Kelsey had him."

"Tell that to Robert," Mickey muttered. "But wait long enough for me to get far from yer side afore ye do, lad."

Gary didn't miss the leprechaun's point.

"Enough of this foolishness!" Robert roared suddenly. With one arm, he heaved his huge sword across the room. It hit the wall with a blinding flash, and hung in place, halfway embedded in the solid stone.

Gary thought for a moment that Robert had capitulated, had admitted that Kelsey had fairly won.

Sensing the truth, though, Kelsey raced back to retrieve the magical shield of Cedric Donigarten, working frantically to get it in place on his slender arm.

Gary started to question the elf's movements, but when he looked back to Robert, he came to understand, came to understand so very much.

Robert began to change.

The human coil warped and bulged; red hair wrapped Robert's head and blended with his mutating skin. A great wing sprouted, then another, and huge claws tore the boots from the creature's feet. Great snapping sounds of reforming bones echoed sickeningly through the chamber; a monstrous, scaly tail slammed to the floor behind the creature and rushed out as it thickened and elongated, seeming almost like a second creature.

"Oh my God!" Gary Leger stammered. "Sonofab . . . Holy Sh . . . Oh my God!" Gary simply ran out of expletives. His mouth worked weird contortions, but no words spewed forth. If Tommy had been standing beside him and had uttered one of his customary "Duhs," Gary would certainly have patted him on the leg for giving him the right word. Nothing in Gary Leger's life, not the volumes of fantasy reading he had done nor any sights he had ever seen, in his own world or in Faerie, could have possibly prepared him for the spectacle before him.

The chamber no longer seemed so large—the dragon had reached fifty feet long and continued to grow, to stretch. Gary remembered the dry lake, Loch Tullamore, and now he understood how the dragon might indeed have "hissed" it away. He clutched at *The Hobbit*, sitting in a pouch on his belt, like it was some protecting amulet, a source of strength and a reminder that others had faced such a creature and lived to tell about it.

But even Gary's amulet could not begin to insulate him from the sheer terror of facing Robert the Wretched. The change was complete then—Robert loomed nearly a hundred feet in length, with spear-like, stone-tearing claws and a maw that could snap a man in half, or fully swallow him, at the dragon's whim.

Gary's knees went weak under him. He wanted nothing except to run away, but knew his legs wouldn't carry him. He wanted nothing except to close his eyes, but he could not, held firmly by the awesome spectacle, the majesty and the horror of the true dragon.

"Enough!" the dragon roared again. If Robert's voice in human form could shake stones, then the power of this blast could surely split them. "The game is ended, Kelsenellenelvial Gil-Ravadry!"

Geno cast a disconcerting look Gary and Mickey's way. "I suppose that the spear will have to wait some time before it gets back in one piece again," the dwarf muttered sarcastically.

"Stupid elf," he added, and his derisive chuckle momentarily freed Gary from his awestricken trance.

"You don't seem too concerned," he muttered Geno's way, his voice cracking several times as he struggled to spit out the words.

Geno gave a resigned shrug. "Robert will not eat me," he replied with some confidence. "Dragons are not overly fond of the taste of dwarfs, and besides, dragons like the pretty things a dwarf hammer might bring." Geno's snort twanged against the marrow of Gary's bones. "He'll eat you, though."

Gary turned his attention back to the fight, which seemed more a prelude to a massacre now. Kelsey's smile was long gone, and so was the elf's look of confidence, even of determination. And who could blame him?

"Can we help him?" Gary whispered to Mickey, though Gary knew that if Mickey told him to charge in beside Kelsey, his quivering legs would betray his noble intentions.

The leprechaun snorted incredulously, and Gary said no more. He finally managed to close his eyes and turned his thoughts inwards instead, calling upon the sentient spear, his most reliable battle ally, for some answers to this nightmare.

* * *

Kelsey braced himself and clutched his sword more tightly, trying to remind himself of his purpose in being there, of the fact that he had known from the beginning of his quest what creature he would ultimately face.

Rationale just didn't seem an antidote to the sheer terror evoked by the sight of the unbeatable dragon.

Serpentine Robert slithered, belly low, towards Kelsey. He gave a swipe of his huge foreclaw, almost a playful swing, like some kitten with a ball of yarn. Kelsey threw his weight behind the heavy shield to block, but still went sliding many feet across the stone floor.

"Oh, damn," Geno muttered; and turned away, thinking the fight at its gruesome end.

"Oh," the dwarf corrected weakly when he looked back, looked at Kelsey.

Somehow still standing and somehow undaunted, the elf stepped right back and ripped off a series of three short jabs into the dragon's extended arm.

The wind from Robert's ensuing laughter knocked Kelsey to the floor.

"Do not make it so easy," the dragon growled. "I wish to play for as long as I might. Who knows when another hero might be as foolish as you, Kelsenellenelvial Gil-Ravadry?"

"How might I aid my friend?" Gary's thoughts asked the sentient spear.

No answer.

He called mentally to the spear several times, insisting that it communicate with him.

"*The fight is not yours*," the spear finally answered.

"I must help Kelsey!"

"*You must not!*" came an emphatic reply. "*The fight is a challenge of honor; events go exactly as they were dictated before the elf's quest was undertaken.*"

Gary started to protest, to argue that no one single warrior could defeat such a beast and that the quest must be abandoned for the sake of Kelsey's life. But then he understood. The spear cared nothing for Kelsey. This battle, carried out properly in accordance with ancient rules, was the sentient weapon's only chance of being reforged.

Helplessly Gary Leger opened his eyes.

Kelsey was on the attack again, rushing in beyond Robert's foreclaws and banging away at the dragon's scaly armor with all his strength. The huge horned dragon head bobbed with bellowing laughter, mocking Kelsey. Every now and then, Robert casually dropped a claw near to the elf, knocking him aside.

But stubborn, incredibly stubborn, Kelsey did not relent, and his persistence paid off.

Robert's lizard-like features contorted suddenly in pain as Kelsey's sword slipped between armor plates and dug deep at dragon flesh. The dragon set his wings into a fierce beat, their wind driving Kelsey back while lifting Robert to his towering height.

Kelsey stubbornly kept his balance, using the great shield to somewhat deflect the blasting wind. He nearly overbalanced when the dragon sucked in its breath, countering the force of the beating wings.

"Here it comes," Gary heard Mickey mutter.

And indeed it did, a blast of fire that seemed to swallow pitiful Kelsey and warmed all the vast chamber so profoundly that Gary, standing many yards away, felt his eyebrows singe underneath his loose-fitting helmet. Robert's exhale went on for many seconds, the white-hot fires pouring over Kelsey, scorching the stone all about the elf's feet.

And then it was ended—and Kelsey still stood! Stone bubbled beside him and the outer metal of the shield of Cedric glowed an angry red, but the elf, even his clothes, and the ground in the protective shadow of that shield, appeared unharmed.

"Damned good shield," Geno said in disbelief.

Robert, too, seemed stricken, gawking at the elf who somehow had held his ground against a blast that could melt stone.

"Ye'll have to do better than that, mighty wyrm," Kelsey chided, apparently gaining some confidence in the proof that the legendary shield could, as the bard's pen had declared, "turn the fire of a dragon's breath."

Robert launched another blast, Kelsey just barely ducking behind the protective shield in time. Now the stone around the elf hissed and sputtered, that sulphuric smell permeated the room.

But when the fires ceased, Kelsey poked his head around the shield—and he was wearing a smile.

Simply surviving Robert's breath was insult enough, but the elf's taunts, and now his smile, sent the dragon into a rage beyond anything Gary had ever imagined.

"Oh, begorra," he heard Mickey whisper, and then came the scraping and pounding of the dragon's charge that tore the cavern floor in its wake.

Claws hammered down at Kelsey, a hit so fierce that Gary thought the elf surely dead. Somehow Kelsey held his ground, but then the terrible maw snapped down, cat-quick, to bite at him. Somehow again—it seemed impossible to Gary—Kelsey managed to dodge, even to smack Robert several times before the dragon got its massive horned head back out of range.

Claws rained destruction, back legs kicked, wings beat down mercilessly, and once, the dragon's tail snapped around with force enough to fell a thick-trunked oak. But Kelsey was ahead of nearly every attack, and those that did connect did no more than slow the elf's own frenzied offense. The slaps of

Kelsey's sword sounded as a tap dance, rhythmical and constant, beating at every target Robert presented to him.

Dragon fire came roaring in again, but the shield repelled it, and Kelsey even managed to close in under the fiery cover and snap off three vicious strikes.

"That's impossible," Gary groaned, turning to Mickey. The leprechaun was too intent on the action to answer him, but Geno replied, tossing a hammer casually off the side of Gary's helmet.

"Shut your big mouth," the dwarf growled, his unexpected anger stunning Gary to silence.

Robert's frenzy did not relent—Gary came to fear that all the mountain would crumble under the dragon's pounding. But neither did Kelsey relent, snapping, slicing, poking, beating at the dragon from every angle, moving with such speed and precision that at times he seemed no more than a thin blur.

A claw sent him reeling backwards, a solid hit, and as he started forward once more, Robert's great maw fell over him. Gary nearly swooned as the dragon's head came up with Kelsey in his mouth.

Kelsey wasn't finished. Somehow, impossibly, the elf had wedged his shield between the dragon's jaws, and Robert's actions now actually worked against the dragon, for now Kelsey was within reach of the beast's only vulnerable area.

With his slender, wicked sword dancing less than an inch from the dragon's yellow, reptilian eye, Kelsey asked evenly, "Do ye yield?"

"I could breathe you to char!" the dragon hissed between its locked jaws.

"And ye'd lose yer eye," Kelsey proclaimed.

Robert made not a move, considering his options.

"I don't believe it," Gary breathed, his voice full of stunned elation. He just shook his head and stared blankly as the god-like dragon obediently lowered the elf to the floor and released him.

"Bring the ancient spear and be done with it!" the dragon roared, stamping his foreclaws, and several stones in the wide cavern did indeed split apart under the force of Robert's outrage.

"Unbelievable," Gary muttered again.

"Keep quiet, lad," Mickey implored him. "Say not a word and get yer part done as quickly as ye can."

Gary considered the leprechaun curiously, wondering why Mickey was so full of intensity and trepidation. Was that a bead of sweat on Mickey's forehead?

Why? Gary wondered, for the greatest trial had been passed—Kelsey had won. The elf had survived the wrath of Robert, had taken blows that would have toppled ancient trees and flattened mountains . . .

Gary abruptly halted his confused train of thought. "Ye'd lose yer eye?" he mumbled under his breath, imitating the accent that Kelsey had used when demanding Robert's surrender. Now he understood Geno's anger at his proclamation that Kelsey's feats were impossible.

Gary turned his attention to the scene before him. Robert had started away, shifting his great scaled body to the side, towards a wide and high tunnel running off of the main chamber. Kelsey stood in the same spot where Robert had released him, impassive, apparently basking in his victory.

Gary looked right through the illusionary elf.

"The first hit," Mickey whispered to him, seeing that he had finally figured out the game.

Gary quickly recalled the events of the battle, the first powerful sidelong swipe that Robert had launched Kelsey's way, then looked to the appropriate side. Crumpled beside a stalagmite mound lay Kelsey, curled in a ball and covered in blood. The elf was alive, Gary could see, and trying hard not to make any move or sound.

"You will need the shield," Geno remarked to Gary. With the illusionary scene dispelled to him, Gary noticed the shield lying where Kelsey had first placed it on the floor, beside the scars of dragon fire and the fast-cooling stone. He wondered how he might retrieve it without alerting Robert to the trick, but Mickey was already taking care of that part. The illusionary Kelsey walked over to the real shield and laid the illusionary shield atop it.

It was all very confusing to Gary—and he didn't understand why the dragon hadn't seen right through the leprechaun's trick—but he went over and picked up the shield and followed Geno and Robert into the side chamber.

He looked back as he exited the room, and watched Mickey's illusionary elf go and sit beside the real Kelsey at the stalagmite mound, the leprechaun going as well to tend to the real Kelsey's very real wounds.

Gary slumped even lower behind the shield when he heard the sharp intake of the dragon's breath. He felt like he had to go to the bathroom—feared that he would embarrass himself right then and there. But he could say nothing. The spear was laid out on a flat stone before him and he, as the prophecies dictated, held tight to its bottom half. Geno had tied the two ends of the shaft together with a leather thong and had sprinkled some flaky substance—Gary couldn't tell if it was metal scrapings or crushed gemstones—along the part to be rejoined. Now Geno stood far back, hammer in one heavy-gauntleted hand and bag of the same flaky substance in the other.

Gary reminded himself that he had not actually witnessed the shield deflecting the dragon's terrible breath, that what he had seen had been no more than one of Mickey's illusions. He peeked up over the rim of the shield, wanting to protest, but saw that he hadn't the time.

Then the flames came and Gary didn't know if he had wet his pants or not—and in that heat, they certainly would have dried in an instant anyway! Great gouts of white fire licked at Gary around the edges of his shield; his hand holding the magical spear warmed and then burned with pain. He held onto the weapon's shaft, though, for Geno had promised him some very unpleasant consequences if he didn't.

And then it was over, suddenly. Gary blinked the sting out of his eyes, almost fainting with relief that the shield had indeed turned aside the white-hot flames. On the flat stone before him, the magical spear glowed an angry orange in the dimly lit room. Immediately the dwarven craftsman fell over it, sprinkling flakes and pounding away, sprinkling and pounding. Geno muttered many arcane phrases that Gary couldn't begin to understand, but from the dwarf's ritualistic movements and reverent tone, Gary correctly assumed it to be some sort of smithy magic, a spell to strengthen the bonding beyond the might of simple metal.

The work went on for many minutes, Geno tapping and banging, chanting and sprinkling still more of the flaky substance on the still-hot metal shaft. Then the dwarf lifted the spear up and looked along the shaft, checking to be certain that it was perfectly straight.

He dropped it back to the stone, gave a few more taps, and lifted it for another inspection. Geno's smile was all the answer that Gary Leger needed. The dwarf backed away and slipped his hammer into a loop on his belt.

The glow dissipated; the spear seemed remarkably cool.

"So now you are in the legends once again, mighty Robert," Geno called to the dragon. "All the world will know that it was Robert, greatest of wyrmkind, who gave the fires to reforge the ancient spear!"

The dwarf's attempt to placate the fuming dragon seemed to have little effect.

"Get you gone from my mountain!" the beast roared.

Gary concurred with Geno's nodding head; they wouldn't have to be asked twice.

"Pick it up," Geno instructed Gary, indicating the spear. With one hand, Gary easily hoisted the long weapon. It seemed even lighter now than either of its previous parts, and even more balanced. If before, Gary had believed that he could hurl it a hundred yards, now he felt as though he could throw it two hundred.

The sentient spear did not communicate to Gary in any discernible words, but Gary could clearly feel its profound elation.

TWENTY-FOUR

CROWS

Twoscore lava newt escorts walked in tight formation right behind the companions, their leveled spears guiding wounded Kelsey and his friends out of the lower tunnels. The dragon had warned them not to go anywhere near the castle on their way out.

"Or ever again!" Robert had roared, and it had seemed to Gary that he directed his warning particularly at Mickey McMickey. Had Robert guessed the trick? Gary wondered, but he dismissed the notion, thinking that the beast would never have let them out if it had.

Truly Gary was glad now to be out of sight of the awesome dragon, and had no intentions of ever coming anywhere near Robert's castle again. He hadn't yet shaken off his fears, though. Fully supporting Kelsey now, he kept looking back over his shoulder, fearing an imminent attack from the lava newt guards.

"Don't ye worry, lad," Mickey told him, noticing his uneasiness. "Robert would not dare to break his oath."

"Never trust a dragon," Geno added. "Unless you have beaten him in a challenge. Even wyrms have some sense of honor."

That's what it always seemed to come down to in this strange and magical world, Gary noted. Honor.

"He's no choice but to let us go," Mickey finished smugly. The leprechaun's gray eyes turned up in a profound smile of victory as he drew another long drag of his pipe.

Gary was glad to hear it, but his face, unlike the leprechaun's, reflected no hint of elation. Kelsey winced in agony with every passing step, and Gary thought the elf would surely faint away. One of Kelsey's arms was badly twisted and possibly broken—and a great tear ran along Kelsey's side, where dragon claws had ripped through armor and skin alike. Blood matted the elf's golden hair and caked on his delicate face, and only the luster in Kelsey's golden eyes, a profound look of satisfaction, showed that he was even conscious of what was happening around him.

Then they were outside—the new day had dawned—on the lower trails of the mountain's east side, far below the barracks of Robert's lava newt garrison. Half of their escorts remained to block the tunnel behind them; the other half took up defensive positions on the sloping road above.

"As if they fear we're heading back that way," Mickey scoffed, seeing the blocking line.

The leprechaun's words and tone struck Gary profoundly. They were free—even Gary realized it fully then. They were free of Robert, and Gary was free of Faerie, for he held the reforged spear. The terms of indenture had been met; Gary could soon go home.

Home.

The word sounded strange to Gary, walking along a towering mountain in a land so unlike his own. It seemed like many years since he had been in Lancashire, seemed almost as if that other world had been just a long dream, as if this land of Faerie was somehow more real.

More real than the plastics factory. More real than the tedium of standing beside the humming grinder, dropping in chunks of scrap plastic and dreaming of absurd adventures.

Gary bit back a chuckle at that notion. Absurd adventures? They didn't seem so absurd to Gary Leger anymore, especially not with an elf leaning heavily on his shoulder, with a leprechaun and a dwarf trotting along beside him.

Gary couldn't bite back his chuckle, despite Kelsey's wounds. He looked back up the mountain path, to the red-scaled lava newts standing solemn guard across the road.

"So tell me how," he bade Mickey as they put even more distance between themselves and the lava newts.

Mickey looked up at him to consider the vague question, staring as if he had no idea of what Gary was talking about.

"You said that illusions were of no use against dragons," Gary clarified, though he guessed correctly that Mickey already knew what was on his mind.

"I said that they weren't about to work well on the dragon," Mickey corrected. "As it is with dwarfs, lad. Not so good." He gave Gary a wink. "But I can always find a bit of use for them."

"It worked perfectly," Gary remarked, both his tone and his subsequent expression revealing clear suspicion. "Too perfectly."

"It was a fight," Mickey reminded him. "Sure'n Robert would have seen right through me tricks if he had the time to think on them!

"But he had a mighty foe before him, and he knew it," Mickey asserted. "Besides, me magic was at its strongest in there." Mickey stopped abruptly and turned his eyes back to the trail before them, as if he hadn't wanted to make that statement.

Gary didn't fully appreciate the leprechaun's slip of the tongue, though, too involved with his own recollections of the battle. "Then we cheated," he said at length. "Robert really won and was under no obligation to forge the spear or to even let us out of there."

Geno kicked him hard on the shin, a blow that nearly sent both Gary and Kelsey tumbling to the ground.

"Give me the elf, then!" the dwarf snorted at Gary. "And you walk back up there and surrender yourself to the dragon! Let your conscience be appeased while your body is being devoured."

Gary never took his glowering eyes off the dwarf as he reached down and rubbed his bruised shin.

"Yer reasoning is right, lad," Mickey put in. "But so's the dwarf. Ye cannot play fair with a beast like Robert—it's not a fair fight to begin with, ye know."

"The end justifies the means?" Gary replied.

Mickey thought over the strange phrase for a few moments, then nodded. "When playing with a dragon," he agreed. "Besides, lad, the real Kelsey had Robert beaten before he ever turned into the dragon. It was Robert who chose the swords for the challenge, and in that fight, Kelsey truly won."

Gary let it drop at that, glad for the reminder and glad that he could agree with Mickey's reasoning. For some reason, he had to feel that honor had been upheld in the challenge. Kelsey patted him on the shoulder then, a minor movement, but one that struck Gary profoundly. He turned to regard the wounded elf, and found, to his surprise, sincere approval in Kelsey's golden eyes.

They continued on down the mountain at as great a pace as they could set with Gary half carrying Kelsey. The castle was soon far behind them, to Gary's relief, but he couldn't help noticing that Mickey kept glancing back that way. It wasn't as though the leprechaun feared any imminent attack (again, to Gary's relief), but rather, Mickey's gaze reflected a longing, a heartache, as a young mother might glance over her shoulder after dropping her child off for the first day of school.

Gary tried to put it all together in private, knowing that Mickey would offer no explanations. He recalled the leprechaun's meeting with the pixie on their first night out of Dvergamal, and only then did he make note of Mickey's remark that his magic was at its strongest in Robert's lair. Truly it had been the finest illusion Gary had witnessed yet—the image of the fighting elf resembled Kelsey in every detail and moved perfectly to compensate for the give-and-take maneuvers of the battle.

But that did not explain to Gary why Robert had been so fooled. The only reason Mickey's illusions had once been able to trick Geno, back in the dwarf's cave when it appeared as though Kelsey had walked into the wall trap, was that Mickey had shown Geno what the dwarf had expected to see. Not so in Kelsey's fight against Robert. Most likely the dragon would have expected what had really happened, would have expected to see a broken Kelsey go flying away after the first claw strike. If Robert was truly an ancient and wise wyrm, a beast befitting the common and apparently accurate legends of dragonkind, he should have seen through the illusion, if not at first, then at least later on, in the lull before he had led Gary and Geno into the side chamber to reforge the spear.

Then why was Robert fooled? And why did Mickey keep looking back up at the castle?

No matter how hard Gary tried, the pieces of the puzzle would not add up.

The trail split in several directions as they neared the bottom of the obelisk-shaped mountain. Mickey took up the lead and headed north. "This way will get us back quicker to the crevice and the giant," the leprechaun explained.

"And to the Crahgs?" Geno asked dryly.

Mickey shook his head. "No need to go back that way," the sprite replied firmly, and his face and the dwarf's lit up at that welcomed declaration. Mickey hopped up into the air and kicked his curly-toed shoes together. "The quest is done, don't ye know?" he said, overly exuberant and looking mostly at Kelsey. "We can take our time in walking now and enjoy the fine weather!"

Even as Mickey landed, his joyous façade slipped and he cast a concerned look back up the trail. Gary understood then why the leprechaun had suddenly acted so full of cheer—for Kelsey's sake. And looking at the pained elf, Gary gave an approving nod to Mickey. Gary held the spear out before him, so that Kelsey might see it in all its reforged splendor. Kelsey's face did indeed brighten, and it seemed to Gary as if his elvish load lessened somewhat, as if some of the spring suddenly returned to Kelsey's step.

"And you'll go down in the legends," Gary remarked to Geno, vying to get the dwarf to join in the celebration, "as the dwarf who reforged the legendary spear."

He felt Geno's spittle splatter against the back of his leg and said no more. He thought again of the prospects of returning home, wondered if he would wake up in some white room with padded walls, or in his own bed, maybe, to learn that it had all been no more than a wistful dream.

His mind played the adventure, from Tir na n'Og to the Giant's Thumb, trying to hold on to the many sights he had seen, the wondrous smells, the fears and excitement. He should have reminded himself that he was a long way from home, a long way from Tir na n'Og even, and that the adventure had not yet ended.

Kelsey cried out in pain. Gary looked around the elf's slumping form to see a small hunk of moving rock, vaguely humanoid in shape, though less than half Gary's height, grabbing tightly at Kelsey's leg. Instinctively Gary released his hold on the elf, trying to use his leg to cushion Kelsey's inevitable fall, but more intent on readying his spear.

"Dwarf magic?" Gary cried out in disbelief. He jabbed the spear against the stone, wincing as it struck, for he feared that the rock might break it once again. Sparks flew as the metal tip connected, and Cedrick's spear slashed right through the stone, its magic blasting the curious little creature to a pile of rolling rubble.

"Dwarf magic?" Gary cried again, but when he looked to Geno, he knew how ridiculous his question, his accusation, must have sounded.

Several rock men surrounded the dwarf, clubbing and grabbing at his arms and legs. Geno's hammers smashed away, each swing sending large chips of his enemies flying.

"My sword!" Kelsey called weakly as more rocks suddenly animated along the sides of the trail and rushed in. Gary held the spear in both hands as he straddled the prone elf, knowing that Kelsey could not begin to defend himself.

"Mickey!" Gary yelled. He slashed and jabbed repeatedly and the air all around him became a shower of multicolored sparks.

"I cannot do a thing against them!" Mickey called back. Gary noticed the leprechaun, floating up in the air beneath his open umbrella, bending his curly-toed shoes under him to avoid the reaching grasp of still more of the creatures.

Metal rang on stone repeatedly, sparks filled the air, but the fearless creatures came on relentlessly, too many to beat back.

"Mickey!" Gary yelled again, fearing that Kelsey would soon be crunched.

A rock man slipped inside the wide swing of Gary's spear and bore down on the man and the elf. Gary had nowhere to run, nowhere to even back up enough to bring his spear to bear.

A single hammer stroke shattered the rock man into a hundred pieces.

Gary looked up from the pile of blasted stones to see Geno, wearing that wide one-tooth-missing, mischievous smile, wading through a sea of broken stones. Rock men closed in on the dwarf from both sides, and, "Bang! Bang!" the path around him was clear once more.

"They are just stones," Geno muttered, and to further display his superiority, he grabbed the limb of the closest creature and bit off its stubby rock fingers.

"What'd I tell ye about that one's meals, lad?" came Mickey's call from above, a sense of relief evident in the leprechaun's tone.

A hammer flew past Gary, connecting on a creature that had closed behind him.

"Keep them away from you," Geno instructed. "Play defensive and protect the elf." Geno smiled as another rock man came into range. He casually reached out and bashed it apart. "Just keep them back," he said to Gary again, "and let the dwarf do what a dwarf was born to do!"

Gary whipped his spear across in a wide arc, back and forth, slashing any of the rock men that strayed too near. Geno, true to his boastful promise, marched all about the perimeter of that area of sanctuary, seeming impervious to the creatures' stone-handed attacks and shattering every opponent with a single stroke. "You have to know where to hit them!" he said to Gary on one pass, tossing a playful wink. As if to accentuate his point, the dwarf absently launched a backhanded stroke that seemed to just nick another of the creatures.

It exploded and lay in a hundred pieces.

More of the area's rocks animated and fearlessly came in at the companions, but with Mickey up high guiding Geno's positioning, the creatures had no chance.

But then Gary felt the ground buck under his feet, as if the whole side of the mountain had shifted. He looked to Geno curiously for some answer, but the dwarf only shrugged his broad shoulders, having no more of an explanation than did Gary.

"Uh-oh," they heard Mickey mumble from above. The leprechaun stared numbly and pointed back along the trail. Gary and Geno, too, dropped open their mouths when they looked back, looked back at the huge slab of humanoid-shaped stone rising up, fifty feet away but still towering over the companions.

"Lead on!" Gary cried to Geno. He grabbed Kelsey roughly and slung the elf right over his shoulder as Geno rushed by, the dwarf, obviously as frightened as Gary, frantically clearing the path ahead of the smaller rock men.

The ground shook with the thunder of a gigantic footstep; Gary didn't have to look over his shoulder to know that the stone behemoth was close behind.

"Do you know where to hit that one? Gary cried to Geno.

"Even if I did, I could never reach the spot!" the dwarf roared back.

Another small rock man appeared in the path ahead of Geno's frantic rush; another rock man disappeared into a pile of broken stones.

"Only one thing stupider than blocking a dwarf's charge," Mickey explained to Gary, floating down near to Gary's shoulder.

"What's that?" Gary had to ask, realizing that Mickey would wait all day for the correct prompt. Another rock man rose before Geno, lifting its arms threateningly for the split second it took the dwarf to reduce it to a pile of rubble.

"Blocking a dwarf's retreat," Mickey answered dryly. Gary shook his head and looked over Kelsey's form to regard the leprechaun. He appreciated Mickey's humor at that dark time, but he noticed that Mickey, glancing back at the pursuing behemoth, did not wear a smile.

Geno continued to keep the path clear before them, cutting a wide swath along the trail, even smashing apart some boulders that showed no signs of animating. But even on a smooth and clear path, Gary, burdened by Kelsey, could not hope to outrun the stone giant.

"*Thou must not throw me!*" came an emphatic cry from the sentient spear, sensing Gary's intent.

Gary didn't bother to answer. When he came to a small climb in the trail—not too great an obstacle, but certainly one that would slow him more than it would slow the pursuing giant—he turned about and lifted the mighty spear in one hand.

"*I am the cause!*" Cedric's spear protested. "*I must be protected!*"

"You've got that backwards," Gary muttered. He aimed for the approaching giant's chest, then realized that the minuscule weapon, powerful though it was, would probably not even penetrate that thick slab deeply enough to affect the monster.

Gary lowered the angle and heaved. The balanced spear's flight was true and the magical tip buried deep in the stone giant's knee. Great cracks appeared around the vibrating shaft, encircling the whole of the giant's leg. The monster stopped its advance and swayed dangerously.

Gary turned and fled.

"You cannot . . . leave . . . the spear," Kelsey, on the verge of unconsciousness, implored him.

"You want to go and get it?" was Gary's immediate reply. He trotted more easily now, trying to keep Kelsey's ride less bumpy and thinking the giant left behind. But then there came a tremendous crash, followed a moment later by another. Gary looked back to see the giant once again in pursuit, hopping across great distances on its one good leg.

"Damn!" Gary spat, and he put his head down and ran on.

"*I warned thee,*" came a distant call in his mind, a reminder that now he had no weapon at all.

Gary was still looking more behind him than in front when he heard Geno cry out in surprise. He glanced ahead to see another gigantic form rushing over to them. At first Gary thought them doomed, thought that another animated stone giant had cut off their retreat. This second form moved right past the companions, though, lowering its broad shoulders and charging headlong into the pursuing giant.

"Tommy!"

Tommy was not nearly as large as the stone giant, and, of course, just a fraction of the animated monster's weight. But the bigger giant was unbalanced with its wounded leg and did not react quickly enough to brace itself against Tommy's powerful shoulder tackle.

The two behemoths tumbled down in an avalanche of flesh and stone, breaking apart the rocks all about them.

"Keep running!" came Geno's cry from in front, but Gary ignored the call. He gently laid Kelsey to the ground and headed back the other way.

"No, lad," Mickey called behind him.

"Oh, begorra," the leprechaun added as Geno, too, rushed by, going to the aid of his friends and spitting curses with every step.

The instant Gary got his hands around the shaft of Cedric's spear, he wondered how smart he had been in returning. The movements of the wrestling giants whipped the shaft every which way—Gary got it in the face once, and only his helmet prevented the blow from splitting his skull. To his own amazement, he did manage to pull the spear free, and he stumbled back a few steps, looking for a vital target.

Geno was already hard at work on the stone giant's shoulder, cracking apart one of the arms squeezing Tommy. Fortunately Tommy was on top of the larger giant; Tommy would have no doubt been crushed if the stone monstrosity had come down on top of him. Still, the giant's constricting arms worked hard on poor Tommy, who could not hope to draw breath under that brutal assault.

Gary danced and dodged, keeping clear of the flailing feet. He poked the spear in whenever he could, but knew that his halfhearted attacks were doing little damage.

Down the path, Mickey cried out, and Gary heard the twang of a bowstring. He looked up to see the leprechaun and the elf huddled under a virtual rain of black-winged crows. Kelsey lay on his back, swiping across with his longbow to keep the birds away and trying to notch another arrow amidst the chaos. Mickey crouched low next to the elf, his umbrella an impromptu shield above him.

"Run on!" the dwarf instructed Gary when the stone giant's arm finally broke free.

Gary rushed off, pausing to jab his spear once into the stone giant's other knee. A hammer spun past him as he bore down on the flock, taking down two birds in its flight.

By the time Gary got close enough to skewer one squawking bird, three more of Geno's hammers had crashed through, showering the area in black feathers.

Free from the immediate assault, Kelsey managed to fire off a few effective bow shots.

But the crows were not alone; more rocks animated and moved in on the group.

"Robert's word isn't so good," Gary grumbled.

Mickey started to reply, to correct Gary, then changed his mind. The leprechaun knew that only the dwarfs of Faerie and one other person, a certain witch, could animate stones so effectively, and Mickey understood the significance of crows flying near to Robert's mountain.

Gary grabbed Kelsey by the arm and got him to his feet as Geno intercepted the approaching stone men.

"Take the helmet," Gary offered, and before Kelsey could begin to protest, he plopped it over the elf's head and moved Kelsey along.

The chase was on once more, even more miserable now with crows pecking and scratching at Gary's face and eyes every step of the way. Mickey found a perch below Gary's shoulder, sheltered by Kelsey's leaning form.

How convenient for him, Gary thought, brushing away a nagging crow.

Something smaller and much swifter than a crow zipped past Gary's head. He looked around to see a falcon tear through the crow pack, emerging with one blackbird in its deadly clutches.

Another bird of prey rushed by, and then another.

"Falcons?" Gary whispered. It didn't make any sense. And when something didn't make any sense, Gary could be relatively certain that Mickey was involved.

"I've always been partial to hunting birds," the leprechaun remarked. His illusion proved quite effective in driving off the flock, and Geno soon had the situation of new rock men fully under control, his crunching hammers battering them to littler and littler pieces.

Even more good news came a moment later as Tommy lumbered down the path, finally free of the stone giant's stubborn grasp, and with no pursuit evident behind him. Limping, the giant still had no trouble catching up with the companions. He came up beside Gary and gently hoisted Kelsey into his great arms, cradling the wounded elf before him.

Gary clenched a fist in victory; all about them the enemy ranks dissipated and fell away altogether.

Mickey was not so exuberant. Nor was the leprechaun overly surprised when they turned a bend in the mountain trail and came face-to-face with a fuming Ceridwen.

TWENTY-FIVE

END OF THE ROAD

Gary heard a small, resigned sigh escape Mickey's lips as the leprechaun turned himself invisible. Gary honestly couldn't blame the leprechaun for his tactical retreat. Looking at Ceridwen, beautiful and terrible all at once in her black gossamer gown, and standing on a ledge against the mountain wall, high enough up so that she seemed to tower over even Tommy, Gary knew that they were doomed.

"Well, giant, what have you to say for your treachery?" the witch hissed evenly. Tommy blanched and trembled so violently that Gary thought the giant would surely fall right over and grovel on the path.

Kelsey pulled free of Tommy's weakened grasp and dropped to the ground, somehow finding the strength to get to his feet and move in at the witch. The elf pulled himself up straight and proud before the evil sorceress, drawing out his magical sword.

"This is none of yer affair!" he growled.

Ceridwen laughed so hard that tears streamed down her porcelain-white cheeks. She snapped her fingers and Kelsey vanished—or at least Mickey's illusion of Kelsey vanished. Gary saw the real elf then, on the ground and crawling doggedly, stubbornly, towards the witch.

Ceridwen paid him no heed. She snapped her fingers again and Mickey reappeared, off to the side of the trail now, sitting atop a flat boulder.

"It was worth the try," the leprechaun remarked, trying to appear unconcerned. He pulled out his pipe and tapped it on the stone.

Ceridwen seemed amused as she watched his movements.

"Ye cannot win, ye know," Mickey went on absently. "For all yer tricks and all yer traps, the spear is whole again. Even yerself cannot break it."

Ceridwen's smile faded, replaced by a glare so cold that it stopped Gary's heart in midbeat.

"That is of no matter," the raven-haired witch replied. "The spear is forged, but it will not be seen again in the wide realm of Faerie."

"Empty promises," Mickey answered, conjuring a tiny flame above his fingers. He took a long and easy draw on his pipe as he lit it. "The word will get out—ye know it will. Once the people of Faerie know that the spear is whole again, they'll play up against King Kinnemore. They'll force his hand and tell him to go and find the thing."

Ceridwen smiled confidently and shrugged. "And so the King will begin a search, and so will the finest knights of the land. But will they come to Ynis Gwydrin? And if they do, do you really believe that they will ever leave?" She looked down to regard Kelsey then, still stubbornly crawling towards her and muttering breathless curses with the little air his injured body could draw.

Mickey returned the witch's shrug, but stopped short of smiling. "But the word will be out," he said. "'The spear is whole!' they'll cry in the streets of Dilnamarra. 'The spear is whole!' they'll whisper in Connacht, through the halls of yer puppet King's own castle. And the Tylwyth Teg, Lady; let us not forget the fair folk of Tir na n'Og. Kelsey's quest is fulfilled. When his kin hear the word, and hear of yer interference, they're sure to unite against ye. They're a tolerant bunch, the Tylwyth Teg, but I'm not for getting them angered at me!"

Ceridwen laughed again, this time an evil cackle. "Then none shall return to deliver that word!" she retorted.

"Damn you!" cried Kelsey, defiantly tucking his feet under him and hurling himself the remaining distance to the witch. His sword flashed across Ceridwen's face, but the stroke didn't even turn Ceridwen's head to the side, had no more effect than to heighten the witch's mocking laughter. Bravely, stupidly, his rage beyond reason, Kelsey drove his sword in again, this time point-first.

Ceridwen caught the blade in her bare hand and held it before her, motionless.

"I have already told you, foolish elf," the witch explained. "Your weapons, even weapons forged by the magic of the Tylwyth Teg, cannot bring harm to me." She released her hold on Kelsey's sword suddenly and slapped the elf across the face with an easy backhand motion that launched Kelsey through the air. He flew a dozen feet, crashing down heavily against the mountain wall, where he crumpled and lay very still.

"Stonebubbles!" Geno roared. "How will you do against my weapons, filthy witch?" The dwarf banged his hammers together and drew back as if he meant to launch them.

A simple wave of Ceridwen's hand loosed a huge slab of rock right above Geno's head.

The dwarf immediately dropped his hammers and managed to get his hands up in time to catch the falling stone. But though he broke the slab's initial momentum, this hunk of rock was too large even for Geno to handle. He stood under it, his legs and arms trembling violently under the tremendous strain.

"How ironic that a dwarf of Dvergamal would die so!" the witch cackled. "A dwarf crushed by a stone! Such a fitting end!"

Gary looked to Geno, to Kelsey, not knowing where he should begin to help.

"Keep still, lad," Mickey whispered to him, coming back to his side and apparently guessing his intent to act. "We'll try to get her to accept a surrender."

Gary wanted to scream "No!" a thousand times in the leprechaun's face, a million times in Ceridwen's face. So many obstacles had been overcome—poor Kelsey should not die knowing that his life-quest had failed, after all. But Gary saw no other course, saw no way to harm the terrible witch.

"Ye must be desperate to come so near to Robert's mountain," Mickey reasoned, trying to make some headway in his discussion with the obstinate sorceress. "Even sending crows—yer calling card if ever ye had one. I'm not thinking that Robert likes having ye about."

"But you have fixed that for me already, haven't you, leprechaun?" Ceridwen spat back. "The spear is forged; thus, the dragon lost the challenge. A hundred years is it, before Robert might emerge from his castle?"

Mickey thought fast to get around the logic trap. "But his minions," the leprechaun started to reply.

Ceridwen's renewed laughter cut him short. "Lava newts?" she scoffed. "And what else, leprechaun? Do tell me. What other mighty minions has Robert the Ridiculous prepared to drive me off?"

"This isn't going to be easy," Mickey muttered to Gary.

"You have done so much for me," the witch went on, ignoring Mickey's remark. "Delivered the forged spear and banished Robert for a hundred years. A hundred years! The Crahgs will again be mine, decades before the dragon can even step out of his castle once more to challenge me."

"So let us go and we'll call it even," Gary remarked.

Ceridwen's smile disappeared in the blink of an eye. "Let you go?" she muttered incredulously.

"If we have done so well by you," Gary began.

"Silence!" the witch roared. "Anything you have done to aid me, you have done inadvertently. I have not forgotten your disobedience." She looked directly at Tommy as she said this and Tommy suddenly didn't seem so large to Gary.

"You were told to remain on Ynis Gwydrin," the witch fumed. "Yet I returned to find my guests gone!"

"Ye must admit that the lad was resourceful in finding a way through yer spell," Mickey put in, in the hopes that Ceridwen would think it better to keep Gary alive and at her side.

If she even heard the leprechaun's words, she made no indication of it. "Gone!" she growled again, her ire rising dangerously.

"And you, giant," she spat. "I took you in and gave you a home! This is how you repay me?" She waggled one finger and a small flame appeared atop it, dancing in the air, growing hotter and larger. "I will burn the skin from your bones, ungrateful beast," the witch promised. "And feed you to my goblins, more loyal by far."

What a pitiful thing Tommy One-Thumb now seemed. The giant who had casually tossed a mountain troll through the air, who had charged fearlessly into the grasp of a stone behemoth much larger than he, fell to his knees before the threats of the sorceress. He tried to speak out, but only undecipherable blabber came past his trembling lips.

Ceridwen snapped her fingers and a burst of flame appeared next to Tommy's head, singeing his hair. He slapped at it wildly, began to blubber and scream out his pleas.

"He hasn't hurt anyone," Gary breathed.

"Easy, lad," implored the leprechaun. "We're not wanting to share a similar fate. We'll go for the surrender."

A sudden thought came over the outraged man. He looked at Mickey, his lips curling into a wicked smile. "Who made the spear?"

Mickey shrugged, seeming confused.

"That's what I thought," Gary replied. There was more to Ceridwen's desires to have the spear than any fears she might hold for the feelings and heroic recollections of her pitiful and unwitting subjects.

"Wait!" Gary cried at Ceridwen, to Mickey's dismay. "You came to retrieve the spear, and it is mine to give." He held the spear out before him, ignoring its sudden stream of telepathic protests. "We overcame so many obstacles to reforge this weapon, many of them inspired by you, no doubt. But we did it, and Kelsey, brave Kelsey, faced down the dragon—fairly. But for all its value, this piece of metal is not worth the lives of my friends."

"Give it to me!" Ceridwen roared, verily drooling at the sight of the magnificent weapon.

"*Yes, do,*" agreed the spear, suddenly satisfied.

Ceridwen's icy-blue eyes widened in surprise as Gary drew back the spear, his face contorted suddenly in open hatred. The witch waved her hand, sending a blast of fire rolling out from her fingers towards the threat.

"No, lad!" Mickey cried, trying to scramble away.

Gary's scream came from the pit of his stomach, emanated from every muscle and every nerve in his entire body. All of his anger, all of his frustration, strengthened his movements as he hurled the mighty weapon. The spear dove into the flames, just a few feet away from Gary by then, and disappeared behind the orange and smoke-gray ball.

The witch's fires blew away the instant before they engulfed both Gary and Mickey, and when the flames were gone, the companions looked again upon Ceridwen, the spear through her belly, pinning her to the mountain wall. Horrified, the witch grasped at the quivering shaft with hands that hadn't the strength to even close about it.

Vile blackness flowed out from the wound, spreading across the witch's gown and down her bare arms.

"I shall repay you!" she spat at Gary, a hollow threat as the blackness spread up her neck and over her face. Her mouth contorted in a silent scream, her hands still trembled over the vibrating shaft of black metal.

Then Ceridwen seemed no more than a shadow against the wall. Gary could see the back of the spear's tip, buried deeply in the stone.

"Would ye look at that?" Mickey gasped.

Ceridwen's final, agonized scream split the air, then there was only the mourn of the wind, and the spear, and the marked stone, covered still, covered forever, by the witch's shadow.

"How did ye know?" Mickey asked Gary.

Gary shrugged. "I did not," he answered honestly. "But Robert claimed that no fires wrought by mortal hands could soften the blade. If he spoke truly . . ."

"Ah, what a fine lad ye are," Mickey chuckled.

Gary looked down at the leprechaun, his green eyes catching Mickey's in a wistful gaze. "I did not know," he said again. "But I had to believe."

"If you are done with your congratulating over there . . ." came a strained call from behind. The startled companions turned to see Geno, his bandy legs finally beginning to bend under the tremendous weight of the fallen slab.

Tommy got to the dwarf first and, with Gary and Geno's help, managed to angle the slab to the side, away from the dwarf, where they let it crash down to the path.

"Lad!" Mickey called from across the trail. They turned to see Kelsey, struggling to his feet with the leprechaun's diminutive support. Gary rushed over and hooked Kelsey's arm over his shoulder.

The elf was surely wounded and surely exhausted, but, looking at the luster in his golden eyes as he regarded the spear, hanging still in the bare stone, it was obvious that he would survive and heal well.

"Ding dong, the witch is dead?" Gary offered hopefully, bringing a smile to Kelsey's bloodied lips.

"Not dead, lad," Mickey corrected. "But she'll do a hundred years on Ynis Gwydrin before she finds her way back out again, and a better land it'll be with both Ceridwen and Robert out of the way!"

"There goes the last buckle for this leg," Mickey said to comfort Gary as the leprechaun helped the man strip out of the bulky armor. Dilnamarra was in sight; the companions had come to the end of their long road.

"Where is the damned elf?" Geno muttered, not happy at all about the unexpected delay. They had come into the region many hours before, but Kelsey, seeing an uncommon number of king's soldiers milling about, had determined that they would wait outside of the town, hidden by a large hedgerow, (it had to be a large one, since Tommy was still with them) until he could determine what was going on. Taking the guise of one of the many beggars of the pitiful region, the elf had slipped out into the fading daylight.

"Another one," Mickey declared, loosening the buckle low on Gary's back. The leprechaun noticed something curious then, and after a moment's consideration, he quietly lifted an item from Gary's belt and slipped it under his own cloak.

"Damned elf," spat Geno, paying no heed to either Mickey or Gary. Geno had actually been quite hospitable after the defeat of the witch, on the uneventful road home north around the dreaded Crahgs, down a narrow pass between them and Dvergamal. But then Kelsey had informed the dwarf that he would not be released straight to his mountain home, that he would have to accompany the group all the way to Dilnamarra in case there arose a question concerning the authenticity of the forging.

A movement to the side turned all of them about. They relaxed immediately, recognizing the slender form of Kelsey.

"King's guards," he confirmed. "All about the keep. It would seem that I am an outlaw, as are you, Gary Leger, and you as well, leprechaun, if they ever figure out that it was you posing as a babe in Gary's arms when we procured the items."

"They gave us the armor freely," Gary protested.

"Aye," Mickey agreed. "But then me illusion on the King's edict went away and Prince Geldion realized the truth."

Kelsey nodded his confirmation.

"How long, then?" Geno interrupted gruffly. "I've a hundred contracts to fulfill before the first snows of winter!"

Kelsey honestly had no answer for the dwarf. "Baron Pwyll remains in charge only of his keep," he explained. "The outlying lands are heavily guarded. I do not know how we might get through to deliver the forged spear."

A moment of silence hung about them as they privately considered their options.

"But if we did get the spear to Pwyll," Gary prompted, "then what?"

"Geldion'd not be a happy sort," Mickey replied.

"But likely there would be little that the Prince could do," reasoned Kelsey. "With the spear in his possession and the armor and shield returned, Baron Pwyll would prove that he was in the right in giving the items to me. The truth would free Pwyll of Geldion's evil grasp."

"Then let Geno deliver it," Gary said casually.

Geno glowered Gary's way.

"They're looking for a man, an elf, and a leprechaun, not a dwarf," Gary reasoned. "Disguise the items and let Geno walk them right into Baron Pwyll."

"It might work," Mickey muttered. "Geno leading a burdened mule, bearing pots"—he held up the helmet of Donigarten, suddenly appearing as a rather beat-up old cooking pot—"and other items less interesting to Geldion than a magical spear and a suit of mail."

"Mule?" Kelsey and Geno remarked together.

"Come here, would ye now?" Mickey asked Tommy. "And kneel down on all fours—there's a good giant."

Geno snickered. "This might be worth the trouble," he said. "And then I am free to return to my home?"

Kelsey looked around and then, seeing no problems, nodded.

"Tommy does not like this," the giant put in, finally figuring out his equine role in the deception.

"Aw, it'll be fine," Mickey assured him.

"That it will," Geno added, giving Tommy a look of sincere confidence. "I will watch out for you. And when we're done, you come along with me to Dvergamal. There are many holes in my mountains. I will find you a proper place for a giant to live—not too near to my people, you understand!"

Tommy's face brightened and he assumed his best mule posture, waiting for Mickey to work another of his tricks.

A few moments later the dwarf tradesman and his pack mule set off, passing through the many guards who indeed were not so concerned with the "mundane" items Geno carried.

"Never did I expect so much of you," Kelsey admitted when he, Mickey, and Gary came to the great oak tree of Tir na n'Og, the very spot where the elf had first met Gary Leger. Kelsey cast an amused look up the tree, to the lair of Leshiye.

Gary agreed fully with the elf's observations. He, too, recalled that first meeting, where Kelsey had stolen him away from his pleasure. It had been an auspicious beginning, to be sure, but now that the adventure had ended, neither would deny their friendship, publicly or privately.

"I am glad that your quest went so well," Gary replied. "And I hope that Ceridwen's fears concerning Cedric's spear prove well founded. The people of Dilnamarra could use a new attitude."

Kelsey nodded, patted Gary on the shoulder, and took his leave, disappearing into the darkness of the thick forest underbrush so quickly and so completely that Gary almost had to wonder if the elf had ever really been there.

"Are ye ready, lad?" Mickey asked. "The pixies'll be dancing in the blueberry patch; I can get ye home this very night."

Gary cast another longing gaze up Leshiye's tree. "Another hour?" he asked, half-serious.

"Don't ye be pushing yer luck," came Mickey's warning. "It's time for ye to get back to yer own place."

Gary shrugged and moved away from the tree. "Lead on, then," he said, but in his heart he wasn't so sure that he ever wanted to return home.

Gary said little on their trek back through Tir na n'Og to the blueberry patch. He wondered again what his return trip might be like. Would he simply awaken, in his own bed, perhaps? Or would he come out of a delusion to the startlement of those concerned people around him?

Truthfully Gary didn't believe either explanation; they seemed no less strained to him than to simply accept what had happened as reality.

But wasn't that exactly what an insane person might believe? Disturbing questions, questions of reality itself, nagged at Gary, but he found he had no time then to contemplate them. Blueberry bushes were all about him, and in sight, too, was the small ring of light within the joyful and mysterious dance of the tiny fairies.

He cast a final look to Dvergamal, where the moon was coming up behind the great and stony peaks. And then, on Mickey's nod, he stepped into the faerie ring.

As soon as Gary had melted away into the enchanted night, Mickey McMickey pulled a curious item out from under his cloak: a jeweled dagger, ancient and marvelously crafted, that Gary Leger must have inadvertently taken from Robert's castle.

The implications of the theft, inadvertent or not, were quite grave, but Mickey tried not to view things that way.

He wondered now how he might use this unfortunate twist to his advantage in his quest to retrieve his bartered pot of gold from the treasure hoard of the wicked wyrm.

EPILOGUE

Gary Leger groaned as he rolled over on the scratchy ground, prickly bushes picking at him from every angle. He managed to roll to a sitting position, smelling blueberries all around him, but it took him some time to figure out where he was. Images of sprites and elfs, dragons and bandy-legged dwarfs, danced all about his consciousness, just out of his reach.

"So it was just a dream," he remarked, trying to hold on to at least a part of the grand adventure. But like any dream, the images were fleeting at best, and entire sections were missing or out of place. He remembered the general details, though, something about a spear and a horrendous dragon. And wearing armor—Gary distinctly remembered the sensation of wearing the armor.

Gary looked down to his side, saw *The Hobbit* lying on the ground next to him, and knew what had inspired his evening adventure.

He realized then that he had missed supper; he worried then how many hours (days?) had passed. Gary blinked at that thought and looked around him, studying the landscape beneath the light of the rising moon. Yes, he was in the woods out back, not in Tir na n'Og.

"Tir na n'Og?" he mumbled curiously. How did he know that name?

Confused beyond any hopes of sorting it all out, Gary scooped up his book and struggled to his feet. He started down the path to the fire road, but changed direction and went across the blueberry patch instead, to the ridge overlooking . . .

Overlooking what?

Gary crept up, alternating his gaze from the widening landscape beneath him to the distant hills.

Hills, he thought, not mountains, and dotted with the lights of many houses.

Still, Gary held his breath as he came to the lip of the small hill, and was then sincerely relieved—and also, somehow sincerely disappointed.

Southeast Elementary School.

"Some dream," he mumbled to himself, sprinting back as fast as he dared to go in the dim light towards the fire road. More sights, familiar sights, greeted him as he rushed along: the cemetery fence; the houses at the end of his parents' street; and then his own Jeep, sitting under the streetlight in front of the hedgerow.

"Where the hell have you been?" his father asked him when he burst through the kitchen door. The remnants of supper sat on the stove and counter. "You'll have to reheat it."

"Reheat it?" Gary muttered curiously, an image of a spear flashing through his mind, and white flames licking at him around the edges of a fine shield.

"Yeah, it got cold. You'll have to heat it up again," his father said sarcastically.

"Hey, I cooked it once," his mother, playing solitaire at the dining room table, added sternly. "If you can't be in on time for . . ."

"You won't believe this," Gary interrupted. "I fell asleep down in the woods."

"Fell asleep?" his father asked with a snicker.

"You're working too hard," his mother piped in, suddenly the concerned hen once more. She shook her head and gritted her teeth. "I hate that place."

It all seemed so very commonplace to Gary, so very predictable—say the seventeen words, Mom. He hadn't been gone a very long time; he was amazed that he had encapsulated so wild an adventure in so short a nap.

He grabbed a quick bite and went up to bed, announcing that he needed the sleep, and also privately hoping to recapture some of that strange dream. Honestly Gary didn't know how he was going to drag himself out of bed the next morning, how he was going to go back to the mundane realities of life around him, back to the grind.

"Well," he told himself, slipping out of his clothes and falling onto his bed, "at least I'll have something new to think about while I'm loading those chunks into the grinder."

Almost as an afterthought, Gary took up *The Hobbit*, opening it to mark the spot where he had left off.

His eyes nearly popped from their sockets.

For Gary Leger looked upon not the expected typeset of a paperback, but upon the strange and flowing script of Mickey McMickey.

ABOUT THE AUTHOR

R. A. Salvatore's first book, *The Crystal Shard*, was published in 1988; in 1990 his third novel, *The Halfling's Gem*, hit the *New York Times* bestseller list. Since then he has written more than sixty novels, which have sold more than thirty million copies worldwide. In addition, Salvatore has numerous game credits, making him one of the most important figures in modern epic fantasy. Among his books are numerous titles in the saga of dark elf Drizzt Do'Urden, the Coven series, the Crimson Shadow trilogy, and many more.

Salvatore spends a good deal of time speaking to schools and library groups, encouraging people, particularly young people, to read. He enjoys a broad range of literary writers, from James Joyce to Dante and Chaucer, and counts among his favorite genre literary influences Ian Fleming, Arthur Conan Doyle, Fritz Leiber, and J. R. R. Tolkien. Salvatore makes his home in Massachusetts, with his wife, Diane, and their dogs. His gaming group still meets on Sunday nights.

SPEARWIELDER'S TALE

FROM OPEN ROAD MEDIA

OPEN ROAD

INTEGRATED MEDIA

OPEN ROAD

INTEGRATED MEDIA

To the memory of J.R.R. Tolkien and to Fleetwood Mac, for giving me elfs and dragons, witches and angels, and for showing me the way to find them on my own.